GUARDIAN ANGEL

Though he was not wearing his helmet or flak jacket, Chaplain Sean Rasmunsen instinctively ran toward the sound of the explosions, and the rising pillars of black smoke. Sgt. Tyler Kraus, his chaplain's assistant, encumbered by the weight of his own protective gear, struggled to keep pace.

"Here, take this," Kraus demanded as Sean paused. "Take my helmet at least."

"But it's your—"

"Don't argue," Kraus scolded. "Sergeants are a dime a dozen, but only God can make a chaplain."

FOR GOD AND COUNTRY

Jerome Prescott

BERKLEY BOOKS, NEW YORK

THE BERKLEY PUBLISHING GROUP
Published by the Penguin Group
Penguin Group (USA) Inc.
375 Hudson Street, New York, New York 10014, USA
Penguin Group (Canada), 90 Eglinton Avenue East, Suite 700, Toronto, Ontario M4P 2Y3, Canada
(a division of Pearson Penguin Canada Inc.)
Penguin Books Ltd., 80 Strand, London WC2R 0RL, England
Penguin Group Ireland, 25 St. Stephen's Green, Dublin 2, Ireland (a division of Penguin Books Ltd.)
Penguin Group (Australia), 250 Camberwell Road, Camberwell, Victoria 3124, Australia
(a division of Pearson Australia Group Pty. Ltd.)
Penguin Books India Pvt. Ltd., 11 Community Centre, Panchsheel Park, New Delhi—110 017, India
Penguin Group (NZ), 67 Apollo Drive, Rosedale, North Shore 0632, New Zealand
(a division of Pearson New Zealand Ltd.)
Penguin Books (South Africa) (Pty.) Ltd., 24 Sturdee Avenue, Rosebank, Johannesburg 2196,
South Africa

Penguin Books Ltd., Registered Offices: 80 Strand, London WC2R 0RL, England

This book is an original publication of The Berkley Publishing Group.

Copyright © 2009 by CKE Associates, LLC.
Cover art by Richard Tuschman. Cover design by Rita Frangie.

PRINTING HISTORY
Berkley trade paperback edition / December 2009

Library of Congress Cataloging-in-Publication Data

Prescott, Jerome.
    For god and country / Jerome Prescott.—Berkley trade paperback ed.
        p. cm.
    ISBN 978-0-425-22845-6
1. Military chaplains—Fiction. 2. Iraq War, 2003—Fiction. I. Title.
PS3616.R46F67 2009
    813'.6—dc22   2009032370

PRINTED IN THE UNITED STATES OF AMERICA

10   9   8   7   6   5   4   3   2   1

The events depicted in *For God and Country* include some violence and rough language—inspired by real events—that may be offensive to readers who enjoy faith-inspired fiction. After much thought, we decided to include a small amount of dialogue that, though potentially offensive, is culturally accurate, helps to capture in an honest way the realities of ministering on the battlefield, and gives a truthful illustration of humanity and warfare, without whitewashing it.

Pro Deo et Patria (For God and Country)

CONTENTS

1

Embrace the Unexpected

"The Lord moves in mysterious ways," Chaplain Sean Rasmunsen said out loud—to himself more than to anyone in particular—as he stepped off the C-130 at Baqubah.

The sweaty, greasy, mechanical smell of the U.S. Air Force transport gave way to the arid dustiness of the Iraqi desert. It all came rushing back. Nothing stung the nostrils like the dust of Iraq. Nothing stung the eyes like the dust of Iraq. Nothing stung the human spirit like the dust of Iraq.

"The Lord moves in mysterious ways," Sean Rasmunsen repeated with bittersweet irony. Eight months ago, he had boarded another C-130—or maybe it was the same one, he couldn't tell—at Baghdad International Airport for a flight to Kuwait that would lead him home after a nineteen-month tour of duty in Iraq.

Now he was back, back in the place that the Americans referred to without affection as "the Sandbox."

Eight months ago, he was "outa here" and glad, but for Sean, "outa here" did not deliver the satisfaction that was assumed and expected by every soldier and Marine that left this dreadful place.

By comparison to his nineteen months in Iraq, his duties back at Fort Jackson were a piece of cake—maybe not a piece of cake with chocolate icing, but a piece of cake nevertheless.

However, thoughts nagged him. He talked to a lot of soldiers as they passed through Jackson—which is the home of the U.S. Army's Training and Doctrine Command (TRADOC), and a crossroads of soldiers coming and going to and from combat assignments overseas. Sean Rasmunsen talked to frightened men and women who were headed to Iraq and to heavily relieved men and women on their way back to the real world. He talked to people who knew people he had known in the Sandbox, and who knew the places he had been—and with whom he had much in common. They had heard the same sounds, and they had smelled the same dust.

But the thoughts nagged him, and they nagged him to action.

He felt as though it were not the voice from inside that was nagging him, but the voice of the Lord nagging. It was the Lord calling him.

It was counterintuitive that the Lord would be calling him back after those bloody nineteen months, but it was equally counterintuitive a few years ago that the Lord would have called a budding accountant fresh out of the University of Missouri into the seminary.

And it was counterintuitive that the Lord should have called a young minister fresh out of the Edredin Theological Seminary to enlist in the U.S. Army as a chaplain. It was all very counter-intuitive, but Sean kept telling himself that the Lord moves in mysterious—and therefore counterintuitive—ways.

But as Jesus told Peter in John 13:7, "What I do thou knowest not now; but thou shalt understand hereafter."

It was His way of telling Peter to do what he was told, and the meaning would be apparent in due course. Sean remembered that he had once delivered a sermon on counterintuition. Embrace the unexpected.

When the dusty heat stung Sean's face as he lugged his gear off the plane, he could be excused for wondering why he had volunteered to come back to this God-forsaken place. However, a quick glance into the eyes of a young airman second class whom he saw on the tarmac told him why. It was precisely because combat zones do look and feel *so* God-forsaken.

He paused and watched as the young man—he was barely past his teenage years—climbed onto the C-130's ramp to help the loadmaster untangle some gear for off-loading.

Sean stepped over and patted the kid on the shoulder and said with a smile, "Keep up the good work, man, you're doin' a good job here."

Embrace the unexpected.

The kid looked stunned. The very idea that a captain should give him an unsolicited pat on the back was counterintuitive, but it made his day. As Sean walked away, the kid was back at work with a grin on his face, and Sean knew why he had returned.

Embrace the unexpected.

As counterintuitive as it was, he was glad to be back in Iraq. The meaning was already becoming apparent.

Sean Rasmunsen's stay in Baqubah was intended to be brief.

It either *would be* brief, or it would be forty-eight hours or so of "hurry up and wait." The U.S. armed services also often moved in ways that were incomprehensible.

As he stood in the long line to present his orders to the officer in charge of travel, Sean had a chance to reflect on the mysterious ways of the past two weeks. Back then—it seemed like an eternity—he was at the U.S. Army Chaplain Center and School (USACHCS) at Fort Jackson, ready for a career of turning fresh-faced seminarians and grizzled old pastors into Army chaplains. His assignment as an instructor with the Chaplain Basic Officers Leadership Course (CBOLC) was open-ended. As a chaplain with hot-zone experience, he was exactly what they needed at Jackson. He had to argue to convince the general—who was also a sagely old Presbyterian minister who had been through Gulf War I—that there were people in the Sandbox who needed him *more*.

The Lord moves in mysterious ways.

Less than two days after the general reluctantly took Sean Rasmunsen's name off the CBOLC syllabus and put it on the active-duty roster, word came that Maj. Mike O'Malley—*Father* Mike O'Malley—the highly regarded chaplain with the 2nd Battalion of the 77th Infantry in the 69th Brigade Combat Team, had been badly injured when his Humvee was hit by an improvised explosive device (IED) near Safaliyah in Diyala Province.

Father Mike was one of those men to whom the term *well loved* had been applied several times by journalists who had ventured out to the wilds of eastern Iraq to interview the troops. They often compared him to Father Francis Duffy of the Fighting 69th Division, who took home the Distinguished Service Cross for his tireless work with the wounded and rattled during World War I.

Normally, there is a transition period when a new guy comes out to take over a chaplain's assignment. Not this time. The 2/77 needed somebody who knew what he was doing, and they needed him plenty quick.

The U.S. Army has recognized the need for a front-line chaplaincy since the Revolutionary War. Indeed, Virginia had established its militia regimental chaplaincy even earlier—by legislative act in 1758 at the request of a colonel named George Washington. The official motto of the U.S. Army Chaplain Corps is the Latin phrase *Pro Deo et Patria*, which translates simply as "For God and Country," but few chaplains lose sight of the fact that their customer base, their congregation, those for whom they truly do what they do, are the individual men and women in uniform with whom they are posted.

All of the literature states that the chaplain's responsibility to his or her congregation is to "honor the dead, comfort the wounded, and nurture the living," but the importance of a chaplain goes far beyond this. In the abstract, chaplains provide a moral compass in the midst of people who are trained for war. Pragmatically, many a wounded or troubled soldier would much rather talk to a chaplain than a shrink, and the U.S. Army knows this.

"We'll getcha all on a chopper soon as possible, Chaplain," the transport officer promised, glancing at Sean's travel orders. "FOB Lex musters over at trailer Bravo Four."

The wait for the CH-47 Chinook transport helicopter was blessedly short. It seemed almost as though the Army had discovered efficiency since Sean's last tour.

The trip to FOB Lex—Forward Operating Base Lexington— in the wilds of Diyala Province brought back the usual memories. The violent jerking after takeoff—evasive action to dodge possible RPG rounds—was all too familiar. So too was the banking and dodging to avoid the deadly pinkish clouds of sandstorms.

The chopper was filled mainly with young men and women on their first deployment. Some had fear in their eyes. Most merely looked exhausted. They all looked young. Very young.

Sean made a deliberate effort to make eye contact and to give everyone a relaxed smile. Noticing the black cross pinned above the name patch on his gray-green camo uniform, they either smiled back or glanced away. Not everyone regarded chaplains in the same way. Some people had bad past experiences with the clergy, and others came from a background with no religious tradition and were unfamiliar with having a pastor in their midst.

"Where you from?" Sean asked, nodding to the young corporal sitting next to him.

"I'm from Jeff City, Missouri, sir," she replied nervously. Like most enlisted troops, she was not used to casual conversations with officers. Chaplains carry officer rank, with the benefits and responsibilities, but they have no command authority—other than the chain of command that runs up through the brigade chaplain back to the chief of chaplains at Fort Jackson. When named in writing, their names are usually preceded by the title *Chaplain*, with their military rank in parentheses. New chaplains are commissioned as lieutenants, and most battalion chaplains are captains.

"I'm from Missouri, myself," Sean said, smiling. "Up in Linn County, the little farm town of Laclede. Y'know, it's the boyhood home of General John Pershing?"

"I'm afraid I don't know of a General Pershing, sir. Is he with the 3rd ID?"

"Is this your first tour?" Sean asked, dropping his reference to his hometown being the childhood home of the commander of American forces in World War I.

He knew that it was her first tour—he could see it in her eyes—so he turned to this question that was always a good icebreaker.

"Yes, sir, it is. I'm in communications, sir. Just got in from Benning."

"That's great. Except for food, there's nothing more important here in the boonies at these Forward Op Bases than communications. I'm in the religion business."

"Yes, sir," she said, nodding to his cross. "I saw that, sir. Is this your first deployment, too?"

"No. Second," he said with a smile. "And you don't have to call me *sir* unless you want to. Most people just call me *Chaplain*, although I've been called other things."

"I hope not to your face, sir," she said, smiling for the first time.

"No," he said with a chuckle. "At least not usually. My real name is Sean Rasmunsen," he said, offering his hand.

"Davis, sir," she replied, nervously shaking hands with the officer. "Braylee Davis."

"Pleased to meet you," he said.

The young first-timers did not seem so young on his last deployment, but of course, they were. So was he. Now, he was a veteran. Back then, he was a twenty-something fresh out of the Chaplain Officer Basic Course. He was more just a Methodist minister with a buzz cut and fresh new lieutenant's bars than anything resembling a soldier. His life had passed the big three-o, and this, along with a slightly receding hairline, made him an old man in the eyes of those enlisted personnel in their early twenties who were deploying for the first time.

Like the takeoff, dropping into Forward Operating Base Lexington was another jolting experience of dodging the threat of RPGs and hoping that everything and everybody reached the ground in one piece.

The ramp dropped and everyone moved quickly. Not, however, as fast as the dust. The ever-present dust swirled into the Chinook faster than the soldiers swirled out. Several of the new people coughed and sneezed, but the crew from Lexington who came aboard to pull off a pallet of freight just ignored it.

In the future, if anyone ever writes the story of the Iraq War without mentioning dust, you'll know that either he was never here or he was here so long that he became oblivious to it.

Forward Operating Base Lexington originally got its name when it was once home to a Kentucky National Guard outfit, but that was many, many rotations ago. The people from "Kaintuck" were long gone, but the name had stayed, although nearly everybody just called the base *Lex*.

"The Lord moves in mysterious ways." Sean laughed as he looked around FOB Lex. During his last deployment at Camp Cottonwood north of Baghdad, they had finally gotten freight containers for people to live in, but here, he would be back to living in a tent. In a way, he was glad to be back in the Sandbox. He found it almost scary that this place actually felt like home.

There were several more-or-less permanent buildings at Lex, most of them ugly concrete, former Saddam-era Iraqi Army bunkers. One of these served as the Tactical Operations Center (TOC), the headquarters for the 2/77 and the attached elements of the 69th Brigade's field artillery and engineer battalions.

The crude welcome sign on the building's entrance reminded

Sean that "home" was no longer within the safe, more politically correct confines of Fort Jackson.

"Where's your weapon, sir?" asked the harried lieutenant as Sean presented his orders to the first desk he encountered inside the busy TOC. Everyone else reporting for duty was carrying his M16 along with his duffel bag.

"Right here," Sean replied. He had a worn paperback copy of the Bible in the folder with his orders. Chaplains in the U.S. Army are never armed, an unquestioned—albeit often discussed—regulation that comes down from the Chief of Chaplains. Neither are medics, although they have been known to pick up a gun to defend their patients.

Back during the Civil War, it was not unheard of for chaplains to carry weapons. A case in point was Milton Haney, the regimental chaplain of the 55th Illinois, who picked up a musket to help his outfit recapture a Union position from the Confederates near Atlanta in 1864. Known as the "Fighting Chaplain," he is best remembered because he was one of four Civil War chaplains to be awarded the Medal of Honor, the nation's highest medal for valor.

"Sorry, Chaplain," the lieutenant said, focusing on the Bible. "I didn't see . . ."

"No worries," Sean told him in a reassuring tone. "That's cool. You got your hands full."

"You're here to replace Father O'Malley, right?"

"I wouldn't like to exactly use the word *replace*," Sean said. "I'm here, I guess, to try to fill his shoes."

"Whatever," the lieutenant said. "He'll be missed, y'know. A lotta guys weren't thrilled about having a Catholic chaplain . . .

y'know, most of us aren't . . . but he was a for-real guy . . . really well liked. Good luck . . . big shoes to fill."

Who would have thought?

Back in the seminary, it was the furthest thing from Sean's mind that he would one day be asking God for the strength to fill the shoes of a Catholic priest.

◆ ◆ ◆

God moves in a mysterious way
His wonders to perform;
He plants His footsteps in the sea
And rides upon the storm.

His purposes will ripen fast,
Unfolding every hour;
The bud may have a bitter taste,
But sweet will be the flower.

Blind unbelief is sure to err
And scan His work in vain;
God is His own interpreter,
And He will make it plain.

FROM THE HYMN "GOD MOVES IN A MYSTERIOUS WAY"
WORDS BY WILLIAM COWPER

2

Welcome to Lex

Sean threw his duffel bag on his shoulder, grabbed the satchel that contained his laptop, and began making his way through the sprawling tent city of FOB Lexington to his—formerly Father Mike O'Malley's—abode.

The tent was eerily empty. There was a cot, a desk, a chair, and a file cabinet. Some random junk lay on the floor, giving the place the look of having been stripped of everything of value in a hurry—which was probably the case. There was a power strip behind the desk, but nothing in the drawers but a few paper clips, a stapler, and several half-used pads of Post-its. The file cabinet was empty except for a nondenominational hymnal and some requisition forms.

High on the wall was a crucifix.

Once, like most Protestants, Sean had been put off by crucifixes. Protestants prefer the cross as representative of Christ without the more graphic depiction of the Crucifixion.

Once, like most Protestant clergymen, Sean would have firmly, but gently taken down the crucifix. However, a lot of things had happened to him on his first tour. Mainly, he had become more ecumenical. Early in the Chaplain Officer Basic Course, the trainees were required to attend the services of denominations other than their own. It bothered him. The liturgical emphasis bothered him. Those with too much emphasis on the hymnal troubled him, as did those with not enough.

He came to Iraq the first time thinking he was a Methodist, but gradually transitioned to thinking of himself more generally as a Christian. He left his first tour thinking of himself as a chaplain, rather than as a minister representing a particular denomination. His biases had blurred as he realized that faith was faith, and it was not always packaged as neatly as he had come to imagine back in the seminary.

Behind the cot was a tiny portable refrigerator that was not plugged in. Inside was a dead scorpion. Sean instinctively scanned the seams around the base of the tent to see whether they were secure. Nobody likes to wake up to a scorpion on his neck or toe—nor on any other part in between.

As he reopened the tent's entrance to fling the scorpion, Sean found himself face-to-face with a young sergeant in battle gear and dark blue sunglasses.

"Afternoon, Chaplain, sir," the man said awkwardly, making a crisp salute. "I was about to knock . . ."

"What can I do for you, Sergeant?" Sean said, smiling at the young man and returning his salute.

"It's what I can do for you, sir," he replied. "I'm your assistant."

"Well, I guess that makes the UMT complete," Sean said, extending his hand.

In the U.S. Army, the basic building block of the chaplaincy is the Religious Support Team. Formerly designated as, and still unofficially called, the Unit Ministry Team (UMT), this building block consists of a chaplain and his assistant. In the "Army of One," the chaplaincy is an army of just two.

Operationally, the chaplain's assistant is just that, but more than that. If the chaplain needs anything, whether it is a microwave oven, a place to hold a memorial service, or a Humvee to take him to another FOB, his assistant scrounges it. Because a U.S. military chaplain bears no arms, his assistant is also his bodyguard.

"C'mon in," the chaplain said to his new assistant. "I'm Sean Rasmunsen."

"Pleased to meet you. I'm Tyler Kraus."

"Welcome. I'd offer you a cup of coffee, but I don't really have . . ."

"Consider it done. Father Mike used to have a table and chairs, too. I'll try to get all that for you, too."

"Great, I appreciate that. I guess Father Mike was pretty well liked?"

"Yeah. Great sense of humor and all that, y'know. Always had time for everybody. Had the kinda personality that really grows on ya. You Catholic, too?"

"No, ordained Methodist," Sean said, noticing that Tyler was looking up at the crucifix. "What about you?"

"Episcopal. We got a lot a guys from all faiths here. I was active in my own church back home, but it's been great getting to know guys—and gals—from all kinds of religious traditions over here."

"Where's home?"

"Oregon Coast. Coos Bay. The lumber industry really crashed out there. No jobs, so I sorta joined the Army to get away. How about you?"

"Laclede, Missouri, originally. Fort Jackson lately. Did a tour at Camp Cottonwood. Nineteen months."

"And you're *back*? Wow."

"Yep," Sean said, nodding.

"What can I do for you, sir? Where would you like to start?"

"To start with, could you show me to the chapel? I'd like to look in there before I unpack."

The FOB Lexington chapel was a sandbagged structure with a peaked roof made of corrugated metal that had been modified from another old bunker from the days of Saddam Hussein. Inside, there were about sixty chairs. Up front was a table covered by a white cloth and a lectern with a microphone. A single unadorned cross flanked the lectern, opposite a pole on which hung a banner with a Star of David.

Three soldiers were sitting quietly at random locations in the room. Two looked up when Sean and Tyler entered the room. One just remained with his head in his hands, in prayer or just asleep.

One of the young soldiers who had looked up walked over to them.

"Are you the new chaplain? Father O'Malley's replacement?" she asked.

"Yes," Sean said, choosing not to plunge into another philosophical discussion about whether the priest could truly be "replaced."

"I'll work on getting that coffeemaker," Tyler said, making his exit.

"I'm Chaplain Rasmunsen," Sean told her in a whisper so as not to intrude on the quiet time of the others. "I just got here to Lex about an hour ago . . . Just getting my first look around."

"I'm Private First Class Alexander, Dayane Alexander. Could I talk to you?"

"Of course, is there someplace we can go?" Sean had been on the ground for just an hour, but he was ready to listen. He just didn't want to be whispering in the back of the chapel while others were trying to have some quiet time in the only quiet place at FOB Lexington.

"You *are* new, aren't you." Dayane smiled.

The someplace turned out to be a room in the back of the chapel.

"Must be hot in here in the summer," he said, making conversation.

"You better believe it," she said, shaking her head and tossing her short dark hair. "It's like an oven."

"How long have you been here at Lex?"

"Last summer," she replied. "Still got a year to go . . . or so."

"What is it that you wanted to talk about?"

"My boyfriend back home." She shrugged as tears began to flood her cheeks. "Jason. He's been, well . . . y'know . . ."

Sean had heard it all before. He had heard enough "Dear John" and "Dear Joan" stories to write a book. Yet every one of them was as different from the last as it was like all the others—and each required his ear.

Dayane's was not unlike so many others. The boyfriend was at home, and she wasn't. Someone else was, some other woman, and Dayane's carefully planned future together with her lover was withering like an ice sculpture in the Iraqi desert.

She had left home for basic at nineteen, and she could be well past twenty-one when she next saw Jason. He would be nearly twenty-five. These years were like an eternity to these kids.

Kids? Here he was, calling the twenty-somethings "kids" again. Sean had been just twenty-five himself back when he had first decided to become a chaplain.

As he spoke to Dayane, the words came smoothly, if not easily. He knew what to say. He had once loved a woman and had seen Nicole drift away. In a split second of self-pity, he had once mused that *nobody* wants to be a preacher's wife these days. Though he had never allowed himself the opportunity to believe that there would someday be a woman who wanted to be a preacher's wife, he told Dayane there *was* someone out there for *her* and that she would meet him, and she would know it when she did.

Ignoring his own example, he drew his words from what seemed like a lifetime of thirdhand experiences molded from a career that had begun with his brief stint as an associate pastor in Kansas City before he joined the service.

He smiled, she smiled, and he assured her that Jesus loved her—and that He would not abandon her. He did not add the phrase *like Jason abandoned you*, although he thought about it. Instead, he just told her that someday, someone many times more her soul mate than Jason would come when she least expected him.

He knew what to say. He had once loved a woman and had seen Nicole drift away. Who wants to be a preacher's wife these days?

As he patted Dayane's shoulder and stepped out into the daylight, he winced at the brightness and made a mental note that he would have to ask Tyler to requisition him some sunglasses. Another thing to add to the list of what he had forgotten to pack as he scrambled to pull things together back at Fort Jackson.

Lt. Col. Folbright had not been at the Tactical Operations Center when Sean had arrived, so he decided to head back over that way. Protocol sort of demanded that the 2/77's new chaplain check in with the battalion commander.

Like any American base in a war zone, Lex was a beehive of activity. Trucks and Humvees were dashing this way and that. A line of Bradleys lumbered past, and the staccato buzzing and thrumming of helicopters was a constant background noise.

The same lieutenant who was on duty previously greeted Sean and took him into the CO's "office," an area separated from the rest of the TOC by a flap of canvas.

The commander returned Sean's salute and stood to shake his hand. He was a big man with a powerful grip. His well-tanned cheeks told Sean that he spent a lot of time in the field. His pale eye sockets said that he spent a lot of time outside during sandstorms with his goggles on.

"Amos Folbright," the CO said, introducing himself. "That's *Folbright* with an O, not a scholarship."

It was obviously not a new joke, but it was disarming.

"And Amos like the biblical prophet," Sean said, going along with the banter.

"You betcha," the colonel said, gesturing for Sean to have a seat. "Father O'Malley told me some stories about him . . . Amos, I mean . . . about how he told folks that religion has gotta be accompanied by action. Quite a guy, my namesake."

"I've heard that Father O'Malley was quite the man."

"You betcha, Padre," Folbright said thoughtfully. "He'll be

missed. We're glad you're here. A battalion can't function without a chaplain, y'know."

"I believe that," Sean said thoughtfully.

"Big shoes to fill. You have more than a thousand troops here at Lex, including the 2/77 and all the guys from the 212th Engineers that are working like hell . . . 'scuse the language . . . to bring Safaliyah into the twenty-first century. Safaliyah. That's a lot of our mission out here. Has anyone briefed you?"

"No, sir, I've just been on the ground for less than two hours."

"Okay then. See now, Safaliyah is *the* big city out there. Most of the guys call it *Saf City*. You may have seen it from the air coming in. It's the biggest town in this part of Diyala. Saddam was really cruel to them even though they're Sunni. A lot of places lost their utilities back in '03–'04. Safaliyah never had a lot of that to start with, and they suffered a lot. We're trying to build things up for the people. They're great people if you get to know them. The engineers are helping them out. At the same time, we . . . I mean the 2/77 . . . we spend most of our time trying to keep the bad guys out . . . the clowns try to sneak in from Iran to cause trouble in town."

"I'm happy to be here where I can be of service," Sean told him. "I'm looking forward to getting out to meet everyone here . . ."

The *krump* of an incoming mortar round interrupted the conversation.

Both men paused, holding their breath.

With the *krump* of a second incoming mortar round, both men, both veterans of this situation, knew the conversation was over.

"Gotta run," Folbright said with concerned calmness as he grabbed his helmet.

Sean ran, too, dashing instinctively toward the point of impact near the perimeter of the FOB.

Several rounds—Sean had lost count after three or four—had hit near the 2/77 motor pool. One Humvee was on fire and another was damaged. The sound of troops returning fire rattled in the background as the chaplain ran toward a place where medics were attending to the wounded.

Thankfully, the injuries appeared minor. One young soldier had a bandage on his wrist, but he had a smile on his face and was joking with the medic.

Just as Sean was about to breathe a sigh of relief, he heard a plaintive appeal over his shoulder.

"Help me . . . I've got the jitters . . . help me *now!*"

It was a call for a chaplain if ever there was one.

He turned to see a Humvee that had just caught fire. One soldier was staring motionless, while another, holding a large and obviously heavy cloth satchel was shouting at him and pointing to the vehicle.

"I got the jitters," she repeated. "Help me get the handheld units outa there!"

He recognized the soldier doing the shouting. It was Braylee—he'd forgotten her last name—the young corporal he'd met on the chopper flight in. He recalled now that she had said she was in communications, and he immediately realized that she hadn't said that she had the "jitters," she had actually told him that she had the JTRS, the Joint Tactical Radio System, whose acronym has the same pronunciation.

The satchel in her hand contained ground mobile base station equipment, but other gear was in the burning truck and Braylee's comrade was not responding to her insistence that it be saved from the flames.

As Sean ran toward them, Braylee dropped the large satchel and lunged into the Humvee. Just as Sean reached her, she pulled out two additional packs and staggered backward, lugging them. Suddenly there was a flare-up, and the vehicle was engulfed in flames. Had anything actually exploded, the chaplain and both of the soldiers would have been toast.

Sean pulled Braylee away from the fire, grabbing the large satchel with his left hand as he went.

"Are you all right?" Sean asked, looking at the young woman from Jeff City.

Except for a dirty dollop of sweat on the tip of her nose, she seemed fine. Not even her narrow, blond eyebrows had been singed.

"I loaded this gear in Benning myself," she insisted. The frightened eyes from the chopper were gone, replaced by the look of exasperation that comes from someone who takes her job seriously.

"We can't afford to lose this, dammit!"

"I think you've saved it, Corporal Davis," he told her calmly, patting her on the back. He remembered her name—now that he had read it on her name patch. "I think we're good here."

She simply glared past Sean, with a nod toward the young man whom she apparently perceived as having frozen when duty demanded action.

Sean turned to him and put a hand on his shoulder. He jumped slightly at the touch, saw Sean's cross, and relaxed slightly.

"Somebody could've been killed, Chaplain," he said.

"But everyone seems fine," the chaplain said. Now would be the time for another officer to begin a lecture about detachment and about letting your training take over, but Sean figured the best thing to do was change the subject. "Where are you from, Private Lockhart?"

"Iowa City, sir," he replied. "Y'know, Iowa City, Iowa."

"Yes, I do know," Sean said, smiling. "I grew up just south of the Iowa line in Missouri."

"Excuse me, sir," Braylee Davis said. "If I could butt in here for a minute, I just wanna say . . . I'm sorry for yelling at you, Kyle."

She extended her hand to Kyle Lockhart; he took a deep breath and shook it.

"Happens to everybody, I guess," she told him. "But, like it's my first day in country and I'm responsible for this stuff, y'know, the JTRS. It's supposed to be replacing the PRC-148 multiband and single-channel SINCGARS out here, but there isn't enough of JTRS to go around, so I'm in big trouble if this gets wrecked."

"*I'm* sorry," he said. "I dunno what happened. Y'know, maybe I was just gettin' a little bit *jittery* . . . ha-ha . . . It won't happen again . . . y'know. I mean it."

"It's a hard place to get used to," Sean said sympathetically. "It's my first day, too. I did a tour up at Camp Cottonwood a while back, but I've been back home for the past few months and it's a real jolt coming into a hot spot."

"But we're all here now," Braylee said thoughtfully. "I guess, like we knew it wouldn't be easy, sir. We just gotta trust each other and everybody who's in this with us . . . umm . . . I guess you'd say we gotta trust in God, I guess you'd say that?"

"I'd say that it's in Him that we put our trust ultimately, but yeah . . . you're right . . . in a place like this, we need to put our trust in our fellow soldiers . . . we're all part of a team . . . and in ourselves. You have to trust that your training has prepared you."

There, he got in the line about training.

"Speaking of being part of a team, sir, I've been looking all over for you since these mortars went off."

Sean looked up. It was Sgt. Kraus.

"You should get used to the idea that I'm going to be where the bombs are falling, Sergeant," Sean told him.

"Yes, sir, Chaplain, sir," he said, nervously unslinging his M4 carbine. "I'm sorry. Father O'Malley was the same way. I'll stay close."

"No need to apologize," Sean said, wincing slightly at yet another mention of his predecessor. He knew that in every situation in life, the new guy finds himself being compared to the guy who came before. He was sure that Rabbi Ira Pearlstein had been compared to Sean Rasmunsen up at Camp Cottonwood after the baton was passed. It was inevitable, but equally inevitably, the new guy always became the old guy sooner or later. Some would call it a parable for the cycle of life.

"Thank you, Chaplain," Kraus said. "Is everything squared away here?"

"Yes," Sean said, scanning the scene of the mortar attack. "It looks as though all is well. One guy went to the aid station, and I want to drop by there, but I think that we're okay here."

He glanced at Lockhart and Davis as if to ask, *Right?*

Lockhart gave the chaplain a thumbs-up, and Davis smiled and said, "Thanks, sir, we'll see you around the base."

"I guess it's 'Welcome to Lex' for all of us," Sean said, smiling, as he and Kraus headed for the combat support hospital.

As the chaplain and his assistant made the rounds at the hospital, Sean spent more time with a young nurse who had felt herself suddenly coming down with the other kind of jitters than he did with the wounded man. The guy was elated, and not the least bit troubled. Sometimes, the relief of surviving a close call is like a euphoric drug.

Finally, an exhausted Sean Rasmunsen returned to his tent, bade his assistant good night, flicked on his battery-operated lamp, and slumped down in his chair. The coffeemaker that he had requested many hours earlier was on the desk. Tomorrow, he'd have to ask Kraus to requisition some coffee—and a proper table lamp.

More than that, he would have to get together a schedule for office and chapel hours. How can a pastor properly begin his ministry without posting a schedule for services?

Sean felt a hundred pounds lighter as he pulled off his ballistic vest. He stared at his cot and his gear, still lying where he had dumped it earlier in the day. The cot beckoned more strongly than the idea of unpacking. Some things are best left for the morning. It had been more than twenty hours since he'd boarded his flight in Kuwait, and he was truly bone weary.

He pulled off his boots, splashed some water on his face, and lay down. The thought of taking off his stinking, sweaty socks was drifting through his mind as drowsiness overcame him.

"Chaplain? Chaplain!"

The voice was almost like a dream.

Where am I? What time is it? Who are you?

"Sir, you better come quick."

"What? Where?" Sean asked, sitting up and shaking his head. A man was in his tent. He could see the man silhouetted in the doorway. The answer was like a push broom for the cobwebs in his brain.

"The morgue, sir."

Outside the sky was black, and FOB Lexington was quieter that it had been during the day. Sean followed the man down the narrow avenue between lines of tents. There were voices in the distance and the murmur of a number of generators, but other than that, the base was like a sleeping village.

It had seemed to all concerned that the mortar attack had caused no serious casualties. Sean had been to the scene himself and it had certainly seemed that way to him. As the man explained, however, a crew had gone in to clean up the site, and they had found someone about twenty yards from the impact point. It was a shrapnel wound.

The light in a morgue is always unnaturally white, verging on greenish. Sean had an unvoiced theory that this lent a sense of unreality to the scene that made death—and all that accompanied it—easier to grasp.

There were many tables. In a war zone, there were always many tables—don't call them *slabs*—in the battalion morgue.

Tonight, only one of these was occupied. Two people in scrubs stood around a single person in gray-green camouflage who was lying on it.

As Sean approached, he had a flash of recognition.

It was Dayane, Private First Class Alexander, the young woman he had met in the chapel a few hours earlier, the young woman whose boyfriend had decided to chart his course on life's seas without her.

She had been in the wrong place at the wrong time.

She had been twenty yards from the point of impact when the mortar rounds came down, but a random fragment of metal that was probably no bigger than a small pair of pliers had been hurled through the air.

Dayane's face looked peaceful. The cliché about closed eyes making someone seem asleep always came to mind at this moment—but the ugly gash that cut across her forehead, parting her short, dark hair, told a different story.

Tomorrow, or three days from now when he was finally located, Jason would learn of Dayane's death.

What an irony this was. The man whom Dayane had loved had—for reasons that Sean could not judge—rejected her, yet the man who had come to get the chaplain was now standing at her side, holding her hand. Tears were literally pouring down his cheeks. Sean had told her that someday, someone many times more her soul mate than Jason would come when she least expected him.

Sean touched the unblemished side of Dayane's forehead and whispered a prayer. The Twenty-third Psalm popped into his head. It always seemed appropriate at times like this.

He realized as he spoke that he didn't know what denomination she was, nor where she was from. He had spoken with her and he had counseled her briefly, but he had not even asked her about herself.

Now he would never have that chance.

As he looked into that quiet face, he said a prayer on his own behalf, asking for strength, asking for guidance, asking for whatever it took to be a better pastor to these young people, to be better every day.

He looked into the sad, dry eyes of the two men in scrubs—they had seen it all too many times—and turned to the sobbing man.

Honor the dead, but comfort the grieving.

With a tour under his belt and a wealth of experience, Sean still felt like a rookie. His ministry was only barely beginning. Welcome to Lex.

◆   ◆   ◆

Abide in me, O Lord, and I in Thee,
From this good hour, oh, leave me nevermore;
Then shall the discord cease, the wound be healed,
The lifelong bleeding of the soul be o'er.

These were but seasons beautiful and rare;
Abide in me, and they shall ever be;
Fulfill at once Thy precept and my prayer,
Come, and abide in me, and I in Thee.

FROM THE HYMN "ABIDE IN ME, O LORD"
WORDS BY HARRIET BEECHER STOWE

3

Duties Ever Near

"Don't talk that shit around the chaplain, dude!"

As Sean passed where they were working, the three soldiers were trading epithets in hip-hop rhyme that would have made a rap singer blush. Once, Sean himself might have blushed, but two weeks into his second tour, he hardly noticed. One of the men had, and he deliberately cautioned the others to tone down their lyrics.

Sean paused to talk with the three, asked their names, and asked where they were from. St. Louis and South Bend were the answers. The one who had admonished the others to dial it down was from Jersey City.

Once, Sean would have asked whether they were Christian, and if so which churches they attended, but most of the troops did not attend specific churches, and Sean had long since come to know that part of being a good pastor was being a good listener, not a good questioner.

Once he would have made a point to lead with his Christian foot, but he had learned that a religious foot at a first meeting could be a wedge. Even for someone raised in a church, it often put a divide between those who attended regularly and those who did not.

If there was one thing that Sean's first tour had taught him, it was that a chaplain's job is better described as that of a pastor, rather than that of a preacher.

Two weeks into his new ministry at FOB Lex, Chaplain Sean Rasmunsen had yet to establish any kind of routine, although a routine of sorts had started to impose itself on him. People were stopping by his tent at all hours, or taking turns with him when he dropped by the chapel each day. His best intentions were to be at the chapel each day at a regular time, but he was always being called here or there. Sgt. Kraus made sure that the clipboard hanging at the chaplain's tent carried a reasonable facsimile of the chaplain's unpredictable schedule.

The only constant was on Sundays. Father O'Malley had held both a Catholic Mass and a nondenominational service each Sunday morning. Sean couldn't take over the former, but he compensated with a second nondenominational service on Sunday night. The Catholic soldiers missed the priest, but understood that this was not a comfy, well-ordered base back in the real world.

Sean had promised that he would make arrangements to import a Catholic priest for Christmas services. He had a friend who was a priest at Camp Victory in Baghdad—another second-tour guy whom Sean had met when they were both in the Chaplain Basic Officers Leadership Course—who promised that he would come out to Lex for a couple of days in December.

Having begun to catch up to the FOB Lex momentum, Sean was indulging himself with a project. He had decided that the chapel needed a choir. His own ability in regard to matters of voice was sadly lacking, but logic told him that among the thousand or so people at the base, there must be at least a dozen or so who could sing.

Two weeks into his ministry at FOB Lex, Sean was doing a little outreach. If it was better to be a pastor than a preacher, it was better to develop a reputation as a good listener than a good proselytizer. Although he generally saved his sermons for those who came for them on Sunday, he had decided that this shouldn't prevent him from actively recruiting for his choir.

Thanks to a couple of cartons of hymnals that his predecessor had ordered, Sean had made a few familiar standards part of his Sunday service, and he turned his ears to spotting a few budding prospects here. Out of the fifty or so people who turned up for each service, he managed to identify several, but the challenge was to get them to agree to a practice schedule.

His initial core group was just four people, including Ashley Mariott, an energetic young specialist who had been the leader of her Baptist church choir back home in Tennessee. He made her the choir director. He needed someone with experience, energy, and the right attitude. She had all three. Someone better might come along later, but Ashley came aboard first, and she got the job.

As he finished his rounds at the hospital and started heading for his tent, Sean decided to make a detour back to the place where he had earlier rapped with the three rappers. One of the men, De Shawn Hughes from Jersey City, struck him as more talented than his apparent choice of musical genre seemed to indicate.

The chaplain found the young soldier alone, changing out barrels on a line of belt-fed M240 machine guns. The barrels required replacement routinely, as the desert dust and grit inevitably got inside. This turned each round that was fired into an abrasive pad, scouring the metal and enlarging the inside diameter by a minuscule amount every time a bullet went through. Eventually, as the caliber of the barrel became large enough, the velocity of each round dropped significantly, making the gun less effective. It then became even dangerous for the operator.

"I couldn't help noticing that you like to sing," Sean said.

"Um, well . . ." De Shawn didn't really know what to say. No officer had ever greeted him with those words. "I just go along with what's playing on whoever's iPod."

"If I'm not mistaken, I'd say that you've had some experience singing songs that didn't come out of an iPod or a radio," Sean said. He was guessing here.

"Maybe. I guess."

"School? Church?"

"Both, I guess."

"Where'd you go to church?"

"Emmanuel Baptist . . . when I was a kid," De Shawn admitted warily. "Haven't been in a long time."

"That's cool," Sean told him reassuringly. "Lots of people I know haven't gone for a long time."

"People . . . they *tell* you that they ain't been to church?"

"Yep. Did you sing in your church?"

"I guess. My grandmother had me doing it."

"Did you like to sing?" Sean asked, handing the soldier a M240 barrel so that he didn't have to reach.

"I guess," De Shawn said thoughtfully, thumbing the barrel release button on the left side of the weapon.

"One of the new things I'm trying here now that I'm at the 2/77 is to start a choir to sing on Sundays in the chapel . . . and some other times, too. Do you suppose you'd like to come and check it out . . . maybe even join us?"

"I can't sing none of those kinda songs no more."

"I bet you could if you practiced," Sean prodded.

"Naw."

"Bet you could."

"How much?" De Shawn said, figuring his comeback would catch the chaplain off guard.

"Twenty bucks," Sean said instantly, catching De Shawn himself off guard. "Deal?"

Two nights later, when the 2/77's choir held its second practice session, De Shawn Hughes was one of seven people who showed up. After Spc. Mariott, the director, he was the second African American, and the first bass voice. He stumbled through the first hymn as he tried to follow the words, but on his third try, he turned in a better than passable rendition.

Sean smiled and left the chapel. He didn't want Ashley to have a backseat driver hovering in the wings. The choir was obviously still rough around the edges, but he could see that she had the raw material she needed.

Her boundless enthusiasm was showing its lack of bounds as "her" choir made its debut on Sunday to an enthusiastic response. Indeed, this performance was the best recruiting tool that his choir had seen to date. The following week's practice brought more than a dozen wannabes.

It came as an immense surprise when Ashley approached the chaplain on Saturday with a concerned expression on her face.

"Chaplain . . . we got a problem," she said.

"What is it?"

"Well, y'know we've been getting a lot of good people showing up for practice," she explained as she fell in and walked with him toward the Tactical Operations Center, where he was headed for a staff meeting. "But we've also got a couple of . . . well . . ."

"Duds?"

"Um, well . . . yes, sir."

"Really bad duds?"

"Um, yeah. Well, there's one in particular. Kyle Lockhart. Nice kid, but he can't hold a tune worth sh . . . um, y'know?"

"Yeah, I know." Sean remembered Lockhart, the kid who froze during the mortar attack on his first night at Lex.

"I don't really know what to say," Ashley said in a tone that pleaded for guidance. "I don't know what to tell him."

"What's the purpose of a music ministry?" Sean asked.

"Music?"

"Yeah, but what's more important than music?"

"Fellowship?" Ashley asked rhetorically after giving it some thought.

"Yup," Sean answered. "Fellowship trumps musical ability in a *church* choir. Lex is not Carnegie Hall. It's a place where people who enjoy singing can express themselves as part of the service. Right?"

"I guess so."

"Back home, did you ever have any duds in your choir?"

"I guess so, but . . ."

"Listen, Ashley, I really don't want to interfere with your running of the choir, 'cause I think you're doing real good, but I'd like to *ask* you to give the kid a chance. Kicking him out can be bad for morale all around. Can you let him stay for the time being?"

"I guess so."

No one knows better than a chaplain the immense gulf that exists between theory and practice. In theory, Sean had been right. Choirs are made up of people who come together for a love of music and the material they sing. In theory, those who come together have a certain basic skill. Those without the skill are usually not drawn to participate. In practice, theories do not often hold.

On Sunday, alas, Kyle Lockhart proved himself to be one of the worst singers that Sean had ever heard—possibly *the* worst he'd ever heard at a church service. The other choir members braced themselves and carried on bravely, but Sean could see people in the folding chairs that doubled for pews glancing at one another and at the choir.

Fortunately, for the finale, Ashley had tapped De Shawn Hughes for a baritone solo in which his budding natural talent truly shone. Only this saved the day for the choir.

After the closing prayer, as everyone was filing out, Ashley shot Sean an *I told you so* glance and he nodded back to her with an *I'll talk to him myself* glance.

"Bless you, Kyle. It's good to see you at church," Sean said, approaching him as the other choir members went their separate ways.

"It's good to be here," he replied. "I used to go to church a lot when I was a kid. Haven't been for years."

"It's good to have you back. I'm sure that He is glad to have you."

"I sure wish I could get the hang of this singing, though," Kyle said, shrugging.

"It's hard, I know," the chaplain said sympathetically. Silently he was asking for higher authority to guide his words. "It's not for everyone. I'm a living example of that. I can't sing two notes that go together to save my life. When it comes to music, I know that my role in the choir is as an audience."

"Me neither. I try real hard and it just doesn't come out the way I hear it in my head."

"I know what you're talking about," Sean said. "It's good to know your limitations, I guess."

"I sure do want to participate, though," Kyle said plaintively. "I really want to make this work."

"What's your background?" Sean asked. "What sorts of things did you do in school? Sports?"

"No, I was too small for sports," he said. "Took a lot of crap for that. It was a small school. Just a hundred and thirty-four in my class. I enlisted to prove myself. Picked up a lotta muscles in basic. Proved myself *to* myself at least. No, I didn't go out for much in school. Worked in the library for three years. Took a lot of crap for that, too."

"What did you do for the library?"

"Just the usual stuff, y'know. Filing, sorting, ordering stuff. That . . . ordering stuff . . . is what I got to be pretty good at. They didn't have any budget for materials, so I found all these places online, y'know, places that provide last year's books and last year's software . . . provide it all to schools for pennies on the dollar, y'know."

"I know," Sean said. "I think I know exactly. And y'know what, I think I know how you can participate."

Sean proceeded to create a situation wherein Kyle Lockhart found himself with no time for choir practice. Within a week, cases of books began arriving at FOB Lexington addressed to "Private Kyle Lockhart, Lex Chapel, FOB Lexington," in care of an APO address that funneled mail from the United States to the troops in Iraq.

Inside the boxes were hymnals and inspirational books, religious software, and computer games. Where once he had found places that sold inexpensive materials to schools, Kyle was now tracking down entities that were bending over backward to *donate* religious materials to American troops overseas.

◆　◆　◆

Do not wait until some deed of greatness you may do,
Do not wait to shed your light afar,
To the many duties ever near you now be true,
Brighten the corner where you are.

Here for all your talent you may surely find a need,
Here reflect the bright and Morning Star;
Even from your humble hand the Bread of Life may feed,
Brighten the corner where you are.

FROM THE HYMN "BRIGHTEN THE CORNER WHERE YOU ARE"
WORDS BY INA DULEY OGDON

4

Saf City

"Let's load 'em up and head 'em out," Capt. Ryan Clark shouted as he climbed aboard the lead Humvee. Inside the vehicles, good-natured banter sputtered to a stop and everyone got serious as the convoy rolled out of FOB Lexington.

Moving "outside the wire," as the troops called leaving the relative safety—and the barbed wire—of the Forward Operating Base, was traditionally an invitation to a myriad of potential hazards. Out here on the road to Safaliyah, as elsewhere in war-torn Iraq, the next few hours would *probably* be boringly routine, but they could just as easily be punctuated by the blast of an IED that could change anyone's life permanently.

Sgt. Tyler Kraus nervously fingered the sights of his M4 carbine and glanced across at his charge. Sitting opposite in the tight confines of the Humvee, Chaplain Sean Rasmunsen smiled and gave his assistant a thumbs-up.

Combat patrols outside the wire were a big part of what the 2nd Battalion of the 77th Infantry Regiment did for a living, and riding along was an increasing part of how Sean saw his job description. Troops tended to respect officers who weren't afraid to dirty their boots, and they were developing an affinity for the young chaplain whom they had seen on patrol as often as they saw him leading services at the chapel.

For Sean, the patrols meant keeping in touch with his congregation at their moments of greatest anxiety. This was the essence of why he had come back to Iraq. For Kraus, this *was* his moment of greatest anxiety. Taking care of yourself was one thing. Riding shotgun for the only unarmed man in the convoy was an order or two of magnitude more challenging.

As Lt. Col. Folbright had told Chaplain Rasmunsen on his first day at FOB Lex, the primary reason that a FOB existed in this corner of Diyala Province was the city of Safaliyah. "That's most of our mission out here," he'd said. Most of the patrols took the troops into and beyond Saf City.

The travel time from the base to the city was short, and the road was clear. Placing an IED on this stretch of paved highway was virtually impossible, but the bad guys had shown great ingenuity in the past. The city streets inside Safaliyah were another matter. Vigilance was a vital necessity.

Over the past year or so, the relationship between the Americans and the people of Safaliyah had changed considerably. A big part of the change here, as elsewhere, was that the Americans had gotten out of their vehicles and had walked among the people. Convoys of armored Humvees and lumbering Bradley Fighting Vehicles were intimidating at best, and guaranteed to create an "us and them" dichotomy between the two sides. Things had gradually changed as Americans had begun relating to the townspeople at eye level.

The Iraqis casually referred to the Americans as the *ulooj*, an ancient derogatory epithet from Arabic literature that has a variety of meanings: "pigs," "bloodsuckers," "infidels," "crusaders." Even after a thousand years, Muslims still have a sour taste for the Crusades. Despite all this, the Iraqis had slowly come to accept the *ulooj*. The epithet lost some of its sting as the two sides gradually began to cooperate.

The Americans were and would never *not* be an alien occupying force—but compared to the alternative, they were benign occupiers. The Iraqis had no use for the alternative. They were fed up with Shiite and Sunni street gangs, and they *hated* the al-Qaeda gangs. Al-Qaeda had come into Iraq packaging themselves as saviors, calling themselves Tanzim Qaidat al-Jihad fi Bilad al-Rafidayn, meaning Organization of Jihad's Base in Iraq (or literally "the land of the two rivers"), making them sound like the local guys they were not. Soon, however, they came to be perceived as bullies whose only interest was their own.

Like the Americans, they were not native to the land of the two rivers, but their cruelty to the people of this land eclipsed what anyone could attribute to the Americans.

To the Iraqis who still felt that the *ulooj* were evil, they were clearly the lesser of two evils when compared to al-Qaeda. More and more Iraqis cooperated with the Americans because there was some truth to the old adage that "the enemy of my enemy is my friend."

In this inconvenient marriage of convenience, the Iraqis found that having the Americans to combat the al-Qaeda threat made them palatable, even welcome. And after all, at *eye level*, when you actually looked them in the eye, the Americans weren't so bad.

On the flip side, the Americans began to see from eye level that the Iraqis weren't so bad, so alien. Just as the Americans were the *ulooj*, the Americans had their own nicknames for the Iraqis. Among the most common, and most tame, was *hajji*, meaning someone who participated in the hajj, the once-in-a-lifetime pilgrimage that Muslims made to their holy city of Mecca.

Sean waved to a group of Iraqi kids as he and Kraus climbed out of the Humvee about a block east of Outpost Bravo, an American forward location on the road that led eastward toward the Iranian border. When the grinning, unarmed American didn't break eye contact, they smiled and waved back.

"*As-salaam alaikum*," Sean said in his best language-school Arabic. The kids giggled at the stilted pronunciation, but at least they understood what he was saying. The locals always appreciated it when the Americans spoke their language.

At eye level, the kids were not hajjis, but simply kids.

Part of being at eye level meant permanently staffing the outposts such as Bravo that the 2/77 had placed around Saf City. Back in the early days, the American patrols headed back to Lex at the end of the day and al-Qaeda sneaked in to punish anyone who'd been friendly to the Americans that day. Once the Americans started hanging around 24/7, it was harder for al-Qaeda to bully the Iraqis.

"*Ismi* Sean," he said, squatting down to talk to the kids as they approached. He always identified himself by his first name because it had just one syllable and was easier to say than *Rasmunsen.*

"*Aish ismika?*" Sean asked in a passably pronounced query as to the names of the kids.

"Bilal," the older boy answered.

A girl identified herself as Naja and nodded to the younger kids, giving their names as they giggled and coyly hid their faces.

"You're like kids everywhere," Sean said with a grin. They didn't understand the words, but they understood the grin and replied in kind. "I wish we didn't have to grow up killing each other."

He glanced at Sgt. Kraus, who was looking beyond the kids toward the houses that were narrowly packed along the side street. He was taking his job seriously. Sean said a quick prayer of thanks for Kraus's vigilance, but added a postscript asking for a day when it wasn't necessary.

Sean handed the kids a couple of packs of chewing gum, and the Americans moved down the street. As Capt. Clark and a couple of squads of troops began a dismounted patrol through the east side of Safaliyah, Sean and his assistant made a stop at Outpost Bravo.

It was a low cinder-block building away from the others, but like the others. Plastic chairs were set around the exterior, and a canvas awning shaded the entrance. No menacing machine gun barrels protruded from the small windows—the soldiers had consciously made Outpost Bravo *not* have the appearance of a pillbox, although it had in fact been reinforced against IEDs and RPGs.

Inside, a slight breeze blew in from the outside, but it was noticeably warmer. As summer approached, this could be a problem. The people inside had shed their body armor as they went about their tasks.

Sean pulled off his helmet as he passed from room to room, greeting the troops. As usual, they were glad to see their chaplain outside the FOB Lex wire, on what passed as front lines in Saf City.

In the last room, a single soldier dressed in a gray-green T-shirt sat before a low folding table set up with piles of electronic gear from which snaked a mass of reptilian cables. She turned as he came in, tossing her blond hair slightly. It was Cpl. Davis, the communications specialist from Jefferson City.

"Hello, Chaplain Rasmunsen," she said, smiling.

"Hi, Jeff City," he replied, more informally than he usually greeted the troops. "You have your JTRS running, I see."

"Yes, I do. It's really a step up from the old stuff we had when I was training."

"It seems that good comm gear is really important out in an outpost."

"It's key," she said, nodding. "Like you said before, except for food, there's almost nothing more important. Can't run the place without it. Like, we can talk to Lex, we can talk to Baghdad, we can even talk to the Air Force."

"Woo-ee." Sean laughed in mock amazement.

"I haven't seen you around much," she said, ignoring her crackling console. "But I guess I've been spending a lot of time out here the last few weeks."

"You oughta stop by the chapel for services on Sunday," he said, doing his job. "We have a really nice choir going."

"That's what I've heard . . . yeah . . . maybe I will."

"You seem to have gotten into the swing of things here in Iraq. When I first met you on the chopper coming in, you seemed pretty stressed out."

"Like I *hate* helicopters," she said. "And that was like the worst flight I've ever been on. I'm happy to be on the ground."

"It's a long way from Jeff City."

"I *know*," she said. "But it's an experience. I don't mind it, do you?"

"No, it's . . . well . . . where I want to be," Sean replied, realizing that this was probably one of the only times during either of his deployments that anyone had asked *him* how he felt. He was always asking others.

"Really?"

"Yeah, really. This is where I think I belong. I truly feel that I was called to be here . . . doing what I'm doing."

"Called? Like by Him?" Braylee asked quizzically, glancing upward.

"Yeah." Sean laughed. "By the Guy Upstairs. Does that seem improbable?"

"Nope," she said. "I've never been called . . . at least that I know of . . . but that doesn't mean I doubt somebody *could* be called, y'know."

"How did a young woman like yourself end up at a place like Outpost Bravo?" Sean asked. "Seems like that was some kind of calling?"

"Not in the same way," she said. "But I guess sort of. My dad was in Nam. He lost his arm, but he came home, got a job, did well at it, raised three kids, never complained about what happened. He was always proud of the country and had a lot of people looking up to him. I guess I sorta called myself to do something like this because of the example he set."

"He must be very proud," Sean told her.

"He died about two years ago," she said. "Just before I enlisted. He would have been, maybe. Guess if he's up there looking down, he's proud. I'd certainly hope he is."

"I'm sure he is," Sean said soberly.

"But the Army's good experience and money to finish college," she said, smiling.

"What were you studying?" Sean asked.

"What else? Communications," she chuckled, gesturing at the sprawling setup on the table. "Maybe radio or television or something. I'm learning how to run all this stuff."

"Well, in any case, I wish you luck, and I hope to have you stop by chapel one of these Sundays," he said, standing up and clutching his helmet. "Don't forget, we have a great choir."

"That's what I've heard," she said, smiling. "I heard you have a great preacher, too."

As Sean and Sgt. Kraus rejoined the rest of the patrol outside Outpost Bravo, Captain Clark was briefing the rest of the men.

"We got some intel on the QT from one of the old guys in the souk in town that there's some al-Qaeda holed up in a place just out of town on the Iran road," Clark said quietly, hoping to stay out of earshot of any eavesdroppers. "He's been reliable in the past, so it's worth checking out."

Ryan Clark was an officer who had earned the respect of his guys. It was not typical for the company commander to head a platoon-sized patrol, but Clark was the type who insisted on leading from the front. Three years out of West Point, he was well into his second tour. He was part of a generation of U.S. Army officers who had begun their careers since the start of Operation Iraqi Freedom and who would carry that experience forward into their service careers. Everyone expected that one day the young captain would be a colonel commanding a brigade, and that eventually he would wear a general's stars.

Clark ordered the vehicles to head west on a road parallel to the road where the supposed al-Qaeda hideout lay. While the Humvees attracted the attention of the potential bad guys, a foot patrol would simultaneously sneak up on them on the road that actually led to the alleged hideout. If a battle was joined, the troops in the Humvee column could intervene quickly.

It was obvious from the tone of Clark's voice that he really wanted to lead the foot patrol himself, but a commander's place was with the main body of troops and with the communications link.

As the foot soldiers moved out inconspicuously, the vehicles drove through the streets of Safaliyah in the opposite direction to give the foot patrol time to get into position before moving back onto the parallel road.

As he studied the random faces of the Iraqi civilians on the street through the bullet-resistant glass window of the third Humvee in the line, Sean realized that he was about to become part of an offensive operation for the first time in his career.

He had ridden on routine patrols before, and he had been on patrols that were attacked, but this was the first time he'd been with troops who were expressly on the offensive. Tyler Kraus had his finger near the safety of his M4. He looked more nervous than Sean felt.

Amid Sean's smorgasbord of emotions were apprehension, a natural apprehension of knowing that you're going into battle, and the conflicted awareness that he was a chaplain and he was part of an attack. He knew that he shared this awareness with countless other American chaplains stretching back through the years, back through Nam, through two world wars, to the War between the States and before.

Overriding the other factors that boiled his adrenaline that afternoon was an unfamiliar emotion—exhilaration. This prospect of a coming fight was—despite his efforts to frame the experience with logic—exciting!

At last, the brief clips that sputtered through the radio told the men in Sean's Humvee that the foot patrol was in position. He could see the target buildings in the distance, squatting among a cluster of date palms. In the warm afternoon light, the scene looked so peaceful—so deceptively peaceful.

He could not see, but he could hear on the radio as the troops—men with whom he had just walked Saf City's streets— kicked in the door of a building.

The crash of a wooden door being shattered was quickly followed by yet another, more sinister, sound. Any American soldier, even a noncombatant like Sean, knows the hollow hammering clunk of an AK-47.

The old man in the souk had been right. Armed gunmen were in the building, and they were reacting to the sudden intrusion of American boot leather.

The Kalashnikovs were answered by the sounds of M16s.

"Go! Go!"

Somewhere up in the lead vehicle, Capt. Clark now ordered a full-on assault.

The distinct sounds of the two automatic rifle types had melded into a swirling, roaring thunder that mixed with the racing of engines and shouts of people in battle.

Sean felt the heaving, jostling, slamming sensation of being inside a vehicle dashing across open terrain. He saw the dust clouds and smelled them as they swirled inside the Humvee. He heard the heavy machine gun fire above his head, and he felt the hot brass cartridge cases splattering everywhere around him.

Suddenly the Humvee lurched to a stop, doors opened, and people were running. Sean felt Kraus push him into the floorboards and climb on top of him.

A bullet crashed against the door frame. Then another. Sean heard the sound of a ricochet as it pinged near his head.

Kraus remained atop Sean.

"Keep your head down, Padre!"

Sounds of AK-47s and M16s ebbed and flowed in that symphony of swirling, roaring thunder.

At last the noise of gunfire died away, overtaken by frantic shouting. Soon this, too, slackened. Now it was more of an excited conversation.

Sean felt the weight of the sergeant and his ton of body armor lift off him. Both men took a deep breath.

"Are you all right?" Kraus asked as Sean coughed out a mouthful of dust.

"Is everyone else all right?" Sean answered, peering toward the building that had just been assaulted.

"Six bad guys down. No good guys hit."

It was a matter-of-fact assessment. The Americans had taken down the enemy with no casualties. As everyone knew, it didn't always work out this way, and this fact should have been a cause for celebration, but the sergeant who was surveying the small battlefield just reported the facts. They had executed their task and had gotten off lucky. Job done.

Sean made his way toward the scene and looked into the eyes of the soldiers. Even for the men on their first tour, the aftermath of a deadly gun battle was not a new experience. They had grown familiar with the sight, though few ever grew truly accustomed.

This is the battleground of the chaplain. He walks with his people as they walk the line, the line between succumbing completely to the horror of battle and the arguably greater horror of taking the killing and the death for granted.

It was the time of the pastor, not of the preacher. He was here to comfort, not to preach. The words were often not easy, but they were usually simple. Often there were no words at all—just a nod, just a pat on the back.

For one young soldier, with a *What the hell did we just do?* expression, there was even a quick, unashamed hug.

The al-Qaeda hideout had been decimated. Sean counted seven bodies. He saw a pile of bomb-making materials in the main part of the house and automatic weapons stacked in a side room.

He stepped outside, where more bodies lay in the brush along a small irrigation ditch. One man was staring at these bodies, his M16 at his side. It was De Shawn Hughes, the soloist in the 2/77 church choir. He looked at Sean and shook his head. Sean just nodded. It was a sobering moment.

"*Aaaalllllaaaahhhh...!*"

Sean was startled by the shout that came from somewhere in

the brush. As he turned, there were gunshots. Somebody near the ditch was firing at him.

"*Arrrrrghh!*"

Sean felt Tyler Kraus body-slam him. He saw the sergeant raise his M4 and open fire.

He watched the 5.56-mm rounds rip into the man in the brush.

He saw blood and flesh hurtling through the air.

"Stay down!" Kraus demanded.

Sean obeyed.

Kraus ran over to the man, looked down, kicked the AK-47 away from his hand, and began probing the brush with the muzzle of his M4.

At last, he returned to the chaplain, satisfied that there were no further gunmen. Only then did he allow Sean to lift his head out of the dirt.

"Are you okay?" Kraus asked.

"I think so, but man, you hit me hard!"

"Jesus!" Kraus said. "Pardon me, I mean . . . You've been hit, Chaplain!"

Indeed he had. The hard blow that he had taken from Kraus knocking him down had apparently been preceded by a 7.62-mm round from the AK-47 that had impacted his body armor about three inches to the left of his sternum. Another five or six inches and it would have hit his arm.

"Jesus," Sean began, taking the Lord's name in an entirely different context than Kraus had. His prayer would be in thanksgiving of a mere bruise to his rib cage. He was thankful also for what this bruise would remind him of—the nature of the combat that so many of his congregation faced—and he was very thankful for Tyler Kraus.

◆ ◆ ◆

O God, the Strength of those who war,
The Hope of those who wait,
Be with our sons gone forth to fight,
And those who keep the gate.

Give to our hosts in battle's hour
Firm hearts and courage high,
Thy comfort give to those who fall,
Thy peace to those who die.

Breathe on our land the spirit calm
Which faith in right bestows,
And in the hours of dark suspense
A faith which stronger grows.

FROM THE HYMN "O GOD THE STRENGTH OF THOSE WHO WAR"
WORDS BY WILLIAM BOYD CARPENTER

5

Understanding

"A chaplain belongs with his people," Sean Rasmunsen told Lt. Col. Amos Folbright as they sat in the boss's office at the Tactical Operations Center. "Can't do my job if I'm not at the job site."

"I don't want my chaplain going down to Saf City and getting himself shot," Folbright said with mock disdain. "It would be bad for morale."

"It seems to be *good* for morale that I *do* get out of the chapel, and outside that wire once in a while," Sean said, smiling.

The 2nd Battalion's commanding officer couldn't argue with that. Having taken a round to the chest had strengthened the chaplain's "street cred" with the troops. Those who had been inclined to think of a chaplain as an aloof character who inhabited a lofty world above and beyond their own mundane world now saw him more as someone with whom they could talk.

More and more of the people who "came by to talk" or who sidled up to him as he made his rounds at FOB Lexington were not regular churchgoers. Some wanted to talk about spiritual things, but most just wanted to have someone to talk to. Sean was reminded of that axiom, learned very early in his first tour, that people would much rather talk to the chaplain than the shrink.

With those who wanted to talk about God, Sean talked about His plan and His message. With the others, Sean just offered insights on relationships and fears and troubles, or just commiserated about how much he also wished he could just take the afternoon off to go bass fishing.

So it was with even the boss. Even Folbright had opened up with some off-the-record conversation about the overall mission of the U.S. Army in Iraq and his thoughts on the troops and their relations with the civilians in Safaliyah.

"I wish we could do more for those folks down in Saf City besides just building them a water treatment plant," he said.

"Every time I go down there, the kids are happy to see us," Sean said. "A pack or two of gum always buys you a dozen friends . . . or at the very least it fosters some goodwill. Maybe we could start with those kids in Saf City?"

"Good idea," Folbright agreed. "But you gotta steer clear of anything religious. I knew a family over in Najaf. Got to know them pretty well. The extremists caught them with some Christian literature and killed them all. That stuff happens all the time."

"I know," Sean said, shrugging. "I've heard of it myself. Trouble is that religious materials are easy to get . . . people *want* to send it . . . they think you need it. They mean well, but . . . you don't know how many times I've had to say 'thanks, but no thanks' to some Christian mission group or other that wants to send stuff for me to pass out to the people . . . prayer books, Bibles, Christian music CDs, stuff for kids . . . I get e-mails all the time. They mean well . . . but they just have no idea."

"So what *can* you . . . we . . . do?"

"Every time I go down there, I see kids kicking around ratty old soccer balls. They just love soccer here, y'know. We could try to get them some sporting goods. That oughta be easy enough."

"Worth a try. Where do you start?"

"I got a guy who helps me out. Private Kyle Lockhart. It's incredible what he can do with the Internet. He can scrounge just about anything . . . and he *has*. Books . . . music . . . computers . . . you name it."

"You say he's a private?"

"Yup."

"We'll have to do something about *that*."

"Thank you, sir."

Sean glanced at the clock and told the boss that he'd have to excuse himself. It was Sunday, and he had places to be—such as at the front of the chapel.

"I see that it's almost ten," he said. "I've got to report to my duty station."

"Very good, then," the colonel said, snapping off a quick and perfunctory salute. "Dismissed."

"Will I see you at services today?" Sean smiled, returning the salute.

"Um, well, um . . ." Folbright sputtered. He was Sean's most staunch supporter at Lex, but not exactly one of his most committed congregants. "Well, um, I guess . . . well . . . what could it hurt? Can't hang around all day with my ass glued to this chair."

◆ ◆ ◆

The service went well. The commander did show up. He took a seat near the back, but he did remain for the full hour and a quarter. As usual, the choir was a hit. When De Shawn Hughes sang his solo, Sean watched his face, measuring the maturity that had blossomed in this big kid who'd come to Iraq as a tough guy in his own sphere, but a fish out of water in the world beyond.

Sean delivered his planned sermon on sharing that was built around the passages in Matthew 25 where Jesus says whatever you do for the least of His brethren, you do for Him. This gave Sean an opportunity to work in a brief mention of the soccer ball project.

Many times, Sean had watched people cringing in their pews during this parable. They also often felt themselves chided for not doing enough for their fellow man. Today, he wanted to give them a proactive project, rather than just a scolding. He wanted to be a pastor rather than a preacher.

Apparently, it had worked. As the closing hymn ended, several people approached him with offers to get involved. Among them, Sean noticed the smiling face of Braylee Davis.

"I'm glad you could come today," Sean said warmly as she gave him a slight hug.

"I heard that you had a good choir." She grinned.

"I hope they lived up to the PR."

"Yeah, it was great," she said. "I especially liked the soloist. It makes me homesick for the First Methodist back home."

"We like to make folks feel at home," he told her. "But I hate to hear it when they're homesick."

"Everybody's homesick," she said more soberly. "At least to some degree. Like I try to make the best of the situation and be at home where I am. That's why this was nice. I'm gonna have to come more often."

"You are always more than welcome," he said.

"I feel welcome, and I liked what you were saying about the kids. When you get that going, let me know. Like I wanna help out. I've made friends with some of the kids down there myself."

"Thanks," Sean told her. "And thanks for that comment about being at home where you are. Maybe you could come to one of our prayer meetings and talk about that. It's real informal. Be glad to have you stop by. Every night at eight . . . right here."

"Well . . . um . . . maybe . . ." she stammered, edging toward the door with a nonchurchgoer's typical reaction to a prayer meeting. "Maybe sometime. Can't tonight. I'm headed back to Bravo for another rotation. Maybe sometime, though. See you at church next Sunday, though . . . for sure."

Sean hated to have put Braylee on the spot. He hated to see her natural positive attitude dampened by the preacher's having nudged too hard. He'd have to keep working to understand how to keep the preacher in the bullpen and the pastor on the mound.

As part of his rounds, Sean always stopped by the phone room. Located in a concrete building near the Tactical Operations Center, it was the place where the troops could use satellite phones to talk with loved ones back home. Almost everyone had access to e-mail at FOB Lexington, but sometimes a few e-mailed snapshots and a text message just weren't enough.

Usually, the conversations were happy, bittersweet reminiscences of birthdays missed and visits by grandparents, or they were confirmations of undying love. Sometimes there were wedding plans.

Occasionally, the line of dialogue went from bad to worse, ending in personal tragedy. There might be the breaking of news of the death of a parent, or the pain of a relationship come to an unanticipated and abrupt end. Sean thought often of Dayane, the girl he met on his first day at Lex, and how things had ended for her.

Part of a chaplain's job, he thought, was to be hanging around at the little coffee place outside the phone room. He'd get a cup and sit down at a quiet table with a newspaper.

"Could I talk to you?"

"Of course," he'd answer this query, which was often nervous and usually whispered. The exchange almost invariably began this way.

"My daughter . . ." a young woman began nervously.

He breathed an internal sigh and a silent prayer. These were not good words when spoken to a minister with such urgency.

"What's your name, Private Schmitt?" Sean asked, gesturing for her to take a deep breath and calm herself. Her surname was stitched on her uniform, but he always preferred to use a first name.

It turned out that Pfc. Kelsi Schmitt was from Fort Dodge in Iowa, and her daughter, Brittany, had been living with Kelsi's mother.

"My ex just came and took her," Kelsi sobbed. "Mom couldn't do anything."

Sean had visions of a wild-eyed crackhead snatching a small baby in the middle of the night, but fortunately things were not quite that bad. Brittany was almost seven, and both of her parents belonged to the same church.

He let her talk. He let her vent. He let her cry.

He offered some words of encouragement, some words of scripture, and a promise to do more than pray for Brittany's safe return to her grandmother.

Sean picked up the sat phone and just called the pastor at the specified church, catching him as he was in his bathrobe, making coffee. It was Sunday and his plate was full, but when Sean identified himself as a chaplain phoning from Iraq, he sat down and they worked out a plan. He'd see Brittany's grandmother at church, and he'd talk to her father that afternoon.

Kelsi was sobbing tears of joy when Sean patted her on the back and left the phone room.

"Thank you," she said. "I can't understand how you could make it seem so easy."

The pastor in Fort Dodge promised Sean an e-mail update in a few days.

Nurture the living.

One small victory.

Sean was in his tent working on an upcoming sermon when Tyler Kraus burst in with the acronym that always wrenches the gut.

"IED," he said, his face furrowed with concern. "On the road to Saf City. Just happened. They're bringing them in now."

Sean sent word to Ashley Mariott asking her to make the evening service a choir event and headed for the combat support hospital.

He and the sergeant passed the helipad just as a Black Hawk was setting down with the first casualties from the explosion of an improvised explosive device and jumped in to lend a hand to the medics who would unload the wounded.

The scene in the payload bay of the UH-60 was nothing short of carnage. The floor looked like the floor of a slaughterhouse. It was worse than what Sean had seen after the al-Qaeda shoot-out—and these were people he *knew*. He recognized faces that had looked at him from his congregation that very morning.

He and Tyler steadied a stretcher while the medical personnel went inside to begin extracting the injured. Best to leave that work to people who knew what part of a broken body could be lifted without exacerbating an injury.

As he waited and caught his breath beneath the deafening noise of the two General Electric T700 engines and the huge blades, Sean looked up into the bay. In the corner, he saw her face and remembered that Braylee Davis had been headed back into Saf City tonight. It was *her* convoy that had been hit. He could barely make out her features in the shadows, but at least he knew that she was alive and sitting up.

"Run, run!" the medic aboard the chopper demanded.

Sean and Tyler ran. They ran to the waiting entrance of the ER. The object on the stretcher they carried hardly looked like a living person, but they knew it was. In the medical triage process, the living with a chance of staying that way are on the first stretcher out. The hopeless have to wait.

Soon the ER was a nightmare of barely organized chaos.

Shouts, screams, and sobs filled the air.

The man whom Sean and Tyler brought in had lost a leg, and doctors raced to save his arm.

Sean watched another succumb on the operating table. He had lost so much blood from so many places that they simply could not stop the bleeding.

Even the living were a bloody mess.

Sean spent the next eternity staying out of the way of the doctors and trying to comfort those who had been stabilized. The line from the chaplain's motto about comforting the wounded came to mind. It was at times like this that he wished he could do more, but was glad for what he *could* do.

One man, obviously in horrendous pain, reached up to grab Sean's hand and simply begged, "Pray for me, man."

Sean did, saying the Lord's Prayer, slowly and deliberately.

The man was making an effort to wrap his mind and voice around the words when his head tipped gently to one side.

Sean gulped, then saw his chest heaving rhythmically. It was the morphine, not the Grim Reaper, that had taken him.

Others were not so lucky.

Sean recognized the mortuary affairs people as they arrived to take the man who hadn't made it.

Gradually, the room grew quiet as the survivors slipped one by one into that peaceful, albeit temporary, place where the morphine interrupts the pain. As people began picking up the brown-stained uniform cloth that had been hacked from the broken bodies, Sean and Tyler stepped out into the night. The dust spewed across the ER entrance by the Black Hawk's rotors billowed up in a ghastly, choking cloud.

As the dust settled, the 2/77's Religious Support Team could take a moment to catch their breath. The chaplain ignored his assistant when he apologized for the tears streaming down his dusty cheeks and complemented Kraus on how hard he'd worked in the ER. Sean felt like sobbing himself, but he knew the tears would not come.

Both men were stained head to toe with drying blood, but where they were headed, nobody would care.

The morgue was as quiet as the ER had been noisy. The whirring of the air-conditioning simply made the room seem all that much emptier.

There were three bodies that the mortuary affairs people had cleaned up to make somewhat presentable. Sean recognized each one. He also recognized their half dozen comrades who stood nearby in silence. Among these soldiers was Braylee Davis. She was the only one who still wore her helmet.

Honor the dead, Sean thought as he pulled out his pocket prayer book.

Tomorrow, these three young heroes, their lives cut short, would be placed on a chopper to go to Baghdad and be placed on a C-17 bound for the United States. Tomorrow, they would be sent on their way by a full-fledged memorial service. Sean would read from his hardback Bible. Taps would be played, and so too "Amazing Grace." Everyone who could, religious or not, would be there. Honoring the dead has always been universal among soldiers. Even for nonchurchgoers, a memorial was a means of tribute, a means of insisting to the living that their departed comrade had not died in vain.

Tonight, however, there would also be a memorial service, a far more intimate one. Sean opened his little book to the Twenty-third Psalm. Even the mortuary affairs people bowed their heads.

When it was over, one of the onlookers, a Catholic, instinctively made the sign of the cross.

The living all came forward to greet Sean—everyone but Braylee Davis.

Sean murmured words of encouragement to each of them in turn, and walked over to where Braylee stood alone.

The blood that covered her uniform was in a pattern that told him she had held someone tightly as he bled to death.

Her face was covered with layers of dust, the outer layer untouched by the tracks of her tears. She had, at some point in the ordeal, simply reached a point of physical shock and emotional numbness, where tears no longer flowed.

"I try to make the best of the situation and be at home where I am," she had said a few hours earlier. Now the situation had overpowered her optimism, her natural exuberance.

Braylee's bloodshot eyes were wide, the pupils dilated. Her complexion, even in the greenish, unnatural light of the morgue, was ghostly and unnatural.

He was about to order Sgt. Kraus to go get a medic to treat her for shock when she looked at him and said, "I just can't stop. I'm falling and I just . . . can't . . . stop."

◆ ◆ ◆

I am not skilled to understand
What God hath willed, what God hath planned;
I only know at His right hand
Stands One who is my Savior!

I take Him at His word indeed:
"Christ died for sinners"—this I read;
For in my heart I find a need
Of Him to be my Savior!

FROM THE HYMN "I AM NOT SKILLED TO UNDERSTAND"
WORDS BY DORA GREENWELL

6

Pour des Enfants du Safaliyah

"Warrom hier? Warrom zelf?" Mareike De Vries asked herself out loud as the Unimog in which she was traveling came to a stop in front of a large cinder-block structure.

"What am I doing in this place?" Mareike asked as the dust and grit stung her eyes, coated her lips, and filtered into her nostrils.

The *place* was the center of the Iraqi city of Safaliyah, and the *why* was *Pour des Enfants du Monde*—"For the Children of the World"—the slogan of the Paris-based NGO known as Organisation École Globale.

OEG (the "Global School") was a small fish in the sea of nongovernmental organizations operating in troubled nations around the world. OEG is a mere minnow compared to the likes of the International Red Cross, the Red Crescent, CARE, the Lutheran World Federation, Oxfam, and Save the Children. Nevertheless, the volunteers that carry out OEG's good works in a dozen countries across the developing world are no less fervent in their commitment to their cause than those in the larger NGOs. Arguably, OEG volunteers were even more committed because they operated against greater logistical odds on a much narrower shoestring.

As Muhammad Tammin of the Iraqi Ministry of Education had once said, "Teachers are fleeing the country on a daily basis, leaving schools without experienced teachers. Educational standards in Iraq have severely worsened."

Somebody had to pick up the slack, and it was the volunteers of the shoestring-budget NGOs.

Mareike De Vries was one of those volunteers, and it was one of those narrow shoestrings that brought her to dusty, forlorn Diyala Province. The only daughter of a successful Dutch electronics engineer in Eindhoven, she grew up comfortably. Seven years as a teacher in an elementary school in Utrecht had given her a good life and a good start on a career in a field that she loved. Yet, as is often the case for people in their twenties, something was missing.

Mareike had first learned of OEG two years ago when she and a friend were trekking in the Pyrenees. They had met a young French couple who had just gotten back from six months with OEG in Sudan. The organization, they explained, had achieved great success operating a school there.

When she got back to Utrecht, Mareike had Googled OEG and found their website. She studied their successes, as well as their failures, and was impressed with what she saw. She exchanged a few e-mails and boarded a train to Paris to visit their offices. Two days later, she applied for a sabbatical from her teaching job.

Mareike De Vries had spent four months in Darfur when OEG asked for volunteers for a special project in Diyala Province. She felt that the call was meant for her.

Now she was part of a four-person team that would spend the next year helping to upgrade the standards at Safaliyah's largest nongovernmental school and bring it into the twenty-first century.

"Good afternoon," said the middle-aged man with the mustache as he opened the heavy gate leading into the courtyard of the school. "We are pleased to have you. Come quickly. Move your vehicle inside."

"Thank you," Mareike said. "But we can just unload here. The driver will be going back to Baghdad first thing tomorrow morning."

They spoke English, the lingua franca of a world made smaller by advances in communications, but a world in which language barriers were merely exacerbated by the ease of communications. English was the only language these two people had in common. Mareike had learned but a few words of Iraqi Arabic, but Mustafa Ilik, headmaster of the Safaliyah School, had zero knowledge of Dutch.

"You don't understand," Ilik told her. "You don't leave vehicles on the *street*. Especially if you are not . . . mmmm . . . native to Safaliyah. This is . . . mmm . . . Diyala."

She gestured to the driver to drive through the narrow gateway. He shrugged, cursed in Arabic, folded down his mirror, and restarted the 2.2-L, straight-six SOHC engine. The other members of the OEG team craned their necks to see what was going on.

In addition to the Dutch woman who had just spent her thirtieth birthday in a Darfur refugee camp, the team consisted of two middle-aged British men and Isabelle Laclerc, a French woman who was about Mareike's age. The two Englishmen, Clive Atherton and Richard Crimm, were retired secondary school science teachers and veterans of many an NGO assignment. Isabelle had been on the OEG staff for several years but had never before had a field assignment. She preferred the Paris headquarters to the filth and stench of the Third World, because, after all, it was *Paris*. However, in order to advance within the organization, she was required to spend time in the field—so here she was.

In much of the developing world, NGOs worked in circumstances where basic education was not just barely obtainable, but where it was almost an alien concept. In Iraq, the challenge was to pick up the pieces after decades of the education system having been designed around supporting the ideals of a dictatorship—and the ensuing years of chaos when that dictatorship collapsed into a void. In many ways, OEG faced greater challenges in Iraq than it did in places such as Darfur, where an educational system simply had not existed.

Mustafa Ilik's admonition that they keep the Unimog off the street proved to have been good counsel. Two cars were stolen within a block of the school overnight. With everything else they had to worry about, stolen cars didn't even make it onto the list of priorities for the Iraqi police.

With their realization of what might have been, the OEG teachers breathed a sigh of relief. However, the vehicle would soon, in fact, vanish from their lives. The Unimog had not been stolen, but the psychological effect of watching it drive away—headed back to Baghdad—was even more unsettling, especially for Isabelle, who began sobbing. Mareike found herself comforting the Parisian girl and ignoring her own sense of sudden isolation.

Warrom hier? Warrom zelf? What am I doing in this place?

Mareike had little time to dwell on herself and her loneliness. It was class time, and she found herself in a classroom on the upper floor of the school, paired with Hala, a pleasant Iraqi woman about her own age, who taught two classes of about forty nine-year-olds each. The plan was that Mareike would teach both of Hala's classes to speak a language alien to all—English.

"Salaam Sabah el khair," Hala greeted her class.

"Sabah el noor," they replied in unison.

Mareike understood the good-morning greeting, but little else of the ensuing exchange as Hala spoke with the children. She did, however, perk up her ears when she heard her own name spoken. She could sense that Hala was explaining what Mareike was doing there.

The children stared at the Dutch woman with a mix of curiosity and amusement. Most were unused to seeing adult women without headscarves. There were a few in Safaliyah—mainly foreigners—but they were rare. Hala, who had been educated in Beirut and seemed to Mareike to be quite open to Western ideals and ideas, was nonetheless never without her own scarf.

"Hal tatakalum Al Engleaziah?" Mareike asked tentatively, inquiring whether anyone spoke or understood the global lingua franca.

The room was a mass of giggles, mixed with a few snickers.

They thought it especially jolly fun to watch the pink-skinned European woman blush.

Most shook their heads at the question, but one little boy answered, *"Na'am,"* meaning "yes."

Encouraged, Mareike asked in English what words he knew.

"Wazzup, dude," he answered.

"What?"

"Wazzup, dude," he repeated.

It was soon apparent that the phrase was the sum of his knowledge of the language. It was going to be a long climb, working with these kids. It was so different from teaching the multilingual suburban kids in Utrecht, but in their eyes, Mareike could see that these kids were just like kids everywhere, and just as deserving of her time as any on earth.

"Wazzup, dude."

Mareike had her work cut out for her.

After class, about a dozen of the kids clustered around Hala and Mareike, curiously asking their Iraqi teacher about the new and unfamiliar European teacher.

A bright-eyed boy asked Mareike a long question in Arabic, apparently assuming that because she had used some Arabic phrases, she knew his language. With this, she realized that she was, in this regard, no different from the boy she knew only as "the wazzup dude."

"Ana la tatakalum Al Arabiah," she admitted to the boy.

"Ana la tatakalum Al Engleaziah," he replied with a grin, as if to say, "Okay, so let's get started."

"My name is Mareike," she said, slowly and carefully, pointing to herself.

"My . . . name . . . isss Bilal," he said proudly, thumping his small hand on his chest.

It was going to be a long climb, teaching these kids, but Mareike felt herself up to the task, and she had a sense that her reward would be great.

◆   ◆   ◆

Each day I'll do a golden deed,
By helping those who are in need,
My life on earth is but a span,
And so I'll do the best I can,
The best I can.

I'll help someone in time of need,
And journey on with rapid speed;
I'll help the sick and poor and weak,
And words of kindness to them speak,
Kind words I'll speak.

FROM THE HYMN "A BEAUTIFUL LIFE"
WORDS BY WILLIAM MATTHEW GOLDEN

7

Smiles and Footballs

"Les Américains viennent!" Isabelle Laclerc moaned dramatically, graphically demonstrating her flair for the flamboyant. *"C'est terrible!"*

"Pourquoi?" Mareike De Vries asked, rolling her eyes. Like Mareike, Isabelle spoke English reasonably well, but insisted on reverting to her native French when she wished to express herself emotionally—which was often.

For her part, Mareike almost never reverted to Dutch, but she humored Isabelle by replying in French. *"Pourquoi pas? Quel est le problème avec les Américains?"*

"Boosh! Boosh! Boosh!" Isabelle shouted, throwing her hands in the air. The surname of America's former president was her shorthand way of expressing all of the many things that she found objectionable about the United States.

Mustafa Ilik had just informed the young volunteers from Organisation École Globale that the U.S. Army was coming to the Safaliyah School later in the day with some sports equipment that had been donated by a company in North Carolina. After two weeks at the school, the OEG volunteers were feeling a bit proprietary about their role, but the more pragmatic headmaster was anxious to accept donations from any quarter.

"I told you so," Isabelle sniffed angrily as they watched the approach of the Americans from a window on the second story of the school. "They come to us like bullies . . . with guns and *camions bruyants.*"

Mareike had to agree that their arrival in a trio of broad-beamed, menacing-looking vehicles made the Americans seem just as sinister as they were often described in the media back home.

The vehicles sputtered to an idling halt, the doors on the middle one popped open, and three men got out. Covered head to toe in gray-green uniforms, they were all large, bulky individuals. Mareike realized that this must be because of the body armor that Americans were said always to wear.

One man unfastened and removed his helmet. He then lifted a large cardboard box out of the vehicle, handed it to the smallest of the men, and pulled out another. As they crossed the street carrying the boxes, only the third man, the one with the blue sunglasses, appeared to be armed.

The man without the helmet spoke to this man, and he lowered his gun, slinging its strap over his shoulder.

Mareike shrugged and the two women headed down the stairway to the courtyard. They found the children curiously swirling around the Americans, chattering and poking at the boxes. The man who had earlier removed his helmet had now pulled off his body armor and was squatting amid the crowd in his T-shirt with a grin on his face.

Mareike noticed the boy Bilal racing toward the American. He was a bright, outgoing boy with whom Mareike had already developed a rapport. He and his sister Naja were eager learners and infectiously happy children, despite the circumstances of having to grow up in Safaliyah at an unsettled time in Iraq's history. Both had already made great progress in learning a few English words.

"Mareike, Mareike!" Bilal shouted excitedly, grabbing her hand. "Friend, friend. Come."

Bilal half-pulled, half-dragged Mareike toward the American in the midst of the crowd, who was by this point bouncing soccer balls toward the children and laughing.

"Friend!" Bilal shouted to the man. "My friend Mareike. My friend Taptin Sean!"

Mareike found herself a few feet from the clean-cut American with the slightly receding hairline. He glanced at her and looked at the boy.

"Bilal, buddy, *tatakalum Engleaziah* these days?"

"*Tatakalum Engleaziah,*" he said excitedly, pointing to Mareike. "Talking English . . . learning . . . Mareike!"

"Mareike, hmm? This must be your new teacher," the man said, looking back at Mareike. "Hi, my name's Sean Rasmunsen."

"Mareike De Vries," she replied, finding herself shaking hands with the friendly soldier. It was her first direct contact with the American military, and it made her nervous. "I'm teaching here at the Safaliyah School. I'm with Organisation École Globale."

"I've read about OEG," he said. "I've heard some good things about what you've done down in sub-Saharan Africa. I'm with the 77th Infantry myself."

"Ummm, I'm glad you have heard good things about OEG," she said. She had heard mainly not-so-good things about what the U.S. Army had done, but this pleasant man seemed to run contrary to the stereotype, so she decided to be polite and not mention this.

"Bilal seems to like you."

"Oh yeah," the man said, smiling. "Bilal and me are kinda buddies. I run into him now and then. We've kicked a soccer ball around a bit, and I told him we were going to get the kids some new ones."

"Soccer?"

"I'm sorry, I mean *futbol . . . Fussball . . .*"

"I'm sorry," Mareike blushed. She prided herself on her English vocabulary, but she had momentarily forgotten the American word for what the rest of the world calls *football*.

"Americans are a strange breed." He laughed disarmingly. "We have a game called *football*, too, but it's not played with the feet like *futbol . . .* or whatever . . ."

"We call it *voetbal* in the Netherlands," she said. "But many at home do say *football*. I'm surprised that Americans would give these balls to the children. I'd think you would give them *American* footballs."

"Don't sell us short," he said, smiling. "Lotta folks in America play your kind of football. I did a little myself in school. I wasn't very good at either kind, though."

"I see," she replied, surprised by his self-effacing manner. Most Americans that she had met or read about liked to brag about their accomplishments.

"Did you ever play?"

"Yes, of course, in school," Mareike said. "Yes, of course."

"Let's get going, then," the American said, standing up and nodding to Bilal, who was prodding one of the new bright white soccer balls with his toe.

Bilal kicked it to Sean, who tapped it toward Mareike, who kicked toward it, her grayish-purple sneaker missing it by barely an inch.

She recovered, and soon the two adults were in the midst of a courtyard filled with screaming kids. For a few minutes, it was as though the dust they kicked up in their play was a million miles from a war zone.

Gradually, the little whirlwind of laughing children spun off to the opposite corner of the yard, and the two adults found themselves merely spectators.

"That was good exercise," he said, smiling, breathing deeply.

"They have boundless energy," she agreed.

"How long have you been out here?" the American captain said, making conversation.

"Only sixteen days," Mareike answered. "We came . . . four of us came . . . to help at the school."

"You're teaching English pretty well," he said. "If Bilal is any indication. How did you get to be an English teacher?"

"You mean because I'm Dutch?" Mareike laughed. "You don't think of Holland as an English-speaking country?"

"Well . . ."

"I have spoken English since I was five . . . Everyone in Holland does."

"Nobody in the United States speaks anything but English," he said. "Except Spanish, I guess, in certain parts of the country.

We always complain that kids should be more conversant in other languages, but we don't ever really do anything about it."

"Could I ask you something?" Mareike asked. She had noticed and was intrigued by the little black cross pinned to his uniform.

"Sure."

"The cross? What does that represent? I don't see that on the uniforms of most American soldiers . . . not that I have seen many American soldiers . . . except in pictures."

"Oh, that goes with my job . . . I'm a chaplain . . . a minister . . . I'm like the hometown pastor for the folks at FOB Lex . . . which is their home away from home."

"FOB Lex?"

"Oh . . . yeah . . . Forward Operating Base . . . Lexington . . . it's where the Americans are based out here near Saf City . . . Safaliyah."

"And you are their chaplain? I have heard of this . . . but it seems strange to find a religious person among those who fight and kill . . ."

"They're just regular people," he said, smiling. "Most Americans . . . like most people anywhere . . . I guess . . . like to go to church . . . or to have some sorta opportunity for a little spiritual reflection . . . I'm there to facilitate that."

"I see," Mareike said, genuinely intrigued by this concept that she had not thought about before.

"What church . . . mmmm . . . are you involved in any church?" he asked.

"My grandparents were . . . my parents, no," Mareike explained. "They were part of the sixties, you know . . . rebelled against their parents' values. I did not go when I was young, but

I have been a few times . . . mainly to the Domkerk . . . Sint Martin in Utrecht . . . I'm, I suppose, rebelling against *my* parents like they did against their parents, maybe. Most people are more secular in Europe now . . . not like my grandparents' time."

"I guess that's the same everywhere," the chaplain agreed. "I used to think, when I was first out of seminary, that it was my job to get everybody into my church, but it's not that simple."

"Why?" Mareike asked. "I thought that this is really what the priests do—make everyone go to church or feel guilty?"

"I don't think so," he said. "I suppose I *used to* think so. I guess maybe at home when you've got people who are too lazy to go to church, but there's a difference between going to a building called a church and making a spiritual commitment. You can *make* somebody go to church, but you can't make somebody make a spiritual commitment. My job is to be there for people, to provide spiritual leadership or spiritual guidance for people when they feel the need and the desire."

"Makes sense, I guess," Mareike said, shrugging.

"The U.S. Army is a volunteer force," he said, smiling. "And religion within it is *definitely* voluntary."

"Good to see you volunteering to be with the children," she said, nodding to the place where a group of youngsters were clustering around Tyler Kraus and Kyle Lockhart, both of whom had removed their sinister-looking helmets. One little girl was wearing Tyler's signature blue sunglasses.

"Lots of the people in the 2/77 are parents," the chaplain told her. "They miss their kids. Lot of them have younger siblings. They're like anybody."

"Do you wish that you could have had children?" Mareike asked.

"Yeah . . . maybe someday."

"I thought . . ." Mareike was confused. "Priests cannot have children . . . be married?"

"Priests can't, but mainly it's just Catholic priests." He laughed. "Most Christian ministers can get married. Rabbis can, too. Mainly it's only the Catholics that don't have a married clergy."

"Are you married, then?"

"No, not yet."

"Why did you sacrifice that, a normal life, to join the American Army?" Mareike asked. She was having a hard time reconciling this man who seemed so kind and thoughtful with the image of the American Army that she had seen on television.

"Why did *you* volunteer to come here?" Sean asked.

"To make a difference," she answered, somewhat startled by his comeback. "As in the OEG charter, it is '*pour des enfants*,' for the children."

"In the big picture, that's why the U.S. Army came," Sean replied. "As much as anybody debates all the nuances, a lot of the reason that the United States came into Iraq had to do with a better life for future generations. I know that it doesn't always seem like that, and it's not *only* about that, as it probably is with your outfit . . . but that's why a lot of us came, and we believe that we can leave it a better place. We're not just a bunch of trained killers."

"Mmmmm . . ." Mareike warily considered what he'd said.

"But what I'm getting at is why *you* came here," he continued. "What made Mareike De Vries *really* want to come to Diyala Province?"

That made her think.

Over the next twenty minutes, the two of them probed their own motivations and those of one another. Not wanting to be a preacher to this woman from a secular background, Sean deliberately did not tell her that he had felt the Lord calling him, describing his own larger-than-life inspiration in more abstract terms.

Just as Mareike was giving the kids the tools they needed to communicate in another language, Sean had been learning a new language, teaching himself to "speak secular," to communicate his own thoughts and feelings in a language that was comprehensible outside his own faith community.

As they spoke, Mareike felt a strange warmness toward this American. He was like a priest in his understanding of the spiritual, but in his relaxed manner he was unlike the priests she knew. His language was a casual American form of English, yet he was someone with whom she could communicate. He was a man her age, a man with whom she could share the confused feelings that she had about spirituality in a secular world—and about the reasons she had stepped in from the secular world of Utrecht to the message—and the songs—inside the Domkerk.

When the time came for the Americans to leave, and for Mareike to convene her afternoon language class, she was sorry to see the chaplain go, but glad that he had come.

"*Les Américains*," Isabelle said disgustedly, reappearing only when the soldiers were out the front gate of the compound. "*C'est terrible!*"

"Is it so terrible that the children now have footballs?" Mareike asked in English, finding herself grinning the relaxed grin that she so liked about the American.

Isabelle looked stunned. Mareike just felt happy, and selfishly wanted nothing to intrude on that.

◆ ◆ ◆

There is sunshine in my soul today,
More glorious and bright
Than glows in any earthly sky,
For Jesus is my Light.

There is music in my soul today,
A carol to my King,
And Jesus, listening, can hear
The songs I cannot sing.

FROM THE HYMN "SUNSHINE IN MY SOUL"
WORDS BY ELIZA EDMUNDS HEWITT

8

Midnight Phantoms

"Darker than a razorback in a coal mine," someone drawled over the roar of the Black Hawk's rotors.

There were some snickers and someone replied, "And jus' about twice as unpredictable."

"Right on."

Plenty of agreement there.

The chopper was flying blind—or so it seemed to the men in the payload bay—into the dark of night.

There was nothing out there in the inky darkness but the occasional red flicker from the second Black Hawk.

It was the usual banter of warriors headed into the unknown. Chaplain Sean Rasmunsen had heard it before. It was the way of the experienced to conceal their fear of the unknown in the presence of the inexperienced. It was probably as old as war itself.

There were a lot of inexperienced kids in the 2nd Battalion these days. By *kids*, Sean was thinking of people only a half dozen years his junior, but kids by their inexperience. They came as others left, a new crop just in time for the blistering, unimaginable heat of summer. A new crop to replace the dead and wounded from the terrible IED attack a few weeks ago and the slow, gnawing attrition of battle.

Some survivors left Iraq without hands, feet, or eyes. Some, like Braylee Davis, the young corporal from Jeff City, left with empty places that you could not see—unless you looked deeply into her empty blue eyes. Sean prayed for each, and he prayed *with* many. When he was alone, he prayed that there would be no more.

Tonight, he prayed for the safe return of his companions and himself. The thought crossed his mind that had he been Catholic, he might have even said a prayer to St. Christopher, their patron saint of travelers.

It seemed to make little sense that the U.S. Army's operational tempo in Diyala Province should increase as the weather began to grow so awful, but someone up the chain of command must have decided so. Someone at some lofty "need-to-know" level in the chain of command at Central Command knew something that mere mortals down at the grunt level at FOB Lex could not know. The soldiers always imagined this exalted personage as someone with a lot of stars and an ample rear end sitting in an air-conditioned room at CENTCOM in Qatar or at MacDill in Florida tapping a touch screen and sending real people into difficult situations.

The more difficult, the more incomprehensible on the need-to-know scale, the more the chaplain knew that he *needed* to be there. Sean had already gone into battle much more often on his second tour than his first, and Sgt. Tyler Kraus had grown accustomed to following his boss into progressively tighter situations.

Ever since that day on the outskirts of Safaliyah, when the sergeant had saved Sean's life, the abstract concept of their respective roles in the Religious Support Team—they still called it the Unit Ministry Team—was abstract no more. Neither was Sean's sense that he had done the right thing by coming back to Iraq.

Suddenly, the UH-60 jerked hard and Sean felt the g-force as his body slammed against the restraints that held him from tumbling headlong into the dark and invisible desert below.

There was a yelp, a couple of coughs, and more than a few expletives. Then there was another jerk. Somewhere up front, the flight crew, with their night-vision gear in place, had determined that it was time to set down and disgorge the two dozen young soldiers of Charlie Company.

The dust seared their eyes and choked their throats. Instinctively, they moved away from the faint red lights within the payload bays, their only point of visual reference in the moonless darkness. By the time Sean had tipped his own night-vision gear into place, the two choppers were already becoming airborne again.

In the surreal greenness of night-vision technology, he watched everyone lifting their gear and walking across the dusty ground toward the other landing zone, where Capt. Ryan Clark was already organizing the troops. The command would be in two sections, one led by Clark, the second by 1st Sgt. Brandon Mosier. The Religious Support Team, comprising Sean and Sgt. Kraus, would be attached to Mosier's squad.

Like any good infantry officer, Clark made good use of his noncoms. It has been said for centuries that the basic building block of unit cohesion in any ground army is its noncommissioned officers, its sergeants. Clark was attentive to molding good operational units around good sergeants, but like any field commander, he had to work with what he had.

On paper, Mosier looked like good material. As with so many 69th Brigade noncoms, he was into his second tour, although much of his time had been spent behind a desk at brigade headquarters. The powers that be had decided that he needed some field experience, so he wound up at FOB Lexington.

Into the moonless night in opposite directions went the two contingents, with the Religious Support Team settling in toward the rear of the column led by Mosier.

Humans are not, by nature, nocturnal. From childhood, we know intuitively that the night is a world of unknowns and potential dangers. There is the dragon under the bed, the unseen mugger, the potential rapist.

Once, the nighttime battlefield was the enemy of all soldiers who were unused to it and a friend to those who mastered the limitations imposed by it. The U.S. Army had suffered in Vietnam when fighting guerrillas who had mastered the night and had responded the way the U.S. Army responds to such situations—with technology. By the end of the twentieth century, the U.S. Army *owned* the night with night-vision technology. Today, that technology is so widely available that the American advantage has essentially vanished.

The dragons under the bed have returned.

It has been written that night-vision technology has turned night into day, but this optimistic assessment was not written by anyone who has actually been out on an all-night patrol. You can see the guy next to you, and you can see terrain features at considerable distance, but the sky is still black, and the shadows are deep and dark.

After the first hour, most of the men in Mosier's patrol had relaxed somewhat. The al-Qaeda infiltrator they imagined under every rock was turning out to be just another rock, and another, and so on.

Two hours passed, and everyone was now starting to imagine another routine and uneventful night ahead.

This sense abruptly evaporated when Mosier suddenly stopped, raised his hand, and dropped to a crouch.

Everyone followed suit. Kraus put his left palm between Sean's shoulder blades, ready to flatten him, and he fingered the safety on his M4. He could flick it off in an instant, but he was just going through the motions.

They all strained their eyes to see what Mosier might have seen, and listened for a snippet of the sound that might have caused him to stop.

It was an unusually calm night. Beyond the pounding of his heart, Sean could hear only the slight and uneven hiss of the desert wind.

At last he heard it. Somewhere in the near distance, someone was talking. It was just a phrase, then silence.

Then Sean heard the sounds of shuffling feet. It sounded like many feet, but he could not make out what was going on. It was not the sound of running feet. It was not even the sound of walking feet. It was more the sound of milling-around feet.

Could it be smugglers unloading something? The closer to the Iranian border you got, the more likely you were to run into smugglers.

The voice returned.

Was it a voice or voices?

Mosier gestured for the squad to spread out and follow him as he began creeping closer to the sound.

Everyone was moving as quietly as they could, but the scuffling sound of American boots was deafening compared to the silence of a moment earlier.

As Sean moved out to keep pace, he could feel Kraus grab him by the collar and tug. His bodyguard wanted him to be far behind when the bullets began to fly.

He obliged, moving a short distance before he stopped. A chaplain would only be a hindrance during a firefight, so he might as well just wait. It would be only in the aftermath that his guys would need him. Nevertheless, as with all troops, waiting is often one of the hardest parts of a battle for a chaplain.

He breathed a sigh and said a short prayer.

"Oh my God," the voice in the distance whispered. "Oh my God."

It was the panicked voice of Sgt. Brandon Mosier.

Sean glanced at Kraus, and Kraus nodded, releasing his hand from Sean's battle gear.

"Chaplain coming through," Sean whispered as he and Kraus moved quickly in Mosier's direction. Everyone else remained where he was.

"Chaplain coming through," Sean repeated as he approached the small rise behind which he could see Mosier sitting on the ground.

As the squad leader turned to him, Sean thought he could see his jaw quivering. He could not see his eyes because of his goggles.

"I killed him," Mosier sobbed.

Sean looked down. Beneath the sergeant was the body of a boy who looked to be about twelve. His light-colored clothing was splattered with something that appeared in the green glow of the goggles to be about the same color and tonal value as the surrounding shadows.

As he reached out to gently remove the combat knife from Mosier's hand, Sean wondered whether it is merely a coincidence that blood looks just like shadows in the phantom world of night-vision gear.

Not too far away, he could see the feet that made the milling-around sound they'd all heard earlier. About a dozen sheep grazed in the scrub at the bottom of a gully.

Mosier had slit the throat of a preteen shepherd boy.

"My nephew . . . " Mosier gulped as Sean put his arm across the sergeant's shoulder. "He's about Jonathan's age . . ."

Sean nodded at Kraus, who moved a few paces behind them to give Mosier the illusion of privacy.

This was scary. For Kraus, the death of the kid was awful, but scarier still was that the squad leader was apparently freaking out. This was no place to freak out, this dangerous corner of a dangerous country where essentially the only way out was the planned rendezvous with Clark at a far distant predetermined helicopter LZ.

"What did I just do?" Mosier whispered.

Kraus gestured for the rest of the patrol to form a defensive perimeter and keep their eyes peeled. Among the men, only the chaplain and his assistant carried the burden of knowing that the person their leader had just killed was not an al-Qaeda sentry but a kid the age of their kid brothers.

"Sergeant Mosier . . . Brandon . . . A terrible thing just happened, but terrible things happen in wartime . . . and the men, a dozen of them, are depending on you to pull yourself together and continue to lead them. Do you understand what I'm saying?"

Mosier nodded.

"Let's say a prayer over the boy," Sean said.

The closure offered by a prayer was often what was needed to help someone move on in terrible moments such as this.

"I can't."

"Why not?"

"I don't know any prayers," Mosier said in an almost desperate tone. "I've never been to a church service in my life."

Sean just asked him to follow along with the Lord's Prayer, thinking about the irony of a Christian prayer said over the body of a Muslim boy who had just been knifed—albeit accidentally—by a man who'd never attended a church service.

Finally, they both said "Amen"—Mosier knew at least *that* word.

Sean whispered for him to stand up and lead the troops while the chaplain folded the boy's hands across his chest and covered his body and face with a cloth that he found nearby. It was less a funeral gesture than a vain attempt to ward off jackals.

Sean knew that despite this horrible mistake, the best thing for all concerned was to keep moving. Nothing could undo the tragedy, and to allow it to disrupt the operation could invite further misfortune.

The chaplain's duty to care for the living, the men of the patrol, meant comforting the wounded. Mosier had no visible wounds; his injuries were inside, but nonetheless they were terribly real.

As they passed the small flock of sheep, still scratching for browse among the rocks, Sean thought of all the New Testament references to shepherds and their flocks and of sheep who'd lost their shepherd. Just as these parables were metaphors, so too was the loss of a shepherd a metaphor for the patrol. Mosier was on the move, but he was still in a state of shock—and his troops were on the verge of discovering that they were a flock with no shepherd.

Sean found himself playing the role of Mosier's puppeteer, walking near him and whispering to him what to do. The unit's cohesion depended on a belief that their shepherd was still functional.

They were just kids, all of them, just out of high school. They looked to Mosier for leadership, and Sean wanted to make sure they got it.

Several times, the first sergeant stopped, imagining that he heard the enemy. He stood still, his teeth chattering—a physical symptom of shock—until Sean assured him that it was just a lizard and it was safe to go on.

They continued into the darkness, guided only by compass coordinates and an urgency to have this living nightmare over. Sean glanced at his watch. Still hours to go before the LZ rendezvous. He prayed that the remainder of their patrol would be without incident.

His prayers were not answered favorably. The next sound they heard was not a lizard.

The old Toyota pickup in the broad gully below had suffered a flat tire, a not unexpected eventuality when crossing an open desert on a moonless night.

The men were armed. Sean could see the familiar silhouette

of at least two AK-47s. One might surmise from the overloaded pickup that they were smugglers, but they might also be gunrunners supplying one or another of the factions or criminal gangs that swarmed throughout Iraq.

Under the circumstances, the prudent thing would have been to let them pass. The problem was that they weren't passing. They were stuck. Three men scurried aimlessly around the stalled vehicle, displaying the same level of mechanical ingenuity as the sheep in the shepherd's herd. Either the truck carried no spare tire, or these guys had no experience changing a flat. The one who seemed to be in charge was berating the others, blaming them for the predicament.

Sean was about to organize the troops to circle wide around the distracted men when one of the young Americans slipped, causing a small avalanche of rocks to cascade noisily into the gully.

The firefight became a firefight the way most do.

Someone opens fire blindly at an alarming sound—in this case, it was one of the smugglers—and someone else nervously returns fire without stopping to think that to fire against someone firing blindly is to reveal one's own position.

The firefight evolved as most do. Soon, everyone with a gun is shooting, and eventually it all sputters to an end.

The Americans had the numeric advantage, as well as the high ground. It ended with one of them having a nasty facial cut because of a ricochet, but no other casualties.

All three of the men at the pickup were dead.

They had indeed been smugglers. Their load was not of guns or bomb-making materials, but black-market contraband headed for a souk somewhere.

As the Americans pressed on, the light of dawn was a hint on the eastern horizon, and soon the night-vision gear came off.

Sgt. Brandon Mosier's patrol reached the LZ ahead of Capt. Clark's men. Despite everything that had happened, they were nearly a half hour early. There was no sign of Clark, but all assumed that it would be just a matter of time.

Mosier pulled himself together and positioned his men for the rendezvous with the Black Hawk. He did it by the book, reverting to his training, to his memory of the field manual. The men, most of whom were frightened kids who had just been through their first firefight, did as instructed.

Mosier sat down on a rock near where Sean was seated and just hung his head.

After the guns, the dust, and the death, it was back to *hurry up and wait*.

"I suppose you think I should be praying or something," he said as they watched the first sliver of the sun crest the horizon.

"Praying for what?" Sean asked, trying to let the tone of his voice show kindness rather than mere exhaustion.

"Praying for whatever you pray for after all this shit," Mosier said despondently. "Sorry for saying *shit*; I know that you're not supposed to say *shit* to the chaplain."

"Most chaplains have heard worse," Sean said, smiling. "Most chaplains have *used* worse words than *shit*. You know, 'good' words and 'bad' words are just a matter of context—but you know all that. And you don't want to talk about words; you mentioned prayer."

"Yeah. I feel like I oughta, y'know, be praying at a time like this . . . but I don't know any friggin' prayers. Can you say *friggin'* to a chaplain?"

"Would you like to know a prayer?" Sean asked, deliberately ignoring Mosier's query. He had long since noticed that when they were around a chaplain, people deliberately used the word *friggin'*—in place of that stronger word beginning with the same letter—as both an adjective and an adverb.

"Yeah, I suppose."

"The one I use a lot is pretty simple. I say it about a hundred times a day. I just take a split second . . . actually a coupla split seconds . . . and say 'Lord, give me strength.'"

"Just like that?"

"Just like that," Sean said, smiling. "Y'know, strength comes from within. We all have the responsibility and the free will. It's just that sometimes—often—we just need His help to give us a hand in pulling it out of ourselves."

"Never thought of prayer like that," Mosier admitted. "I always thought that you asked Him to kill the demons."

"You can, but it's like a parent-and-child relationship. It doesn't do you much good if your mom kills the dragon under the bed for you. It's better for you if you master the dragon for yourself. Of course, sometimes you need a little help, and there's nothing wrong in asking."

"I never went to church, y'know," Mosier said. "Guess I woulda learned all that before."

"Well, we have chapel at Lex twice on Sunday, and get-togethers nearly every night," Sean replied.

"Ahhh, I think it's probably too late for me," he said, tears running down his cheeks. "I just killed a kid, and I can't get his face outa my mind . . . same age as Jonathan . . . and then my patrol just blew away a batch of hajjis who were nothing but petty criminals."

There needed to be a moment of silence. There were no words that were right. There was no telling him that it was going to be okay. He wasn't ready or able to hear that. It was time to listen. Talking could come later.

Sean just placed his hand on the sergeant's back, between his shoulder blades, as Kraus had done for him last night. He hoped that even through the Kevlar, he would feel some comfort in the gesture.

It needed to be a moment of silence—and of silent prayer.

◆　◆　◆

The dawn is sprinkling in the east
Its golden shower, as day flows in;
Fast mount the pointed shafts of light:
Farewell to darkness and to sin!

Away, ye midnight phantoms all!
Away, despondence and despair!
Whatever guilt the night has brought
Now let it vanish into air.

FROM THE HYMN "THE DAWN IS SPRINKLING IN THE EAST"
WORDS ATTRIBUTED TO AMBROSE OF MILAN IN THE FOURTH CENTURY

9

Opposites Within

"When you start having an unplanned routine, does that mean you've been at something too long?" Sean Rasmunsen asked Tyler Kraus as they drove into Saf City.

"Is that a philosophical question, Padre?" Kraus asked from behind the wheel as he maneuvered the Humvee through the narrow streets, constantly wary, constantly ready to take evasive action. He had taken to using the age-old U.S. Army nickname for chaplains. Lt. Col. Folbright was the only other man at Lex who used the term.

"I dunno. I was just thinking that when I first got to Lex I was running around reacting. I had no real schedule; it took me a couple of weeks to have more than just one chapel service on Sunday. Now we have our regular town visits."

His reference was to their customary Wednesday visits to the school in town where the OEG teachers were working. The initial impulse to get some soccer balls for the kids had evolved into one of the success stories of Sean's modest ministry in Iraq.

Soccer balls had led to other equipment and eventually to cheap laptop computers. The kids loved it, and so did their families. This had a ripple effect throughout the Safaliyah community. Even the imam from the local Sunni mosque stopped by to guardedly offer his appreciation. The hierarchy within the 69th Brigade liked it, and so too did the powers that be up the chain of command. It was "hearts and minds." Anything that fostered good relations with the "average Iraqis" furthered the ultimate mission of stability in this unstable country.

Sean liked it, too. His visits to Safaliyah and to the school were a way of catching his breath with something completely different, a break in the routine ups and downs at FOB Lex.

The ups were many, and so were the downs.

Sergeants came and sergeants went. Young Pvt. Kyle Lockhart, who had started scrounging religious materials for the chapel, was now Sgt. Kyle Lockhart and responsible for an amazing flow of things that were being donated to the people of Safaliyah. Who would have predicted a shipment of ten thousand toothbrushes?

Sergeants came and sergeants went. Sean had baptized Sgt. Brandon Mosier the same day that he testified at the inquest into the sergeant's having knifed the young shepherd.

Sean told it as he'd seen it.

Was it murder or a dreadful mistake made by a frightened man, barely not a kid? That was up to a court-martial that would be held half a world away.

◆ ◆ ◆

In the meantime, there were these weekly visits to the school, to Mustafa Ilik and to the two European women with whom Sean had been working. They were like night and day, those two women. The French girl was almost impossibly beautiful, but almost impossibly arrogant and abrasive. The Dutch girl was also quite attractive, but cursed with a complexion that did not coexist well with the desert sun. Her work ethic, on the other hand, was a better match for her responsibilities at the Safaliyah School than those of her colleague.

The two women reminded Sean of a lot of officers he had met in his U.S. Army career. Isabelle Laclerc was a delegator. Mareike De Vries was a doer. Isabelle Laclerc's style was to complain until those around her got tired of it and fixed the problem. Mareike De Vries was not afraid of getting her hands dirty. Her work at the school had helped transform it from merely a sanctuary of calmness in a turbulent town into a place of hope and happiness where the children really did grasp the notion that their future *could* be brighter. Indeed, it *would* be if nothing interrupted the momentum that OEG, and especially Mareike De Vries, had set in motion.

In the beginning, both women had regarded the Americans at arm's length, but they'd eventually gotten used to them showing up from time to time. Sean had even started to develop a rapport with Mareike. She was pleased that he deliberately spent time with the children, rather than just roaring in to drop off crates of gifts. Both she and the American chaplain had developed a genuine affection for the kids, and had become quite friendly with several, especially young Bilal.

Sean and Mareike had also become quite friendly with one another. She had never imagined a friendship with an American soldier, but he was not, as they say, like all the rest. Whereas most Americans walked the streets in helmets and body armor, he showed up in an open-collared shirt or often just a T-shirt. He also always wore a cap with the logo of one or another American Major League Baseball team. His caps had become his signature, as did his always leaving the school bareheaded. Some lucky Iraqi kid always got a cap whenever "Chaplain Sean" came visiting.

With this in mind, Sean and Kyle Lockhart had started teaching the kids to play baseball in the soccer field behind the school. At first, the Americans did all the pitching, but gradually, the kids—both girls and boys—filled in all the positions. Kids who had not known English a few weeks ago were now shouting phrases like "Out at first" and "Double play."

Isabelle had ignored the "decadent American" sport, but Mareike had watched a few times. Today she had asked to play. When she managed to hit a single in the eighth inning, she felt that she was finally mastering "bass-bol."

"Having fun?" Sean asked as the game ended.

"It's a very complicated sport," Mareike said, shrugging. "But I'm beginning to grasp the idea. The children really like you. I can't imagine the priests at the Domkerk getting dirty with the children."

"I bet they would if they could make the kids grin just by sliding into home," Sean said, smiling himself.

"That is a very strange thing to see for the first time." Mareike laughed. "I thought that you were joking or something."

"Nope. That's how it works."

"The children appreciate you very much," she said as they returned to the courtyard of the school.

"I appreciate being able to spend time with them," Sean told her. "It reminds me that this country has a future, and that we can make a difference in breaking the cycle of pessimism. I want them to have a positive view of what life can be when you get beyond the cycles of dictatorship, intimidation, bloodshed . . . and then more intimidation, bloodshed, and on and on and on."

"As I saw in Sudan, it is a challenge that seems sometimes insurmountable. I joined OEG with sincere hopes, dreams even, of accomplishing much. Sometimes it works; other times it seems as though it cannot be done. The climb is so steep."

"I understand," Sean admitted. "In my own work at the 2/77, I sometimes feel there is so much to do, so many people to look out for. I pray that I'll have the intuition to know what needs to be done, and the strength to actually do it."

"Are your prayers answered?" Mareike asked.

"Yes, I believe they are."

"I don't know if I believe in talking to God."

"Sometimes talking isn't everything," Sean said, shrugging. "Sometimes I just take a moment and listen. I guess what I'm saying is that it's more like a conversation."

"I'll try that," Mareike said, looking into Sean's eyes.

"Keeps the loneliness quotient down."

"I suppose that it can be very lonely among the thousand people and you are the only minister—the only man of a thousand with your responsibilities."

"If you put it like that," Sean replied with a smile. "Do you get lonely?"

"Some ways, yes . . . some ways, no." Mareike said, shrugging. "Like you, I sometimes feel alone among others. My isolation is my language. I do not speak English well; my thoughts are in Dutch."

"I disagree that you don't speak English well," Sean replied. "But I agree about sometimes having thoughts unlike many people around me."

"That makes you lonely?"

"Mostly, y'know, I really don't have much time to get lonely."

"Sometimes you can be lonely in a crowded room," Mareike replied. "Didn't someone famous say that?"

"I think a lot of people have said that, and even more have *felt* it," Sean said. "There's no cure-all for it, but part of pastoring, part of my job, is to try to make everybody feel welcome in the crowded rooms at the churches and chapels and prayer services where I work."

"And do people welcome *you*?"

"You welcomed me here to the school," he said. "You and Mr. Ilik, and Hala, and everyone—even Isabelle; when I first met her, she seemed a little bit . . ."

"Arrogant?" Mareike laughed.

"Well, Americans call it . . . well, she was a little bit stuck up."

"Stuck up?"

"It's a figure of speech. I guess it means arrogant or conceited . . . or maybe a symptom of loneliness?"

"You are being charitable." Mareike smiled.

"I guess that's part of being in my business," Sean replied.

"You are a most unique American," she said as they climbed the stairway to her classroom. "You and Tyler. You must remember the image that we have in Europe of Americans: rich and superficial. It is so good for us to see what Americans are like behind our stereotype—not just sport, but getting involved in the lives of children. Boys like Bilal are really starting to look up to you."

"I'm glad," he said. "I think they look up to *you* . . . and the OEG folks, too. I think that sometimes it takes outsiders to bring in the light."

"Same as what you said about ending the pessimism," she said.

"Americans and Europeans, working together for a common goal." Sean laughed. "Who'da thought?"

"I'm glad that I got to know you," she said, suddenly squeezing his hand. "You are a wonderful man."

"Umm . . . you're a wonderful lady," he said, surprised and even stunned by her sudden display of intimacy.

It felt good, he admitted to himself, her touch and the way in which she intended it. He had read that European women were less reticent than American women in expressing such feelings, but perhaps that was just another stereotype, and Mareike was unique. For the moment, this did not matter.

Alone in the empty classroom, that moment belonged to them.

He returned her gesture, squeezed her hand, and found himself looking into her eyes. Her expression told him that this was one of those moments when a relationship between two people could change irrevocably and *would* change if nothing interrupted the momentum.

They were two people who had given so much of themselves to others. They had selflessly given their counsel, their emotions, and their love. Suddenly, they were in a moment in which all of that tide of emotion could come crashing back. All he had to do was let it all hit him like one of those waves in which he had splashed along the South Carolina shore many months ago.

The wave struck. He responded to her touch with a hug, and she replied to his hug with a kiss, a heat-of-the-moment response in a heated moment.

Both Mareike and Sean knew at once that the kiss was a bridge too far. Both knew that it must end, but neither wanted it to—so it didn't.

For Mareike, there was the sudden realization that she had just grabbed and kissed a man of God. Despite all that he had told her, she couldn't get it out of her head that Sean was like the priests she had known back home, where it was always considered blasphemy to kiss a priest. Despite this, she wanted so much to kiss him—*and* it felt so good.

For Sean, there was a cascade of memories that went back to Nicole, who had told him that she could not be a preacher's wife. There was a split second of self-pity, several seconds of joy at how the crashing waves of Mareike's lips filled that empty void, and the realization that he had given his life to a calling and somehow his emotional being was not his to give.

Maybe Nicole had been right. Maybe there really was not room for both this feeling of selfish, personal delight and the duties of his calling.

Both sensed the reticence of the other, but neither really wanted to acknowledge it.

The heated moment gave way to the awkward moment.

Finally, it was Mareike's turn to break the ice.

"I've never—never kissed a priest before."

"I'm not a priest," he said reassuringly.

"But . . . you know what I mean."

"Yeah, I know what you mean."

The awkward moment gave way to a moment of silence and then another.

Sean wanted to say something about how a kiss like that implies a relationship or desire for a relationship—and it's hard to imagine how someone who gives himself a hundred percent to a calling that is more than a job can give any of himself to any other relationship.

But he did not say this.

Nevertheless, his expression betrayed his thoughts.

Mareike read them in his face.

"You look like you're about to say something overly analytical," Mareike said, her arms still around Sean's neck.

"By nature, I guess I'm analytical," he said, not questioning the mystery of intuition that allows a woman to correctly intuit a man's innermost thoughts.

"I guess I analyze things in order to figure out in my own mind how to deal with them . . . you know."

"Am I a *thing* to deal with?"

"No . . . I didn't mean that," Sean answered defensively. "My life, and how things inside it all fit together . . . that's what I mean."

"Am I a thing inside your life?" Mareike said, her face softening into a smile.

"Past few weeks . . . getting to know you . . . and now this . . . I wish you could be . . . I wish that I could find a way to reorganize the things I have to do . . . There's so much . . ."

Sean had suddenly, but for just a moment, felt whole. A long-sidelined empty void had been filled, but as the wave ran out, he found himself being pulled in two directions. The power of the two opposite directions each pulled him to throw himself toward them completely. He had come to Iraq sensing that his ministry there would be his life, and he'd *returned* to Iraq knowing that his ministry among these men was his life. Now, suddenly, something had happened. A new element had come into a life that had seemed already filled to overflowing.

Now he just felt speechless, unable to think of the right words to say.

"You are not the only one who has a life with things to piece together," she reminded him.

"I understand, but . . . I guess what I'm saying is . . ."

"That you are saying too much," she said, kissing him quickly and flicking her tongue playfully across his lip. "You *are* being analytical."

Sean felt an electric jolt up his spine. He just stared at Mareike, thinking how beautiful she was, with her long blond hair cascading haphazardly across her shoulders, and her once-sunburned nose starting to tan.

His thoughts and all the pieces that had only moments ago been neatly ordered were spinning within his head as though in a prairie cyclone.

Only a couple of hours ago he had casually told Tyler Kraus that his life had become routine, and that he wondered what that feeling meant. Now his head was really spinning and he had no idea what *this* meant.

For Mareike, too, there was the spinning sensation of having found herself pulled into the mystery of falling in—or at least *toward*—love with a man of God. Not long ago, she had not believed that there *was* a God.

Before either had a chance to say anything, there was a commotion in the hallway and Hala, the Iraqi teacher, came in with Bilal. One of the several beneficiaries of Sean's baseball cap giveaway, he was wearing his prized Kansas City Royals cap. He took much pride in this cap, because he was Sean's pal and he knew that the Royals were Sean's "home team."

"Bilal has brought something for both of you," Hala said in her halting, but nonetheless comprehensible English. Smiling, she handed a piece of paper to Mareike.

Sean glanced at the note, sheepishly admitting to himself that beyond knowing that it was written right to left, he knew absolutely nothing about written Arabic.

As Mareike traced her finger over the letters, Hala realized that it would be a good time to step in to translate.

"This is an invitation from the parents of Bilal and Naja," she said slowly, carefully picking her English words. "They wish to invite Sean and Mareike . . . two people of whom their children speak constantly . . . to come to the family home for *ashaa* . . . the evening meal . . . next week."

* * *

Strange and mysterious is my life.
What opposites I feel within!
A stable peace, a constant strife;
The rule of grace, the power of sin:
Too often I am captive led,
Yet daily triumph in my Head,
Yet daily triumph in my Head.

Thus different powers within me strive,
And grace and sin by turns prevail;
I grieve, rejoice, decline, revive,
And victory hangs in doubtful scale:
But Jesus has His promise passed,
That grace shall overcome at last,
That grace shall overcome at last.

FROM THE HYMN "CONFLICTING FEELINGS"
WORDS BY JOHN HENRY NEWTON, FROM *OLNEY HYMNS*

10

Always Alone,
Never Alone

"Chaplain, Chaplain!"

Urgent shouts aroused a dog-tired man dozing not on his cot, nor even at his desk, but in a chair at the FOB Lexington morgue. "Chaplain, Chaplain!"

Urgent shouts aroused a dog-tired man who had just prayed over the mortal remains of two young soldiers who had died a needless, useless death in a faraway place. Death in battle, though no less tragic for families and friends, carried at least an aura of sacrifice for a noble cause. Death in the preventable rollover of a Humvee driven too fast carried only the lamentable aura of pointlessness.

"Chaplain, Chaplain!"

The young soldier awoke Sean Rasmunsen from his trance-like slumber in the place where exhaustion had deposited him.

He was needed in the combat support hospital.

"What happened?" Sean asked as they headed out into the dusty daylight. "Was it an IED? Another accident?"

"Not sure," the man said nervously, as though he was more sure than he wanted to admit, but didn't want to talk about it.

In the hospital, he was led to a place where a man on a gurney had been wheeled out of the sight of other patients. At first it looked as though he might be dead, but then Sean noticed the restraints that bound both wrists.

"Massive abdominal injuries," was the doctor's grim reply to Sean's quizzical glance. "Hmmmmm. . . . uhhhh . . . self-inflicted."

The words just hung heavily in the cool, clear air—so much cooler and more clear than the outside world, or the tent where young Lance Gullie had just tried to blow out his guts with an M16.

"Officially, I didn't say that," the ER doc told Sean under his breath, qualifying the term *self-inflicted*.

To himself, Sean said simply, *Lord, give me strength*.

Suicides are a hard subject for anyone to grasp. They are hard for civil society just as they are for the U.S. military. They are especially hard on families. Suicide carries the dark impenetrable cloud of shame and disgrace that casts all of those left behind in its humiliating shadow.

The suicide rate among service personnel had increased by about twenty percent after the turn of the century, since those men and women began going into combat in Iraq. Here, the stress and uncertainty of the war zone coincided with ready access to weapons. Under such circumstances, grim thoughts can turn quickly to grim actions. As Lt. Col. Elspeth Ritchie, a psychiatrist at the U.S. Army's Uniformed Services University of the Health Sciences in Bethesda has said, "It just takes a second to pull it out and put it to your head and pull the trigger."

At least with Lance Gullie, it had been abdominal injuries, not a head wound.

"That which you didn't officially say," Sean asked. "Are you pretty sure?"

"The angle of the rifle and the way he was found indicate that it was."

"How is he doing?"

"Resting comfortably, as we say in this business," the doctor said, looking at his patient sadly. "The muzzle was pressed against his belly, but it entered at an angle and missed the kidney on that side by about an inch. It's awkward to pull the trigger of an M16 at arm's length with the muzzle pushed into your belly."

In recent years, some have cried "cover-up" when a U.S. Army suicide is officially classified as a "non-combat weapons discharge" or a "non-hostile gunshot wound," but what do you tell the family? Would a soldier's family find it easier to think that he died cleaning his gun, or to embrace potential shame and ridicule of having it officially announced that he did it deliberately? Worse still is to be told the latter when it was the former. It is a hard call, nearly always made at the field level, not in a comfortable, air-conditioned Pentagon office.

In any case, it's a no-win situation for the family left behind.

"Could it have been accidental?" Sean asked.

"Could have been." The doctor shrugged, glancing at the restraints. "But I didn't send for you because I thought that."

"How long before he wakes up?"

"At least an hour."

"I'll be here," Sean promised. He knew why he was there. Most soldiers would rather be comforted by a chaplain with whom they could speak confidentially than have to explain to a psychiatrist whose notes would head straight into their medical records. In most cases, a chaplain is just as qualified as a shrink. In many cases, he or she is much *better* qualified to counsel a man—or woman—on the edge.

As part of his training, Sean had become certified in suicide prevention, and he was glad of this because the need had indeed arisen—not often, but too often. He never knew how many he had thwarted—just as the various measures taken by the highway patrol cannot tell you how many traffic fatalities they deter—but he hoped there had been more than just a few. However, he *did* know how many had occurred on his watch, and those two deaths during his first tour still gnawed at him on sleepless nights.

Lance Gullie would, by his own failure, have a second chance.

"Lord, give me strength," Sean said. "Give me strength to comfort this man . . . and Lord, give *him* strength . . . and allow him to hear what I'm going to say in the spirit in which it's said . . . Amen."

Anyone's first reaction on coming off sedation is to wonder where they are. For young Pvt. Gullie, the second was about the restraints. First he tugged angrily, and then the realization set in and he slumped back.

"Lance, I'm Sean Rasmunsen," the chaplain said. He recognized the young man, but only as one of the many faces that he had seen on his rounds—he had made an effort to make eye contact with everyone at FOB Lexington, regardless of whether they showed up at the chapel.

"Yeah, I know," he replied glumly, looking away. "I've seen you around."

"Doctor says you're gonna be okay." Sean smiled.

"Great," Lance said as though he'd just received some very unwelcome news. "I even screwed *this* up."

"You wanna talk about what happened?"

"Whaddya want me to say?"

"Whatever you want to say."

"If I said I wished I hadn't missed, would you tell me that was a sin?"

"You want me to say that?" Sean asked. "Would it feel better?"

"Huh? Well it *is*, ain't it?"

"It's not my job to pin blame on . . . to judge . . . somebody I hardly met, I don't know what happ—"

"I'll tell you what happened. I am so tired of being trapped in this *place*. I want out. I wake up every morning in this place. I can't escape! I just want *outa here* . . . any way I can!"

Sean had heard it before. People feel so helplessly trapped that death seems to be the only way out, an escape that is preferable to the pain of continuing on.

"I don't care if it's a sin," Gullie continued. "I just can't go on. Tell me this: Does it matter if some punk with an IED blows me up, or if I blow me up? I'm still dead, right?"

"God gave you life, and he kept you alive—" Sean began, biting his tongue for letting himself sound too much like a preacher.

"I don't care," Gullie shouted, tugging at the restraints. "I don't even know that's true . . . Even if it is, you gotta die sometime. Life is only worth living if it's worth living—right? If it ain't, you gotta have the right to get yourself out! Right?"

The dark logic of the argument indicated only that Gullie had given it some thought.

Fall back on your training. Remembering his suicide prevention course, Sean realized that this was the point when his job was to just shut up and listen. Gullie had something on his mind—plenty on his mind—and Sean's best course was to just let him continue to vent his feelings, to jerk at the restraints, and to articulate the dark thoughts that had taken him to the edge.

Sometimes what men on the edge really need most is to have someone just listen to all of the dark thoughts that they have bottled up within themselves.

At last, Gullie sighed deeply and sank back to the gurney, his rant spent. Though he was far from fully rational, he did now understand that the restraints would not be moved regardless of his angry thrashing. Just as his spirit had felt so impossibly trapped, so too was his body trapped. Just as his attempt to escape his life had failed, the restraints had suspended all possibility of escape from the gurney.

"I really screwed up." He sobbed. "My whole life. I really screwed up. I even screwed up offing myself. I'm a screw . . . *screw-up*. I'm crazy. You think I'm crazy, don'tcha?"

"You're not crazy," Sean said quietly, so quietly that Gullie had to quit moaning in order to hear him. "You're not a screw-up. You just got to the point where your aching outstripped your ability to cope with your pain."

"You think I committed a sin, don't you?"

"Like I said, it's not my job to judge you."

"All you mean is that you're passing me off and God's gonna let me burn in hell for sinning, right?" Gullie said in a half-taunting, half-hopeless tone.

"No, I don't mean that," Sean told him. "God's got an infinite capacity for forgiveness. My job is to help you get through whatever it is that made you want to give up, and to help you put your life back together so it's worth living."

Gullie just sighed hopelessly and shook his head back and forth. It was the only extremity that was unrestrained. Arguably, it was the extremity most in need of restraint.

It was now Sean's opportunity to speak, to offer recognition of a man who felt isolated and forgotten. It was his turn to get to know Lance Gullie, not as a failed suicide, but as a person with hopes, dreams, and unbearable pain.

It was now time to take the causes of the pain apart, separating them into pieces that Gullie could deal with one at a time. He promised the anguished soldier that he was there—and would be there—for him.

Lord, give me strength, Sean asked silently. *Lord, give him strength.*

It was a long night, but the sedation took Gullie to sleep, and Sean could stagger off to his tent and crash for a couple of hours himself. The suicide watch would continue, but the restraints would eventually come off.

Sean awoke to the anguish of Lance Gullie's loneliness and how it had pushed the kid to the edge. As he felt his mind wrestle itself awake from the hard sleep borne from exhaustion, he watched almost as a bystander as his thoughts drifted spontaneously to the discussion of loneliness that he'd had with Mareike De Vries last week.

His mind drifted often—at these moments at the cusp of sleep when his subconscious still was the master control of his thoughts—to Mareike De Vries. He thought often of what she had come to mean to him. She was a fresh ear, a fresh voice; she was disconnected from all other aspects of his life and work.

For Sean, Mareike had become that someone with whom *he* could talk about his own personal loneliness. He had found great comfort in being able to share his thoughts and to talk with someone who was not part of the 2/77, not part of the U.S. Army, and not even an American. It was like a breath of cool, fresh air to step outside his routine and share his feelings.

They had become close friends and confidants against the backdrop of mutual misperceptions of one another's culture. She had assumed Americans to be self-centered and superficial. He had always assumed that Europeans fit the stereotype that fit Isabelle, but he found Mareike to be just the opposite.

She had become symbolic of the secret and seldom-seen Sean Rasmunsen who lived in that narrow breathing space that existed apart from all else.

Was the fact that his mind drifted so naturally and so easily to Mareike De Vries a symptom of something missing from his life—and from his *ministry*?

Were his thoughts of her and what she represented a manifestation of his need to have a refuge from the pressures and sadness that he experienced almost hourly at FOB Lexington, and wherever American soldiers went?

He admitted to himself that he truly enjoyed her company,

and he knew she felt the same way—but were their conversations and the bond he sensed merely a coping mechanism?

Was it simply a case of two lonely, stressed-out people drawn together just because their circumstances meant they had no one else, no place else? Were they just unconsciously using one another?

And having considered all that, Sean wondered whether he was, as Mareike had suggested, merely overanalyzing a natural and straightforward situation?

Sean thought often of her smile and her words, and tried not to think of her hand on his and of their kiss. In his world, physical manifestations of affection such as this were not taken—or given—lightly.

By the strict regulations of his own conscience, he had definitely gone too far—though *technically*, he had done no wrong.

By the rules of every major religion in America, a pastor should *never* become involved in a physical relationship with a member of his congregation—but Mareike De Vries was *not* a member of his congregation.

By U.S. Army regulations, an officer, especially a chaplain, should *never* become involved in a physical relationship with a fellow service member—*but* Mareike De Vries was *not* in the U.S. Army. She wasn't even American.

By U.S. Army regulations, a service member should *never* become involved in a physical relationship with a resident of a foreign country in which the U.S. Army is operating—*but* Mareike De Vries was *not* Iraqi.

Though each of these rules was routinely broken, Sean could never imagine himself breaking any of them—and he had not. Still, by the standards of his own conscience, his own personal code of conduct, he felt pangs of guilt. He felt that his turning toward thoughts of Mareike like a houseplant toward a window—never mind the *kiss*—were diverting his attention from his true purpose, his calling.

Sean was torn. Was his faith not the sanctuary into which he could retreat? Prayer still provided the solace that he sought, but his mind kept turning toward Mareike, the warmth that these thoughts provided, *and* to next Wednesday.

Did this reaching beyond his ministry mean that he had reached a spiritual crossroads in his life?

Sean Rasmunsen had felt called to return to Iraq, to risk himself physically in a dreadful place in order to provide solace for the men of his service. Was his meeting Mareike De Vries part of this calling, or merely a distraction?

And once again, Sean wondered whether he was, as Mareike herself had told him, indulging in overanalysis.

Sean had put a visit to Lance Gullie atop his agenda for the morning. He found the soldier lying quietly, an IV tube taped to his arm, monitors attached someplace beneath the sheets. The restraints were off, although he was in a place where he could be constantly observed by the staff.

When he saw Sean, tears welled up in his eyes and he reached out. The IV tube halted this gesture, but Sean came close.

"You saved my life, man," Gullie sobbed, grabbing Sean's hand. "You talked me back from the friggin' edge. You saved me, man."

"I'm really glad that you're feeling better," Sean said sincerely.

"When I get outa here, I'm gonna come to chapel every friggin' Sunday, man."

"I'll look forward to seeing you," Sean said. "In the meantime, I'm going to come by and see you here every day."

They talked for about ten minutes—nothing special, just talk, just to let Gullie know that somebody cared. It reminded Sean of a Hallmark card, an almost perfect ending to a night of anguish that had almost cost a man his life in a needless act of desperation.

"If only all the trials of life could always be resolved so easy," Sean muttered to himself as he left the hospital.

Maybe it was the Lord cutting him some slack. Last night he had breathed a prayer for strength, for himself and for Lance Gullie. This morning, he said one in thanksgiving as he made his way to the chapel.

Inside the sandbagged structure with a peaked roof made of corrugated metal that had been modified from an old bunker, Ashley Mariott was rehearsing her choir. Sean quietly grabbed a folding chair in the last row and listened as they sang an old hymn by Ludie Pickett. She had taught at Asbury College in Kentucky, coincidentally located just a twenty-minute drive from the namesake city of FOB Lex. Though the hymn was from more than a hundred years ago, in the last decade of the nineteenth century, it seemed to summarize perfectly all of the soul-searching that Sean had done since the darkest hours of last night.

◆ ◆ ◆

I've seen the lightning flashing, I've heard the thunder roll.
I've felt sin's breakers dashing, which almost conquered my soul.
I've heard the voice of my Savior, bidding me still to fight on.
He promised never to leave me, never to leave me alone!

No, never alone, no never alone,
He promised never to leave me,
He'll claim me for His own;
No, never alone, no never alone.

FROM THE HYMN "NEVER ALONE"
WORDS BY LUDIE CARRINGTON DAY PICKETT

11

Island of Serenity

"La chaleur d'étouffement . . . the smothering heat." Isabelle Laclerc moaned. "It saps my strength."

"Mais qui," Mareike De Vries teased, answering her French colleague's English with Isabelle's native tongue.

Teasing, too, in the suffocating blanket it spread across Safaliyah and its inhabitants, was the Iraqi summer weather. Its brutality crept up quickly each day with the rising of the sun, smothering all who tried to undertake the simplest of daily tasks. But beneath that blanket, life went on. People lived their lives and dreamed their dreams.

Woensdag—Wednesday—came, and with it came Mareike's nervous anticipation of seeing Sean Rasmunsen again.

She had come to Iraq to give of herself to children caught up in a maelstrom of war and military occupation. The last thing on Mareike's mind had been the thought of falling in love—especially with a man of God, especially with a man of God whose paycheck came from the army of occupation.

After Mareike broke up with Piet two years ago, the last thing on her mind had been the thought of falling in love—with *anybody*. She neither wanted nor sought another romantic entanglement.

Had she thrown herself into work that was so emotionally demanding that she could not spare a cubic millimeter within her heart to contain love for any man?

She had.

Did this leave her vulnerable, her guard down, when it happened without warning?

Apparently.

This man of God was such a marked contrast to Piet, a man so obsessed with his identity as an agnostic that he had become an evangelist for secularism. In her youth, Mareike had been just as strident, but she had changed. She and Piet had grown apart as she sought that ambiguous something in the meaning of life.

She tried the church, but only as someone dips a toe into a cold stream. And she had not dipped her toe into one in many months when suddenly this man of God had come into her life. She certainly did not seek such a man to complete her life, to provide an ambiguous something that was missing in her life—but it had happened.

Of course, love does not come according to a plan. The cold, then warm, tingling that she felt on her skin when he looked at her that day when they had first touched was not something that she sought. Had she thought about it rationally, it would never have happened.

What was it about him that overcame all judgment?

What was it that made her succumb to the desire to *kiss* a man of God?

It was so dreadfully inappropriate, but it felt so dreadfully *good!*

"You are infatuated with the American priest," Isabelle taunted as she noticed Mareike daydreaming. "I can tell. I see it in your eyes. He comes on *mercredi* . . ."

"He is not a priest," Mareike said disgustedly. "He is Protestant."

"Oh, so it is not a sin to love a *Protestant* priest?"

"I don't 'love' the Protestant priest," Mareike lied, her blush inflaming her fair cheeks.

"She don't 'love' the Protestant priest." Isabelle laughed. "I envy you finding love with a handsome man in this hellhole."

Was that it? Mareike wondered. He *was* handsome. Was that all there was to it? Did she find herself falling in love with Sean Rasmunsen *despite* his being a man of God? Or, dare she believe that it was *because* he was a man of God?

Falling in love with a man of God was complicated. Protestant clergy were allowed to fall in love and get married, but there was still something dark and mysterious about this. It was like sailing into an unknown world on an unknown sea. Nobody that Mareike had ever known had fallen in love with a man of God. Nobody had ever even mentioned it.

Mareike had her own feelings, and she knew that he had feelings toward her—but there was something about his manner, his reaction, and his reticence that she could not comprehend. As good as it felt, she had that nagging sense that loving such a man was somehow inappropriate. It was almost like falling in love with a man who was already married, although even that was a poor analogy. How could a mortal woman compete with the love that this man felt for *God*?

Whatever the case, the reality was that Mareike could not spend her time musing about the mysteries of love. The reality was that she had thrown herself into work that was so demanding of her time—if not her emotions—that she could not spare a moment to muse.

The heat brought an envelope of listlessness into Mareike's classroom. Eager learners who usually battled one another to answer the teacher's questions lay their heads on their arms and stared at Mareike with half-opened eyes. The lone ceiling fan simply did not cut it, and Mareike breathed a silent prayer.

"God, if you're listening," Mareike said in the halfhearted way of people who really don't believe in prayer. "Or Allah, if you're listening . . . send somebody down here to install some air-conditioning in this place."

When, after lunch, a breeze began ruffling the papers through opened second-story windows, she felt herself pausing to wonder.

The Americans came, as they always did, in the afternoon. Alone with her thoughts, Mareike had pondered romantically about the abstractions of love. However, in a courtyard full of children, and in the presence of the Americans, she felt a little silly pondering romantically about abstractions.

Reality crept in like a tidal wave.

Every woman *dreams* of the ideal man who will sweep her off her feet and carry her away into endless, ideal bliss. However, every woman *knows* that in reality, life and work are so demanding that there is rarely a spare cubic millimeter to contain even finite ideal bliss.

"I'm looking forward to meeting your parents tonight," Sean told Bilal as the usual ball game came to an end. He noticed a spark of understanding in the boy's eyes even before Hala translated the words.

"Right on," Bilal said, giving Sean a high five.

"You're doing a great job with these kids," Sean told Mareike.

"Phrases such as *right on* are learned from you," she replied with a smile. "And yes, he is looking forward to this night, to the *ashaa*, the dinner at their home."

"Me, too." Sean grinned. "It'll be interesting. I understand that their dad is an important official in city government."

"Yes, he's a deputy director of public works in Safaliyah," Mareike confirmed. "He recognizes the value in building bridges to the outside world. He is genuinely pleased that his children are learning English and befriending outsiders."

"I'm looking forward to befriending his family," Sean said. "It's good that we can sit down with people for a meal. It's kind of what we in my business call *fellowship*."

"Here's to fellowship." Mareike smiled, holding up a plastic bottle of water.

Sean, Mareike, and their entourage left the school about an hour after the children left for the day. Mustafa Ilik had worked out the logistics for the party, which would include Hala as an interpreter, and Tyler Kraus—because his job was to ride shotgun for Sean. Tonight, however, there would be no shotgun, nor his usual M4 carbine, just a discreetly concealed SIG P228/M11, a compact 9-mm automatic pistol.

Typically issued by the U.S. Army to its Criminal Investigation Command, the M11 is small enough to be easily concealed, yet its thirteen-round magazine would give Kraus some reasonable, close-range firepower if he and Sean ran into bad guys. If not, it wouldn't intrude into what everyone hoped would be a "normal" dinner party.

To underscore the idea of normalcy, both Sean and Tyler shed their body armor for the occasion.

To underscore the necessary notion of what passes for normalcy in Iraq, Mareike donned the lavender headscarf that she always wore outside the confines of the school. She dressed all in black, except for her customary grayish-purple sneakers. Hala, despite her apparently having an open mind toward nontraditional customs, always wore her headscarf. Mareike had never even seen her hair.

For Tyler Kraus, it was a strange experience, driving through the streets of Saf City in a regular car with two women in headscarves in the backseat. When he was at the wheel of a Humvee, people more often than not noticed the vehicle, often pausing to stare at him warily as he passed. Tonight, nobody even noticed the 1989 Mercedes as they headed out of the city center toward the middle-class residential area where Bilal and Naja lived with their parents.

Compared to the Humvee, the Mercedes was light to the touch, although it had been retrofitted with steel plate by a Saddam-era official before having been "liberated" by Mustafa Ilik in the confused days of 2003. Apparently the former owner had never complained about the loss of his car. Also apparent was that the armor plate had not prevented his being relieved of his officialdom.

To call the neighborhood *modest* would be accurate for most towns in the Middle East, but for Safaliyah it was the nice part of town. Located on a hill not far from Outpost Bravo, it had paved streets and a little bit of vegetation. To call the streets *tree-lined* would be an overstatement, but as Sean got out of the car, the smell of eucalyptus stinging his nostrils was a welcome variance from the usual chalky bite of the Iraqi dust.

A pleasant, middle-aged man met the Mercedes at the gate to the little enclosed courtyard that surrounded the house and introduced himself in Arabic as Jihan al-Qamar, the father of Bilal and Naja.

"As-salaam alaikum," he said happily as they stepped from the car.

"Alaikum as-salaam," Mareike replied, giving the usual response to the typical greeting of "Peace be upon you."

"Good even-ning," Jihan's wife, Minya, said, exercising a carefully learned English phrase as she appeared at the door.

"Masa el noor," Mareike replied, exercising her own carefully learned Arabic phrase.

Unlike Hala, Minya wore no headscarf indoors, so Mareike slipped hers down around her neck as she stepped into the house.

The visitors presented gifts. The women had brought a plate of pastries, the Americans—feeding a stereotype—brought technology, in this case a pair of iPods preloaded with noncontroversial, easy-listening instrumentals.

When gifts had earlier been discussed at the school, Isabelle had cynically predicted that "Mareike's Protestant priest" would bring Bibles. She knew that such a gift would have been at the same end of the faux pas spectrum as the typical Western dinner party gift, the bottle of wine. Nevertheless, she said it merely to taunt Mareike. Isabelle was jealous about not having been invited. Mareike was pleased to see that Sean had a bit more cultural sensitivity than Isabelle gave him credit for.

The children appeared, excited to have the people from their two worlds together in the same room. Bilal, proud to showcase his new English words, attempted to translate, and Jihan knew a few words as well. However, as things progressed, they more and more deferred to Hala to provide the bridge between the two worlds.

For Sean and Mareike alike, it was an entirely new experience to be in a comfortable Iraqi home, a place that was as untouched by the war as it could be in Safaliyah. Sean's life in the country was spent on the streets, in combat zones, or on American bases that were deliberately molded as generic replicas of American bases anywhere. Mareike's days were spent in a school building where every item of equipment was precious or nonexistent. Her nights were spent in a spartan dormitory setting listening to Isabelle complain about the amenities they lacked—which were, by Parisian standards, many.

By comparison, the al-Qamar home was like a welcome refuge, with neat furniture, ornate carpets on the floor, and even a houseplant or two. The thick walls insulated the interior of the home from the blistering heat of the fading summer day.

As the introductions were complete, tea was offered, and the hosts expressed great interest in the respective homelands of the foreigners. With the two Americans, they were surprised by the great differences in climate and culture between Coos Bay, Oregon, and Linn County, Missouri. Mareike was fascinated with Sean's stories of Missouri, but mainly because of her fascination with the man.

"*Bismillah,*" said Jihan as they sat down for the appetizers, which consisted of lamb kebabs on wooden skewers.

Everyone answered "*Bismillah,*" which means "in the name of God." Sean was initially caught off guard, but remembered from his seminary studies that Muslims, like Christians, say a blessing before a meal. He readily spoke the Arabic word, just as he went along with the blessings favored by any Christian denomination. The words, he figured, were heard and understood by the intended listener in the spirit in which they were offered. The Lord, needless to say, is multilingual.

As they began, Bilal was admonished by his mother to remove his Royals baseball cap. She apologized to Sean, knowing that it was his home team, but explained that hats should not be worn by boys at the table. Tyler offered his signature blue sunglasses, which Bilal perched atop his head with his mother's reluctant acquiescence. Everyone smiled.

Just like kids everywhere.

Mareike noticed that as he was eating his kebab, Sean seemed uncharacteristically quiet. It was something no one else seemed to observe, but Mareike had.

In fact, as he ate the meat, the thoughts of that terrible night in the desert, the knife and the shepherd boy, were tracing through the pastor's mind. He pondered and he wondered. *When,* he asked himself, *will there come a time when all Iraqis can live as this family is tonight in this home?*

◆   ◆   ◆

As they were sipping from the soup bowls that Minya presented, Jihan turned his attention to inquiring about Sean's line of work. With Hala interpreting, he respectfully explained that it was surprising to him that there were men of the Book—of the Bible—in the armed forces of a secular nation such as the United States.

"God willing, I mean no harm in asking," Hala translated, "But I am curious to know about this."

"I take no offense." Sean smiled as he slowly explained. "I'm happy to talk about it. God willing, you'll find that my explanation makes sense. There are a great many religious people in the United States, and the people in our armed forces are representative of the people who make up our country. For many of these people, religion—and exercising it—is an important part of their lives. The Army recognizes this; they have for more than two hundred years, in fact. So they have people like me—ordained ministers—to serve as chaplains."

"Your job then is to enforce religious teachings?"

"Not exactly," Sean answered cautiously. "My job is to provide a religious grounding for those who want it . . . those who feel they need it. Just as we all said 'in the name of God' as we began this meal, and as you say that as you begin many tasks, many Christians begin their meal with a blessing. I guess I see my role as one who leads my people in prayer instead of pushing them to prayer."

"Do you see yourself first as a man whose loyalty is to your army or as a man of the Book?" Jihan asked pointedly.

"The Book," Sean answered quickly, seeing that Jihan understood his answer without the translation, despite Sean's having used the English word. He knew enough Arabic to know that *kitab* was the literal word for "book," but he knew enough about Islam to know that *al-Kitab* was used as a reference specifically to the Qur'an. He didn't want any confusion about his associating himself with that specific book.

"I'm first and foremost a man of the Book," Sean continued. "I was a Christian minister before I joined the U.S. Army. I suppose, that like any man of the Book, my first loyalty is to God . . . but a close second is my loyalty to the people I serve, the people in the Army. I have a loyalty to my country, and to the Army, but my first loyalty after that to God, is to the *people* in the Army."

"Are they all Christians, as you are?"

"Most are, but not all. There are Jews and Muslims and Buddhists. Most chaplains are Christian, but not all. There are Jewish and Muslim and Buddhist chaplains in the U.S. Army."

"How can you be a minister to a Jew or a Buddhist?" Jihan asked. "How can a Buddhist be a chaplain for a Christian?"

"Just as we all sat down together here tonight . . . Christian and Muslim or whatever," Sean began. He was not sure if Mareike really considered herself a Christian, despite her having said she attended church, and he didn't want to exclude or include her where she felt uncomfortable. "We all sat down to a wonderful meal and we joined our voices 'in the name of God'; so it is in my ministry. I try to find common ground, because I believe we are all seeking God. I know that I have people from a lot of faith traditions come into my chapel. I know that their spiritual needs differ; I know they come because they have spiritual needs."

"He asks to describe what sorts of spiritual needs?" Hala said.

"This week, I had one of my hardest," Sean explained. "I had a young man who wanted to kill himself. I had to convince him that his life had value, even if this was not apparent to him at the time. I couldn't tell him that God didn't want him to be dead, because that would be like scolding him. I had to persuade him to look within himself to find the worth in his life and what it might mean for others for whom his life was also important."

"This is remarkable," Jihan said.

Sean noticed that Bilal had paid close. attention to his words. The boy, though a boy, seemed to understand what Sean had tried to tell Lance Gullie, and it seemed to make sense to him. As with kids growing into adults everywhere, it was the realization of the promise that their lives had value.

Sean also noticed the expression on Mareike's face. Hers was more complex, and hard to read.

If Mareike's expression was complex, it was because the wheels in her head were turning, trying to grasp the complexity that she saw in this man whose simple words and simple message were so much more than they seemed. He was remarkable. He was remarkable, indeed.

As the main course was served, the casserole dish called *kibbe batata*, she watched the man move on, turning the tables back to Jihan al-Qamar, guiding the conversation toward an interest in Jihan's life. What sort of work did he do? What challenges did he face in things that he faced each day?

Mareike took her turn, bringing Minya into the conversation with talk of the children. She told some funny stories, and Hala laughed as she translated. She told of her hopes and aspirations for them. She told of the optimism that came with the fall of Saddam Hussein, and of the guarded hopes that she and her family now held for a future that was different from the recent past as well as from the Saddam past. They knew that the future would be different. They hoped it would also be *better*.

By the time that the coffee reached the table and the children, like children everywhere, were sent to bed, a camaraderie had been established. Despite the language barrier, and Hala's inability to keep up with all the conversation, a bond was forming. Six people from distinctly contrasting backgrounds and different religious traditions had found, at least for a moment, common ground to smile and to laugh.

In the warm glow emanating from behind fringed lampshades, Mareike sensed herself enjoying a brief respite on a small island of serenity. In the man toward whom she was drawn more and more each moment, she sensed that she had found a quiet sanctuary.

◆ ◆ ◆

I cannot tell thee whence it came,
This peace within my breast;
But this I know, there fills my soul
A strange and tranquil rest.

I cannot tell thee why He chose
To suffer and to die,
But if I suffer here with Him
I'll reign with Him on high.

FROM THE HYMN "HIDDEN PEACE"
WORDS BY JOHN S. BROWN

12

Another Day Begun

Each step was almost painful. The smothering heat robbed Sean Rasmunsen of his strength. How hot was it? It had been nearly 115 when the sun came up. He didn't want to know what it was now. As he made his rounds at FOB Lexington, Sean kept a smile on his face, sharing a positive word with everyone who made eye contact—despite the overwhelming urge to wilt like a water-starved houseplant.

His thoughts turned often to Wednesday night, and how enjoyable it had been to sit down with the family of his young friends, Bilal and Naja. How wonderful it was to sit around the al-Qamar family table and break *khubaz*—the traditional Iraqi flatbread served with date jelly. It was a welcome relief from U.S. Army food, or from American-style food. Also welcome had been the opportunity to sit down with Iraqis and share a conversation to the point that everyone seemed to forget how different they were, and to be able to concentrate on what they all shared.

This morning, as he had said grace for a dozen soldiers who'd gathered with him for breakfast, Sean had thought about how they had all said "in the name of God" before their meal at the al-Qamar home—as though there were no religious differences.

He had thought a lot about that, about religious differences and how that contributed to the war and the misery into which this part of the world had been plunged. It was not just the differences between his own faith and Islam, but here in the Sandbox, it was the brutal bloodshed traded by Sunni and Shia. Both follow the teachings of the prophet Muhammad, but they haven't agreed on exactly *how* to do so since the time he died. Both say *bismillah* when they sit down to eat, but they're willing to kill one another—over religion—the next day.

His thoughts had already started turning into notes for this Sunday's sermon. If the Catholics and Protestants in Ulster could bury the battle-ax, was there hope for the Middle East? Perhaps.

He had thought long and hard about Mareike De Vries as well, selfishly wishing that she could hear his sermon. He had been thinking a lot about her, and trying to sort out his thoughts and feelings. More than ever, when he let his mind drift, it drifted to her. Was it truly love that he felt?

He wished that he had had some time alone with her on Wednesday—to talk, of course. He wished that he could have had some time alone with Mareike on Wednesday to hold her near him and to taste her lips, but he hid those thoughts, which were not thoughts, but feelings. His loyalty on this earth, as he had said on Wednesday, was to his troops.

He deliberately did not use, even in his own mind, the term *flock* for his congregation. It only brought back memories of that night, that terrible night, and that shepherd who had died so needlessly. It would become just another memory that could not be buried, but could be filed in a place within him where retrieval was by means of thoughts, but not feelings.

Sean found himself making a quick pass through the chapel and lingering long at the hospital. They had a fan at the chapel, but they had air-conditioning at the hospital.

It was amazing how good seventy degrees could feel. He would have to get Sgt. Lockhart to work on getting some of this climate-control magic for the chapel!

On his agenda for the day, Sean had a baptism. It was the first one in more than a week, but some weeks he had several. During his first tour, Sean had been amazed by the number of unbaptized soldiers who wanted to become part of an organized Christian community, but soon he took it in stride. Back when he was a kid, and later in the seminary, he had been surrounded only by people who had already been baptized. Since then, he had been surprised by how many unbaptized people he met, but his worldview had expanded a great deal.

He now realized that there were many good people in the world who would probably never be baptized, but who lived naturally, and not through dogma, by the most basic of Christian beliefs—to love others as oneself. Nevertheless, the minister in him was still pleased when someone asked. As a pastor, he was happy to oblige.

As a human being in an environment where it had been 115 at

sunrise, he looked forward to the baptism for selfish reasons. An excuse to have water poured over you was certainly welcome. He recalled the story of a U.S. Navy chaplain named Michael Baker who baptized a Marine Corps sergeant in the Euphrates River. The sergeant asked for it because the Euphrates is one of the four rivers mentioned in the Bible as flowing from the Garden of Eden. Sean would have enjoyed that—both for the symbolism and for the dip in cool river water—but there were no rivers anywhere near FOB Lex. In the rainy season, there were a few streams in the area, but these had long since dried up for the summer.

Some Christian denominations believed in total immersion, as Jesus had been baptized by John, whereas others allowed for the symbolism of the sprinkling of water. Sean believed that the symbolism *may* be adequate, because the true baptism took place in a person's acceptance of a role in the church, but he also believed that there was symbolism in not stopping at the halfway point. If a baptism was worth doing, it was worth doing all the way, even if the immersion involved ten gallons of desalinated seawater in a plastic container trucked in from Kuwait.

Derek Holder was waiting for Sean in his office. He sat quietly, fumbling with his cap and staring at the ground. Lots of guys were jittery about getting baptized. It was that symbolism thing.

"Don't be nervous, Derek," Sean said, trying to cheer him up. "It's only water. On a day like this, it oughta feel pretty good."

"Yes, sir, it oughta," the soldier said, barely glancing up.

"Are you having second thoughts?" Sean asked. Far worse than not baptizing someone was baptizing someone who was reticent about the idea.

"No, sir. I mean kinda, sir."

"You don't have to call me *sir*," Sean assured him. "What do you mean by 'kinda'?"

"I mean I'm kinda not sure, y'know. I'm kinda not sure I'm worthy."

"What makes you think you're not worthy?"

"You can't baptize a sinner, can you?"

"Everybody's a sinner. Imperfection is just as much human nature as perfection. You just gotta work on one and against the other."

"Where do you draw the line?" Holder asked. "Where's the line between a sorta, y'know, a little-white-lie kind of sin and a really big whopper of a sin?"

Sean saw the warning flag. Any sentence containing a phrase like *really big whopper of a sin* was definitely a signal that something was truly troubling this kid.

"You wanna talk about it?" Sean asked, slumping down in his chair to make his body language less that of an authority figure with captain's bars on his collar. "Anything you wanna talk about with me is in confidence."

"Don't matter, sir. I'm in pretty deep. I thought if I joined up with you guys and became Christian and all, that would make things kinda change for me, but I know now that it ain't gonna happen, y'know."

"Sometimes it's better to talk about it. Maybe things aren't so hopeless as you think."

"Man, sir, I don't know . . ."

"Try me."

"Is it a sin to snitch on somebody when you promised to keep your mouth shut?"

"Depends. I think you know inside whether it's right or wrong in your case."

"Is it a sin to snitch on an officer if he gives you an order?"

"I think you know the answer."

"Okay, but there's thousands of dollars involved."

"Involved in what?" Sean asked. He was getting very curious about Holder's secret.

"They're taking stuff, y'know. Lots of stuff. Computers. Phones. Other stuff."

"Who is? From where?"

"Lieutenant Stahl and Captain Prieto," Holder answered. "They got this thing. Goes all the way back to Baghdad. They're taking all this computer stuff out of shipments headed out to the FOBs, like here at Lex."

"What are they doing with it?"

"They got a fence down in Saf City who pays 'em for it. Guess they ship it across the border into Kurdistan or Syria or somewhere."

"How are you involved?"

"I'm in Quartermaster, y'know," Holder said, shrugging. "I just unpack it and repack it. Shipment comes in that's got four of something in a carton, I just make it three of something and pad it out with bubble wrap. They got some guy who forges paperwork and it all looks normal."

"And then they take it into Saf City and sell it?"

"Yeah. Stahl takes a patrol down. I'm in the same Humvee. He gets out. I get out. He sees his guy. I carry the stuff. Guy gives him money . . . American money . . . Lots of hundreds."

Sean took a deep breath. The last sentence underscored the enormity of this caper that Derek Holder himself had called a "really big whopper of a sin." What could be done? Sean decided it would be best to appeal to the man's already troubled conscience.

"What do you think oughta be done about this?"

"I dunno," Holder said, staring at the floor and looking as though he were about to cry. "I don't suppose we can just pretend it never happened?"

"It seems as though you're saying that it's *still* happening. Right?"

"Yeah."

"What do you think . . . what does your conscience tell you oughta be done?"

"I guess we better tell somebody." Holder shrugged, a tear streaming down his cheek. "I guess I oughta come clean about this."

"I guess," Sean agreed.

The commander of the 2nd Battalion of the 77th Infantry never left his chaplain waiting longer than it took to finish a phone call or say "dismissed" to whoever happened to be in his office. Lt. Col. Amos Folbright ran a tight ship and a tight schedule, and Sean made it a practice of staying out of his way unless it was a scheduled meeting or a matter of urgency. As a result, getting a prompt audience with His Highness was nearly always possible when Sean came calling.

When he had heard the story, Folbright felt incredulous and by no small measure stupid.

It was not that Stahl and Prieto were stellar officers in the mold of a man like Ryan Clark—because they weren't—but neither were they particularly the dullest pencils in the 2/77's drawer. Not in his wildest imagination had Folbright imagined such a thing could be taking place on their watch and under *his* nose. His first reaction was that Derek Holder was making it up to get back at the officers. It was not unknown for a soldier with a grudge to implicate an officer in some imaginary transgression.

"Do you have any *proof* of these allegations that you can offer?"

"Not exactly, sir," Holder admitted.

"These are serious allegations," Folbright pointed out. "Are you aware that there are serious penalties for making untrue allegations of this scale?"

"Yes, sir."

"How can you convince the colonel that it's true?" Sean asked. He was sure that the young soldier was not lying, but he also knew the repercussions of unproven, or unprovable, accusations.

"Okay, pull over here," the captain demanded. "Stop the vehicle next to that building and set up a perimeter."

"Yes, sir."

Capt. Jacob Prieto had nearly finished his second tour in Iraq, winding up his overseas commitment as a company commander. He already had his next assignment, to CENTCOM at MacDill AFB, and by Christmas, he'd be a major. Nearly every officer in the Army, and certainly everyone who planned to go anywhere within the service, had done time in the Sandbox. Most found it stressful and unpleasant, but many found ways to make lemonade out of the bitterness. Prieto had. It wasn't exactly an ortho-dox way of making lemonade, but he felt he deserved the sweet fruits of his sideline activities.

Inside the building, the man known only as Ali bade Prieto to sit down for a cup of sweet mint tea. Prieto disliked mint tea, but it did taste better than hot dust, and drinking it was part of the ritual.

"It's a very warm day," Ali said in English.

"Must be a hundred and twenty in the shade," Prieto replied.

"I don't know your temperature scale." The old Arab shrugged.

"It's the same as fifty in Celsius, I think."

"Indeed, warm . . . hot."

More than his dislike of the mint tea, and perhaps more even than the weather, Prieto disliked the small talk and the ritual. *Why*, he asked himself, *can't we just get on with it?*

At last, the tea was finished, and the transaction began.

Prieto peeked out the door and nodded to the young soldier standing next to the Humvee. He then stepped back inside and waited as Derek Holder came into the room carrying two large, nondescript cardboard boxes.

Ali struggled to his feet. He was a large man, and standing up from a low chair was always a struggle. He opened the top box and rustled through the bubble wrap.

"Hewlett-Packard," he exclaimed happily. "You are reading my mind. My people will be so pleased."

The big man took a quick look into the second box and pulled a battered manila envelope out of his pocket.

Derek Holder watched as Prieto took the wad of worn Ameri-can currency out of the envelope and began to count it.

The sound of the door opening made him lose track.

Prieto glanced up, angry at the rude disruption.

"Lot of money there," Lt. Col. Amos Folbright observed casually. "You boys playing cards or something?"

Prieto's suntanned face lost its color.

"By the way, Captain," Folbright said, nodding at the boxes. "Do you have a list of serial numbers on that stuff?"

It was yet to happen, but it was obvious by the end of the day that Capt. Jacob Prieto's job at CENTCOM would be reassigned to another officer. Meanwhile, in a town in the Kurdish north of Iraq, frustration rose as certain people were unable to reach the man in Safaliyah known as Ali. Soon, however, that would be the least of their worries, but that was a matter for tomorrow.

At FOB Lex, the baptism did not take place that day, but that too was a matter to be revisited another day. Sean had suggested immunity from prosecution in exchange for helping with the evidence, and Folbright had signed off on it. It was always hard to say no to a chaplain, and Sean had made a point of asking for favors only on rare occasions.

Sean had also made it a point not to look at a thermometer until the sun was a red disk on the distant horizon. It was only 107. Soon, perhaps, a cool breeze would begin blowing.

He paused to reflect on the day. Poor Derek Holder. His "really big whopper of a sin" had been merely the tip of a really big whopper of a black-market operation. Should he get a medal for being the catalyst that shut it down, or should he be condemned for having been part of it?

As far as the Uniform Code of Military Justice was concerned, he'd probably wind up with a get-out-of-jail-free card but would spend many months being called and re-called into courts-martial. As far as Sean was concerned, a life had been saved from ruin. One day soon, a baptism would finally take place, and for one man's life, it would be a true beginning.

It had been a long, hot day. It had been a long, hard day. Tomorrow another would follow.

However, each was not just another day, it was a unique day. Like each short life, each long day has unique value, and today was one that Derek Holder would remember for all his days.

◆　◆　◆

Another day of toil!
To Thee we yield our powers;
Keep Thou our souls from guilty soil
Through all the passing hours.

Another day of fear!
For watchful is our foe,
And sin is strong, and death is near,
And short our time below.

FROM THE HYMN "ANOTHER DAY BEGUN"
WORDS BY JOHN ELLERTON

13

Lies and Choices

"Loved ones are the anchor to which a soldier overseas can cling in times of anguish, but only in the abstract, because it is our thoughts of them to which we cling. We can find solace only in our thoughts of them, and in disembodied voices.

"Loved ones are a curse that torments a soldier overseas, because the thoughts of them that fill the mind often bring more pain of separation than solace."

Pfc. Kelsi Schmitt mulled these words that were spoken by Chaplain Sean Rasmunsen from the pulpit in the FOB Lexington chapel.

Her mind wandered, and she did not hear him speak of these feelings being an allegory for our thoughts of the Lord, whom we know only in the abstract, though we know Him nonetheless.

Talk of loved ones made Kelsi Schmitt's mind wander to Fort

Dodge in Iowa, and to her daughter, Brittany. She longed to feel her touch and to hear her voice, and to hear it *not* as a disembodied voice on a satellite phone.

She heard the chaplain's voice, and she remembered that night when he had been there, that night when she felt herself falling off the edge of the earth. She remembered his calm voice and calm manner and how he had made things right. Her ex had taken Brittany. He might have taken her out of state and into oblivion, but the chaplain had talked to the minister at home and he had talked to her ex—Kelsi could not say his name, even in conversations within her own head—and he had brought her back to the home of Kelsi's mother.

"How's Brittany?"

"Oh . . . she's fine," Kelsi said, smiling. She had lingered after the service, and the chaplain had recognized her. She was impressed that he remembered Brittany's name. "She's with my mom now. She just finished first grade."

"Great, you must be proud," the chaplain said cheerfully.

"I missed her graduation."

"Sorry . . . but there'll be more, and you won't miss those. Your mom was there, and that will be a special memory for them both. It's good for her to have a grandma there on those special days."

"Yeah, I guess," Kelsi said, shrugging. "I don't mean that it's a bad thing that my mom is there, but she's doing my job, and I miss Brittany. Guess I miss my mom, too . . . it hasn't been real easy with her lately. We've had some 'issues,' but I do really miss her."

"Of course."

"Do you have kids?" Kelsi asked. "I never asked you that night when were talking."

"Nope."

"Do you want to?"

The chaplain looked startled, as though he had not thought of something that was the embodiment of Kelsi's impressions of completeness in life.

"I guess that would be a good thing . . . someday."

"You don't sound too sure," Kelsi probed. "Are you a minister who . . . I mean . . . y'know, are you allowed to have kids and all?"

"Yeah."

"Then it ought to be a good thing."

"Children are a wonderful thing," the chaplain agreed. She wondered if he meant it, or if he was just saying so. "They are a blessing."

"Like you said in your sermon," she said, smiling. "A blessing and a curse . . . a curse because you can miss 'em so much, right?"

"Yeah, right."

"Do you miss your family?" Kelsi asked, catching herself as the words left her mouth. "I mean . . . I'm sorry . . . Like I didn't mean to get personal with a chaplain or anything."

"That's okay. It's always okay to get personal with a chaplain. It's part of our job. Yeah, I miss my family."

Sean Rasmunsen realized that he probably missed his family less than most, and for the first time in a long time, he felt guilty about it.

His older sister had a corporate job at a bank in Kansas City. She had an attorney husband, a largish house in Overland Park, and two kids, almost teenagers. Sean sent her an e-mail now and then, to which she replied tersely on her BlackBerry. His father was still on the farm, a few miles north of Laclede. They spoke occasionally on the satellite phone. To Sean's dad, blackberries were still things that grew on bushes, and the last time Sean spoke to his dad, they were just becoming ripe.

"Yeah, Dad, I wish I were there, too," he'd said. A blackberry would taste good, he'd thought, fresh and tart against the dust of the desert.

"Do you miss your mom, too?" Kelsi asked.

The chaplain got a faraway look in his eyes.

He missed his mother often. Her words came to him from time to time when he was writing his sermons. She had been his moral compass when he was a kid—not in a Bible-quoting sort of way, but in a practical, you-oughta-know-better sort of way.

He missed his mother often, but he would not hear her words again until he passed through what the poets call "the pearly gates," but pastors describe with less tangible metaphors.

What, indeed, was heaven like?

"She's passed away," Sean said. "But yeah, I miss her. Someday, if I do have kids, I'll wish that they could have known her."

"Someday they will," Kelsi said. "In heaven . . . right?"

"Yes, absolutely." Sean smiled, thinking it a good image to hang on to.

"What's heaven like?" Kelsi asked.

Sean cringed; it was a hard question, an impossible question.

"The theological shorthand answer is that we'll know when it's time to know," Sean told her. "In the meantime, we can be pretty certain that it's a place where there is not nearly as much dust in the air as there is here at Lex . . . and not as hot."

"Not as hot." Kelsi laughed. "That's for the *other* place . . . right?

"That's what they say," Sean said, smiling. According to many, if there was a heaven, there also had to be a hell. It's what the Taoists called yin and yang.

In any case, he was glad that she took his flippant answer about heaven not being as hot as the desert as a joke. He guessed she understood that she had asked the unanswerable.

The mortar shells began falling as the last of the people were leaving the chapel.

Though he was not wearing his helmet or flak jacket, Sean instinctively ran toward the sound of the explosions and the rising pillars of black smoke. Tyler Kraus, encumbered by the weight of his own protective gear, struggled to keep pace.

"Here, take this," Kraus demanded as Sean paused. "Take my helmet at least."

"But it's your—"

"Don't argue," Kraus scolded. "Sergeants are a dime a dozen, but only God can make a chaplain."

"Thanks," Sean said, strapping on the helmet before resuming his dash to the perimeter. Sean didn't know how many times he had lugged his helmet and flak jacket to chapel, only to lug it back to his tent. Today he hadn't bothered, and he wished that he had.

The scream of counterfire rounds was in the air as they reached the flaming remnants of several vehicles that had been hit. Usually the mortar attacks were harmless. The Americans called it "shoot-and-scoot." Bad guys would sneak in close, let go a few blind shots, and scamper away into the desert. Today, they were either very lucky or very good at calculating a trajectory.

Sean had counseled the mortally wounded and he had seen the dead. He had watched men be shot, and he had watched men die.

He had never before seen a man blown up.

Some people say it's like a rag doll being tossed in the air, but most people these days don't have much experience with rag dolls.

Some people say it's like the movies, but it's not.

Sean did not know until he reached the man's side that two people had been caught in the blast. The second was a young woman. With her slender face and short, dark hair, she looked a little bit like Kelsi, but her eyes were brown, not green.

"Don't worry, the medics are here," he said, taking her hand in his. He reached for her right hand, but took her left. It looked as though she no longer had a right hand.

"It's gonna be all right," he lied soothingly as he squeezed her hand. He felt something and glanced down. It was a thin gold ring with a microscopic diamond.

Like Kelsi, she was on the arc of a relationship with a man she loved. She was in that hopeful beginning phase, when the future lay ahead. Kelsi, though about the same age, was on the downhill side, past the anticipation of a wedding, past the anticipation of a first child, and already through the custody battle to that place where a child had been kidnapped by the ex.

"Docs are gonna fix you up," Sean said, compounding his lie as she looked into his eyes, desperate to believe him.

She started to speak.

As Sean leaned closer to hear her words, he felt her grip on his hand relax.

There were no words, but the eyes continued to stare.

Sean looked up. Tyler Kraus was looking silently at the pool of blood in which his boss knelt.

"Where . . . ?" Sean said, looking around for the injured man whom he had seen blown up, not like a rag doll, but like nothing he had ever seen.

"Gone," Kraus said. "Off to the hospital . . . triage."

Triage indeed. Sean and the sergeant were alone in the killing field. The medics had taken one look at the young woman—with her right arm ripped out of her shoulder and the brachial artery running like a garden hose—and they had decided to put all their attention on the man.

Should I have done that as well? Sean asked himself. *Should I have exercised spiritual triage?* When confronting two wounded people who needed his comfort, did holding the hand of one at the moment of her death trump focusing on the man who might live?

Why was he asking himself this?

Lord, give me guidance.

Sean received not a few stares as he walked into the ER drenched from his waist down in the sticky, drying blood of the young woman—a woman whose fiancé would later that same day be hearing the lies of a chaplain telling him that she had not suffered.

Rarely does one see panic in the eyes of ER surgeons when just a single patient lies under their care. Today was such a day, and it was Sunday at that.

There was little about the man that could be called intact.

They had brought in his legs, but not on the same stretcher as his body. As with the dead woman, the man's right arm had taken some of the worst that mortar shrapnel can dish out.

Sean slumped into a chair. There was nothing for him to do until the fellow was stabilized—and Sean knew better than to get in the way of ER docs.

Tyler Kraus handed Sean a bottle of water. It was blessedly ice cold. He took a long drink and sighed a long sigh. As he caught his breath, he caught sight of the man's left hand. The sparkle of the gold wedding band stood out in contrast to the red of the fresh blood.

Oh Lord, save this guy.

In some measure of time between a half hour and eternity, the man was stable. The bleeding from the arteries in the stumps of his thighs had been clamped off, and morphine had dulled the agony.

"I'm Chaplain Sean Rasmunsen . . . Looks like you're doing well, Logan," Sean told the man in an upbeat tone, reading his name from the tag that the doctors had affixed to his IV. Logan was another guy he knew by sight, but he was another guy whom the chaplain had never seen in the chapel.

"I guess . . . " came the muffled, groggy reply.

"Is there anyone I can call?" Sean asked, looking at the man's wedding ring. "Anybody who'd like to know that you're doing good?"

"Mmmm," Logan mumbled. "Yeah . . . I guess?"

"I suppose I can get . . ." Sean started to say that he could get his wife's contact information from Logan's file.

"Yeah . . . you know Kelsi?"

"Kelsi?"

"Yeah . . . Kelsi Schmitt . . . you know her?"

"Yes I do . . ."

"Tell her . . . tell her to come here . . ."

"You got it," Sean told him.

Having overheard the conversation, Kraus nodded and headed out the door.

"Sergeant Kraus is gonna go get her," Sean told Logan. "Is there anybody else . . . anything else I can do?"

"No . . . can't think . . ."

Lord, give me guidance.

Kelsi Schmitt burst into the room about ten paces ahead of the chaplain's assistant.

She ran to the bed where the injured man lay, tears streaming down her cheeks.

"Logan!" Kelsi screamed. "Oh no! It can't be true."

He murmured something that sounded like "baby" as she kissed him repeatedly on the forehead.

She reached beneath his body, trying to lift him, trying to hug him. Two nurses sprinted to his side and pulled her away.

Sean held her, hugged her, and patted her back.

"I love you, Logan!" Kelsi screamed. "I love you. Don't leave me . . . dammit . . . don't please leave me *now* . . ."

Lord, give me guidance, Sean pleaded.

It was obvious to Sean, painfully obvious, that a married man and a lonely girl had found love and companionship in a distant place, thousands of miles from their reality and *his* wife.

What could he do?

Sean would comfort them, and pray for them.

For Logan, if he survived the night, there would be many prayers to be said, and thanks to be offered.

For Kelsi, there would be a conversation. She was not the first woman to fall in love with a married man, and she would not be the last, but she was a member of his little flock—*there*, he had used that word he tried to avoid—and she was his to counsel.

Lord, give me guidance. Lord, give me strength.

Kelsi Schmitt was at his side as Logan Moore breathed his last.

She sobbed and shivered when the nurse looked her in the eye and nodded.

It was about ten minutes later, at nearly 4 A.M., that Sean got the word. He had asked to be notified if it happened, and he came as soon as he could.

Kelsi was still in the ER when he arrived. So too was Logan, although the mortuary affairs people came in on Sean's heels.

As they packed him up, Sean held Kelsi again and patted her back.

Lord, give me guidance. Lord, give me strength.

Lord, give us both *guidance and strength.*

"I'm so sorry for your loss," he whispered. "I know that you and Logan had . . . um . . . well . . . a special relationship."

"Was it that obvious?"

"Yeah, it was . . ."

"It's not every day that you lose a baby brother." Kelsi sobbed.

"Brother?"

"Yeah, you said it was obvious . . . you didn't think—?"

"No, of course not," Sean lied.

Of course he had. His mind had contrived a scenario that was so easily contrived, of a faithless husband and a vulnerable girl. Sean cursed himself for being so judgmental as to assume that they were having an affair, so sanctimonious as to assume that this could be the *only* logical conclusion to be drawn.

"I mean, I didn't know your brother was here at Lex."

"Neither did I."

"What do you—?"

"Oh my God, I didn't know." Kelsi sobbed, squeezing Logan's hand. "She never told me . . . She never told me . . ."

"What? Who?"

"Mom."

"Your mother didn't tell you that your brother was here at Lex?"

"Mom didn't tell me," Kelsi said, desperately shaking her head. "She never even told me . . . that I even *had* a brother."

"Maybe we oughta go get a cup of coffee," Sean suggested, putting his arm around Kelsi's shoulder.

"About a week ago, I got an e-mail," Kelsi began as Sean poured her a cup in the area that functioned as a sort of waiting room inside the hospital. "She said that I oughta look up a dude named Logan Moore who was here at Lex. I asked her why. She said, 'Because he's your brother, that's why.' "

"You didn't know about him?" Sean asked. "I mean growing up, you didn't know you had a brother?"

"No, she never said. What happened was that she split up with my real father way back when I was two. We moved. He took Logan. Mom took me down to Fort Dodge. He took Logan out west someplace. I never saw my real father. I don't remember if I even ever saw a picture of him. He died in prison when I was about six."

"And your mother lost track of Logan?"

"Yeah, I guess. Somebody took him in. Relatives of my real father. They raised him."

"What made your mother wait until last week to tell you?"

"Just found out, I guess. You know how people can look up what happened to people on the Internet? Guess she was doing that? She just sent me an e-mail. She said she hadn't stopped crying since she found out. She was so sorry that she told me about it this way. She was so ashamed. The coincidence is that he ended up here at Lex, same as me."

"Did you have a chance to talk with him . . . before . . . ?"

"Yeah . . . twice," Kelsi said, breaking down into sobs.

Sean put his arm around her shoulder, comforting her.

"I just talked to him two times," Kelsi said through the tears. "He thought I was lying to him. He thought it was some kinda *joke*. He couldn't believe it. The people who raised him didn't tell him nothing."

"Did your mother . . . ?"

"Yeah, she e-mailed him and told him the whole story. I saw him yesterday. He had e-mailed the people who raised him, and they told him that they thought it was true. They remembered that they'd heard Logan's dad had a daughter somewhere, but they had never mentioned it to him."

"I'm so sorry to hear about that," Sean said. "It's always awful when families get torn apart . . . always."

"We were so happy yesterday," Kelsi admitted. "Neither of

us had brothers or sisters. We both thought we were only children. We both thought we really had something . . . and now we won't . . . we won't ever . . . ever . . . ever!"

"I'm so sorry for your loss," Sean said. "I know that those are empty words, but—"

"But the one you gotta be sorry for is Becca, Rebecca Jo—Logan's wife. She's seven months pregnant . . . with . . . my nephew, I guess."

"Do you want me to . . . ?"

"No," Kelsi said, wiping away the tears. "No, I'll call her. It's like, y'know . . . family. One part of me wishes I hadn't ever met Logan last week . . . that I never had to know a face that was my brother's face, and have to watch that face while he died. Another part of me is thankful that despite all this stupid pain . . . I'm gonna have a *nephew*."

"That's a great way of looking at things," Sean said. It was true. It really was.

"I'm never gonna let that little boy grow up not knowing about part of the family he has. He's gonna know Brittany and Brittany's gonna know her cousin and they're gonna grow up knowing each other."

"Is there anything that I can do?" Sean asked.

"Yeah, you can pray for me."

"Of course."

"You can say a prayer that tells Him that you want Him to guide my tongue to say the right words to Becca and know that when her little boy comes into the world that I'm gonna be part of his family."

A trace of mist was clouding Sean's eyes when he nodded.

◆ ◆ ◆

Order my footsteps by Thy Word,
And make my heart sincere;
Let sin have no dominion, Lord,
But keep my conscience clear.

My soul hath gone too far astray,
My feet too often slip;
Yet since I've not forgot Thy way,
Restore Thy wand'ring sheep.

FROM THE HYMN "O THAT THE LORD WOULD GUIDE MY WAYS"
WORDS BY ISAAC WATTS

14

When Love Shines In

Janis Schmitt had suffered as no mother should have to.

No mother should suffer the pain of having a child missing from her life for a quarter of a century, of knowing, but not knowing.

No mother should suffer the pain of having a long-lost child rediscovered, only to lose him irrevocably a couple of weeks later—without ever having had a chance to be reunited face to face.

As much as Sean felt the pain of young Kelsi, or of Logan Moore's young widow and her unborn child, his mind kept coming back to Janis Schmitt. For her, it was not simply the pain of loss, but also the pain of a lifetime's mistake.

Perhaps she'd had no choice. Just as Sean knew that he'd jumped to an erroneous conclusion when he'd seen Kelsi kiss

Logan Moore, he didn't want to paint Janis Schmitt into the corner of having voluntarily tossed away a child. There are irresponsible twenty-year-old mothers who abandon children, and there are twenty-year-old mothers who have circumstances thrust upon them that are beyond their comprehension and beyond their control. There are a lot of circumstances over which twenty-year-old mothers have absolutely no control. Sean would give Janis the benefit of the doubt.

Still, the pain of a lifetime's mistake haunted Sean. He thought of all the biblical references, all the way back to Abraham's having to make the irrevocable choice to kill Isaac. That time, God emerged like the cavalry, with a sign that it was all just a test—a biblical air-raid drill. It wasn't always that easy.

The Lord moved in strange ways with His air-raid drills.

Indeed, as Sean and Tyler Kraus headed to Saf City for their weekly visit to the Safaliyah School, the chaplain had a lot of things on his mind. Despite his best efforts to balance his thoughts among his responsibilities, Mareike De Vries crowded out all others. It was Mareike De Vries and what she had come to represent that dominated his thoughts, especially when he went into Safaliyah. Spontaneously and almost uncontrollably, these thoughts came to him. Like a warm and unexpected ray of sunshine on a cold day, they came to him and they were *most* welcome.

Today, as the pain of a lifetime's mistake still haunted Sean, he wondered about a relationship that *could* happen. The door had been flung open, and it seemed to Sean that it was up to him to slam it shut again—or else to just walk through it. Which choice, if not chosen, would he count as a lifetime's mistake?

◆　◆　◆

Today, all was not right at the school. The children were running about as though something bad had happened, and the staff was shooing them back into classrooms.

Mustafa Ilik was not in his office, which was unusual. He was *always* in his office.

"Where's the headmaster?" Sean asked, spotting Isabelle Laclerc. "What happened? What's going on?"

"They went to the mosque," Isabelle said, shrugging, in her diffident manner. "It's Crimm . . . Ree-shard."

"What happened to Richard?" Sean asked, recognizing the name of one of the British math teachers.

"He was kidnapped," Isabelle said. "By whom I do not know. Someone said the mullahs knew who it was. Mustafa went to the mosque to ask . . . and I suppose you wish to know where is Mareike?"

"Where *is* Mareike?" Sean asked. He knew that Isabelle knew that there was "something" between him and Mareike. He saw no reason to pretend to her that this was not true, but he tried to conceal his panic at the thought that she, too, had been kidnapped.

"She went to the mosque as well."

"When?"

"Fifteen minutes, more or less."

"Is there anything we can do?"

"Maybe you should go to the mosque as well?"

It took only five minutes for the chaplain's Humvee to reach the mosque.

Normally, American troops gave wide berth to mosques in

Iraq, but Sean had been here before. He had made a courtesy call on the mullahs when he first arrived at FOB Lexington, hoping to speak with them man-of-God to man-of-God. They'd responded less enthusiastically than he had hoped, but more cordially than he had feared.

"You sure you want me to wait outside?" Tyler Kraus asked insistently when Sean climbed out of the Humvee and laid his helmet on the seat.

"Yeah," Sean said. "It's a tough call, but I don't think it would be a good idea for you to stroll into a mosque with an M4 under your arm."

"I could leave it in the car," Kraus said. "I hate to see you wandering around this place by yourself."

"I'll be okay . . . really," Sean assured him. "I don't think the mullahs are gonna shoot me in their house of worship."

"Yeah, right," Kraus said cynically.

Unspoken was that Kraus himself was going to be sitting alone here in Saf City as well.

The cool quiet inside the mosque felt good. It made Sean realize—as if he needed a reminder—how very hot it was out on the streets of Safaliyah.

"As-salaam alaikum." Sean said, smiling, as a man in a white skull cap approached with a scowl on his face.

"Alaikum . . . as-salaam," the man said hesitantly, eyeing Sean's military uniform.

Stumbling through the words as best he could in his pidgin Arabic, Sean asked whether Mustafa Ilik and the woman from the school were there.

"Na'am," the man replied reluctantly, gesturing for Sean to follow him.

He was led to where the headmaster was standing in the middle of a room, arguing with three men in turbans who were lounging on a long, low couch. As Sean entered, the three men glanced at him and scowled. He recognized the largest of the three as Mullah Yazid, with whom he had met many months earlier.

Mareike was standing nearby, her head and most of her face wrapped in her pale lavender scarf, the same one he had seen her wear to the al-Qamar home. When she saw Sean, her eyes lit up. It was nice to be welcomed by at least someone in the room.

Mustafa Ilik was glad to see him as well.

"Richard has been kidnapped," the headmaster told him in English.

"Yeah, I heard that. Is there anything I can do?"

Ilik turned to the three mullahs and, pointing at Sean, explained in Arabic that this man was an American chaplain.

Yazid remembered having spoken with Sean and told Ilik that he had been honored by the courtesy shown by the chaplain.

He waved his hand, gesturing that Sean was permitted to sit down. As an afterthought, the headmaster was also invited to take a seat in one of the several chairs in the room. Mareike remained standing. As a woman, she was not even officially there.

"Do you know where the Englishman is?" Sean asked Yazid.

"We know the people who have him," Yazid replied in English.

"Why do they have him?" Sean asked.

"He is an infidel." Yazid shrugged as if to add, "but of course."

"Why do they want him, these people who have him?" Sean asked.

"They are poor men. Men without jobs."

"That is quite unfortunate," Sean said, commiserating with the plight of the kidnappers. "One's heart goes out to them."

Yazid nodded soberly.

"I'm sure that they are reasonable men. I'm sure that arrangements could be made."

"Perhaps. But the man *is* an infidel."

"Certainly, as a man of God, may Allah's name be praised, you could convey to them that he is a human being whose life is deserving of their respect. Is not all life sacred in His eyes?"

For an hour, Sean and Yazid double-talked back and forth. It had quickly become apparent that Richard Crimm was sweating it out, blindfolded in a basement somewhere, not because of his being an infidel, a nonbeliever, but because his kidnappers knew that Organisation École Globale would pay to get him back.

Like Sean, Yazid understood why Crimm had been taken, but like Sean, he never actually articulated this fact. Both men knew that all but the most naive NGOs—just like the multinational corporations—had an undiscussed contingency fund in a bank account somewhere to cover such emergencies . . . to pay ransoms.

At last Yazid picked up a cell phone, placed a call, and left a message.

Within moments, the phone rang.

There were heated words on the part of the mullah, and finally an exchange of pleasantries. He closed his cell phone and nodded to Sean.

◆　◆　◆

"I was very frightened," Mareike admitted to Sean when they had returned to the relative safety of a room on the top floor of the school that served as an office for the OEG personnel. "All I could think of was poor Richard being beheaded."

"Me, too," Sean admitted. "I'm glad that we were able to defuse the situation."

"*You* were," Mareike said in a cross tone, as though correcting an errant student. "It was *you*. You persuaded the mullah to accept money for Richard's life."

She looked so beautiful with the golden desert light streaming through the window, catching the side of her face and lighting the golden hair that tumbled across her shoulders. She had pulled off the lavender headscarf and wore it loosely around her neck. She was dressed head to toe in black, clothes appropriate for a woman entering a mosque.

The exception was her trademark sneakers. Sean smiled when he thought about that day when he had casually referred to them as purple, and how she had insisted, in a faux indignant tone, that they were not purple, but *aubergine*. He smiled as he remembered how they had laughed when he had reminded her that this was a French word, and that Mareike always complained about Isabelle's insistence on using French.

"Why are you smiling?" Mareike asked.

"Oh, I'm thinking happy thoughts . . . mmmm . . . thinking about how nice you look and how it's a relief to know that Richard is going to be all right."

"I thought maybe you were laughing at me for giving you credit for persuading the mullah to accept money."

"It was always about the money, only the money." Sean shrugged modestly. "I think that's all the kidnappers really wanted. Mullah Yazid understood that, too. He deserves a little bit of credit, himself, I think. In the end, it was *him* who persuaded the kidnappers to settle for twenty grand in U.S. dollars instead of a million. I just hope that it won't be too much of a hardship on OEG."

"They can afford it."

"Throughout the scriptures there are people who put a dollar value on a human life," Sean said. "Today it was the kidnappers who set the price and OEG who paid it . . . or who will pay it as soon as they can get it wired."

"I just hope that Richard is safe," Mareike said thoughtfully. "Until the money comes tomorrow."

"I'm praying for that," Sean said.

"Me, too," Mareike said.

"I thought you were still a little bit skeptical about prayer, Mareike." Sean smiled, relishing the sight of the beautiful woman seated near him.

"That's your impression of me?" Mareike smiled back. "I'm more of a believer than you give me credit for."

"You are?"

"Yes, Chaplain Sean. I prayed today, and my prayers were answered. When I went to the mosque with Professor Ilik, I was very frightened. I was frightened a little for myself as well. That is no place for a woman—a Western woman. I prayed that some way, you would come to the school and come to the mosque . . ."

"Me?"

"I feel safe and protected with you around, Chaplain Sean."

With that, she reached out and wrapped her arms around his neck, pulling him toward her.

Sean was startled, unready for her move. He had wrestled for weeks with his feelings toward her, arguing with himself over whether to succumb to emotion. He had not yet resolved his deep inner conflict, not yet resolved to plunge headlong into the warmth of a relationship with Mareike.

"What is wrong?" Mareike asked, pulling back from her embrace. "I'm sorry if I am being too forward. Don't you . . . don't you . . . am I wrong to feel that you have an affection toward *me*?"

"No, that's not wrong . . ."

"What is wrong, then?" Mareike said sadly, almost desperately. "Why do you flinch when I hug you?"

"It's that I'm a minister . . . I'm not supposed to have feelings of my own."

"But you do, don't you?" Mareike said, calling him on the emotions that they both knew lay within him.

"I'm not supposed . . . I have a thousand souls that I'm responsible for."

"And this means that you must shut out the feelings that you have for *me*—feelings that I know you have? I see it in your eyes."

"There are hundreds of men and women who look to me to be their moral compass . . ."

"What do you mean by *moral compass*?"

"Oh boy, that's . . . I mean it's a matter of ethics and right and wrong . . . of conscience . . . of doing what your conscience tells you is a moral absolute. For people who are religious, a chaplain can represent the presence of God, but for everybody, the chaplain has to be the moral compass. A chaplain has to walk a narrow line because of what he has to represent."

"Am I somehow *outside* your morality?" Mareike asked indignantly, tears starting to trickle down her cheeks. "Look at me! I'm just a human being . . . I'm just a woman. I'm not immoral, I'm not evil . . . *am I*? I'm not a Salome, not a temptress sent to lure you into evil like Satan did to Jesus in the book of Matthew."

"I didn't *mean* that," Sean stammered insistently. "A moral compass isn't a preacher scolding people to follow some arbitrary code of conduct. It's being a sort of anchor point for people, an anchor point when they're under pressure, when everything is in turmoil."

"*I'm* in turmoil," Mareike said angrily. "I fell in love with a man who was so good and caring, a man who the children love so much because he gives of himself, a man I love. Now I'm talking to a man who thinks he is above everyone else, a man who finds me immoral, a man who cannot even hug me."

"*Love?*" Sean asked.

Things were spiraling out of control.

She was not evil. She *was* just a woman. She was a woman whom he had not allowed himself to love, but who was willing to allow *herself* to share her love with him.

How long could he resist? The answer was that he should not resist at all.

Sean had built himself into an emotional fortress to protect himself from the pain around him, the pain of disappointment, of loss, of hopelessness, of death, and of suicide. He had built himself into an emotional fortress, and someone was breaking down the fortress walls.

"Yes, *love*," Mareike said, staring him in the eye. "Yes, *love*. I love you, Sean. I love you so much it hurts . . . and it hurts me so badly to see that you cannot let yourself love *me*."

"But I do, Mareike," he said. "I do love you."

She stared for a moment in what seemed to be disbelief, and then she reached out to hug him.

He did not recoil. He hugged her back.

"I want to be with you always," Mareike said.

"Oh, how I wish that it could be," Sean said.

"Why can it *not* be?" Mareike said, pushing him away, the anger returning to her voice.

"My life is not my own. My life is and will always be a life of serving others. That would be a miserable life to drag someone into."

"Who do you think I am?" Mareike asked indignantly. "Do you see me strutting on the streets of Paris wearing Prada? No, I'm here in the dust and deprivation of a county at war, sharing *myself* with children. I don't *have to* be here. I didn't *have to* be in Sudan—a place which, by the way, is so much worse than here that I cannot tell you. Do you think I am someone who runs away from service to others?"

"I suppose . . . not."

"*Of course not!* You sharing your life with others is what I love . . . *part* of what I love about you."

"I love you, Mareike. I love you, too," Sean said. She looked so beautiful, not in Prada, but in her aubergine sneakers.

"My love," she said, tears of joy welling in her once-angry eyes. "My love . . . my love."

The emotional fortress that he had built around himself had been breached, and Sean saw himself in the rubble, helping the beautiful Mareike roll away the stones.

The emotional fortress that he had built around himself remained, but a crack had been created, and through that crack streamed sunlight so warm and so pure.

As they kissed, Sean felt as complete and fulfilled personally as he had felt complete and fulfilled spiritually on the day of his ordination.

His heart rejoiced.

◆ ◆ ◆

How the world will grow with beauty, when love shines in,
And the heart rejoice in duty, when love shines in.
Trials may be sanctified, and the soul in peace abide,
Life will all be glorified, when love shines in.

When love shines in, when love shines in,
How the heart is tuned to singing, when love shines in,
When love shines in, when love shines in,
Joy and peace to others bringing, when love shines in.

FROM THE HYMN "WHEN LOVE SHINES IN"
WORDS BY CARRIE ELIZABETH BRECK

15

Coming Home

Thin and pale, he stood in the doorway to the chapel.

He was so thin and so pale, it would have been easy to joke that he was practically invisible—but he was so thin and so pale that you didn't feel like joking.

"When I get outa here, I'm gonna come to chapel every friggin' Sunday, man."

Those were the words that Lance Gullie had spoken to Sean Rasmunsen that morning when he thanked the chaplain for talking him back from the edge, the edge of self-destruction.

Lance had made good on his promise, but he had been out of the hospital for just one Sunday.

He might have gone home even sooner, had Sean not intervened. Typically, the wounded were sent to a succession of combat support hospitals that began at the Forward Operating

Base, then led to Baghdad, to Germany, and finally to the States. The doctors passed their patients up the line as they were stabilized medically, but Sean feared that Lance Gullie was not ready emotionally for this grueling ordeal. As the steps unfolded, Sean knew each would be more impersonal than the last.

Sean had seen a man who had shoved an M16 into his gut, and he had sat with this emotionally fragile nineteen-year-old as he anguished about his desperation, his fears, and his shame.

"Guess I'm goin' home, Chaplain," Gullie said in a soft voice so distant from the voice with which he had ranted on the terrible night as he stared into the abyss—and failed in his effort to cross the deadly threshold.

"How are you feeling, Lance?"

"Good, I guess."

"I'm glad that you had a few weeks to recover . . . to get back your strength before they sent you back."

"Yeah, I guess."

More than getting back his physical strength, Sean was thinking of Lance's emotional strength, and his spiritual strength. Massive abdominal injuries had been the outward manifestation of the massive trauma in his mind and spirit. He had been lost that night, and Sean hoped that he had at last found himself.

"Glad you could make it to chapel on Sunday." Sean smiled, walking over to him and patting him on the back. Oh boy, was this poor kid *thin*. Sean could feel his shoulder blades through his shirt.

"I'm glad I could get to chapel at least once before I gotta go home."

"I'm glad that you could come, too. It was great to have you as part of our fellowship."

"Yeah . . . y'know . . . I don't feel so alone anymore. I dunno what it is but, y'know, it's good . . . it feels good to be a part of a bunch of people like that."

"We try," Sean said. "The idea is exactly that. I want to have a space where people can be part of something and not feel so empty and alone."

"Yeah. I sure wish, y'know . . . I wish I woulda started coming here a lot sooner. Maybe I wouldn't have did it, y'know . . . had my 'accident,' y'know."

Sean knew. He knew all too well. The injury that nearly caused Lance's death was being listed as a "non-hostile gunshot wound." If he had died from this wound, there would have been an investigation, but as it was, the CID—the U.S. Army's Criminal Investigation Command (formerly Division, hence the still-used acronym)—would not try to peg Lance's "accident" as a suicide attempt. Legally, because nobody but Lance saw it, it would be hard to prove. The Army would rather let it slide than accuse someone of trying suicide if there was any doubt.

Sean knew, and so did Lance.

It was like getting a second chance—*exactly* like getting a second chance.

"Y'know . . . I know that I sinned pretty much big-time," Lance said, casting his eyes toward the ground. "I hope, y'know, that the Lord's gonna kinda overlook that."

"Maybe not overlook, but *forgive*," Sean said, trying not to do so in a judgmental tone. "The Lord's capacity for forgiveness is infinite, but it's not a free pass. We have to work to redeem ourselves."

"I don't have no capacity to do anything infinite," Lance said, looking away.

"He knows that. He knows that you're human. He expects only that you do the best you can with the abilities that He has given you."

"Uh-huh."

Sean felt himself walking the tightrope between preaching and pastoring, between nurturing and pointing out responsibilities yet to be fulfilled.

"I know that you can make Him proud," Sean said. "I'm sure that you will."

"Sure gonna try," Lance confirmed, looking up at Sean.

"What are you gonna do when you get home?" Sean asked, changing the subject.

"Discharge, I guess."

"Yeah, I know, but after that?"

"Get a job. Go. home and get a job. My uncle's in flooring. Said he'd give me a job."

"That sounds good."

"Laying carpet's better than nothing, I guess."

"When you leave here, you'll be going through all sorts of transitions, changes, between here and home," Sean said. "Are you going to be all right?"

"Yeah, I guess."

"You said when we talked after chapel on Sunday that you're not feeling so alone and freaked out like you were."

"No, sir, I'm feeling a whole lot better. Like, y'know, I feel a whole lot stronger. I know I sure don't look it, but I feel like I'm stronger . . . I'm moving on. I feel like I'm really gonna be able to do it."

"That's great news."

"That's what my mother says, y'know. She's real glad I'm

coming home. She was pretty worked up—y'know, bummed, when she heard that, um, that I got shot."

"A mother would be expected to get pretty bummed to have her son shot."

"Yeah, y'know . . . I haven't exactly told her what happened."

"Will you?"

"I guess so, y'know."

"You'll know what to say when you see her. Let the Lord guide you. You'll find the words."

"I guess."

"She'll be understanding. Trust that your mother will understand."

"I guess. Anyways, she'll be glad to have me home."

"You said you're gonna get involved in your old church back home, too. Trinity Lutheran, wasn't it? I'm glad to see that," Sean said, changing the subject.

"Yeah, I feel like a real churchgoer . . . thanks to you."

"I hope you'll find the kind of fellowship there that will make you feel part of something . . . part of a community."

"Yeah, y'know, I hope so . . . I think so. And y'know what?"

"What's that?"

"There's this girl," Lance said sheepishly.

"A girl? Tell me about her."

"Name's Kacie."

"Pretty name."

"Yeah. I knew her in high school. Well, I kinda sorta knew her a little bit. So I got her e-mail from a guy who knew somebody and I wrote to her."

"Mmmm." Sean smiled. "You wrote to her, did you?"

"Sure did, y'know. Wrote to her and told her, 'Remember me?' and all that, and she said she did, and I said I'm coming home and all."

"What did she say?"

"Well, I told her that I was lookin' forward to going back to Trinity, y'know, and she says, that's funny, on account of she goes there, too. It was her mother's church and she started going."

"What else did she say?" Sean said. He had by now bought into the story and was anxious to find out whether Kacie was going to be more than just a fellow parishioner.

"Yeah, she said we ought to get together and all."

"Great."

"Yeah, I sent her a picture of me and all, y'know, and she says I look 'cute' in a uniform."

"That's a good start," Sean said, smiling. He was so happy for Lance, and how happy he seemed by the prospect of someone to go home to.

"She said she remembered me in high school a little bit, but she says I'm a lot cuter now that I'm a soldier."

"Did you ever ask her out in high school?"

"Naw, she was a sophomore the year I graduated. She ran around with this bunch of girls, y'know . . . all giggling and pointing. I guess I was too shy. I really was kind of a skinny little punk in high school. The sophomore girls always had their eyes on jocks anyway, y'know."

"Yeah, I know," Sean said, nodding.

"What was it like for you in high school, Chaplain? Did you know that you were gonna be a chaplain and all? Guess you probably didn't."

"Not in high school, I didn't," Sean confirmed. "I guess like most people, I was just trying to figure things out. It was a small town, and we lived out in the country, so I didn't have too much of a social life like the kids in town had."

"What about girlfriends and all?" Lance asked. "I don't know if it's okay to talk to chaplains about girlfriends, though, is it?"

"It's okay to talk about just about anything with chaplains," Sean confirmed. "And yes, I had a girlfriend in high school. It was sort of, though—you know—she lived in town. I had another girl that I liked, but she lived way over in Marceline, so we didn't really have much of a relationship."

"What about after high school? I mean, you're a pretty old guy; you probably had some girlfriends since then."

"Well, there *was* Nicole," Sean said. He figured that part of his job was to commiserate with members of his congregation, to personalize his own experience in order to make them more comfortable.

"What happened to Nicole?"

"Didn't want to be a preacher's wife," Sean admitted.

"Guess you gotta give up a lot for that, y'know. I guess you're sorta on duty 24/7, aren't you?"

"Comes with the territory."

"You got a girlfriend now?" Lance asked.

Sean felt himself blushing, and he couldn't stop. Having been triggered by the young soldier's query, the thoughts of Mareike, the warm and beautiful thoughts of beautiful Mareike poured into his mind like a flood.

"Ha . . . I can tell!" Lance said, a big grin spreading across his face. It was the first time he had ever seen Lance grin like that. It was enough to make Sean glad that he had blushed.

"Who is she? Ahhh, come on, tell me! Is she in the Army?"

"No, she is absolutely *not* in the U.S. Army," Sean said emphatically.

"How long you been going out?"

"We've known one another for a while."

"What's her name?"

"I'm not sure I can—"

"C'mon, you asked me and I told you Kacie's name."

"Mareike . . . her name is Mareike."

"That's an interesting name . . . sounds kinda old-fashioned."

"I suppose so. I can't—I shouldn't say any more."

"Yeah, I understand," Lance said, smiling. "You don't wanna jinx it."

"No, I definitely don't want to jinx it."

"I'm really looking forward to getting home and starting a life," Lance said. "Maybe Kacie will be part of it, or maybe it'll be somebody else. I'm just glad I have a life to get started on."

"You don't know how happy I am to hear that," Sean said. "When we first talked, you weren't very happy with the life that God gave you."

"I didn't *want* my friggin' life that night," Lance said. "I didn't want it because it all hurt so bad, but you told me that it was worth having and worth fighting for, and it *is*."

"Of course it is," Sean replied. "I know that sometimes it takes a crisis to put things into perspective like that, but I'm so glad that it worked out as it has."

"You saved my life, man," Lance said soberly. "You saved my life and gave me the rest of my life. It's like having a gift, y'know."

"I know, and I'm glad that *you* know."

"Thanks, man. Thanks from the bottom of my heart, y'know.

Without you, there'd be nothing at all. Because of you, I have my whole life back. It's like walking into a sunny day."

"I'm really glad, *really* glad," Sean said, patting the soldier on the back.

"Well, I guess I better get goin' here, y'know," Lance said. "Been nice talking with you and all, but I got a chopper to catch."

"You still got my e-mail?" Sean asked as they parted.

"Sure do."

"Stay in touch. Send me an e-mail when you get back home. Tell me if the Royals got a chance at the pennant."

"You got it, Chaplain."

Sean finished unpacking a recently arrived case of contemporary Christian songbooks, set them aside for Ashley Mariott, his choir director, and headed out to do his rounds. He was nearing the hospital when he saw the big CH-47 Chinook lifting up from the helipad on the far side of FOB Lexington. He paused a moment to watch the helicopter as it flew into the sweltering distant skies and headed toward Baghdad. He knew that Lance Gullie was aboard, and Sean couldn't stop thinking about his terrible ordeal and what he had ahead of him. He thought of Lance Gullie and how he had so fully embraced the life that he had once wanted to discard.

Sean said a prayer for Lance Gullie, and continued on.

Inside the combat support hospital, two soldiers were being treated for heat prostration, and a young woman was writhing in pain from a scorpion bite.

There was always something, but today, at least, that something included neither hostile nor non-hostile gunshot wounds. Sean said a prayer of thanksgiving.

He assured the young woman that the medication would neutralize the scorpion's venom, and that soon the Vicodin would allow her to forget the pain. She was still too uncomfortable to believe that this was possible, but she nodded politely and thanked the chaplain through clenched teeth.

Leaving the hospital, Sean headed across the base toward the Tactical Operations Center for his every-other-day-or-so reality check with Lt. Col. Amos Folbright.

"Hear that you're doing a real good job at that school down in Saf City," the colonel said after Sean sat down. "Those do-gooders down there have nothing but praise. I heard that you stepped in when one of their teachers got kidnapped, and they got nothing but praise about that, too. They've told their bosses up in wherever they're from, and it's been passed over to Brigade, and Brigade has run it back down to me."

"I've tried not to let it impact my work *here*," Sean said.

"No, I mean I think that you're really doing a great job out here at Lex, too," Folbright said. "Don't want you gettin' a big head or anything, but I'm really happy with the way things are going. I gotta admit that when Father Mike left, I was pretty skeptical about this new guy—the new guy being you—skeptical that the new guy could live up to what he meant to us out here. But you have really done it, Padre."

"I'm glad of that," Sean replied.

"Yeah, y'know, I've actually started going to your services."

"I've been seeing you," Sean said with a smile.

"Really like your choir."

"That's Specialist Mariott's doing," Sean said, plugging his choir director. "She's the one who really makes those kids shine."

"They're really first rate, y'know. I used to come in just to listen to them. Lately, I've been starting to listen to your sermons."

"I know," Sean said, smiling. "I've seen you out there on Sundays—and you seem to be paying attention. I'm really glad that you're liking what you're hearing."

"Another thing I need to talk to you about is—"

Suddenly, a fresh-faced young sergeant barged through the tent flap into Folbright's inner sanctum.

"Colonel, we just got news—" he began.

"Sergeant, can't you see I'm talking to the Padre here?" Folbright said, obviously perturbed at the interruption. "I'm sittin' down here with my spiritual advisor."

"I'm sorry, sir, sorry, Chaplain," the man said. "But I thought you'd better know right away, sir."

"What's that?"

"The chopper, sir, the Chinook that just took off from Lex about a half hour ago, headed for Baghdad . . ."

"What about it?"

"It went down, sir. Two Black Hawks from the 160th were in the area. They saw it go down."

"Are they picking up survivors?"

"No survivors, sir. They slammed into a rock cliff. Nobody made it."

• • •

Coming home, coming home,
No longer in the path of sin to roam;
I'm coming home, coming home,
Lord Jesus, I am coming home.

Like a father seeks a wayward child,
Thou hast sought me o'er the desert wild,
Sick and helpless, by my sin defiled,
I am coming home.

Tell my mother what her boy has done,
God has spoken to her wayward son;
To be faithful till my crown is won,
I am coming home.

FROM THE HYMN "COMING HOME"
WORDS BY ALFRED HENRY ACKLEY

16

Just a Hallmark Moment

Their roles had reversed. Even if it was for just a moment, their roles had reversed.

The pastor whose life was devoted to counseling others had no one with whom to share his anguish, on whose shoulder he could lay his weary, worried head.

This was, she felt, what distinguished true relationships from merely personal interactions.

Mareike De Vries was glad to be able to be that shoulder.

The death of this man named Gullie had hit Sean Rasmunsen harder than he had expected, harder than many others.

He told her about Lance Gullie and about his suicide attempt, unburdening his heavy heart of his mixed and conflicted feelings. They talked about the Christian view of suicide, and about the truly horrendous inner torment that leads a person to knock willingly on death's door.

He told her about Gullie's turnaround. Mareike had no idea what a "Hallmark moment" was. It was another of those peculiar things about American culture, one of many about which she was learning. She hadn't known about Hallmark moments, but she had gotten the idea from Sean's description.

To take a man's hand and walk with him back from the abyss on the road from despair to hope, and then to have him die so pointlessly because of a rotor gearbox malfunction, was a terrible blow. It had struck Sean in an unexpected way. It had struck Sean hard.

Mareike was glad that she could reach out her own hand to the man whom she loved. She found herself telling the minister that perhaps it was somehow God's plan.

"I never expected myself to be saying this," she told him as she held his hand in hers. "Two years ago, even one year ago, I would never have imagined myself telling anyone that anything might be part of God's plan . . . certainly not telling this to a *minister*."

"It's pretty ironic, I know," Sean said, grinning, almost laughing at the irony. "In the Army they have a saying about your number being up. A lot of people use that idea to explain sudden deaths that make no sense . . . deaths that leave so much sense of meaninglessness."

"*Number being up?* That's another American expression." Mareike laughed. "I'm learning so many American expressions by being with you."

"It means that your time is over, that it is your time to die."

"Like a higher authority has decided that—"

"Like a higher authority has decided that it's time to come home."

Mareike nodded.

Sean squeezed her hand.

"Now that you've learned all of our quaint expressions, have you ever thought about coming over to the United States?" Sean asked.

"Of course," Mareike said. "People in Europe—most people in Europe—are very curious about America. Most find your worldview very confusing, but we are nevertheless curious to see what it's all about: New York, Miami Beach . . ."

"What about the middle of the country?" Sean said rhetorically. "You ever think about the heartland, out on the prairie, the wide open spaces?"

"Mostly people in Europe think of New York, and Las Vegas, and Hollywood."

"I'd like to show you my part of the country sometime," Sean said.

"I would like to have you show me your wide open places, sometime," Mareike said, smiling.

"Neither of us will be in Iraq forever," Sean said. "A year from now, we're both gonna be somewhere else, both gonna be a long way from here. I'm . . . what I'm saying is that I'm really going to miss you."

"I will miss you, also, Chaplain Sean."

"You know that people always say that they will stay in touch, send e-mails and all . . ."

"I will send you e-mails, Sean," Mareike said, almost patronizingly. "I'll come to America to see your wide open places. Have you ever been to Nederland?"

"No," Sean said. "The only time I was ever in Europe was on my flight back to the States after my first tour. I was in Germany for twenty-four hours. Sure, I'd be happy to visit the Netherlands. I want to. I want to see where you're from."

"Good, I want to show you my country, my places," Mareike said. "It is wide and open, too, not so wide and open as Missouri, I suppose, but you would be surprised. I hope that we can spend more time together."

"I wish that we could . . . I mean . . . get to a place where we could never be apart."

"You want that we should live together?"

"Yeah . . . I guess I was thinking that maybe when we both finish up our work in Iraq, maybe you'd consider being a preacher's wife?"

"Is this a formal proposal? Are you meaning marriage?"

"Yeah. Mareike De Vries, I love you. Would you be my wife?"

"You seem so nervous," she said, smiling. "You're so cute when you are nervous. I never expected to be asked to be a wife while I was sitting under a bare lightbulb in an empty classroom on the top of a concrete building in the middle of the desert."

"Not very romantic, I guess," Sean said dejectedly.

"Oh, no," she said. "It is *very* romantic."

With that, she wrapped her arms around his shoulders and gave him a long and passionate kiss.

As Sean felt her tongue exploring his lips, he realized that he had crossed the line, leaving a world in which his total being was at the service of his congregation, and entering a world in which he would have to share that total being with one person above all others.

He had not come to this moment lightly. Despite a marriage proposal far clumsier than he would have liked, he had anticipated such a moment long and hard. There was love—intangible, burning love. But more than that, he sensed that her values paralleled his. She had left a good life to share herself with Iraqi children. It was something that he admired, and at which he stood in awe. While he retreated each night to the relative comfort and safety of a fortified military base, she spent her days and nights in a world that some would characterize as privation.

The happiness of the moment flooded into the moments that followed, as they both interacted with the children on the schoolyard. In two minds, the afternoon became almost a template for a life together. They imagined sharing the work, the selfless, caring work, giving of themselves to make the lives of others a little bit better.

Sean noticed that Mareike was smiling a little more than usual, and laughing a little more easily than usual.

Someone fell—it was a little girl.

Sean and Mareike both unconsciously hastened to pick her up.

As she scampered back to play, none the worse for wear, their eyes met.

For a split second they had this small child between them, Sean lifting her arm, Mareike brushing off some of the insidious Iraqi dust.

Both sensed what the other was thinking.

A future lay before them, a future together, and it was good.

• • •

By vows of love together bound,
The twain, on earth, are one;
One may their hearts, O Lord, be found,
Till earthly cares are done.

As from the home of earlier years
They wander, hand in hand,
To pass along, with smiles and tears,
The path of Thy command.

With more than earthly parents' care,
Do Thou their steps attend;
And with the joys or woes they share,
Thy loving kindness blend.

O let the memory of this hour
In future years come nigh
To bind, with sweet, attractive power,
And cheer them till they die.

From the hymn "By Vows of Love Together Bound"
Words by Eleazor Thompson Fitch,
in *Connecticut Congregational Psalms and Hymns*

17

Mook

In his private prayers, as in his sermons, Chaplain Sean Rasmunsen always prayed for peace in his corner of the war zone, and in his private prayers, he often was given cause to breathe a thank-you.

During his months at Camp Lex, Sean Rasmunsen had watched Safaliyah gradually turn from a town on the edge to a city of relative calm. He was thankful, not only on behalf of Mareike, his love, but also for all the kids—especially for his buddy Bilal, and Bilal's sister, Naja. He was also thankful on behalf of his fellow Americans at Camp Lex. Each day that turned into weeks without a combat death was cause for thanksgiving.

Not deserving yet of prayers of thanksgiving was the situation in the town of Muqdarubah, about forty klicks southwest of Safaliyah. Sectarian squabbles exacerbated by both al-Qaeda meddling and organized crime had made it and kept it a troubled and dangerous place.

Sean had never been inside "Mook," as the troops called it, although he had flown over it a few times. He did, however, know of its reputation for lawlessness.

The 69th Brigade Combat Team had decided on a show of force, with the hope that it would settle things down. The idea was that the local detachment of the Iraqi Army's Diyala Operational Command would be less likely to lose control of the situation if the presence of American muscle could be rallied on short notice.

None of the Americans at FOB Lex had been around back in the winter and spring of 2007 when the insurgents were so powerful that they captured Baqubah, the capital of Diyala. They had not experienced this, but the difficult fight to regain control of the province still loomed large in the institutional memory of the brigade—and of the 2nd Battalion of the 77th Infantry.

Nobody wanted to see any corner of the province experience a repeat of that type of bloodshed, nor of the dozens of mass graves that al-Qaeda had filled in the area during that terrible period in Diyala's troubled history.

Capt. Ryan Clark, the young West Pointer whom everyone respected as a leader, would take Charlie Company out to Muqdarubah, their armored Humvees backed by four M2A3 Bradley Fighting Vehicles that the brigade had sent down for the operation.

Not widely known was that the show of force was to be of relatively short duration. They'd be in and out in seventy-two hours. The planners at the brigade level had decided that if they moved around a lot within the city and made enough noise, there would be an intimidation factor, a *lasting* intimidation factor.

Sean had been in Folbright's office when the battalion commander briefed Clark on the plan. He could see by the way that Clark's jaw clenched that he didn't think a *quick* show of force, however noisy, could do the job. Sean could tell from the kinds of questions that Clark asked that he felt that a job worth doing was worth doing right.

"If it's only a three-day mission, maybe I could tag along," Sean suggested. "I'd be back before Sunday. The guys might appreciate my being there."

"I dunno," Folbright said. "Mook's a dangerous place."

"Glad to have you aboard," Clark said. "If the colonel gives you the green light."

"Well . . . " Folbright said. He had the authority to order Sean to remain behind, but he was reluctant to stand in the way of his chaplain's volunteering. "You are so authorized."

Before dawn, the troops moved out, rolling through Camp Lexington's gates in a long line of armored Humvees, with the four Bradleys located in pairs at the center and the rear of the column. Sean and Tyler Kraus rode in the back of the Humvee driven by Spc. Dustin Grob. They were immediately ahead of the first of the big fighting vehicles. The sound of its treads, when he was used to being around vehicles with tires, was deafening.

It had been a long time since Sean had been on the road in the same column as a Bradley, and he had forgotten about the noise and the imposing size of the big armored vehicle. Though smaller than a main battle tank, it was much larger and heavier

than a Humvee. It was also a lot slower than a Humvee, and
the column puttered along at barely more than thirty miles per
hour.

"So this is the famous Mook," Kraus observed as they crossed
a narrow canal and entered the city. "Looks like we have an
audience."

"Guess the hajjis got the word that we were coming," Grob
observed as they looked at the curious people lining the streets
to gawk at the American vehicles. "News travels fast in a war
zone. It sure travels a lot faster than thirty miles an hour."

Sean watched the kids staring at the big, powerful American
vehicles and thought of Bilal and his sister. In Safaliyah, they
were now growing up with an impression of Americans as people who brought soccer balls—correction, *foot*balls. What did
these kids in Mook think? Were Americans just *ulooj* outsiders
who roared around their town with big, frightening machines,
then drove away?

Sean watched as the mud huts of Muqdarubah's outskirts
gave way to larger and larger cinder-block buildings as the convoy pressed on toward the city center. He saw a building that
more or less reminded him of the school in Safaliyah, and of
how much he missed Mareike De Vries.

He was glad that someone else was driving. He knew that
they were headed to a rendezvous with the Iraqi National Army
somewhere in the heart of Mook, but after all the twists and
turns, he was completely lost. One street of cinder-block struc-
tures and staring civilians looked like any other.

"Pretty big town," Kraus said, echoing Sean's thoughts. "Figured we'd have been downtown by now."

"Hope the colonel knows where he's going," Grob shouted over the noise of the Bradley. "I sure don't. I'm just following the guy in front of me."

At last, they arrived in a sort of city square. Sean watched the vehicles turn and maneuver as though part of a huge thundering, clanking square dance, the Bradleys taking up positions on the corners of the cluster of parked vehicles. Huge clouds of dust billowed up, and he thought it a wonder there wasn't a collision. By the sounds of the expletives bellowed from the front seat by Dustin Grob, there were a couple of close calls.

As the dust started to settle, Sean stepped out of the Humvee. About twenty yards away, Capt. Clark was saluting an Iraqi colonel in front of what appeared to be a Saddam-era police station. Behind him were about a hundred troops in Iraqi uniforms. As he looked around, Sean saw a cluster of kids about Bilal's age watching them from the head of a narrow alley.

He waved and smiled, then started walking toward them.

They watched him curiously for a moment, then bolted like a flock of startled birds, running up the alley and away from the Americans.

Sean felt a firm hand on his arm.

"Better wait until we get the lay of the land, Padre," Tyler Kraus said. "This ain't Saf City. They don't know that you're a good guy out here."

"Yeah, I guess you're right," Sean said. Part of him wanted to thank Kraus for the reality check. Another part wanted to find the kids and tell them that their familiar reality need not be the only reality that was possible. He knew this was naive, but still he wanted to do it.

"Sir, the captain wants to see you," a young soldier shouted to Sean. "Wants a quick meeting for all the officers."

"Thanks," Sean shouted as the young man double-timed it to the nearest Bradley to repeat Clark's invitation to the lieutenant perched on its hatch.

"Here's the skinny," Clark said, holding up a handful of maps. "Muqdarubah is roughly divided by these canals into three sections. We're gonna patrol each of these sections in force, with an Iraqi Army contingent in the lead. Lieutenant Burris leads the northwest contingent with one of the Brads, Wright goes southwest with another Brad, and I'll lead the rest into the larger section on the east side of town. The Iraqis will take the lead because they know the way around. Just follow their lead, keep track of your position on your maps, stay in touch with the other contingents, and have lots of fun. Any questions?"

"Where do you want us . . . the UMT?" Sean asked Clark after he had disposed of a few mainly procedural questions.

"You guys can come with my column," Clark said. "Just stay ahead of the Brad like you did on your way down here."

As they moved out, Grob moved the Humvee into the line two Humvees back from Clark's. Ahead were five or six Polish-made Dzik-3 armored cars, the trucklike 4×4 that the Iraqis called *Ain Jaria.* The reason this vehicle that the Poles had dubbed *Wild Boar* was called *Water Spring* by the Iraqis was lost on the Americans. Of course, what kind of a word is *Humvee*?

Again, Sean became completely lost. He *sort of* knew where they were in relation to the center of town after their second turn, but after the sixth, he was hopeless. It didn't help that the streets were so narrow and everything below the third floor of the buildings was in shadow. At least Spc. Grob had a map.

"Do you suppose they're properly impressed by our show of force?" Kraus asked wryly, looking up at people leaning out on their balconies to watch the passing Bradleys.

"They can't help being impressed by our noise and dust," Sean shouted. In the narrow streets, the reverberation of the noise made by the six hundred horses inside the Bradley's Cummins diesel engine was deafening.

Sean knew and understood that the function of tramping around the town in this way was to intimidate the thugs who intimidated the regular people, the families of those kids who had run away from him. However, he also realized that the people themselves were intimidated by this show of force. Like so many soldiers in American uniforms, he longed for the day when shows of force were no longer necessary in Mook, just as they were less and less necessary in places such as Safaliyah.

Like so many soldiers in American uniforms, he knew that such a day would be the day when they could all say good riddance to the Sandbox.

Since that day when he and Mareike had first pledged their love, Sean's thoughts had begun soaring—when he allowed his thoughts to soar—to notions of an ideal life in an ideal world. He imagined days filled with enriching lives of service side by side, just as he and Mareike continued to discuss each Wednesday afternoon. As the column twisted its way through Muqdarubah's streets, he fantasized about a ministry *here* in Mook, a ministry in which he and Mareike could bring happiness and stability to *these* kids, as they had in Safaliyah.

The startling jolt of the Humvee hitting a pothole slammed Sean out of his momentary reverie and back into the real world of the here and now.

In the real world of the here and now, his real ministry among *other* kids, among *these* kids in their late teens and early twenties, kids in American uniforms who looked to him for stability, for reassurance, for an explanation of a personal conundrum—and for a kind word. Many of them even looked to him for spiritual guidance.

In the real world of the here and now, his fantasies of an ideal future had no place. Someday maybe, but not today.

◆　◆　◆

When through the whirl of wheels, and engines humming,
Patiently powerful for the sons of men,
Peals like a trumpet promise of His coming,
Who in the clouds is pledged to come again.

When through the night the furnace fires aflaring,
Shooting out tongues of flame like leaping blood,
Speak to the heart of love, alive and daring,
Sing of the boundless energy of God.

FROM THE HYMN "WHEN THROUGH THE WHIRL OF WHEELS"
WORDS BY ANGLICAN PRIEST GEOFFREY ANKETELL STUDDERT-KENNEDY,
WRITTEN WHEN HE WAS A BRITISH ARMY CHAPLAIN DURING THE FIRST
WORLD WAR

18

Foes That Would the Land Devour

The explosion lifted the front of Sean's Humvee about two feet off the ground.

At first, when he saw the sheet of flame and felt his helmet slam into the vehicle's frame, he thought that they had been hit. But now he could see that it was the Humvee directly ahead of them that had been hit.

Someone shouted, "Direct hit!"

Someone else shouted, "IED!"

Nobody was sure.

Sean felt dizzy. He felt a lump in his throat the size of a football.

His head slammed the frame again as Grob jerked the wheel and made a sharp turn to the left.

Someone shouted, "Evasive action!"

Lots of other words were being shouted, none of them what you might hear at chapel.

Off to the right side as they turned, Sean could see the other Humvee. Actually, he saw only a blackened silhouette of part of the vehicle. It flickered in the midst of a dirty orange fireball like a candlewick inside a candle flame.

The black sooty smoke that swirled around the flames obscured their view of what might have happened to the Humvee, just as the furious flames sealed off the narrow street. Taking evasive action on a side street appeared to be their only choice.

Sean breathed a prayer for the men inside the fireball, men beside whom he had stood just an hour ago, men whom he recognized from chapel, men who recognized him and who had asked, "Howzit goin', Chaplain?"

He breathed a prayer for the men, guiltily admitting that he'd asked God for a merciful death. To have survived this conflagration would have been a hell on earth no man or woman deserves.

Off the left side of his Humvee, in that split second of a turn, Sean saw the Bradley that had been behind them. He imagined what it had been like to have slammed to a sudden stop inside the steel box of a Bradley. Inside, the gunner was starting to swivel the turret to the left.

Whumpwhumpwhump!

They heard the thud of the Bradley's M242 Bushmaster cannon as the gunner fired a burst of 25-mm rounds.

Sean didn't have a chance to see where they impacted. Kraus had shoved his head and shoulders toward the floorboards and had climbed on top of him.

It was the job of the chaplain's assistant to protect the chaplain's life with his own. Sean appreciated this devotion beyond words, but *wow*, was it uncomfortable to be tied in a knot on the bottom of a moving vehicle with two hundred pounds of sergeant and body armor on top of him!

Sean's only sense that actually sensed anything useful was that of feel. He felt Kraus's weight; he felt the pain of his legs bent at an uncomfortable angle and the jostling of the Humvee zigging and zagging. All he could see was an up-close view of dust, grease, and discarded gum wrappers. All he could hear was a confusing, earsplitting mush of whumps, whacks, grinds, and zings reverberating in the narrow streets.

He had no idea where they were or exactly what was going on.

He sensed that they were under attack, and that they had been fired upon, but he wasn't sure.

It might have been a roadside bomb that had destroyed the Humvee. However, if this were the case, why would the Bradley gunner be returning fire?

Maybe he was just as confused as Sean was. Maybe he did not know exactly what was going on, either.

Sean felt the Humvee moving quickly, first in a straight line, and then there came a sharp right and a sharp left.

For a few moments, the gunfire had subsided, but now he heard the sounds of automatic-weapons fire in the near distance. These were followed by sounds that Sean prayed were *not* bullets hitting their vehicle. If they hadn't been before, they were now definitely under attack.

There was the sound and smell of 5.56-mm rounds being fired very close, as Chase Wellman, the soldier riding shotgun in the front seat, opened up with his M16.

Sean felt the Humvee slow down to a crawl, then speed up. They made a sharp right turn, another sharp left, then two rights—or was it three?

Suddenly they stopped.

So too had the sound of gunfire.

After the cacophony of the preceding minutes, it was eerily quiet except for the sound of idling engines.

Sean felt the weight lifted from his back as Kraus got up. He took a deep breath and was rewarded with a mouthful of swirling dust.

"You okay?" Kraus asked.

"Perfect," Sean said, coughing the dust out of his lungs. "Never been better. What happened? Where are we?"

"Ambush," Kraus said, answering a rhetorical question in a tone that implied it to have been a no-brainer answer. "I dunno, where *are* we?"

"I dunno either," Grob answered. "I really wasn't following the damned map. I was just tryin' to get away from the shooters. Guess it worked. There's nobody shooting down here where we are now."

"Wherever *that* is," Wellman added.

Sean sat up and looked around. Ahead of them lay only a narrow street and clouds of dust. It made a turn about thirty yards ahead, and he could see nothing around the bend. Behind them another Humvee was idling. He could see no other American vehicles.

"Is anyone hurt?" Sean asked.

"Not in our car," Grob said, sucking on a bleeding finger.

"Let's check with the others."

As Tyler Kraus scanned the buildings, his M4 carbine at the ready, Sean walked back toward the other Humvee.

"Everybody okay?"

"Yeah. We took a couple of hits, but no damage that I can see."

As Sean leaned down to talk to Alex Rojas, in the driver's seat of the second Humvee, he noticed a familiar face looking at him from the back of the vehicle. It was Pfc. Kelsi Schmitt, the young mother from Fort Dodge, Iowa, who had lost her brother just after being united with him for the first time. She looked back at him with fear in her bright green eyes. She had been through a lot in the past few weeks—never mind the past few minutes.

He smiled a pastorly smile at Kelsi and returned to the other vehicle.

"I guess we better mount up and get back to the Brad?" Grob said, looking at Sean and hoping that the officer would either confirm that this was the right course of action or tell him what to do.

"I think that's probably a good idea," Sean confirmed, trying to appear decisive. "Do you have any idea where they are . . . which way to go?"

"Head toward the sound of the shooting?"

In the distance, they could now hear small-arms fire punctuated occasionally by the sound of a large-caliber round.

Nobody was shooting at them for the moment, and the thought of heading back into the firefight was pretty unappetizing. Nevertheless, they knew that keeping the overall force from being scattered was essential.

"I shouldn't have run," Grob whispered to Sean. "I friggin' panicked. I shouldn't have run."

"Let's go get back to work," Sean said, putting his hand on Grob's shoulder. "Let's catch up with Captain Clark."

Grob had taken fire and he had run. Seven people in two vehicles were alive because of what he had done, but what had happened to the others because these soldiers ran away from the firefight?

"How can we find Clark?" Grob asked nobody in particular. "I hear gunfire coming from over there now, too."

"I think that must be the Humvee that was ahead of us," Sean said, pointing at a column of smoke between the buildings. "If we can get over to there, then at least we know which way Clark was heading at the time of the ambush . . . maybe we can follow his trail?"

"Sounds like a plan," Grob agreed.

Driving toward the sounds of the shooting, and toward the black smoke, was easier said than done. As they traveled, the smoke was often hidden from view by the buildings, and the sooty column had begun to dissipate as the fire burned itself out. At the same time, the noise of the gunfire seemed to be coming from every direction, bouncing and echoing off the adobe and concrete facades of buildings.

"What's that?" Wellman asked in a startled tone.

"Oh man, what a friggin' mess," Grob replied.

They came around a corner to face the aftermath of yet another firefight. The Iraqi Army had lost—big time. Two Dzik-3 armored cars were parked at the side of the street, looking as though they had been discarded in a junkyard. The armor on the *Ain Jaria* is designed to withstand hits from 7.62-mm rounds from an AK-47, and the armor on these two *had* withstood such hits—a lot of them. Unfortunately, each of the vehicles had taken a hit from a rocket-propelled grenade. One had been hit in the engine block, the other in the driver's-side door.

"We gotta stop," Sean said as Grob steered wide to get around these forlorn wrecks.

"Why?" Grob asked.

"Because there might be survivors," the chaplain replied urgently, as backseat drivers often do.

Several bodies in gray uniforms lay on the ground and in the open doorways of both vehicles. Between them, the two vehicles could have carried as many as two dozen personnel, but thankfully only about half that many bodies were visible.

"We don't know if there might be someone inside the trucks who needs first aid," Sean said as he and Kraus tumbled out a rear door on the lead Humvee.

"Can we please make this quick?" Grob asked nervously.

Kelsi Schmitt and Chase Wellman joined the chaplain and his assistant in the grim task of checking the pulses of the men who lay strewn on the packed dirt of the street.

"Owweee!" Wellman grimaced as he leaned inside one of the Dzik-3s. "It really stinks in here."

"Check 'em all," Kraus admonished as he took a deep breath and leaned into the second vehicle.

"Honor the dead, comfort the wounded, and nurture the living," Sean muttered to himself as he touched neck after neck looking for a wounded man among the dead to comfort. He found none.

Both Kraus and Wellman shook their heads as they hopped from the two Dziks. Nobody had survived.

Sean bowed his head for a quick prayer, and when he looked up, Kraus was the only other American still on the street and he was pushing Sean toward the door of the Humvee.

"I got hold of Clark's command post on the radio while you were checking those guys," Grob reported when they were moving again.

"Where are they?" Sean asked.

"I'm not sure. The way they described it, they're not far past the ambush. I think if we can get there, I can find them."

"*How* are they doing?" Kraus asked.

"Taking fire," Grob said. "They circled their wagons and dug in until the cavalry shows up. I guess they're sending tanks down from Lex or something."

He went on to paint a story of confusion reigning throughout Mook. Two of the three contingents of the task force—Clark's and that headed by Lt. Randy Burris—had been hit simultaneously, and the third detachment was attacked a short time after. Fortunately, they had the small measure of warning that came from knowing about the earlier attacks.

Grob and the other Humvee were not the only elements of Clark's eastern contingent to be separated from the main column after the attack.

Clark had now organized a defensive perimeter some distance from the point of the original attack. He was dug in, waiting for help to arrive. The two wayward Humvees were not exactly the help that Clark would need, but if they could reach him, there would be more strength in numbers.

It took what seemed like an eternity of missed turns and dead-end streets, but the Humvees driven by Grob and Rojas finally returned to the point where it all had started.

The Bradley was gone. Perhaps it had reached Clark. Perhaps not.

The destroyed Humvee, barely recognizable as such, was smoldering, but the fire was much smaller and they were able to squeeze past on the narrow street.

Sean repeated his earlier silent prayer, asking the Lord for a quick and merciful death for the soldiers in the Humvee. He added a somewhat more optimistic prayer for the guys in the Brad—wherever they were.

"Uh-oh, we got us a problem," Grob said, looking in his mirror.

Sean looked back. The other Humvee had stopped and the soldiers were getting out.

Grob shifted into reverse and scudded back to where they were.

"What's wrong?"

"I spoke too quick," Alex Rojas admitted. "Y'know, when I didn't think we'd been hit too bad. I spoke too quick. Took one in the oil pan, I guess. Damned engine seized."

No sooner had the three people from the second Humvee started to squeeze into Grob's vehicle than they heard the pops of gunfire.

"Somebody's shootin' at us!"

Kapow kapow kapow!

"Duck."

Kapow kapow!

"Take cover."

Kapow kapow kapow kapow!

"Everybody in . . . let's get moving."

Kapow kapow!

"Arrrhh . . . I'm hit!"

Kapow kapow!

"Let's get moving."

Once again, Sean found his face shoved into the grit and gum wrappers on the Humvee floor—this time with not one, but five people on top of him.

"Bobby's hit!"

The ferrous stench of blood filled the vehicle. Sean could hear the squishing sound of blood-soaked fabric and the gasping and moaning of someone who was badly injured.

Once again, Sean felt the lurching of a vehicle traveling at less than thirty miles per hour trying to dodge 7.62-mm rounds coming at supersonic speeds.

Abruptly, amid the popping and whizzing sound of gunfire, came the sickening sound of metal crumpling and the sensation of the Humvee coming to a sudden stop.

Grob had hit something.

The tires screamed and the Humvee moved a little.

Grob threw it into reverse and tried to back up.

The tires screamed, the Humvee jerked backward, and they hit something else.

The tires screamed and rubber burned.

Sean choked on the black, burning stench.

The Humvee shook violently but had neither forward nor backward motion.

They had reached the end of the line.

"Everybody *out* . . . let's get moving."

Spc. Grob was out of the Humvee and pointing toward a doorway at the end of the street into which he had turned to dodge the enemy gunfire.

"Let's take cover . . . down there! Behind that door!"

They moved as fast as they could. Sean and another man carried Bobby—Pvt. Robert Budner, the wounded soldier—while Tyler Kraus brought up the rear, moving backward, his M4 trained on the place where the alley peeled off the main street. At any moment, he expected bad guys to round the corner shooting.

Suddenly the gunfire began, but it came from ahead, not behind them.

At least one shooter was firing from a window adjacent to the door behind which Dustin Grob had decided they should take cover.

It was just their luck that the random doorway at which they hoped to knock for sanctuary was perhaps one in a hundred that was already an al-Qaeda sanctuary.

Dustin Grob was through running. An hour ago—or a half hour or an eternity—his Humvee had been attacked, and he had run. He had turned mere evasive action into a headlong dash in an unknown direction. He could logically justify his actions, but deep down inside, he understood his motivation. It was panic. It was near cowardice. Nobody saw this as well and as clearly as he did.

Dustin Grob was through running.

He raised his M16 and poured a stream of jacketed lead into the window.

The firing stopped.

Grob ran, not from the gunman, but *toward* him.

He didn't even bother with the door; he just crashed through the window.

The others followed. They heard the pop of gunfire inside the building.

Chase Wellman shouldered his way through the door.

"Hold your fire!" Wellman screamed urgently. "There's hajji civilians."

As the others entered the room, they saw Dustin Grob standing over the lifeless bodies of two bearded men. Blood and brass shell casings littered the floor.

In a dark corner, almost invisible, sat a little cluster of people. It took a moment for Sean's eyes to become used to the darkness, but he could make out a woman, her head shrouded in black but her long narrow wrists and hands unmistakably female. With her were two small children with absolute terror in their expressions.

From another room came the sound of a young girl screaming.

Raising his weapon, Grob carefully pushed aside the drapery covering the doorway and entered the room.

The child shrieked.

"Oh my God!" Grob shouted. "I shot a kid!"

Sean followed him into the small, windowless room. Lying on a low bed was a girl of about twelve. She screamed again as Sean came in, wrapping herself in a blanket. As in the other room, blood was spattered all over the place.

As Sean started toward her, he felt a firm hand on his forearm. He turned, expecting to see Tyler Kraus. The sergeant was always tugging him back from what he feared were dangerous situations.

It wasn't Kraus; it was Kelsi Schmitt.

"You guys need to leave," she said firmly, pushing Sean and Grob toward the doorway.

Surprised by the unexpected, Sean complied, lending a hand to Kelsi's in tugging Grob out of the room.

Back in the main room, first aid was already being administered to Bobby's bloody leg wound.

Sean suggested to Grob that for the sake of the civilians, he ought to find something to cover up the dead insurgents.

With that, Sean removed his own helmet to make his appearance less impersonal, and he smiled at the woman and two small children, holding up his hands to signify that he meant no harm.

He sat on the floor near them and spoke in a quiet voice, trying to appear as calm to the people as the entry by the Americans into their home was anything but.

"As-salaam alaikum," Sean said.

The woman just nodded.

Sean exhausted his limited Arabic vocabulary and continued speaking in English. He was sure that they couldn't understand his words. He just hoped—and prayed—that they could understand his tone and his intentions.

He looked into her eyes, the rest of her face still covered, as she stared at the cross on his uniform. Sean couldn't tell whether she understood that he was a chaplain, or whether she just thought it to signify that he was a "crusader," that common derogatory term for *ulooj* Western soldiers in the Middle East.

After a few minutes, he reached into his pocket for an American granola bar, which he offered to the kids.

They looked to their mother for approval, she nodded, and they took the bar.

She pulled the veil from her face and seemed to relax a little bit. Her eyes drifted toward the two bodies that Grob was covering with a sheet. Her expression was one of disgust. She spat in their direction, and Sean asked her, *"Mein?"*

She looked at him and, understanding the Arabic word for "who," she answered, "Al-Qaeda," in an angry, quavering voice.

No faction among the many who battle one another in Iraq is more hated and more feared by average Iraqis than al-Qaeda.

At that moment, Kelsi stepped from the other room. Carefully folding back the drape that covered the doorway, she tossed her helmet onto the ground.

"I hit her . . . and I'm real sorry," Grob said sadly, looking at Kelsi.

"No," she said, looking him in the eye. "You didn't hit her."

"But, what?"

"She was, ummm . . ."

"You mean . . . ?"

Kelsi nodded. It had been a sexual assault. The woman's older daughter had been raped in her own home.

"By them?" Grob said, nodding at the corpses on the floor. Had this been part of al-Qaeda's master plan for intimidating the people of Muqdarubah, or something far simpler and far baser?

"Guess so." Kelsi shrugged.

The mother's eyes met Kelsi's. The language barrier was insurmountable, but by the look on her face, there was no doubt as to what had happened here.

◆　◆　◆

From foes that would the land devour,
From guilty pride and lust of power,
From wild sedition's lawless hour,
From yoke of slavery,

From blinded zeal by faction led,
From giddy change by fancy bred,
From poisonous error's serpent head
Good Lord, preserve us free!

FROM THE HYMN "FROM FOES THAT WOULD THE LAND DEVOUR"
WORDS BY REGINALD HEBER

19

Daylight Dies Away

"At least he's alive," Capt. Ryan Clark said grimly, looking at his executive officer as he logged off and stepped away from the JTRS.

The task force commander had plenty to be concerned with this afternoon—but *at least* the 2nd Battalion's chaplain was alive, and, for the moment, he was in a safe location.

"There are seven people holed up in a building around the corner from the location of the initial attack," Clark explained to his exec. "They have one guy wounded. We gotta get a patrol back there to secure them. Send two Humvees . . . driver and gunner only. We'll have them try to squeeze those people in and get 'em back here."

Clark and his men had come to Muqdarubah for a show of force and had discovered that the whole town had been infiltrated by al-Qaeda. It was like trying to slice a brown spot off a piece of fruit and discovering that the entire thing was inhabited by insidious bugs.

A signature tactic for al-Qaeda, dating back well before 9/11, had been striking simultaneous targets, and today in Muqdar-ubah, they had taken a battle plan from their usual playbook. Clark had split his task force into three segments, and each had been attacked in a separate corner of the city.

How did they know exactly where the Americans would be?

Because, Clark surmised, the Americans had all been following Iraqi Army units, and al-Qaeda had somehow gotten wind of the Iraqi Army battle plan.

Had it been an inside job?

Had some disgruntled someone within the Iraqi Army tipped off al-Qaeda to the routes that the three American columns would take through the city?

Possibly. The Iraqi Army was filled with former insurgents of every stripe and was well known to contain bad pennies and plenty of double-sided coins.

However, from what Clark himself had observed, al-Qaeda RPGs had blasted the Iraqi *Ain Jaria* armored vehicles with a fury equal to what they dished out to American Humvees. For the most part, there was no love lost between al-Qaeda and the Iraqi troops.

The force led by Lt. Randy Burris in the northwest part of the city, which was attacked at the same time as Clark's column, had been especially hard hit. Burris himself was a casualty, having taken a bullet to a forearm that nicked an artery.

Of the four Bradley fighting vehicles to enter the city that morning, only the one that was assigned to Lt. Bob Wright's contingent was still functioning. Unlike Burris's, Wright's force had managed to defeat their ambush fairly easily. Clark had ordered them to get to where the Burris team was under attack and to reinforce them.

Clark himself had lost one of two Bradleys. An RPG round had knocked the track off the other one, but its gun was still able to return fire, so he was using it as fixed artillery. He had dug in his force into a fairly secure defensive position, but that was all that it was. He was hoping for air support to back him in a breakout attempt, but therein lay a problem. Urban environments were a nearly impossible battleground for Air Force bombers, and even for helicopter gunships.

Clark understood that he might have to be satisfied with a stalemate until reinforcements arrived overland—and that would not be until early tomorrow because there were no main battle tanks at FOB Lexington. They'd have to be brought in overland from brigade headquarters.

"How is he?" Sean Rasmunsen asked, looking at the injured Robert Budner, who lay on a mat in the corner, covered with blood.

"Bobby's okay," Chase Wellman said. "Y'know . . . okay as he can be, considering. He's asleep. Guess the morphine's got the pain under control. We've got the bleeding stopped. He's lost a lotta blood, y'know, but the bleeding *is* stopped. He didn't get hit in an artery or nothing."

As Sean knelt next to the injured man, watching his chest rise and fall, Bobby's face was no longer twisted in pain as it had been a half hour before. Sean breathed a prayer of thanksgiving.

"Thanks, God," he whispered. "Thanks for pulling Bobby through . . . this far."

As Sean knelt next to Bobby, he overheard Dustin Grob on the JTRS.

"What? Hey, man . . . that can't be . . . what are you gonna do? Oh, man . . . what are *we* gonna do?"

Hearing one side of the conversation, and this in a pessimistic tone, made things seem especially bleak.

"Bad news?" Sean asked guardedly.

"Bad news, sir. That relief column that they were gonna send? Y'know, to get us outa here? Well . . . they got ambushed. One Humvee got wasted and the other had to pull back. There ain't nobody comin' for us, at least not 'til they figure things out. We're supposed to sit tight . . . sit tight and wait."

"We *can't* do that," Chase Wellman said. "We got Bobby in a bad way. We gotta get outa here."

"Sir, what *are* we going to do?" Dustin Grob asked the chaplain.

Seven Americans and four Iraqi civilians, among whom two were injured, sat together in a house in the crowded old part of Muqdarubah, trying to answer that age-old question: *What next?*

"What are you asking *him* for?" Wellman interrupted.

"He's an officer."

"He's a noncombatant," Wellman clarified. "Right, sir?"

"Right," Sean confirmed. "I think that what an officer who *was* a combatant would tell you is to obey the order that you were given . . . y'know, to stay put."

"It's not exactly an order," Wellman suggested. "It was a sorta 'do-nothing-till-we-figure-it-out' kinda thing, y'know. I figure we got three choices: We stay here until help arrives, or we make a run for it, or else we send someone for help."

"Making a run for it is not an option as far as I can see," Kelsi said. "We've got a wounded man. We can't move very fast carrying Bobby, y'know. And we've got four civilians that if we left 'em and al-Qaeda got 'em . . . well, y'know we *can't* leave 'em."

Everyone nodded, glancing nervously toward the cloth that covered the doorway to the room where the older girl was taking refuge from the throng that was sitting around the main room of her home.

"I say we send somebody for help," Grob said. "It was my screw-up that got us here . . . I'll go. Besides, I don't . . . I can't stand it, y'know, just sitting around."

"Nobody feels more antsy just sitting around than me," Sean said. "I would much, much rather do *something* than *nothing*, too, but, y'know, sometimes following orders is the toughest choice."

"Yeah . . . you're right," Grob admitted after a long silence. "They do know we're here. Going for help wouldn't get Bobby outa here any faster."

"What do you suggest we do in the meantime?" Wellman asked, looking first at Grob, then to Sean.

"I'd suggest we take a moment for prayer," Sean said. "Take a deep breath and say a prayer of thanks that we got this far . . . and another prayer . . . asking that we get *all* the way home."

"I *have been* praying," Kelsi Schmitt said, tossing in her two cents.

"I'm praying for Bobby," Rojas whispered, crossing him-

self. "Not that I'm thinking about last rites, I just want to . . .
y'know . . ."

"Amen," Kelsi said, wiping the beads of sweat from her
forehead.

Sean thought about his own job description. He thought of
Bobby, and thanked God that he was at the moment comforting
the wounded, not having to honor the dead. He looked around
the room, thinking about his duty to nurture the living.

"I suggest that it wouldn't be a bad idea for us all to say the
Lord's Prayer," Sean said.

Everyone nodded, except Tyler Kraus, whose eyes were peering outside, watching the street.

"Our Father, who art in heaven," Kraus said without looking
away from the window, then pausing for everyone to catch up.

Everyone knew the words. Even nonchurchgoers had heard it
and could follow along with the words.

Except for the usual stumbling when some said "debts" and
others "trespasses," it went well. Everyone seemed a little bit
more relaxed when they had finished.

Rojas, who was apparently the only Catholic in the group,
crossed himself, and added another prayer. For Catholics, the
Hail Mary is not a type of play in football, but a prayer often
said back-to-back with the Lord's Prayer.

"*Santa María, Madre de Dios,*" he said quickly. "*Ruega por
nosotros pecadores ahora y en la hora de nuestra muerte* . . .
Amen.*"

Sean knew that the last line, *ahora y en la hora de nuestra
muerte*, translated as "now and at the hour of our death." He
prayed that hour would long be postponed.

Rojas looked at Bobby and crossed himself again. He was frightened for Bobby. He was frightened for them all.

Outside, the shadows were growing long as the day neared its end. Soon it would be dark, and in a war zone, bogeymen really *do* inhabit the night.

Eleven people crowded together by chance in a tiny house on the back street of a place called Mook prepared for a long night of watching, waiting, and, if possible, resting. Five armed Americans prepared to defend themselves and the others. The defense would be simple, though possibly not so easy. If anyone discovered them and attacked them, they would just use all the firepower at their disposal to stop the bad guys from getting at them. The simplicity in the defensive plan was that the only way in or out of the place was through the front door or the broken window next to it. There was a small slit of an opening in the tiny kitchen, but it was more of a vent than a window.

The Iraqi woman, the mother of the children, had relaxed somewhat as she listened to the Americans saying prayers. They were strange prayers in strange languages, but they *did* sound like prayers. She had heard that the American Christians prayed to the prophet Jesus, but not to Allah. This she could not understand, but at least Jesus *was* a prophet.

Sean could sense that their prayers had set her mind slightly at ease. He hoped—and prayed—that the experience might make some small difference in the Iraqi perception of Americans.

Maybe it had put a human face on these outsiders whom the Iraqis called *ulooj* and al-Qaeda called the "foreign devils." It was an irony that despite being mainly non-Iraqi themselves, the al-Qaeda thugs insisted on calling the American devils *foreign*. Sean wondered how the woman felt now, knowing that her daughter had been raped by al-Qaeda and not by the *ulooj*—the "bloodsucking pigs." He noticed that the injured girl, who had emerged from the other room to lie at her mother's side, was now fast asleep.

Though the mother and her teenage daughter seemed at ease, the younger girl began sobbing when it grew too dark inside the house to see.

"Sorry, little one," Sean said in a soft voice, hoping that his tone, if not his words, would be comforting. "We really gotta keep the lights out. There are bad guys in the neighborhood, and it's best they think nobody's home here at your house."

Comfort the wounded, Sean thought to himself, *comfort those wounded emotionally by darkness both real and metaphorical.*

"They'll sure know somebody's friggin' home with the kid squealin' like that," Grob said in disgust. Sean had noticed that he was another one of those who deliberately used the adverb *friggin'* in the presence of a chaplain, thinking it more acceptable than that stronger word beginning with the same letter. Sean, however, was not bothered by his choice of vocabulary, but his tone of voice.

"Cool it," Sean whispered. "You're freaking her out . . . Your making her start to think that you're mad at her is sure not gonna calm her down."

"Yeah, okay, but they're gonna hear the kid wailing and know somebody's here."

"At least they won't know from that there are a bunch of

ulooj in here," Kelsi said. "Lots of little kids cry at night. I have a kid at home who's not much older than she is."

"Kids cry at night, but we oughta cool it with the chatter," Rojas suggested.

"Shaddup, all of you," Tyler Kraus hissed. "We got hajji out there."

There was the abrupt gulp of a roomful of people holding their collective breath, and all eyes were trained on the window.

In the pale ambient moonlight from outside, they could see Kraus hold up four fingers.

Those close enough to peer out could see at least two figures moving up the street past the incapacitated Humvee.

Inside, Sean could hear the barely audible clicks of the safeties on the M16s being flicked off. He prayed that fingers would not squeeze triggers without a clear target. He figured that Kraus could see what he was doing, but cringed at the thought of four other nervous people in a dark room with assault rifles on full auto.

In the corner, he heard the sounds of the mother muzzling her terrified daughter.

After an interminable amount of time had passed, they heard the tinkle of a bell, the kind that shepherds put on one animal in a flock so they can tell where their livestock are in the dark.

Soon the sound of many small feet passed and Kraus gave a thumbs-up.

All clear.

Everyone gave a sigh of relief, and safeties were reengaged.

Even in a war zone, day-to-day life goes on.

Watching the shadows of the shepherds as they moved past made Sean think of that other terrible night in the desert, the night that Sgt. Brandon Mosier knifed a shepherd boy. He said a prayer for them both. He knew that the boy was in a better place, just as he knew that with the memory of that night eating him alive, Mosier was not in a better place. He prayed also for a time when shepherd boys would herd their flocks with no fear of sharp steel across their throats.

"I'm reminded of Psalm Ninety-one," Sean whispered as he looked around the room and sensed the palpable tension. "You shall not fear the terror of the night . . ."

"Nor the arrow that flies by day," Kraus added.

"Nor the pestilence that roams in darkness," Sean continued. "Nor the plague that ravages at noon."

"I sure hope we're outa here by *noon*," Wellman interjected.

"We will be," Sean said encouragingly.

Outside on the street, strange sounds still kept the soldiers on edge, and fear of the unknown kept them from sleep. It was very dark out there, and in a war zone, bad things happen at night.

◆ ◆ ◆

Now that the daylight dies away,
By all Thy grace and love,
Thee, Maker of the world, we pray
To watch our bed above.

Let dreams depart and phantoms fly,
The offspring of the night,
Keep us, like shrines, beneath Thine eye,
Pure in our foe's despite.

FROM THE HYMN "NOW THAT THE DAYLIGHT DIES AWAY"
WORDS ATTRIBUTED TO AMBROSE OF MILAN (FOURTH CENTURY)

20

Inner Strength

Nobody saw it coming.

Tyler Kraus might have—Tyler Kraus *should* have—but he had dozed off. Dustin Grob had promised to relieve him at midnight, but he had slept through the changing of the guard.

Nobody saw it coming.

Two silhouettes stood in the open doorway, two silhouettes carrying silhouettes of AK-47s.

In fairness to Kraus, there was nothing that he could have done, aside from opening fire and revealing the place where the Americans were hiding.

Through the night, while he was still awake, Kraus had seen people out there a half dozen times, but none had shown any interest in their hiding place.

And so it was, until these two, for some unlucky reason, had noticed that someone had broken the hinges off the door and that it was merely propped over the opening. They wondered why, and they checked it out.

For their trouble, the two silhouettes with AK-47s found themselves in a darkened room where eleven people slept. This was not unusual for Muqdarubah, but the American uniform was. They noticed the fabric pattern of this American uniform, and then they saw another, then another.

Naturally, one of them said something to his startled companion, and in a split second, one of the American uniforms stirred, and then another, then another.

Sean awoke to see the silhouettes and to hear the safeties coming off.

Kapow kapow kapow!

"There's hajjis in here."

Kapow kapow!

"Get him!"

Kapow kapow kapow kapow!

Sean smelled the stinging stench of burned powder and heard the sound of running feet.

"He's getting away!"

Kapow kapow!

The running feet were farther away now.

Kapow kapow kapow kapow!

There was a short moment of silence before many voices piled atop one another in the darkness.

"Anybody hit?"

"I got one."

"Did the other one get away?"

"Did you hit him?"

"Dunno . . . maybe."

"Anybody hit?"

"Just a nick . . . I think."

"Oh . . . Mother of God . . . it's Wellman!"

"What happened?"

"Is he okay?"

There was the sound of night-vision goggles being put into place. All eyes turned to Chase Wellman.

He lay in the center of the room, partially covered by the dark blue shape of a fallen al-Qaeda gunman. Blood was everywhere.

Kelsi Schmitt was already doing mouth-to-mouth.

"Get some light in here," she shouted. Someone turned on a flashlight. Sean switched on a small, bare-bulb table lamp.

In the corner, the two smaller children were crying uncontrollably. The teenage girl had an expression of horror unlike anything that Sean had ever seen. He longed to console her but realized that the last thing she needed right now was an American uniform wrapping its arms around her.

"He's not breathing," Kelsi said.

"No friggin' pulse," Dustin Grob confirmed sadly. "No friggin' pulse."

"Are *you* all right, Padre?" Tyler Kraus asked, the sound of panic in his voice. Sworn to protect the chaplain with his life, he had fallen asleep on the job, and in so doing, he had allowed a bad guy with an AK-47 to come within inches of his charge.

"Yeah, Tyler, I'm fine," Sean said, trying to sound calm. "I'm really fine. Did the other one get away?"

"Yeah," Tyler Kraus replied nervously "I might've clipped him. Not sure."

"Who clipped Wellman?" Grob asked, looking around the room. The sinister undercurrent was that Wellman's death might have been a friendly-fire accident. With four nervous Americans firing assault rifles in a dark room, it was not beyond the realm of probability.

"Don't ask!" Kelsi said, covering the dead man's face and shoulders with his flak jacket. "It won't do anybody any good."

"We need to know," Grob insisted.

"No we don't," Kelsi insisted. "Just shut the f— up and push the door closed."

Stunned by the firm order from the usually meek private first class, Grob complied.

After Sean had said a brief prayer and Alex Rojas had recited the Hail Mary in Spanish, all eyes turned back to watching the outside.

Ahora y en la hora de nuestra muerte.

The screaming children had become sobbing children, and eventually the sobbing subsided.

"What time is it?" Rojas asked.

"About one thirty when I looked a few minutes ago," Sean said.

"Gonna be a long night," Grob said grimly.

"It's *already* a long night," Kelsi corrected him.

Sean was just thankful for this being the coolest part of that long night. When the burning desert sun rose, so too would the temperature of sweating bodies encased in body armor. Then, too, the heat would accelerate the decomposition of the four dead bodies that now lay within the room.

Rojas said he wasn't tired and offered to take over the post at the window.

Sean decided to hunker down and try to catch some more sleep, and he ordered Kraus to do the same.

"He'll be back, y'know," Grob said. "That dude that got away. He's gone for help. He'll be back . . . we'd better be ready."

"We *know* that," Kelsi said caustically.

She sounded frightened, covering anxiety with sarcasm.

Together, they were like a couple of kids, barely out of high school, bickering almost for the sake of bickering.

For Sean, from the perspective of his age, the twenty-some-things *were* like a couple of kids, barely out of high school.

Sean awoke with a start.

It might have been the snoring. Everything else was still.

It might have been the stench. Even before decomp begins, the gases that belch from dead bodies can make a small space unbearable. Even with the ventilation provided by the glass having been smashed out of the window, it was dreadful.

Eleven—now ten—sweating bodies crowded into a small dwelling that was the size of a lot of suburban living rooms had its own effect. So too did all of those people sharing a bathroom that was really just an alcove, covered by a curtain, that was the size of a phone booth. At least they had indoor plumbing.

Sean promised himself that if they got through this night, he would do what he could to better the life of their accidental hostess and her frightened family. Nurture the living.

What, Sean wondered, had happened to the children's father?

Had he been killed in this war? Had he been killed by the terrorists? Had he been killed by insurgents? Was he one of the insurgents himself?

Rojas sat in the moonlight, staring out the window, his M16 propped on a chair, its barrel pointed outward, ready for action.

Everyone else was dozing fitfully, except Kelsi. She sat on the floor in the corner, her own M16 propped against her left knee. She had taken her helmet off, and in the faint reflected moonlight, her face looked like that of a little girl. Her expression was one of concern, not of fear.

Long ago in Fort Dodge, Iowa, this young mother had decided to join the service. It was a job. It was security. It was health care for a little girl named Brittany. Now it was more than that; it was what soldiering has been since long before Joshua at Jericho, since long before the dawn of recorded history.

"How you doing?" Sean whispered.

"Awesome . . . just wonderful," she replied cynically. "And you, sir?"

"I'm fine . . . awesome," Sean said. "All things considered—considering that things *could* be worse."

"Is God gonna get us outa this?" Kelsi asked pointedly.

"If it is His will," the chaplain said. "He moves, as you know, in mysterious ways."

"If I pray that he'll get us out . . . y'know . . . do you suppose that my prayers will be answered?"

"I believe in the power of prayer," Sean said. "I pray that *your* prayer will be answered . . . but I believe that sometimes He calls us—like he called Chase Wellman—from this earth at times and in ways that those around us can't fathom."

"I'm still gonna pray that we get outa this."

"Me, too," Sean said, smiling.

"Are you scared?" Kelsi whispered.

"Yeah, a little; hard not to be," Sean admitted. "You?"

"I was earlier. Now? Not so much . . . Maybe I'm numb, but y'know, I just don't feel scared anymore. After Chase was killed, I just don't feel like feeling scared. Worried? Yeah. Scared? Not really."

"I know how you feel," Rojas interjected. "Y'know, I think it's that at night nothing seems so real, y'know? It's like a video game or something. It's like it's happening to somebody else."

"Hopefully, nothing—nothing more—will happen to *anybody* else tonight," Sean said.

"I'm just not scared anymore," Kelsi said, holding up one of her hands to show that it was not trembling. "And it feels weird. Do you suppose it's shock or something?"

"Maybe—just maybe—it's God's way of giving you the strength to deal with a trying situation," Sean suggested. "Sometimes when you ask for strength, either consciously or instinctively, He answers your prayers."

"Could be," Kelsi said thoughtfully, pausing long to form a thought. "Like I sure never expected that I'd ever be here . . . y'know, in a place like this. It's like that girl I used to be back then, that mom who used to pick Brittany up from day care . . . she's not me—she's somebody else, not me. That girl who lay there on the floor watching cartoons with Brittany, that girl who didn't get that job at the phone company—like, she's another person. She's not me, she's somebody else . . . y'know, like Alex says."

"She *is* another person," Rojas agreed. "Like this dude sittin' here looking for hajjis is not *me*, man."

"I dunno, y'know, how I'm gonna tell Brittany about all this," Kelsi said. "Maybe I won't have to. Maybe she'll just *hear* that it happened."

"Don't think *that*," Sean said.

"Her father's not so bad." Kelsi shrugged, speaking without emotion. The analytical side of her mind was beginning to imagine Brittany without her mother. "I mean, he was a real SOB to me and all, but he was—still is, I guess—a good father to Brittany. Funny thing, y'know—all the fights we had . . . y'know, after watching Wellman get shot, all those fights don't seem all that bad, at least by comparison."

"It sure does put things into perspective," Sean agreed.

"I like, y'know, really never imagined this," Kelsi said, shaking her head at the irony. "A year ago, if you woulda described this night in this place, I would have said 'no *way*, man.' A year ago, I hadn't ever even handled a gun, much less an M16. But here we are and it still ain't even over."

"Amen," Rojas agreed.

"What gets me," Kelsi said, "what gets me the most is that, like, I don't feel the least bit freaked out. My ex keeps Brittany out until after nine, I come *unglued*, but I'm sitting here in this toilet surrounded by dead people, and guys outside who wanna kill me—kill us *all*—and I just, y'know . . . I just don't know. I don't feel freaked out."

"Most people don't get tested as you have tonight," Sean said. "Maybe the Lord is responding to an extraordinary situation by giving you extraordinary strength."

"Like here we are walking through the valley of death," Rojas whispered. "Like, y'know, in the Twenty-third Psalm."

"Or *sitting* in the valley of death," Kelsi said, almost chuckling.

"Sometimes it's while we're sitting in that valley, when we're in our darkest hour, that's when the Lord is closest to us," Sean said.

◆　◆　◆

The darkest night to Him is light,
And thro' the shine or shade,
He speaks in tones of tender might,
"My child, be not afraid."

Child, be not, be not afraid;
Child, be not, be not afraid
The darkest night to Him is light,
And thro' the shine or shade.

From the hymn "Be Not Afraid"
Words by Alfred J. Hough

21

I Shall Not Be Moved

The fear of bogeymen coming by night faded with the first purple promises of dawn, but with the promise of light came the prospect of a burning sun and rising temperatures—and bogeymen coming by day.

In the distance, they could hear the sound of gunfire—fierce gunfire. Apparently Capt. Clark's command was still under attack from the bad guys. There was also the sound of helicopters, which meant that the besieged troops had some backup. However, an attempt to reach Clark's position on the JTRS brought only the static of uncertainty from the radio, and expressions of concern and doubt on all the American faces.

"I wouldn't worry about it," Sean said. Everyone had looked to him for words of encouragement. "No news doesn't *always* mean bad news."

"I dunno," Dustin Grob said, shaking his head and ripping open an MRE. "Maybe we got forgot. Sure sounds like they got bigger fish to fry."

"They know where we're at," Sean assured him. "They've probably got somebody coming for us right now. I'm sure Colonel Folbright has sent more troops down to relieve us. We made it through the night. The worst is behind us. We're cool."

"Cool's the first thing I'm gonna do when I get back to Lex, man," Rojas said. "Cold shower and a cold beer . . . then another cold shower and another cold beer . . ."

"Don't get me started thinking about that." Grob laughed.

Kelsi smiled.

Tyler Kraus did not.

Sean saw hope in the lightening of the mood, but he was worried about his chaplain's assistant. He sensed that Kraus was feeling guilty that he had failed to protect the chaplain last night. It was quite evident that this deeply troubled him. Sean wanted to take him aside, but there was no aside to take him to in the crowded rooms of the small shack.

"Bobby's waking up," Kelsi said, turning to the injured man.

"Where are we, man?" Bobby asked.

"We're camped out in Mook, Bobby," Kelsi explained. "It's all gonna be fine."

"I feel like I'm on fire," he said, wincing. "My leg feels like it's on fire, man."

"That's a good sign," Kelsi lied. "Means you got feeling in your leg."

"It really, really . . . hurts."

"Gonna give you something," Kelsi promised, looking up.

"We don't have no more morphine," Rojas said nervously.

"Got some in the Humvee," Grob said. "I'm sure there's some in the Humvee. More MREs, too . . . I'll go get 'em."

"Are you sure?" Sean asked.

"Sure, I'm sure," Grob assured him.

"I mean, are you sure that you want to go *out there?*"

"Why not?" Grob said. "We haven't seen anybody out there in that alley for hours. An hour from now there's gonna be all sorts of village people out there running around."

"That's funny." Kelsi laughed. "Village people?"

"I meant village people, not *the* Village People. I mean the people that, y'know, people that live in Mook . . . the *Mook* people. What would *you* call them? Mookians?"

His absurd characterization was met by that giddy laughter that always seems to emanate from those who are sleep deprived. Even Bobby Budner attempted a chuckle.

"Don't worry, Bobby, Dustin's gonna be right back," Kelsi said.

"Now's the time," Grob said.

"Dude's itching to go out and score some drugs this morning." Rojas laughed.

"That's *real* funny," Grob snarled.

"Everything's funny today," Bobby said weakly, coughing when he tried to laugh.

Clutching his M16, Dustin Grob started down the alley toward the wrecked Humvee, which lay in the predawn shadows looking so dark and gray and lifeless. Yesterday, these fifty yards had seemed so much shorter when the Americans were all running.

There were still sounds in the distance—shooting and shouting—but in the alley, the only noise was from a small animal scuttling through some garbage that lay in a pile and a little bird fluttering in a small, withered olive tree.

At the corner of each building, he looked left and he looked right. He knew that it was an exercise in futility. If someone was hiding there, if someone was going to ambush him, they would do it long before he had a chance to look around a corner.

As he reached the Humvee, it began to look as though his whole mission was an exercise in futility. At some point yesterday, or during the night, someone had looted the vehicle. It was like coming out in the morning to find that somebody had broken into your car.

The doors were wide open, but of course the Americans had left them open as they'd made a run for it yesterday. So too, however, were the lids and doors to all the boxes and compartments within the vehicle. A bag of MREs that he knew he'd left behind had vanished. The mounted .50-caliber machine gun remained, but the ammo boxes were gone and there was evidence that somebody had tried to get the gun itself off its mount. They hadn't figured out how.

Grob reached beneath the seat and breathed a sigh of relief. The looters had missed the backup medical kit.

Giving a thumbs up to Alex Rojas in the distant window, he headed back.

About a third of the way to the house, Grob heard an ominous sound behind him.

He turned just as a burst of 7.62-mm lead splattered in his direction.

The sound of the rounds impacting the building beside him rattled in his ears. Dust and flecks of cinder block chipped off by ricocheting bullets filled the air, showering his face.

His first instinct in that split second, which stretched into slow-motion eternity, was to take cover.

As he dove behind a low stone wall, he felt the sting of having been hit in the ankle.

There were more shots and more impacts as he tried to fold himself into the smallest possible target.

Peering through the window, Rojas had seen at least five gunmen a split second before they saw Grob. The shout of warning was still stuck in his craw as the shooting started.

They had been coming to attack the house and had unexpectedly come across Grob.

"Only thing we can hope for is that they think he's part of a larger patrol and not one of us," Rojas said as he unleashed a few rounds of his own. "They'll think they're outnumbered . . ."

"And they get outa here?" Kraus added, pouring a stream of lead in the direction of the al-Qaeda punks. "Wishful thinking!"

"Was he hit?" Sean asked.

"Can't tell. He didn't fall . . . he took cover . . . so we can hope," Rojas said.

Bullets began ripping at the door.

As Rojas and Kraus blasted away at the bad guys, both Kelsi and Sean tried again to raise Capt. Clark's command post on the JTRS.

"Can't get through," Sean growled in frustration. "Why did it work yesterday? Am I doing this right?"

"Far as I can tell," Kelsi said, looking at him and closely at the machine.

"Mother of God." Rojas gasped as a well-aimed fusillade

blasted through the window, ripped into the opposite wall, and sent a cloud of masonry fragments and shrapnel swirling into the room.

The Iraqi civilians screamed and began sobbing.

"Hey, we got civilians in here!" Rojas shouted.

His words were answered only by another hail of bullets.

This time, they missed the window and hit the wall.

"At least the walls are bulletproof," Sean said hopefully. As the words left his mouth, he realized that the walls could stop a bullet, but probably *not* a rocket-propelled grenade. He prayed that the enemy would not bring such a weapon to bear.

"There's a *bunch* of 'em out there now," Kraus shouted as he jumped up to fire a burst from his M4 carbine.

"They're closing in on us. Keep your heads down!" he added as he ducked back down behind the safety of the bulletproof wall.

"Long as we got these walls, they can't hit us," Rojas said.

"Until they work their way up here and just jump through," Kraus said. "Remember how *we* got in here."

There was a brief pause in the firing and Rojas jumped up to take a few shots.

A couple of shots came in return, but not the heavy firing of earlier.

"Gettin' awful quiet out there," he observed.

"They're figuring out what to do next," Kelsi said, sighting her M16 through a crack near the door. "They're taking a breather . . . they're figuring out how to finish us off."

"How's Dustin?" Sean asked, changing the subject. "Can you see him down there?"

"Saw where he went down, but haven't seen him since then," Rojas replied. "Maybe he's hit? Maybe he's just trying to stay low."

Suddenly, they heard the unmistakable pop of an M16 being fired.

"There he is," Kraus said. He, like the others, was happy to hear that the man was still alive.

The firing of the lone M16 was answered by a chorus of AK-47s, and the three armed Americans opened fire from the house to cover Grob.

There was a bloodcurdling scream, and everyone looked at one another. Grob had been hit, perhaps fatally this time.

Why had he done it, knowing that he was cut off and surrounded? He should have just stayed down, but he opened fire, obviously to take some sliver of pressure off his comrades in the house.

Having hit Grob, the AK-47s began shooting at the house again, and the men at the window ducked down.

Kelsi squeezed off two more rounds from her position and saw a man fall. It took a moment for the reality to hit her. She had just shot a person!

The reasonable facsimile of that girl who lay there on the floor watching cartoons with Brittany, of that girl who didn't get that job at the phone company, had just shot someone with a burst of high-velocity bullets.

As she was processing the realization and watching this person writhing in the dirt about forty feet away, another man came to drag him out of the line of fire. She shot at the second man, and he fell across the first man.

The second man did not move.

Was he dead? Probably.

The scene looked almost comical—a wounded man squirming like a bug beneath the dead weight of what had been a human being.

Nobody came for the two downed gunmen, but their being hit elicited another furious hail of al-Qaeda gunfire, which in turn elicited another round of screaming and sobbing on the part of the woman and children.

"Can't they see—can't they *hear*—that we got civilians in here?" Rojas asked.

"They don't care," Kraus answered.

Rojas fired another burst and ducked as the enemy returned fire.

"We better conserve our ammo for when they get close enough to come through the door and window," Kraus suggested.

He looked at Sean. For the first time, Sean realized that their situation was untenable. Within an hour or so—perhaps sooner—the Americans would run out of ammunition to defend themselves. Shortly thereafter, the enemy would realize this.

If someone didn't come to their aid soon, the Americans would all be dead.

"If we could get behind them, we might have a chance of turning this thing around," Kelsi said.

"Well, there's no way that's going to happen," Kraus said. "There's only one way out of here, and they're pointing their guns right at it."

"There's a window in the kitchen," Kelsi said.

"*Where?*"

"By the stove," Kelsi said, standing up and pulling back the curtain that separated the main room from the closet-sized kitchen. "Right there."

"That? Nobody can get through *that*."

"I could," Kelsi observed, setting down her M16 and starting to unfasten her body armor.

"You can't be serious," Kraus said.

"Oh, yes I can," she said. "Without this crap I can wriggle through there. I've been staring at it for an hour. I'm a size four. I know I can."

"You're nuts."

"Don't argue with me, Sergeant," Kelsi said firmly, as she stripped down to her T-shirt. "You tell me how we're getting out of this and I'm all ears . . . but you *can't*, can you? There's no other way."

Kraus looked at Sean.

"I'm afraid she's right," Sean said. "She is slender enough to get through, and it looks like our only chance."

Rojas dashed into the kitchen, climbed onto the stove, and carefully removed the metal screen from the opening. It was incredibly small.

"Do you see anything outside?" Kraus asked. "They might be watching for us to do this."

Rojas carefully slid a broom handle through the hole and wiggled it, expecting to hear from a trigger-happy hajji.

Nothing.

"They're not dumb enough to think that somebody can actually fit through there." He laughed.

"Okay, lemme up there," Kelsi said. "We're wasting time."

With the men holding her, Kelsi slid her legs into the opening.

Slowly, they pushed her through as Sean prayed that she would not get stuck halfway.

Her hips made it, and so did her torso.

As her head went in, they let go, knowing that her center of gravity was already outside.

Kelsi could see only where she had been. Beyond the wall, her feet dangled in midair. It was a strange feeling, not knowing how far she was from the ground. She held the inside of the aperture until she had balanced her body, then pushed and let go.

The fall was about two feet, but she was through!

She looked up as the buttstock of her M16 emerged. Standing on a pile of bricks, she grabbed it and pulled it out.

Next came spare ammunition magazines. She grabbed some as others tumbled to the ground.

Next came her flak jacket.

Halfway through the hole, it stopped.

She jumped up and tugged on it.

"Push harder," she said.

"I am," came the muffled reply.

It didn't take long to determine that the body armor was inexorably jammed in the opening. It could be neither pushed, nor pulled—from either side.

"Sorry," came a voice from inside.

"That's cool," Kelsi said, taking stock of the situation.

The sun was just coming up as she moved down a narrow, deserted alleyway with her rifle in her arms and magazines shoved into all of her pockets. It was strangely peaceful with the early sunlight touching the foliage of a line of small fruit trees.

She had to admit that it felt good to be moving around without a hundred pounds of Kevlar hanging on her shoulders.

Quietly and carefully, she circled wide, passing through quiet streets as the city came to life.

She smiled as she passed black-clad women and bearded, elderly men who looked at her with bewildered expressions. Here they were, going about their business within a city at war, and here was a young woman in a T-shirt wandering around with a gun. This was the last thing they expected to see. Americans always wore armor—didn't they?

At last, Kelsi was at the opposite end of the street. She saw the Humvee and took cover near it. Ahead, she could see the backs of the al-Qaeda shooters. She counted at least nine. Four others lay immobile on the ground, including the two whom she had shot herself.

So far, the plan had worked. Somewhere, Kelsi had heard someone say that in war, no plan survives the first shot intact, so she began crawling toward the enemy as quietly and as carefully as she could. She wanted to be so close that it would be hard to miss, and be there before she fired that first shot.

She reached Dustin Grob. He was badly injured and could barely move. He started to say something, but she touched a finger to her lips.

Closer to the enemy she crawled.

If they turned, they might not see her at first. She was so heavily camouflaged by crawling in the Iraqi dust that she imagined herself looking like just another old burlap bag.

At last, she found her place of concealment and composed a short prayer. Kelsi prayed not for herself, but for the safety of the others, sort of implying to the Lord that they would be safe if she was successful.

Just as she picked out her target, the al-Qaeda were all in motion.

Running and shooting, they had rushed the building where her comrades crouched.

Kelsi squeezed the trigger once, twice, three times.

One fell, and then another.

She had hit two, then three, but the others now turned back toward her and Grob.

At first, they fired at the place where Dustin lay, thinking that he had been the source of the gunfire.

Kelsi fired and they saw her.

She missed, and the hail of gunfire forced her to take cover again.

In the distance, she could hear M16s being fired from the house. The bad guys were taking fire now from two directions, but they were also dishing it out.

Bullets were hitting near Kelsi, but the al-Qaeda were also shooting toward Grob. Didn't they realize that he was incapacitated?

Apparently not.

It was good, Kelsi mused, to see the enemy just as confused as she often felt.

Grob lay there helplessly as they moved back down the alley. In a moment or two, they would be close enough to have a clear shot over the small slab of masonry behind which he had taken cover.

Instinctively, Kelsi jumped up and ran toward Grob as bullets plinked and plonked all around him—and around *her*.

She grabbed his arm on the run and began dragging him toward a space between two buildings. He was incredibly heavy, but she got her hands under his armpits and somehow managed to drag him to safety.

The gunfire was coming fast and furious now, but she hadn't been hit. She interpreted this as their being really bad shots.

She glanced back to the street from the place where she had dragged Grob. She could see them, two of them, tantalizingly close, skulking behind a small tree next to a building. They were so near.

She decided that she was not going to back off and let them get to Grob, and to the others. There was only one thing that she could do.

She decided that they had to go, and she had to make this happen.

Taking a deep breath, she shoved a fresh magazine into her M16 and prayed that God would be at her side.

For the two jihadists, the sight came as a startling surprise. A slender woman in a T-shirt, her hair flying, was running straight toward them firing a gun.

One paused and felt a slug impact his body just below his left clavicle.

The other raised his AK-47, aimed, and squeezed the trigger.

◆　◆　◆

Though the tempest rage around me,
Through the storm my Lord I see,
Pointing upward to that haven,
Where my loved ones wait for me.

I shall not be moved,
I shall not be moved,
Anchored to the Rock of Ages,
I shall not be moved.

FROM THE HYMN "AS A TREE BESIDE THE WATER"
WORDS BY ALFRED H. ACKLEY

22

Take a Sad Song

Sgt. Tyler Kraus had shoved Chaplain Sean Rasmunsen into the corner of the space that passed for a kitchen, and had *ordered* him to keep his head down. A moment ago, when their eyes had met, Sean had the distinct impression that Kraus expected it to be the *last* time.

Hey Jude, don't make it bad . . . take a sad song and make it better . . .

It's funny, the way certain things pop into your mind at ridiculously incongruous times. It is not your whole life that flashes through your mind, but random milestone moments, and random, incongruous thoughts.

The Catholics have this practice of praying to saints, a practice that many Christians consider plain and simple idolatry. Many people hold firmly to the idea that praying to saints is not sanctioned anywhere in the Bible, and that praying to anyone other than God is idolatrous.

Sean had grown up believing this, but in the seminary, he had some long discussions with a priest. He explained that the prayers Catholics—and Orthodox Christians—say to saints are not prayers of adoration or worship, but pleas for intercession. Sean didn't really understand why Catholics couldn't just pray directly to God, but he had come to believe that praying to saints was not necessarily sinful. Faith is faith.

Catholics also had patron saints, who were saints connected to places and things. St. Christopher was the patron saint of travelers until the Catholics downgraded him, and St. Patrick is the patron saint of Ireland. Sean himself had even been tempted a time or two to ask St. Christopher to lend a hand of intercession. Lots of people who aren't Catholic celebrate patron saints. England recognizes George as its patron saint, even though it's officially Anglican—and nearly everyone celebrates St. Valentine's Day. Of course, Sean also knew about St. John of Capistrano, because this Franciscan friar had been dubbed the patron saint of military chaplains.

Another saint who always stuck in Sean's mind was St. Jude, commonly known as the patron saint of lost causes.

Rarely had a cause seemed so lost as the one in which Sean and his companions now found themselves in a little hovel in a place called Mook.

They were outnumbered, and soon they would be out of ammunition. Soon they would be overwhelmed, and soon they would be dead. It was a lost cause if ever there was one. Sean figured that it couldn't hurt to have St. Jude praying for them, just as he prayed for everyone around him.

Hey Jude, don't make it bad . . . ask the Lord to make it better . . .

The gunfire from the other room was continuous, as was the sound of the enemy's metal-jacketed rounds chewing at the wall beyond the window, and at the front door.

Just as Kraus had demanded that Sean take cover, Sean had grabbed the Iraqi woman and her two smallest children and had forced them into the corner behind him, where he tried to shield them with his own body and body armor.

The older daughter, who had been raped by two of the al-Qaeda gangsters yesterday, had run screaming to another room. Sean prayed that she had not been hit by any of the bullets ricocheting around these small rooms.

Sean knew that Alex Rojas had been hit, but not yet incapacitated. He knew that Alex was continuing to return fire against the attackers.

Kapow kapow kapow!

"Low on ammo, man," Sean heard Rojas tell Kraus.

Kapow kapow!

"I know—me, too."

Earlier, Sean had heard some banter between the two riflemen that contained the age-old phrase "save the last bullet for yourself." It put a lump in his throat. Al-Qaeda *did* take prisoners, but they didn't last long.

Hey Jude.

Kapow kapow kapow kapow!

A pause.

Was that it?

Kapow kapow!

No, their dwindling stock of ammo continued to hold.

Incoming rounds chewed into the walls of the tiny kitchen where Sean and the others were.

They ricocheted off the cast-iron stove and riddled pots and pans that hung on the wall.

One shot perforated a bag of rice or wheat or something, and a thin stream of grain began trickling onto the floor like a straw-colored waterfall.

Hey Jude, don't make it bad, Sean thought. What could it hurt to ask for Jude's intercession? Sean and his companions needed all the help that they could get.

"Saint Jude, hope of the hopeless," he whispered, paraphrasing the Catholic prayer he had borrowed from his priest friend. "Pray for us . . . and help us ask Him to make it better."

Kapow kapow kapow kapow!

"What's she doing? She's got Grob . . ."

Who? Sean wondered.

Could it be Kelsi?

Of course, it had to be Kelsi.

Had she made it?

Had she actually outflanked the bad guys?

She had!

Kapow kapow!

"Did you see that?"

Kapow kapow kapow kapow! Kapow kapow!

"I can't believe it!"

Kapow kapow kapow kapow! Kapow kapow!

"Look, she's . . ."

Kapow kapow kapow kapow!

"Kelsi!" Rojas screamed. "What the hell you doin', girl?"

Kapow kapow! Kapow kapow!

"Oh man! Cover her! Cover her!"

Kapow kapow kapow kapow! Kapow kapow! Kapow kapow!

"Oh no . . . man!"

Kapow kapow kapow kapow! Kapow kapow!

"I got one!"

Kapow kapow kapow kapow!

"Take that, you . . ."

Kapow kapow kapow kapow!

Another pause.

Was *that* it?

Hey Jude, don't make it bad, Sean thought. *St. Jude, hope of the hopeless, pray for us . . . pray for Kelsi. Lord, listen to me and Jude here . . . and make it* better.

There was a pause in the sound of gunfire.

"I can't believe—" Rojas started to say.

"She got two of 'em," Kraus said.

"Maybe that third guy, too," Rojas added.

Kelsi?

Was she all right?

Sean could hear the sound of Rojas putting down his weapon.

Was it over?

"What happened?" Sean shouted, standing up.

Kraus and Rojas remained crouched at the window. Kraus was still aiming his M4, but his finger was off the trigger.

The wooden front door, broken off its hinges the night before, now lay in splinters, chewed to firewood by the fusillade of 7.62-mm slugs from the al-Qaeda gunmen.

Inside, the children screamed hysterically.

Outside, beyond the door, the street was littered with bodies. Sean caught his breath and counted them.

Two. Four. Six. Eight.

Oh no!

Amid the al-Qaeda lay a figure in the gray-green uniform of the U.S. Army, a bloody gray-green uniform.

Kelsi!

"Padre, *no!*" Tyler Kraus screamed. "It's not *safe* out there . . . *stop!*"

Sean dashed into the street, running as fast as he could.

He didn't hear Kraus's footsteps behind him. He wasn't paying attention.

Kelsi looked so small, lying there without her body armor.

With her head tilted and her dark hair brushed back from her cheek, she looked as though she might be asleep.

Sean succumbed to the overwhelming urge to pick her up, to take her to safety.

Her limp body seemed so light.

As he stared at her closely, he started to be sick.

Her torso had been chewed mercilessly by the AK-47 fire. Blood squished and pooled against his chest. Her arms dangled uselessly. They were mere sinews, barely attached to her shoulders.

Amazingly, her eyelids flickered and he found her green eyes fixed on his own.

Her face seemed so peaceful, as though her body no longer registered any pain.

"We did it, huh?" Kelsi said in a whisper, almost smiling.

"Yeah, Kelsi," Sean whispered. "*You* did it."

"Remember that time?" Kelsi asked.

"Yeah, I sure do," he said, not knowing exactly which time she wanted him to remember.

"I asked you . . . y'know," she said, coughing weakly as several tablespoons of blood spurted out of her mouth and washed over her narrow chin. "I asked you . . . what's heaven like?"

"Yeah, you did," Sean said, remembering and trying not to begin sobbing.

"You said we'd all know someday—?"

The blood pooling in her mouth gave her voice a gurgling sound.

"Like we were saying . . . y'know, I think it's gonna be a whole lot *better* than here," she said, smiling.

"I'm sure of it," Sean said, thinking about seven-year-old Brittany and feeling tears begin to flow.

"Take a sad song and make it better," Sean hummed as though it were a lullaby. "Remember to let her under your skin, then you'll begin to make it . . . *better*."

Around him, the dust began to swirl, great clouds of it, mixed with chunks of dirt and pieces of rock. The dry dust blew across Kelsi, landing in the pools of blood and softening them. Her eyelids fluttered again, as though the dust were getting in her eyes.

Sean looked up. One, two, three UH-60 Black Hawk helicopters were swirling above. The morning sun on their tan hulls made them look as though they were made of gold.

The strokes of the rotor blades seemed to be singing, echoing Kelsi's words.

Better, better, better, better, better, better, better, better, better . . .

One of the choppers was slowly settling down on a patch of open ground just a short distance from where Sean stood with Kelsi in his arms.

It surprised Sean to find himself marveling at how strange the soldiers in the payload bay looked in their clean uniforms, with their uniforms so untainted by bloodstains.

◆ ◆ ◆

Swing low, sweet chariot,
Coming for to carry me home,
Swing low, sweet chariot,
Coming for to carry me home.

If you get there before I do,
Coming for to carry me home,
Tell all my friends I'm coming, too.
Coming for to carry me home.

FROM THE TRADITIONAL HYMN "SWING LOW, SWEET CHARIOT"

23

A Hand on Her Shoulder

No mother should then have to receive the call that Chaplain Sean Rasmunsen placed on the satellite phone that day.

Janis Schmitt had suffered as no mother should have to.

"I dunno, y'know, how I'm gonna tell Brittany about all this," Kelsi had calmly told Sean last night. "Maybe I won't have to. Maybe she'll just *hear* that it happened."

Janis Schmitt would now have to tell Brittany what had happened to her mom. It would fall to her to try to choose the words. Janis Schmitt had suffered as no grandmother should have to.

◆ ◆ ◆

Sean had held Janis's only daughter on the fifteen-minute flight back to FOB Lexington, staring down at her green, unblinking eyes.

After the long hours of pain and darkness, it was an almost absurdly short flight. Bobby Budner made the flight, and so too did Dustin Grob. The medics had stabilized him en route, and they got a transfusion going, but they only finished what Kelsi Schmitt had started. The tiny woman from Fort Dodge had dragged him out of the line of fire. *She* was the one who had saved his life.

Sean had held Kelsi on the flight back to FOB Lexington, staring down at her face, which was amazingly untouched in the storm of projectiles that had most literally cut her small body to ribbons.

Would her body armor have saved her?

Who knows? Sean could not begin to count the wounds.

Probably not; many of the bullets that had struck her arms would certainly have severed arteries.

Kelsi's face, looking so young and so peaceful, seemed almost to be smiling as he handed her off to the mortuary affairs guy at Lex. He leaned down and closed her eyes for the last time.

Tyler Kraus suggested that Sean ought to get himself looked at for injuries. He had so much blood on him that it was impossible to tell whether he also had been injured.

"I gotta make a phone call first," was all that Sean had said.

"It's two o'clock in the morning in Fort Dodge," Kraus said, putting his arm on Sean's shoulder. "Let's go get cleaned up."

◆ ◆ ◆

Sean had finally reached Janis shortly after Brittany had boarded the bus for her summer school program. Macaroni art would be made that day for a mommy who was never coming home.

He summoned forth the best words that he could offer, and still they felt shallow. He heard Janis sob, he heard her gulp for air, and he listened patiently as she composed herself, then fell again into the abyss. It was all too familiar.

Honor the dead. Comfort those left behind.

Sean still had the phone number for the pastor at Janis's church. He had spoken with the man back when the ex had taken Brittany. Sean promised Janis that he would give him a call and ask him to stop by. Maybe he could be there when Brittany got home. Janis had thanked him.

He told Janis that Kelsi had not suffered, and she thanked him for saying that—although her tone said that she thought he was lying.

Strangely, Kelsi really *hadn't* seemed to suffer at the last. Sean hadn't stopped to wonder why until he confronted Janis's disbelief.

Was there a logical reason that she felt no discomfort despite her body having been shredded?

It could have been shock. Perhaps it was massive nerve damage or a severed spinal cord.

Did there need to be a logical reason?

What if there wasn't one?

Deep inside, he knew the answer. Sean knew that his prayers had been answered in a mysterious, incomprehensible way. He knew that there was another hand on Kelsi's shoulder this morning, another hand to show her the way home.

Sean finished his call to the pastor in Fort Dodge and put down the satellite phone. His head should have been spinning from the mixture of exhaustion, grief, and sensory overload, but he felt strangely calm. Maybe it was the endorphins that his body was generating, or maybe it was four hours of solid, uninterrupted sleep, or maybe it was something else. Perhaps this clarity and tranquility was drawn from the same source that had calmed Kelsi as they all sat in that room.

He and Tyler Kraus headed out to make the rounds. Lt. Col. Amos Folbright had requested a briefing from Sean, but the first stop was the combat support hospital to check on Dustin Grob and Bobby Budner. The irony was that Budner, the wounded man who was the catalyst for Grob going to the Humvee for morphine, was going to pull through. For Grob, it was still touch and go.

As he walked into the hospital, Sean smiled and nodded at the people whom he passed. It was his usual routine, and it typically was met by a return smile, and often a greeting. Today, several people stared at him with strange expressions on their faces.

"What is it?" Sean finally asked a doctor whom he knew pretty well. "Why's everybody looking at me funny? Do I have something in my teeth?"

"No, Sean," the doctor said with a grin. "It's all over the Internet. Haven't you seen it?"

"Seen what? I've been kinda busy the last couple of days . . . haven't had much time to be surfing the Net."

"Let me show you," someone said.

Sean stared in disbelief.

Everything in the world was public now, and instantaneously so.

On the doctor's laptop was a picture of Sean on the Reuters website. It had evidently been taken from the Black Hawk that had picked them up that very morning. He was holding Kelsi in his arms, his body turned so that the cross insignia on his uniform was perfectly centered. He was looking upward with a resolute expression on his face. The caption said something about a brave chaplain committing a soldier to God.

Sean was dumbfounded.

What should he think?

What was he supposed to think?

It struck him as terribly off-putting. On one hand, it was a reminder of a bloody mess that was already burned into his mind, and the sight of which made him sick. On the other hand, nobody likes to see candid pictures of themselves.

"That's awful," Sean said sadly. "I can't look at it. It's just awful . . ."

"It's horrible, but it's a powerful picture," the doctor said approvingly.

"I hate to say it," Tyler Kraus said. He, too, was seeing the image for the first time. "But it's *you*. That's how people see you . . . You're the man, Padre."

Sean just shook his head and moved on to visit the wounded from the night before.

For Bobby Budner, the long night in the house in Muqdarubah was oblivion. He had no memory, no knowledge of what had happened.

For Dustin Grob, it was a nightmare burned into his psyche as though with a branding iron.

"Man, I really screwed up." Grob gasped. "I got all those people killed. If I hadn't wrecked the Humvee, and if . . ."

"Don't say that," Sean said, looking down at the man who was bandaged head to toe. In many places, the blood still soaked through the dressings. He'd already had surgery and would be on a fast track to the U.S. Army medical center in Germany by this time tomorrow. The doctors hadn't even started to worry themselves about whether he'd lose his legs. They were just trying to keep him from losing his life.

"It's not your fault. You didn't get anyone killed. You did the best you could in a bad situation. You were a true hero going out for medical supplies like you did."

"Got myself shot . . . and that got Kelsi shot . . . and . . ."

"She was a brave soldier, just as you were."

"Chaplain, she saved my life," Grob said insistently, despite being short of breath from a perforated lung. "You gotta tell people that . . . you gotta tell people she was a real hero."

"You were *both* heroes out there," Sean assured him.

"You gotta tell . . ." Grob said painfully. "What she did, y'know . . . can't catch my breath . . . Chaplain . . ."

"Yeah?"

"Chaplain . . . ask God . . . to help the docs . . . help fix up . . . my lungs . . . okay?"

"You're in my prayers."

Sean's rounds at the hospital did not end with Dustin Grob. The Battle of Muqdarubah had resulted in the worst casualties that the 2nd Battalion of the 77th Infantry had suffered in more than two years.

The American show of force in Muqdarubah had been no secret, even if the operational details had been. There would be plenty of recriminations to go all around, but somehow al-Qaeda had learned the details and had decided to launch a major ambush. In the end, they had paid dearly, but so too had the Americans and the Iraqi Army. One did not want to think about what would happen to the al-Qaeda bad guys when the Iraqi Army caught up to them in the smoldering wreckage of the Battle of Mook.

Out of that smoldering wreckage came the bodies of nine dead Americans and more wounded than had been inside the FOB Lexington combat support hospital since Sean had been there.

It was after the dinner hour when Sean finally arrived at the Tactical Operations Center for his meeting with the battalion commander.

"It's been a busy day," Folbright said.

"Pretty busy for the folks at the hospital," Sean replied.

"A whole lot busier," Folbright added. "They're gonna be doing an all-nighter . . . How are *you* doing?"

"Guess I'm pretty tired," Sean admitted. "Didn't sleep too well when I got back . . . got a few hours, but woke up early and couldn't get back to sleep. Hope I can get a couple more hours tonight."

"Saw your picture on the news," Folbright said, nodding toward his laptop.

"Oh, that," Sean said, shaking his head.

"Looked pretty good, I thought. Your fifteen minutes of fame."

"Glad it's over," Sean said, glancing at his watch. "The fifteen minutes, that is."

"That's what I wanted to talk to you about," Folbright said, leaning across his desk. "What that girl did . . . they say she was a hero."

"She volunteered to go out and outflank the enemy. That took a lotta guts."

"Pfc. Schmitt was the only one who volunteered to do that?" Folbright asked. "Nobody else would go?"

"Nobody else *could*," Sean explained. "There was a hole, a sorta vent, in the back of the kitchen. It was the only way out except through the front door. Pfc. Schmitt . . . Kelsi . . . was the only one of us who would *fit*. It was so tight that we couldn't even push her body armor through after her."

"So she went into action knowing she had no protection?" Folbright asked, beginning to take notes.

"Yeah . . . I never saw her again until . . ."

"I think she deserves to be written up, don't you?" Folbright said, looking at Sean as though for guidance. By *written up*, he meant a formal request for a posthumous medal.

"I'm not sure what the exact criteria are," Sean said. "But I do think that some form of recognition is certainly in order in Kelsi's case. You oughta talk to Sergeant Kraus; he saw more than I did."

Kraus, who was waiting outside Folbright's office, was summoned into the inner sanctum. After an exchange of salutes and pleasantries, the colonel invited him to sit down and tell the story of what he saw from the window as Kelsi had outflanked the al-Qaeda gunmen.

"She got three or four of them right off the bat," Kraus explained. "Then they opened fire on her and on Grob. She dragged him out of the way. Don't know how a girl that size could lug all that dead weight, but . . . y'know."

"Go on," the colonel said, continuing his scribbling of notes.

"Man, that's when it happened," Kraus said, almost teary eyed.

"What happened?"

"There was a couple of them by a tree. We just could *not* manage to hit 'em from where we were . . . me and Rojas . . . we just couldn't. They were shooting at us and she just rushed 'em. All of them . . . behind the tree and everywhere . . . they just turned and opened up on her. I saw her get hit but she kept coming."

Folbright had stopped taking notes and was hanging on Kraus's every word.

"Well, she got two of them . . . even though . . . I saw the rounds hitting her . . . I saw her arm get hit, y'know . . . her bare arm. She was just wearing a T-shirt . . . and even though she got hit . . . she kept shooting with her other arm."

The lieutenant colonel uncapped a water bottle and handed it to the sergeant, who took a long slug and a deep breath before he continued.

"Finally, after she had got two of them down . . . and both her arms were just blown apart, she dropped her gun . . . and she dropped to her knees. Then the bastard, sorry about my language, Padre . . . he just kept shooting. All the time, she was just staring at him. All this took about five seconds . . . but it seemed like an hour. Me and Rojas were just blasting away trying to hit this guy and finally we did. I remember his head just going *poof* in a pink cloud . . . turns out he was the last one standing."

"And where was Pfc. Schmitt by this time?"

"The next thing I remember after the blood and brains of this guy hitting the ground was Chaplain Rasmunsen running like hell, sorry Padre . . . out toward where she was. I guess she was all the way down by that time."

Sean nodded.

"Sir, are you gonna write her up for a medal?" Kraus asked.

"Yes, I am . . . Distinguished Service Cross for sure," Folbright said, nodding.

"Medal of Honor's more like it," Kraus said. "Begging your pardon, Colonel . . . sir."

Sean thought about it that night.

He thought about Kelsi, he thought about her medal and he tried *not* to think about that picture circling the world on the Internet.

Mainly, he thought about his conversation with Janis Schmitt. She had lost both a son and a daughter, and would probably never fully come to grips with this.

A medal would be issued, and it would be given to Janis Schmitt, probably in a ceremony, probably with flags and with colonels hovering about. Brittany would be at her side, and after the hugs and handshakes were over, there would be questions. Brittany would want to know what and where and *why*.

Medals are issued by the living to honor the dead, so that individual heroism will always be part of the collective memory.

Personal memories are kept alive in the hearts of those who need no medals as reminders.

Two decades after she had watched Kelsi begin the second grade, Janis once again would be going to back-to-school night in a second-grade classroom. The flags would now have been furled, the colonels gone back to wherever colonels go.

Janis would stand alone.

Someone would ask, "Where, umm, is Brittany's mother?"

At every step of her growing up, Brittany's grandmother would have to revisit an empty hole in their lives with an explanation of why Brittany's mother could not be there.

"Oh, I see . . . umm . . . I'm *so* sorry to hear that."

The subject would be changed, the emptiness merely reinforced.

What medal issued by a mortal government could fill such emptiness?

Sean's last thought before sleep overtook him was of that hand that had been on Kelsi's shoulder this morning, that hand that had shown her the way home.

He knew that in Janis's most lonely moments, that hand would be on her shoulder as well.

◆　◆　◆

After the mist and shadow,
After the dreary night,
After the sleepless watching,
Cometh the morning light;
Beautiful, soft and tender,
Leading the soul along,
Over the silent river,
Into the land of song.

After the thorny pathway,
After the storms we meet,
After the heart's deep longing,
Joy and communion sweet;
After the weary conflict,
Rest in the Savior's love,
Over the silent river,
Safe in the home above.

From the hymn "After the Mist and Shadow"
Words by Frances Jane "Fanny" Crosby

24

The Home of True Peace

"*Les Américains sont incompétents,*" Isabelle Laclerc said peevishly. "*Les Américains sont hors de commande.*"

"You blame the Americans for being out of control at the Muqdarubah Uprising?" Anders Hortling asked.

"*Mais qui*—but of course. They have their Army, they could make us safe, but the children do not feel safe after the American Army is so badly pummeled in Muqdarubah this week."

"Has this caused your enrollment to change?"

"But of course. The children are afraid to come out of their houses," Isabelle assured the Danish journalist.

"I see children in the classroom today."

"Not so many as usual. They're frightened."

Had Hortling arrived in Safaliyah just two days earlier, he would have found a much quieter town, and certainly more children in the classroom. Mustafa Ilik had approved his request for a visit before the upheaval in Muqdarubah had created a tide of refugees and a mood of uncertainty in this corner of Diyala Province.

It was a case of good timing for Hortling. He had arrived in Safaliyah the day after the debacle in nearby Muqdarubah, so there was plenty to write about. Indeed, the media was already saying that this was the worst thing to happen in Diyala Province since the insurgents captured Baqubah back in 2007. This comparison may or may not have been the case, but the media had characterized it thusly, so it must be true.

"It's not the Americans," Mareike De Vries told Hortling as she came into the room to collect materials for her next class. "It's al-Qaeda."

Isabelle gave her an icy look that asked, *Whose interview is this, anyway?*

"This is not just my opinion," Mareike said, as much to make Isabelle angry as to straighten out the journalist.

"Whoever is to blame, it is very difficult." Isabelle shrugged, lighting another cigarette.

Mareike would have liked to stay to debate Isabelle and to share another opinion with the young Dane, but she had a class to teach.

Isabelle *was* right about one thing, though; it had been a difficult few days. Some of the children had stayed away, and so too had several of the Iraqi teachers. There had been no direct threats in Safaliyah, but the news from Muqdarubah was unsettling, and Muqdarubah was only forty kilometers away.

Just as everyone considered the geography of Diyala and the proximity of Safaliyah to Muqdarubah, geography was the class on Mareike's agenda for the day. The subject, in its abstract and academic sense, was not Mareike's specialty, but she was able to follow along with the lesson plan that had been prepared by the absent Iraqi teacher. Curiously and coincidentally, this week's lesson was on the United States, and the class came on Wednesday.

With Wednesday came Sean's weekly visit to the blessed normalcy of the school in Safaliyah, and the sweet island of warmth that characterized his relationship with Mareike De Vries.

His visits to the school were timed for the afternoons, as the older kids streamed outside to kick the footballs around and to continue to experiment with that curious American sport played with bags laid out on a diamond-shaped field.

This Wednesday, however, the routine had changed. Because of the heat, outdoor time had been scheduled for the morning, so the Religious Support Team arrived to find the children and their teachers in the classrooms.

He found Mareike in the classroom and lingered near the doorway, watching as she attempted to explain the American Midwest to Iraqi nine-year-olds. It was amazing to see a Dutch woman communicating, mainly in English, with Iraqi kids about a country none of them had ever seen.

Mareike saw him in the doorway and felt the excitement of his welcome presence. As she glanced at him, she also realized that the man with the growing relevance in her life had a unique relevance for the daily lesson in the classroom.

She gestured for him to come in and come to the head of her class and to speak to them. They recognized him immediately as the guy who showed up every week to play ball, and their smiles registered their pleasure.

Sean began with the Minnesota Twins baseball cap that he was wearing, and pointed to the Twin Cities on the map that was taped to the wall. This began his discourse on the Mississippi River, which flowed between the twin cities, and the great prairies that surrounded it as it flowed south. He told of how the Mississippi was once called the "Father of Waters," and explained why. The kids wanted to know if America's Father of Waters was as big as the Tigris or the Euphrates and he told them that it was.

For Sean, it was an opportunity to put the recent horrors of Muqdarubah out of his mind. For Mareike, it was a chance to sit back and watch the man she loved interacting with the children. Would it happen? If their relationship continued, would it include children of their own? Where would these children be when they were nine-year-olds? *Am I getting ahead of myself?*

The lecture ended with a lucky little girl being rewarded with the prized baseball cap, and the kids all rattled off to their next class.

"You were in Muqdarubah," Mareike said as she gathered up her things. "I saw the picture of you on the Internet."

"It was terrible out there," Sean said.

"The young woman in the picture . . . did she . . . ?"

"She died."

"So sad."

"Yeah . . . she had a daughter a little younger than the kids in this class."

"That is so lamentable . . . poor child," Mareike said sadly. "It is the ones who are left behind for whom we feel the worst."

"On that subject, I want to ask your help . . . and Hala's help."

"Of course," Mareike said. "What is it?"

"The ones who were left behind . . . there were many lives disturbed and disordered by everything that happened over there," Sean said. "We took refuge in a house over there, seven of us . . . and there was a family, a mother and three children. The older daughter was raped by the al-Qaeda creeps who took refuge in the house before we did."

"And you want to go back—"

"And do anything we can for them," Sean said, finishing her sentence. "And sooner rather than later. I don't know the language, I don't know the customs—but you do, and certainly Hala does."

"You are so generous to go back there after such a terrible battle."

"Their home got wrecked," Sean said. "I promised myself I'd do something. I scrounged a bunch of stuff; it's loaded in the Humvee."

Mustafa Ilik was reluctant to agree to let two of his teachers run off to Muqdarubah when he was shorthanded, but he agreed to listen to Sean's story. Shrugging his shoulders, he said simply that he'd wish he had if he didn't, and told them to go with Allah's blessing.

The chaplain's duty to nurture the living was a concept that was not lost on the headmaster.

It seemed like weeks since Sean had first driven the forty kilometers to Mook. Not driving in a convoy slowed by the presence of the heavy Bradleys made a big difference, and less than an hour after they piled into the vehicle, they were rolling through the outskirts of the city.

What a difference was made by those couple of days. The 69th Brigade had pulled out all the stops, surging an entire reinforced battalion into keeping the peace. Helicopters were overhead, and Sean counted four Abrams main battle tanks. He lost track of the number of Bradleys, but noticed two of those with which he had first entered the city. Their battered hulks were on flatbed trucks, ready to be hauled out and back to Baghdad—to be either repaired or simply scrapped.

He presented his orders to the MP directing traffic, and asked directions to the company of 212th Engineer Battalion, which was tasked with reconstruction.

The major in charge looked at the orders drafted by Lt. Col. Folbright and complained, as Mustafa Ilik had, that he was shorthanded. However, orders are orders, and having registered his complaint, he told four of his guys to load up and follow Sean into the city.

Sean noticed that Tyler Kraus tensed up and swallowed hard as they retraced their route through Mook. He felt the same way. Reliving the nightmare was beyond painful. Ever since the battle, Kraus had been far less communicative than usual. Now he was practically mute.

From the rear of the Humvee, Mareike and Hala sensed by the silence and the looks cast between the two men that it had, indeed, been a nightmare.

If driving the streets was hard to do, turning onto the small street in which they'd endured the ordeal was brutal. The wrecked Humvee was still there, still waiting for someone to pull it onto a flatbed truck and haul it away.

The bodies of the dead were all gone—one of the first things that had been done after the battle ended had been to remove the dead—but a sickening brown stain still soiled the ground where Kelsi Schmitt had become a hero. Sean felt the MRE churning up from his gut, but managed to choke it back down.

At the end of the street, they saw her, shrouded in black, tending a campfire near what had once been a doorway. Two small children sat nearby watching trancelike as the American vehicles rumbled toward them.

"Look at that place," Kraus said in disbelief. "I never even bothered to look back at it when we pulled out . . . I guess I was too busy lugging Wellman out to get him on the chopper."

"It looks like a . . ." Sean started to say, trying to grasp the incredible bullet damage to the facade of the little home. "It doesn't even look like a house. It looks more like . . . like a cave."

Sean ditched his helmet in the seat of the Humvee and walked toward the house carrying an open box of rations.

"As-salaam alaikum," Sean said, smiling.

"Alaikum . . . alaikum as-salaam," the woman replied warily after just staring at him for a moment. It had to have come as an incomprehensible shock that one of the faces from that hellish night should reappear so soon—and especially the one with the cross pinned to his uniform.

She was confused yet further by the presence of the two women, an Iraqi and a Westerner. The last Western woman she had seen on this street had gone away in tatters, blood pouring from her body.

"As-salaam alaikum." Hala smiled. *"Kaifa halak?"*

"Alaikum as-salaam," the woman replied, and then she responded to the query as to how she was doing by explaining

at some length all the reasons why she was *not* doing very well at all.

She was glad to have someone to whom she could spill her concerns, to unburden herself of her misery and that of her family.

Hala explained that the Westerners had come with supplies to repay her for the involuntary hospitality that she had shown them. Hala also explained that if the older daughter had not seen a doctor, the Westerners would get her taken to one who would be sensitive to her religious concerns.

The woman peeked into the box of MREs that Sean had set on the ground and glanced toward the Humvee, where Hala had indicated there were yet more such goodies.

As the two Iraqi women communicated, Mareike smiled at the children and held out her hand in a gesture of friendship. The little girl shyly withdrew, but the boy touched Mareike's hand.

The sun shone and a slight breeze ruffled the leaves in the trees. It was another blisteringly hot day, but the breeze took the edge off.

Finally, after a spirited conversation, Hala turned to the Westerners.

"Fahima wishes me to go inside and speak with Amena," she said. "I should go alone, just myself."

Sean nodded.

Fahima. Amena. The names behind the faces. You spend a night in someone's home and leave without knowing their names. It felt not a little bit creepy.

"Sir," the engineer sergeant said, approaching Sean. "Sergeant Kraus was just filling us in on what happened to y'all here the other night. I'm sure sorry about that, y'know . . . but this place is a real mess."

"Can you fix it up?"

"Sure, we can set a window . . . shouldn't be hard to scrounge a new door. We could frame that in; could do it in a couple hours if we had all the stuff. Get out the masonry drill, throw in a few lag bolts. You'd have a solid door, probably better than what they had."

"We got Quikrete in the truck," an engineer private first class added. "We could clean up the front and get all those holes patched pretty fast. We could do it right now. What's it like inside?"

"Pretty messed up last time I was in there," Kraus said sadly. "More wall damage."

"We'll take care of that and scrounge up some paint. Ought to go pretty fast."

"She'll need a new stove, too," Kraus continued, nodding at the smoldering campfire. "We brought a propane one out from Lex to tide her over."

"Let's get started," the private said. "I'll get the Quikrete."

As he headed back to the truck, Hala emerged from the house and gestured for Mareike to come in and join her. The smaller children had lingered outside while Mareike was there, but as she entered the house, they did as well.

"I'm just as happy to wait out here," Kraus said, deliberately looking away from the building. "After what happened . . . y'know . . . I don't want to be reminded."

"I know what you mean," Sean said, nodding.

"Figure they're probably talking about female stuff," Kraus said. "After the daughter, Amena, got, y'know, assaulted."

"Yeah," Sean said. "If she hasn't had a doctor look at her, we need to get a medic, a female medic, over here. In the scheme of things, that's probably a lot more important than getting Quikrete on the front of the place. You can't put Quikrete on the holes in somebody's soul."

"Being back here . . . y'know, I've been thinking," Kraus said, whispering awkwardly. "Y'know, I didn't do a very good job of being a bodyguard for you in this thing."

"Is that what's been bothering you?"

"Yeah."

"You did *not* let me down," Sean said, making eye contact. "We got ambushed; it was out of your hands. You did what was necessary; you did what you could. You did everything you could."

"I fell asleep on the job," Kraus said. "I fell asleep on guard duty . . . I fell asleep at my post."

"At the last, when we thought it *was* the last . . . you shoved me into a corner of the kitchen and told me to get down. You were ready, you and Rojas; you were ready to give your lives. Remember the line from John 15, where He says that a man shows no greater love than to lay down his life for a friend?"

"Yeah."

"Well, that was *you*," Sean insisted. "You were *living* what John *wrote*."

"I was fighting to defend me, too," Kraus admitted.

"Yeah, but you were the guy with the gun; you *could* do that. I was the defenseless Padre depending on you to show 'no greater love.' Y'know what I mean?"

"Yeah . . . thanks, man."

Hala and Mareike stepped out of the house, and with them

Fahima. For the first time, Sean saw a relaxed expression on her face.

"Fahima asked us about you," Mareike told Sean. "She wanted us to tell about the strange 'crusader' who carries no weapons."

"It's the cross, isn't it?" Sean smiled, pointing to his collar. Fahima nodded.

"We told her that you were a man of the Book," Hala said. "We told her that you were not a warrior. She said that you had led the other *ulooj* soldiers in prayer. She could not understand the words, but she understood that it was prayer."

"I'm glad that you understood that," Sean said, looking at Fahima as Hala murmured a translation. "I wish we could have met under different circumstances. I mean, I wish we could have met before that terrible thing . . . y'know . . . that happened to Amena."

With the translation, Fahima nodded.

"I wish, too, that I'd had this with me that night," Sean said, taking a folded sheet of paper out of his pocket.

As he glanced around, the Americans knew that it was time to bow heads.

"*Allahumma ya mowlana antas-salaam, wa minkas-salaam,*" Sean said, addressing God and saying that He was eternal life and everlasting peace. "*Wa ilaika yarjaus-salaam, haiyyina rabbana bis-salaam, wa adkhilna daras-salaam, tabarakta rabbana wa-ta'laita, ya zal jalali wal ikram.*"

Simply put, the prayer, taken from the Qur'an, asked God to grant people a life in the home of true peace.

For the first time, he saw the trace of a smile on Fahima's face.

There were tears in Mareike's eyes.

◆ ◆ ◆

Now that the daylight fills the sky,
We lift our hearts to God on high,
That He, in all we do or say,
Would keep us free from harm today.

So we, when this day's work is o'er,
And shades of night return once more,
Our path of trial safely trod,
Shall give the glory to our God.

From the hymn "Now That the Daylight Fills the Sky"
Words attributed to Ambrose of Milan (Fourth Century)

25

Outside the Wire

"Sure have seen a lot of changes down here in Saf City," Sgt. Tyler Kraus observed. "I remember when—"

"You're talking like an old-timer." Sean Rasmunsen laughed.

"I *feel* like an old-timer," Kraus said. "Been in this place for more than a year. I've been in the same tent at Lex longer than I was in either of the apartments that I had when I was trying to go to school in Eugene."

Kraus had rarely mentioned his failed year at the University of Oregon, and Sean took it as meaning that the young man was looking again to the future and to resuming his education.

"Are you thinking of going back to school when you get out of the Army?" Sean asked.

"I dunno." Kraus shrugged. "Maybe. After Eugene, I went back to Coos Bay to get a mill job. When that didn't work out,

I joined this outfit. Maybe I oughta think about a career in the Army."

"That's a thought."

"*Not.*"

"We'll miss you," Sean said.

"I'll miss working with you, too. Can't say I'll miss the Sandbox, though. Hope we can stay in touch."

"Me, too," Sean agreed.

It was a routine day outside the wire. When Sean Rasmunsen had first come to FOB Lexington many long months ago, the U.S. Army outposts in Safaliyah had been like the fictional Fort Apache.

A lot had changed. Despite the nearby Muqdarubah Uprising a few weeks earlier, Safaliyah remained secure and well on its way to some sense of normalcy.

When Sean and Tyler had first met Jihan al-Qamar, the father of Bilal and Naja, the deputy director of public works in Safaliyah was playing catch-up. His department was concerned mainly with staying on top of repairs to infrastructure damaged in the ongoing violence. In recent months, however, he had been turning to new construction.

Today, as part of his "hearts and minds" rounds in Saf City, Sean had been invited to participate in the dedication of a new bridge. It was not a big deal, just a two-lane bridge paralleling another two-lane bridge that relieved a traffic bottleneck by having two lanes going in each direction. It was pretty routine stuff, but for Safaliyah it was like a bridge toward the future.

Mullah Yazid, the head man at the big mosque in Safaliyah, would be there, and the U.S. Army, whose 212th Engineer Battalion had been involved in the project, had suggested that it might be a good idea to have one of their own men of the Book present as well.

"It's all just politics, isn't it?" Kraus said, more as an observation than a question.

"Essentially, but it's nice that we've reached the point where it's politics, not war. It's also nice that they're being inclusive. I know that Yazid likes to run the show in Saf City, which is his prerogative. His mosque is here. It was here before we came and it will still be here long after we're gone, so I respect his right to be territorial. I'm glad that Jihan had a hand in inviting us."

"He's a good guy," Kraus observed. "But there's a lot of good guys in Iraq. Who would have thought?"

"Most people here just want to get on with their lives after all those years of Saddam's thugs, and then more years of insurgency and unrest, and of having us here, too."

"It'll be good to get back to Coos Bay," Kraus said, smiling.

"You're starting to see the light at the end of the tunnel, then?" Sean grinned.

"After breathing dust for more than a year, I'm looking forward to the ocean fog, you betcha. Also looking forward to more involvement in the church. I've learned a lot here."

"Maybe there's a seminary in your future, then?" Sean said.

"Never can tell. It's crossed my mind."

It was with a touch of sadness that Sean pondered the prospect of breaking in a replacement for Kraus. The Religious Support Team—the Unit Ministry Team—wouldn't be the same without him, but the team's loss might prove to be a seminary's gain.

◆ ◆ ◆

Kraus parked the Humvee, and the two men strolled over to the bridgehead where people were starting to gather. Mullah Yazid had not yet arrived, but they recognized Jihan al-Qamar standing with some people from his department. At his side was his son, Bilal.

When the boy saw Sean, he came running.

"Chaplain Sean, what's up?"

"Hey, buddy," Sean said with a grin, giving him a high five. "Good to see you here. Your dad's done some good work."

"My father has built a bridge," Bilal said proudly, nearly as pleased with his mastery of Sean's language as he was with his father's feat of engineering.

"And a wonderful bridge it is, too." Sean smiled.

Jihan greeted the two Americans warmly and told them through his interpreter that they had been strangers from his home too long.

"Yes, Chaplain Sean, Ty-ler," Bilal said excitedly. "Will you please come at my home?"

"Of course," Sean said, smiling. "Please tell us a time and day that works for you. We are always happy to accept your hospitality."

That having been said, Sean was introduced to several other Iraqis and the Corps of Engineers major who was on hand for the formalities.

"Wes Burns," the major said, accepting Sean's salute and shaking his hand.

"Sean Rasmunsen with the 2/77," the chaplain said, introducing himself and nodding at the bridge. "You guys have done a good job here."

"Bigger deal than you'd think, just looking at it. Most of the credit goes to the Iraqis, though. Time was that we'd have done most of the work on a deal like this, but about all we did was to give 'em some technical advice and bring in some heavy equipment for about a week."

"That's good to hear."

"Yeah. Seems like you know this guy," Burns said, nodding at Bilal.

"We go way back. Bilal's been one of my best buddies since I came out to Diyala. His dad's one of the guys you worked with on the project . . . Jihan al-Qamar?"

"Oh yeah. One of the brightest. Him and all the guys like him here. They're the future of the Sandbox, y'know."

"I know."

"Speaking of guys," Burns said, looking around. "Wonder when the mullah's gonna show up so we can get the show on the road."

"He'll be along in due course," Sean said, looking up and around and down the street that headed into the center of Safaliyah.

"What's that?" Burns asked, pointing down the street.

"Guy's coming awful fast," Tyler Kraus said, fixing his eyes on a car that was accelerating toward them about two blocks away.

It was one of those ubiquitous white cars with orange fenders that one sees everywhere on the streets of Iraqi cities.

"Taxi driver," Burns said in disgust as the car came closer and closer. "Crazy taxi driver in a hurry to get somewhere."

"I don't think so," Kraus said, dropping to one knee and shouldering his M4 carbine.

Everyone in the crowd had started to scatter now as it became apparent that the car was coming directly at them.

Kraus squeezed off a burst, trying to aim for the tires.

Having missed, he quickly raised the muzzle, aiming for the grille and the radiator beyond.

There was a cloud of steam, and the car seamed to veer away slightly, heading toward where the Religious Support Team had parked their Humvee.

Hitting it a glancing blow, the car with the orange fenders exploded in an orange fireball.

"Everybody okay?" Sean shouted as the last of the fragments were hitting the dusty street.

"That was good shooting, man," the major told Kraus.

"Thank you, sir," he replied modestly. "But it looks like we're gonna need to catch a ride back to Lex with you guys. That clown totaled our ride."

"No problem."

The scene could have been described as orderly chaos.

The crowd had moved away from the bridgehead as the Iraqi police began to form a perimeter around the burning automobile.

Sean could see Jihan al-Qamar shaking his head in disgust as he shooed his young son away from the fire.

This had to have been an awful blow for him, to have worked so hard toward this moment only to have it marred by another random act of violence by those who would deny Iraq's people the normalcy they craved.

"Looks like that puts a damper on the festivities," Wes Burns said. "Probably best that we just withdraw and let the Iraqis handle the situation. We'll get you guys transportation back to base."

"Thanks—and yeah, I suppose you're right," Sean said sadly. "I'd just like to go say a few words to Jihan before we take off. Y'know, a little moral support."

Sean had nearly reached Jihan when he heard a shout from somewhere behind him.

"Look . . . Look out!"

What?

Where?

He looked around, fixing his eyes on a dark blue Toyota. Like the taxi, it was accelerating toward the crowd.

It was the mark of al-Qaeda, a coordinated attack by two car bombs.

From behind him, Sean could hear the popping sound of police gunfire as they began shooting at the car.

People were shouting and running.

Suddenly he saw someone stumble and fall. He was in the path of the oncoming car.

It was Bilal!

"Oh God . . . No!"

He tried to get up, but he stumbled again.

A twisted ankle?

Sean ran toward him, but he was so far away and the car was coming so *fast.*

Sean—and everyone—watched in horror as the car bore down on the boy.

There was no hope.

Suddenly Tyler Kraus was there.

He was running, it seemed, faster than anyone had ever run.

He grabbed Bilal by his belt, lifting him as a person would lift a lightly packed backpack, and he tossed the boy through the air as though he were no heavier than a lightly packed backpack.

Bilal was still airborne when the Toyota struck Kraus with a gut-wrenching *crack*.

There was a cloud of dust as the car swerved—and then came the detonation of the bomb in an immense eruption of fire and smoke.

Sean felt the heat of the shock wave and the sensation of being knocked off his feet.

◆ ◆ ◆

Where is my wandering boy tonight—
The boy of my tenderest care,
The boy that was once my joy and light,
The child of my love and prayer?

O where is my boy tonight?
O where is my boy tonight?
My heart o'erflows, for I love him, he knows;
O where is my boy tonight?

Once he was pure as morning dew,
As he knelt at his mother's knee;
No face was as bright, no heart more true,
And none was so sweet as he.

O could I see you now, my boy,
As fair as in olden time,
When prattle and smile made home a joy,
And life was a merry chime!

Go for my wandering boy tonight;
Go search for him where you will;
But bring him to me with all his blight,
And tell him I love him still.

FROM THE HYMN "WHERE IS MY BOY TONIGHT?"
WORDS BY ROBERT LOWRY

26

Tour of Duty

Sgt. Kyle Lockhart found the chaplain sitting in a folding chair in the back row, listening as Spc. Ashley Mariott rehearsed a traditional gospel medley. Sean smiled when he saw Lockhart come in.

"Don't you just *love* Edwin Hawkins?" Sean whispered. "Lotta folks think of 'Oh Happy Day' when they think of him, but he's got a great songbook."

"Yes, sir, I agree," Lockhart said, looking toward the front of the chapel. He found the chaplain lost in his own world. He guessed that his allowing himself to become so totally absorbed in the choir and the music was a sort of coping mechanism. He guessed that a man who, as a pastor, had been through all of the things that Chaplain Rasmunsen had seen would need a place, a means to detach himself.

"It's very moving," Lockhart said, nervously shaking the chaplain out of his reverie. "The hospital called, sir . . . y'know, they just had a critical come in."

"Sorry," Sean said. "I've been a little distracted. I really appreciate you keeping me on top of it."

"That's my job, sir."

It actually wasn't, but at the moment, the job was vacant and the young sergeant from Iowa City was doing his best to take up the slack. Since the violent death of Tyler Kraus, Lockhart had gone all out to fill the void in the Religious Support Team. He had, in fact, been a second chaplain's assistant for many months, handling many of the behind-the-scenes clerical duties while Sgt. Kraus had concentrated on his role as Sean Rasmunsen's bodyguard and right-hand man.

They both missed Kraus and felt his loss.

Beyond the pain of losing someone who had become a friend, it is a strange sensation when someone who was always around no longer is. Even though you insist to yourself that you hadn't taken him for granted, you begin to realize that maybe you had.

At the ER, a young man lay on a gurney, three people in pale green scrubs busily attending to him.

As the chaplain and his de facto assistant approached, one of the trauma docs looked up. She wore a mask, but Sean could tell by the look in her eyes that this wasn't a good one. There had been so many like this over the many months. He had not exactly become numbed to watching these young lives teetering on the brink, but he had come to develop his mechanisms for coping.

This young man's tortured face was one that he recognized as a regular at Sunday chapel. He was part of the contingent that was still battling the Muqdarubah Uprising, and his luck had run out. His number had come up. It might have been an IED or an RPG. Sean didn't ask. Nor did he ask the extent of his injuries. He could see enough to know what he needed to know.

"Chaplain . . . I'm so glad to see you," the kid said, forcing a smile. "Halleluia and all that . . . Thank you for coming."

"I'm glad to be here."

"One thing . . . can you please . . ."

"Sure, what is it?"

"Tell them," he began, looking up at Sean with a worried expression. "Tell them I did my job . . . I held on as long as I could . . . tell my mom . . . tell my stepdad . . . tell 'em I'm just a guy . . . but I did my job . . ."

"Absolutely."

"One more thing . . . if you can . . . please . . ."

"Of course."

"Just, y'know . . . please just pray for me."

"Definitely, man, I sure will, I sure am," Sean promised.

"Thank you . . . Thank God."

"Do you want to pray together?" Sean asked.

"Yeah . . . but I can't think of any prayers, y'know."

"Why don't you just tell the Lord what you're thinking and we'll make it into a prayer," Sean said, holding his uninjured hand.

"I just wanna get better and go home, Lord."

"And Lord, hear our prayer as we ask for your hand in getting this man home. Amen," Sean added.

"Amen," the young man said as Sean felt his hand go limp.

Sean glanced at the doctor with whom he had previously exchanged glances. While the two doctors formally recorded time of death, she looked at Sean with an expression of deep sadness.

"It's hard, I know," Sean said, putting his hand on her shoulder.

"It's cumulative," she whispered. "It's hardest when it all just seems to pile up."

"I understand," Sean assured her.

"I *know* you do," she said as they stepped out of earshot of the other doctors. "If anybody does, I'm sure that it's you."

"If you ever want to talk . . ."

"Thanks, I will. I'll find you . . . I *will*."

"I've been thinking," Sean said when he and Lockhart had left the ER. "I've been thinking that I'd like to put your name in for chaplain's assistant."

"Thank you, sir," Lockhart said enthusiastically.

"You've been doing a good job all along—a *great* job, actually—and I know that you'd like this to be official."

"Yes, sir."

"You've got all the qualifications: rank and experience, not to mention your enthusiasm, so my filing the paperwork should be no more than just a formality. It should be through in a couple of weeks—bureaucracy time, y'know."

"I know, sir. Thank you, sir."

"Y'know, as I've said before, you don't have to call me *sir*. I'm just a chaplain."

"No, sir—I mean yes, sir."

"If you're gonna be a part—an official part of the Unit Ministry Team, you can just call me *Chaplain*."

"Yes, Chaplain; it will be an honor."

"How are you on your rifle proficiency?"

"I don't shoot much; I've always been a logistics guy."

"You're gonna have to get caught up. Unfortunately, being my bodyguard is a big element of your job, when we go outside the wire . . . y'know."

"No problem, sir . . . I mean Chaplain."

"Safaliyah is pretty quiet now," Sean said. "Huge change from when we both first were out here, but there are still surprises."

"I know," Lockhart said, bowing his head slightly at Sean's obvious reference to the incident that had cost Tyler Kraus his life.

"I know you're up to it," Sean said encouragingly. "Now why don't you take your weapon and get in a little practice, while I head over to the TOC to see why the colonel sent for me."

"I was sure sorry to hear about Sergeant Kraus," Lt. Col. Amos Folbright said. "I know that you guys were close."

"Thanks, Colonel," Sean said. "He will be missed—more than I would have realized. I'll miss him for selfish reasons, but yeah, he was a good man, one of the best. He might even have gone into the ministry himself."

"He *is* in a better place," Folbright suggested.

"Yeah, that's true," Sean said. "But it's still hard, always hard to see a young life—a promising life—ended so soon, and so violently."

"How's that Iraqi kid who he saved from the car bomber?"

"Bilal? Oh he'll be okay. He got a broken arm, but broken bones in kids that age heal pretty easily. Tyler must have tossed him forty feet. I don't know where he got the strength. Maybe it was partly the concussion from the blast that pushed Bilal that far. It sure knocked me about ten feet."

"I'm glad about that," Folbright said. "I mean glad that the kid's gonna be all right. I know that you're kinda friends with the family. Tell 'em that if there's anything we can do . . . anything *I* can do . . ."

"Thanks, Colonel, I will."

"I still think that we've made a lot of progress down there in Saf City," Folbright said. "Maybe it's just wishful thinking, but I hope and I believe that this is just an isolated incident, and not the beginning of a change for the worse."

"I hope so," Sean said. "I pray so."

"Like the Lord told my guy," Folbright observed thoughtfully. "Like the Lord said to the prophet Amos, the days are coming when the reaper will be replaced by the plowman, and the planter by the guy who's stomping the grapes. The best is still to come."

"That's from chapter nine of the book of Amos," Sean replied. "It's also where they talk about rebuilding ruined cities. I pray that the kids like Bilal will get to grow up in a rebuilt city—in a rebuilt land."

"Moving right along," Folbright said, "I have some good news for you."

"Good news is always the best kind." Sean smiled.

"Well, you're getting outa here . . . you're getting outa the Sandbox."

"*What?*"

"Orders came in about an hour ago," Folbright said, putting on his reading glasses and picking up the printout of an e-mail.

"It's from the chief of chaplains, General Tom Kline, at Fort Jackson. You may know him?"

"Yeah, well, I've met him. He gave a couple of lectures when I was in the Chaplain Basic Course. I think he was deputy chief back then. What'd he say . . . why?"

"That picture of you that got taken over there in Mook—the one that's been circulated all over?"

"Yeah," Sean said. "I hate that . . . it should have been a private moment."

"They tell me that with the Internet, there's no such thing as private moments these days," Folbright said. "At least in this case, it shows you being heroic."

"Pfc. Schmitt was the hero, sir. It was not *me*."

"The general is calling you 'inspirational.' That's what it says right here. That's why he wants you back at Fort Jackson . . . It's part of the morale and welfare mission at the Chaplain Center."

With that, he handed Sean the paperwork.

"My ministry is *here*," Sean said with disbelief.

"Your *tour of duty* is here at Lex," Folbright said sympathetically. "But I'd say that your ministry is with the men and women of this service—and wherever the chief of chaplains thinks you'd be the most effective."

"This just takes a minute to sink in," Sean said, looking at the orders. "I wasn't expecting . . ."

"I'm not happy to see you go," Folbright said. "I'm happy for *you*. You're not only getting your ticket out of Iraq, you're getting a ticket to new and pretty decent opportunities, careerwise. I wouldn't be surprised if it isn't *Major* Rasmunsen by the end of the year."

"It's not about rank."

"I *know* that. I know that you're committed to service that's above and beyond what the rest of us in the Army are doing. It's just that . . . well, think of it this way: With each step up the ladder, your opportunities for service expand."

"I know *that*," Sean said. "It's just hard, really hard, to leave a place where you've become emotionally invested . . . like I have at Lex."

"In any case, you'll probably not be happy to know that the guys back at the Chaplain Center, the guys in the Basic Course . . . they're putting your picture up everywhere."

"This is all getting out of hand."

"You knew when you enlisted that there would be orders that didn't make sense at the time," Folbright said. "It's not our job to wonder why."

"I guess in this case, I know why, and that's what's so troubling," Sean said.

"The *why* being that you don't want to be an 'inspiration,' that you don't want to be used as a showpiece?" Folbright said with a nod.

"You nailed it."

"Maybe they *need* you back there. At least that's what they've decided."

"When I think of the chaplain school, I just don't think of myself as an inspiration."

"How so?"

"They have a museum at the Chaplain Center—and in that museum, there's an old kapok life jacket. Sir, do you know the story about the Four Chaplains?"

"Yeah, it rings a bell . . . there's a stained-glass window at the Pentagon chapel."

"And one at West Point and one at a bunch of other Army chapels, too. The Four Chaplains were on a troopship called the *Dorchester* . . . This was one night back during World War II. They were in the North Atlantic, and a Nazi submarine torpedoed the ship. Most of the guys—there were nearly a thousand— had their life jackets off because it was a hot night."

"So when the ship started going down they were out of luck?" Folbright asked.

"Yeah, and the Four Chaplains gave up their own four jackets and helped find others and get them passed out. They were just young guys, just lieutenants. The story made a big impression on me . . . I even remember the names. There was a rabbi named Alexander Goode, and a Catholic priest named John Washington, and two Protestants named George Fox and Clark Poling. Fox was a Methodist, like me."

"And they all went down with the ship?" Folbright asked, knowing the answer.

"They continued to counsel people and pray with them until the last," Sean said, nodding. "The guys who survived said it was about the bravest thing they ever saw . . . They gave up their lives. It's like in John's Gospel, when Jesus says that there is no greater love than to lay down your life for other guys."

"Like Sergeant Kraus did?"

"Exactly like Sergeant Kraus did," Sean said. "Guys like him, guys like the Four Chaplains, they're the heroes, not me. I can't go back and pretend to be a hero in *their* shadow."

"But go back you must."

"In that same museum, there's a shot-up chaplain's kit," Sean continued, ignoring Folbright. "It belonged to a priest named Charles Watters. He was a chaplain with the 173rd Airborne in Vietnam. He was with an outfit that was under attack, and he went out again and again to carry guys to safety. I mean *again and again*. He was carrying guys on his shoulders. He was aiding the medics when he was killed. He earned a Medal of Honor. These guys are the *real* hero chaplains. All I did was scoop up a poor kid after the shooting stopped . . ."

"You're selling yourself short, Padre," Folbright said, bullying his way into the conversation. "Your Four Chaplains inspired others because of what people *saw*. You have an opportunity to help inspire folks because of what *you've* seen. You're not a stained-glass window; you're a guy who has been through it. That picture of you that they've all seen gives you cred."

"I guess I feel like I'm being pulled out of this place just as I'm starting to hit my stride."

"Nobody stays in the Sandbox forever," Folbright said with a wink. "There's still a world out there—and it's your turn to rejoin it. Maybe, y'know, just maybe it's all part of *His* plan."

"Which one of us is the chaplain again?" Sean said, appreciating the irony and finding himself grinning ever so slightly.

◆ ◆ ◆

Only an armor bearer, firmly I stand,
Waiting to follow at the King's command;
Marching, if "Onward" shall the order be,
Standing by my Captain, serving faithfully.

Hear ye the battle cry! "Forward!" the call;
See, see the falt'ring ones, backward they fall;
Surely my Captain may depend on me,
Tho' but an armor bearer I may be.

FROM THE HYMN "ONLY AN ARMOR BEARER"
WORDS BY PHILIP P. BLISS

27

Feu de la Passion

"Four days?" Mareike asked incredulously. "How can this be?"

"I thought it would take a month or so for them to get another chaplain out here," Sean said. "I've always been told that Uncle Sam's Army has a *shortage* of chaplains. I guess they're recruiting them a little faster than they were a few years ago."

Mareike De Vries stared at Sean Rasmunsen, trying to find the words. Their relationship was like a conversation interrupted in midsentence. A few kisses, talk of a life together, and suddenly—*this*. They had known that a moment like this would come, but neither expected it to come like this, and to come so suddenly.

◆   ◆   ◆

Outside, Sgt. Kyle Lockhart was having an equally awkward time with the kids. They wanted to know why Tyler Kraus was not there. They missed the man with the blue sunglasses.

He explained that the man with the blue sunglasses was gone, and the new guy with the shiny—prematurely balding—head was taking his place. He wondered whether Bilal had told the other kids anything about what had happened at the bridge, but they said Bilal was not there, either. He had broken his arm, and his parents were keeping him and his sister at home for a while.

Kyle knew a little bit about soccer, having played in elementary school, and soon he was making a reputation of his own among the children.

"Come on, play ball with us," Kyle shouted, when he noticed Isabelle Laclerc watching them from a doorway.

"I have a class beginning soon." She shrugged, grinding a cigarette with her toe and lighting another. "You need Mareike . . . she is *la femme jouant des jeux*."

"Oh come *on*," Kyle said. He had met Isabelle a time or two when he had accompanied Tyler and Sean on their regular Wednesday visits. He regarded her as snobbish and stuck-up, but with her Parisian manner and stunning beauty, she was the kind of woman upon whom a man could not help fixing his gaze.

She must have reconsidered, because she tossed her partially smoked cigarette on the ground and joined the game. The children laughed and giggled, knowing well the reputation that Isabelle had for avoiding sports.

When the game ended and the children scampered away to their classes, Isabelle lit another Gauloise.

"I'm sorry to hear about the death of your friend," she said, exhaling a cloud of blue smoke and folding her arms.

"Thank you. So are we. We'll miss him."

"So unfortunate."

"Yep."

"He was a nice man . . . for an American, of course."

"I thought you said that you had a class."

"Oh—that? I said that only to avoid playing football."

"But you played, after all."

"*Mais oui,*" Isabelle said, shrugging. "Why not?"

"You don't like sports?"

"Not my 'thing.'"

"Your friend Mareike, she likes to play."

"She's Dutch."

"Huh?"

"Dutch women lack that certain . . . savoir faire."

"French women don't lack . . . ?"

"Of course not. French women are . . . how do you say—?"

"I get the picture," Kyle said. She was beautiful—magazine cover beautiful, perfume ad beautiful—but she was arrogant beyond belief.

"*D'accord.*"

Isabelle took another long draw on her cigarette, exhaled dramatically, and touched Kyle lightly on the arm.

"Let me ask you a question," she said in a conspiratorial whisper.

"Okay . . ."

"The chaplain? I suspect that he and Mareike are lovers. Do you believe that this is true?"

"If they were, why would that be any of my business?"

"I've seen the way in which they look at one another. . . . I've seen *le feu de la passion* . . . the *fire*."

"I haven't seen the *feu* of *anything* myself," Kyle said.

"I've seen it in Mareike's eyes. They *are* lovers."

"In her *eyes*?"

"*Oui*, but of course. Ask him yourself."

"Have you asked *her*?"

"A woman *knows* these things . . . a woman *sees* these things. I see it in the eyes."

"But she didn't actually *say* anything?"

"*Non*." Isabelle shrugged, lighting another cigarette.

Kyle Lockhart found it hard to believe that on his first day on the job—more or less—as Sean Rasmunsen's assistant, he was standing in a courtyard with a chain-smoking French woman discussing whether the chaplain was having an affair with a teacher at a school in Iraq. It struck him as verging on sacrilege.

Inside the school, two people who had in fact expressed their mutual love faced a major obstacle on the road both had intended to travel together—indefinitely.

"I'm so . . . *overweldigd* . . . *geschokt* . . . *stunned* by this," Mareike stammered, defaulting to her native language as she tried to process translations to the English while her head was spinning.

"I came here knowing and accepting that I would have to tolerate hardships of all sorts," Sean told her. "I never imagined the irony of enduring the hardship of *leaving* . . . the hardship of being apart from *you*."

Being apart. Mareike's head was still spinning as she looked into his eyes, the eyes of this man she loved. She saw the sadness in his eyes through the prism of the tears that welled in her own.

She heard the sound of his voice, but found it hard to process translating the words.

"*Warr* . . . where is Fort Jackson?" she asked finally, trying to get her bearings emotionally.

"South Carolina . . . near Columbia in South Carolina," Sean said. He was also trying to get his bearings, trying to intuit Mareike's demeanor. She had said tearfully that she didn't want to see him go, but her mood had now changed to one that seemed almost angry.

"What will you be doing in Fort Jackson?"

"Basically, anything that the chief of chaplains orders me to do."

"But it has been so sudden," Mareike said, obviously exasperated at having a situation to which she had grown accustomed suddenly spinning out of her control. "I thought that you would be at Lexington for—"

"Until after the first of the year," Sean said, completing her sentence.

"Can't you tell them that you cannot go . . . that you are needed *here*?"

"That was my first reaction, too," Sean told her. "My first reaction was to resist change. From their perspective, I'm sure that it would seem counterintuitive that I'd want to stay here rather than get out of the Sandbox, out of Iraq. I do feel that I have given a lot, and I have a lot still to share with the troops out at Lex."

"You must tell them this."

"I have," Sean said. "I had a conversation with Colonel Folbright. I told him, but then *he* told me . . . His take on this is that the people going through the Chaplain Course back at Fort Jackson need people who've been here, who've seen this place. He thinks that they need me to go back there and to share what I've seen and experienced out here, to share it with new recruits who will follow in my footsteps. I suppose that I *do* have a lot to give them."

"It's about that picture, isn't it?" Mareike asked. "The picture of you and the young soldier . . . on the Internet."

"Yes, in part."

"I cried when I saw that picture," Mareike said. "I cried because of her painful death. I cried because someone I loved was so close to such pain . . . and mostly I cried because I knew that you no longer belonged to me."

"*What do you mean?*" Sean gasped. It was his turn to feel stunned.

"I read the things that were said about you on the Internet. I read the words that were written by people who do not know you, people who have never felt the warmth of your touch, the warmth of your kindness."

"A lot of that was pretty embarrassing," Sean said. "It's not *me* they're seeing; it's an abstraction, a symbol."

"A parable?" Mareike asked, looking him in the eye. "Is that not an accurate description, using a word from the *Bible*?"

Sean was speechless. It was a word that was disturbingly accurate. It was a word from his own lexicon, but a word that had eluded him in his search for a way to get his mind around his embarrassment over this disembodied parody of himself.

"But you *have become* this chaplain who they see in the picture," Mareike insisted. "You have become this man."

"I'm still me."

"Yesterday, you *were* . . . but today you *are*, as they say, *larger than life*. You have to accept this."

She paused, not knowing what else to say.

Sean paused as well. She was right, just as Folbright had been right. Something bigger than himself had been thrust upon him. It was a crossroads in his life, and he knew it.

"You could come," Sean said. "You could come with me to Jackson."

Could I? Mareike asked herself.

No.

"I have a commitment here," she told him. "Just as you have a commitment there."

"But we had spoken of sharing a life," Sean said. "We were . . . I thought we were starting to plan . . ."

"I would be too *egoistisch*, as we say in Nederlands, too self-ish, if I insisted that you would share yourself with me when you must give so much to your own people."

"But—"

"You are larger than life; I cannot be part of your life now," Mareike said, tears streaming down her face. "It's like all those reasons you said when we talked about whether ministers and priests should be married."

"But there is nothing to prevent me as a Methodist minister—"

"You belong to *them*, Chaplain Sean," Mareike said, wiping her tears. "I saw it when I saw that picture. There is something bigger in your life . . . that I cannot compete with. It would be unfair to you."

Mareike fought the urge to tell him that she wanted to travel with him to the ends of the earth—to Fort Jackson and beyond—but she realized that she could not. He did, in fact, have a new role that was larger than a life they might have shared.

"You could come," he said. "You could join me at Fort Jackson."

"What could I do in Fort Jackson?"

"There must be something," Sean said, realizing that he had not given much thought to this.

"Can I teach English in an English-speaking country?" Mareike argued. The voices inside her heart screamed at her to accept his invitation and give herself to the man she loved, but she resisted. She found the words, and with those words she argued both with him and with the Mareike within her who loved this man so much.

"I feel my *own* dedication to something bigger than myself," Mareike explained as the voices in her heart screamed for her to stop pushing herself away from this man. "I sacrificed a great deal of comforts to go to Darfur—to Iraq—because I, too, felt a *purpose*. But I cannot see a place for myself at a military base in the United States. I have never been to the United States. I do not understand the military life. I would feel so alien, so out of place."

"I understand."

"Then you will understand why I cannot go to Fort Jackson to be merely an *accessory* to *your* calling."

The roar of the voices inside her heart was deafening. Insinuating that she felt like an accessory to his calling was a cruel thing to say to such a caring and even-tempered man. She unconsciously put her hands over her ears to silence the voices even as she fought back tears.

"*Nee!*" screamed the voices. "*No!*"

"I fear that it cannot be," Mareike said. At last she was being honest with herself, although the voices in her head had won out over those within her heart. "I cannot go with you to a military base. We talked of living in the wide open places, where we could be part of something equally—but a military base? I would have no place."

"Are you saying that you can't be—that I must choose between you and . . . ?" Sean asked.

"No—I feel I do not want to be saying this," Mareike said. "Because I love you . . . but maybe, maybe I *am* saying this; maybe I *am* being *egoistisch*."

"Maybe you're being honest," Sean replied in a dejected tone.

"Maybe I am telling myself that *I* must make the choice," Mareike said. "Maybe it is *I* who must choose . . . who must make this difficult choice."

"You have to be honest and true to yourself."

"I want to be true to you," Mareike said as her heart ached. "But I cannot be true to myself in a military base."

"I understand."

"And I cannot ask you to choose, so *I have chosen*. You're right, you have so much to give . . . and Fort Jackson is where you must be. You have told me many times that you felt 'called' to return to a ministry here in Iraq, even though it seemed so counterintuitive . . . yes?"

"Yes, I believe I was, and yes, it was counterintuitive."

"You said that you were torn between the intuitive and the counterintuitive?"

"Yeah . . . what are you getting at?"

"I'm getting at this: You are now torn by your *calling*. You're being *called* to Fort Jackson."

"Called?" Sean wondered. "To *Jackson*?"

"Could it be that you were called back to Iraq so that you could be called to share your experiences?"

"What about . . . what about us, what we have shared . . . might have shared?"

"You belong *there*," Mareike told him with sadness in her eyes. "As we have talked, things happen for a purpose, yes?"

"Yes?" Sean said sadly.

"*Nee!*" screamed the voices in Mareike's heart. "*No!*"

She longed to be the focus of his life, but she knew he was no longer hers. He belonged to a calling that was larger than himself, larger that what might have been for the two of them. In reality, perhaps she really could *not* share this. Perhaps it really would be best for Sean if he were to go alone. For her to think otherwise, and for her to pull Sean away from his calling, would indeed be *egoistisch*.

"The work that you did here . . . what is the biggest purpose that can come of this?" Mareike said sadly, realizing that in the near future at least, Sean must accept a calling, and accept it alone. "You have seen, you have experienced things that you must share with others. You have seen things in these past months that you never saw on your first tour of duty outside Baghdad. As your colonel said, you *must* share this experience with others."

"I know," Sean admitted, both to her and to himself. "Deep down inside, I guess I know he's right . . . you're probably right."

"*Nee!*" screamed the voices in Mareike's heart. "*No!*"

"Could it be that *I* was called," Mareike began, tears in her eyes. "Could it be that God had a plan for *me*? Could it be that I am called on this sad day to knock sense into your head and make you see *your* calling?"

"But—"

"I am *one* person whose life you have touched. At Fort Jackson there will be *so* many."

"I hope we can . . . someday . . . maybe," Sean stammered.

"Go with God, my love." Mareike said, giving him a hug that carried a sense of finality. At the same time, though, her eyes told him of the undying love that her heart longed so desperately to share.

That afternoon, Kyle Lockhart intended to observe for himself this *feu de la passion* between the chaplain and the Dutch woman that Isabelle Laclerc claimed to have seen.

It did not happen. The chaplain appeared, and he joined Lockhart and the children in a game of baseball. However, he did not see the Dutch woman.

When the game was over, Sean gave his blue Los Angeles Dodgers cap to a lucky girl who had previously caught a pop fly. The ritual of the awarding of the cap was usually the cue for the kids to take off, heading back to class or to other activities, but today was different.

Sean gathered the children around and told them with obviously heartfelt sadness that today was his last Wednesday. Next week on this day, he would be back across the ocean, back in America.

There were sighs and moans of disappointment. There was a

feu de la passion after all, Kyle Lockhart realized; a bond had formed between these kids and the new ball game they had learned. A bond had formed between these kids and their unlikely American pal.

Now, to the dismay of all, this bond had to be severed.

Kyle Lockhart was thinking back to that song he'd heard, the one where you don't know what you've got 'til it's gone.

Sean Rasmunsen was thinking the same thing.

♦ ♦ ♦

Life's evening sun is sinking low,
A few more days and I must go
To meet the deeds that I have done,
Where there will be no setting sun.

While going down life's weary road,
I'll try to lift some traveler's load;
I'll try to turn the night to day,
Make flowers bloom along the way,
The lonely way.

FROM THE HYMN "A BEAUTIFUL LIFE"
WORDS BY WILLIAM MATTHEW GOLDEN

28

Just a Quick Visit

Few things in life are the cause for greater joy or greater sorrow than the beginnings and endings of deep personal relationships, the types of relationships where the word *love* is frequently whispered.

A chaplain is almost never summoned in the beginnings, but it is a part of the chaplain's rounds to counsel those experiencing a relationship's end. Countless chaplains have counseled countless soldiers grappling with the final agonizing moments in their relationships.

In such cases, a chaplain's words of counsel often contain such phrases as "higher purpose that we can't understand" and "someday, someone." Once upon a time long ago, a relationship had ended for Chaplain Sean Rasmunsen himself. It had ended because someone did not want to be a preacher's wife.

Today, a relationship had ended with someone who would have willingly been a preacher's wife, but who said she could not be a soldier's wife—but Sean was both.

Another phrase that often arose was "irreconcilable complications."

Sean had wrestled long and hard about his feelings for Mareike De Vries, and every which way that he had analyzed it, she was his "someday, someone."

Perhaps, however, as Mareike had pointed out so vividly, a man who had given his life to both his flag and his ministry could not truly share this life with *any* "someday, someone."

Sean had always thought of his calling as something bigger than himself, bigger than his personal desires, bigger than himself merely as a man. Was this simply proof of what he already knew—or should have let himself know?

Was there a "higher purpose" in this, or was it merely a rationalization?

Was there a modicum of self-pity in his—and Mareike's—rationalizing that there really *wasn't* room in his life for his job as a chaplain *and* his desire for a personal relationship?

Was this the reason that the Catholics insisted that their priests remain celibate?

As he anguished and fussed about his conversation with Mareike, Sean tried not to think about his last farewell to the kids. One day, God willing, he might be able to rekindle something with Mareike. He believed that she would one day be open to such a possibility, and perhaps there would one day be room in his life for a "someday, someone."

With the kids, it was another matter. He knew that he would never see the kids again. Barring the extremely unforeseen, he would never again after today set foot in Saf City. He especially wished that he had been able to say good-bye to Bilal, his buddy, but the al-Qamars had been keeping their kids out of school since the incident at the bridge. He understood why, but this could not stop him from wishing things were different.

"Lord, give me strength," he whispered. "Lord, give me strength and give Bilal a future; give him a chance to grow up in a world that is as free from strife as . . ."

He meant to end his prayer with "as Laclede, Missouri," citing the town where he had grown up. But instead, looking out the window at the reality of Safaliyah's streets, he concluded with "as possible."

Sgt. Lockhart hadn't heard the words very clearly over the sound of the Humvee's engine, but he knew it was a prayer, and he added his own "Amen" to Sean's.

Sean thought about Fahima and her children over in Muqdarubah and prayed that they too would one day live in an Iraq that was as free of violence as Safaliyah had been before the car bombs at the bridge.

Again, Lockhart nodded an "Amen."

Having made his final visit to the school, Sean had decided that they should pay one last call on Outpost Bravo, the U.S. Army's presence on the road that stretched eastward from Safaliyah toward the border with Iran.

"We'll just stop off for fifteen minutes to say hello and good-bye, and then we'll be back to Lex for dinner," Sean said. "Y'know, I'm actually gonna miss this place."

"Saf City?" Lockhart replied. "No way."

"Yes, way. It's been great to see how far they've come toward reclaiming their town from the bad guys. They're really great people."

"Yes, sir," Lockhart replied in a tone that said he'd meant to add, "if you say so."

There were a few soldiers across the street talking to some locals, and others mingling with Iraqi cops outside the cinder-block facade of Outpost Bravo.

They parked the Humvee beside some other vehicles, and Lockhart shouldered his M4 as Sean greeted the men near the entrance to the blockhouse.

De Shawn Hughes, the baritone in Sean's chapel choir, was on duty. He gave Sean a high five and said that he'd heard that the chaplain had been summoned back to the States.

"You and Specialist Mariott will have to put on a good show for the new chaplain," Sean said, smiling.

"Won't be the same," Hughes insisted. "It just won't be the same without you up there."

"If I had my way, I'd hang out here until all of you went home, but it's not a decision that was mine to make."

Wow, he hated giving that excuse.

"We'll be having a big sendoff for y'all on Sunday," Hughes promised.

"I'm looking forward to it." Sean grinned. "I hope that when the new guy shows up, you'll put on just as big a show for him."

"Ain't no chaplain like Chaplain Sean," Hughes winked. "Folks are sayin' that all over—even folks what don't get to chapel all that much."

"You'll be saying the same thing about the new guy in six

weeks," Sean said, dismissing the comment. He wondered if "the new guy" would be identified by name before Sunday. He wondered if he'd have a chance to meet him, as he had not with Father Mike O'Malley.

As he stooped to enter the building, Sean felt as though a huge hand had suddenly placed itself on his back and shoved. He reached out to slow his fall and felt the sting of his palms hitting the floor.

A split second later, the earsplitting *whump* of a sound hit him. Explosion.

"Oh no!" Sean heard someone shout.

He felt someone tugging on his flak jacket and looked up. He half-expected to see Tyler Kraus, who had always attended to him in emergencies such as this, but it was Kyle Lockhart. Kraus had had the upper-body strength of a man who'd grown up an Oregon logger. Lockhart was a clerk, so Sean was on his feet before the lad had managed to pull him very far.

"What happened?" Sean asked when they were safely hunkered down.

"Explosion," someone said, reiterating the obvious.

Sean lifted himself up to look out one of the slits that functioned as windows in the enclosed courtyard adjacent to the blockhouse in the Outpost Bravo compound.

Tyler Kraus would have had his hand on Sean's helmet, shoving him to the ground. Kyle Lockhart merely peeked over his shoulder.

Out in the street, people were running everywhere. Across the way, where he had earlier seen the group of Americans talking with locals, was the gutted, blackened, burning wreckage of what must once have been a small delivery truck.

Sean said a prayer for the guys he had seen out there, first for their safety, then for their souls.

Somewhere in the distance, they heard the sound of a fire engine. There was a time, back in 2007 and before, when such a sound was never heard on the lawless streets of Diyala's small cities. A car bomb would explode and there would be no fire engine wail, only the wail of the injured. But times had changed— by small increments.

Sean relaxed a little as he saw American soldiers near the burning vehicle—standing, walking American soldiers. The Iraqi police were herding people away from the exploded bomb, trying to maintain order. It was another sign that, although things were not as good as they could be, they were better than they had once been.

"I hope they didn't get none of our guys," Lockhart said.

"Me, too," Sean said.

As the flames lessened somewhat, they saw some injured people on the far side of the blast site, and they recognized De Shawn Hughes walking across to help out. With him was another man whom Sean knew as a member of Ashley Mariott's choir. Sean had spoken with David Menini a time or two and had discussed his having been in the youth choir at his church back in Torrance, California.

As the fire truck arrived, the chaplain and his assistant stood up.

"Let's go get a closer look," Sean said as the fire engine arrived on the scene. "Let's see if there's anything we can do."

Lockhart nodded, and the two men began moving toward the entrance to the courtyard.

Suddenly, the concussion from a blast even larger than the first knocked them to the ground. They felt the heat of a fireball burning close to Outpost Bravo.

Out of the corner of his eye, Sean saw a fragment of torn red metal. The second blast had targeted the fire truck.

Sean's immediate thought, obviously, was a memory of the dual car bombs at the bridge that day, but he had little time to dwell on that.

"Incoming!" shouted another soldier within the blockhouse.

Kapow kapow kapow kapow! Kapow kapow!

"We're taking fire!"

From inside the blockhouse, the shouts of American soldiers mingled with the pop and crackle of small-arms fire. Outpost Bravo was under attack.

"Better get inside," Lockhart said, grabbing Sean by the sleeve.

Kapow kapow kapow kapow!

Inside, the elements of normalcy that Sean recalled from previous visits to Outpost Bravo remained. There were posters on the wall and empty Coke cans laid out casually on the table. People usually hung out here in a relaxed fashion, but suddenly they were all at the windows, feverishly firing their weapons.

The ripping sound of an M249 squad automatic weapon echoed with teeth-rattling volume in the enclosed spaces.

Rrrrrrrrrrrrrip! Kapow kapow kapow! Kapow kapow!

"Got 'em pinned down."

Kapow kapow kapow! Kapow kapow!

"Where?"

Rrrrrrrrrrrrrip! Kapow kapow kapow! Kapow kapow!

"Across there by the gas station. Fifty yards at least."
Kapow kapow kapow kapow! Kapow kapow!

It was a positive sign, Sean thought. In a firefight, having that much open ground between your own position and the enemy was a good thing.

The gunfire lessened a bit.

"How many of 'em?"

"Dunno . . . half a dozen at least," replied another young American voice.

It was now apparent that the dual car bombs had been harbingers of an assault on Outpost Bravo, an attack that these brave young American soldiers were aiming to thwart.

"Is everybody safe in here?"

Sean recognized Lt. Jeremy Gamblin. He was a new guy, fresh out of ROTC at the University of Missouri. Sean had seen him at chapel a few times, and they had shared a few stories about "Mizzou," but they hadn't gotten to know one another very well.

Somebody shouted from the courtyard that they still had three guys outside the wire.

Kapow kapow kapow! Kapow kapow! Rrrrrrrrrrrrrip!

"Can you see 'em?" Gamblin shouted.

"No, sir. Might have took cover over across the street where the cops are."

"If you do see 'em, give our guys covering fire to get back over here if they need it."

"Yes, sir."

Kapow kapow kapow! Kapow kapow!

"You okay, Chaplain?" Lt. Gamblin asked Sean.

"Perfect. I'm doing great. How are *you* doing?"

Rrrrrrrrrrrrrip! Kapow kapow kapow kapow!

"Guess we got a little excitement here today."

"Guess so," Sean said, smiling bravely.

Kapow kapow kapow! Kapow kapow!

"Sir, we got wounded out there," shouted one of the men in the courtyard.

"What are the Iraqi cops doing?" Gamblin asked, ducking out of the blockhouse.

"The cops have disappeared."

Rrrrrrrrrrrrrip! Kapow kapow kapow kapow! Kapow kapow!

"Sir, we got a problem."

That didn't sound so good.

Sean heard these words just as sudden and frighteningly nearby gunfire erupted in the courtyard.

Kapow kapow kapow! Kapow kapow kapow kapow kapow kapow!

"The shooters are trying to outflank us," Gamblin said urgently.

Kapow kapow kapow kapow! Rrrrrrrrrrrrrip!

"Negative!" shouted someone from the opposite wall inside the blockhouse. "They ain't outflanking nothing! We got hajjis on *both* sides. *Three* sides! We're gettin' hit from *all over* here."

Rrrrrrrrrrrrrip! Kapow kapow kapow! Kapow kapow!

"Polar Bear, this is Bravo," Gamblin said, grabbing the JTRS. "We've had two car bombs go off down here and we're taking

fire from all sides. Request backup . . . repeat, request backup.
Can you get an Apache out here?"

*Kapow kapow kapow kapow! Kapow kapow!
Rrrrrrrrrrrrrrip!*

"Bravo, this is Polar Bear," crackled the radio. "We'll get to
you when we can . . . little backed up here . . . simultaneous attacks all over town . . . over."

Kapow kapow kapow kapow!

For the first time, Gamblin looked worried. He looked just
like the kid that he was. In his early twenties, he was at the age
when many people from his high school graduating class were
assistant store managers at a Wal-Mart or a Walgreens somewhere—if they weren't still bagging groceries. Here *he* was, in
a life-or-death predicament, leading a squad of eleven soldiers
who were under attack from a determined foe and shooting live
ammunition.

*Kapow kapow kapow! Kapow kapow kapow kapow kapow
kapow!*

The young officer scurried back and forth, trying to assess
the situation and figure out what to do next. There wasn't much
that they *could* do, other than what they were already doing—
that is, to return fire and wait for an attack helicopter to tip the
balance, or for the enemy to get tired of shooting and melt away
into Safaliyah's streets.

Kapow kapow kapow kapow! Kapow kapow!

The good news was that they were hunkered down within a
well-fortified position—and they had plenty of ammunition.

Rrrrrrrrrrrrrrip! Kapow kapow kapow! Kapow kapow!

Sean compared the situation to that desperate night not so

long ago in Muqdarubah. The differences were marked. Today, there were no civilians inside their position to worry about and no wounded Americans—at least not yet. On top of this, they were within a few minutes of FOB Lexington by air for the attack choppers—and the outside world knew exactly where they were.

Kapow kapow kapow kapow! Rrrrrrrrrrrrip!

Compared to Muqdarubah, this was not so bad.

Kapow kapow kapow kapow kapow! Kapow kapow kapow!

Sean was relaxed, but when he glanced over at Kyle Lockhart, he saw a young man who was beyond frightened. Aside from the odd "shoot-and-scoot" mortar attack on the Lex perimeter, he had never been under fire, and the poor guy was petrified. He remembered the first day that he had met Kyle. It was on their mutual first day at Lex, when this young man had frozen during a mortar attack. He also remembered Braylee Davis, who had been so cool under fire during that same attack, but how she had later gone home with posttraumatic shock after another deadly incident.

Kapow kapow kapow! Kapow kapow!

"Don't worry . . . just relax." Sean smiled. "It's gonna be okay. We're cool. They'll have some firepower on the bad guys very soon. We're gonna be fine."

Kapow kapow kapow kapow! Rrrrrrrrrrrrip!

"Never been shot at before," he said nervously.

Kapow kapow kapow kapow! Kapow kapow!

Sean was about to offer more words of reassurance when somebody outside began shouting.

"They're closing in!"

Rrrrrrrrrrrrrip! Kapow kapow kapow! Kapow kapow!

"They're all around us," someone else said as he cut loose with a burst of M16 fire.

Kapow kapow kapow kapow!

"We're *surrounded*!"

Kapow kapow kapow kapow! Kapow kapow kapow kapow!

That comment, combined with the tone in which it was made, left Kyle Lockhart shaking.

Kapow kapow kapow! Kapow kapow! Rrrrrrrrrrrrrip!

"They're getting close on three sides!"

Kapow kapow kapow kapow kapow! Kapow kapow kapow!

"Keep 'em down . . . keep the SAW on those ones that are behind the fire truck!"

Rrrrrrrrrrrrrip!

"Let 'em have it!"

Rrrrrrrrrrrrrip! Kapow kapow kapow! Kapow kapow!

"They're everywhere out there!"

Rrrrrrrrrrrrrip! Kapow kapow kapow!

"Don't let 'em get any closer," Lt. Gamblin ordered.

Rrrrrrrrrrrrrip! Kapow kapow kapow kapow kapow!

Then, turning to Sean, he asked: "Do you have any words of encouragement for us, sir?"

"The Twenty-seventh Psalm," Sean suggested. "Where it says that though a host should encamp against me, my heart shall not fear."

"No fear!" someone shouted, squeezing off a few rounds at an enemy crouching out in the street somewhere.

Kapow kapow kapow! Kapow kapow! Rrrrrrrrrrrrrip!

Sean put his hand around his assistant's shoulder.

Kapow kapow kapow!

"Never . . . never been shot at before," Lockhart repeated, jumping with a start when a barrage of 7.62-mm projectiles clattered through a window and hit the opposite wall.

Kapow kapow kapow kapow kapow!

"Don't let the fear . . . the enemy inside . . . get at you," Sean advised, sneezing slightly as the pulverized plaster dust stung his nose.

Rrrrrrrrrrrrip! Kapow kapow! Kapow kapow!

"Who's supposed to be protecting who, huh?" Sean smiled.

Kapow kapow kapow kapow kapow!

"I'm sorry, sir, I'll get hold of myself," Lockhart said, bravely sitting up and abandoning his slumped posture.

Kapow kapow kapow kapow! Kapow kapow!

Sean winced and swallowed hard as a chunk of masonry chewed loose by an enemy bullet struck his cheek.

Kapow kapow kapow! Kapow kapow!

"Keep your head down, sir," Lockhart said, maneuvering his body between Sean and the windows through which the gunfire was coming.

"You too, Kyle."

◆　◆　◆

Surrounded by a host of foes,
Stormed by a host of foes within,
Nor swift to flee, nor strong t'oppose,
Single, against hell, earth, and sin,
Single, yet undismayed, I am;
I dare believe in Jesus' Name.

What though a thousand hosts engage,
A thousand worlds, my soul to shake?
I have a shield shall quell their rage,
And drive the alien armies back;
Portrayed it bears a bleeding Lamb
I dare believe in Jesus' Name.

FROM THE HYMN "SURROUNDED BY A HOST OF FOES"
WORDS BY JOHN AND CHARLES WESLEY

29

Cup Runneth Over

"Man down! Man down!"

Kapow kapow! Kapow kapow kapow!

Chaplain Sean Rasmunsen crawled across the Outpost Bravo floor, keeping his head down, finally reaching the side room from which two soldiers had been returning fire against the enemy. He arrived ahead of the medic and leaped forward, pushing on the injured man's ruptured artery.

Control the bleeding, Sean murmured, *keep him from bleeding out until the medic can get here.*

"Lord, give us a hand."

Kapow kapow kapow kapow kapow kapow kapow! Kapow kapow!

Though it was unspoken by the Americans surrounded at

Outpost Bravo, it was clear to all that they faced a determined foe. It was not a simple, cowardly "shoot-and-scoot" attack.

Kapow kapow kapow! Kapow kapow!

Al-Qaeda wanted to make a point, more to the people of Safaliyah than to the Americans. The point was as old as protection rackets anywhere. The Iraqis in Safaliyah had embraced the Americans as friends—so long as the Americans could be perceived as protectors. To destroy the Americans at Outpost Bravo would be a long step toward destroying this perception of the Americans as protectors.

Kapow kapow kapow kapow! Kapow kapow!

This day had been chosen as the day on which al-Qaeda would do all that it could to shake and degrade the confidence of Safaliyah's people in the Americans. Today, all across Safaliyah, fierce attacks carried this message forward.

Kapow kapow kapow! Kapow kapow kapow kapow kapow!

The medic finally wriggled into the room where Sean knelt with the injured man, here to do his best to save a life.

For the microcosm that was Outpost Bravo, there was little perception of the overall strategic situation. In fact, the idea of the strategic situation was the furthest thing from anyone's mind. It mattered little what might be going on elsewhere in Saf City at this moment. It mattered only that this microcosm of Americans was in a life-and-death struggle—and that these men and women were surrounded.

Kapow kapow kapow! Kapow kapow!

"There's two more hajjis over there on the right . . ."

Kapow kapow kapow kapow kapow kapow! Kapow kapow!

"I see 'em . . . just can't hit . . ."

Kapow kapow kapow kapow kapow!

"Look left . . . by the tree . . . two more."

Kapow kapow kapow kapow!

"Jeez . . . they're all around . . ."

Kapow kapow kapow!

"Like bugs . . ."

Kapow kapow kapow kapow! Kapow kapow!

"Two on the far left . . . getting ready to fire. . . . I got the fat guy . . ."

Kapow kapow kapow! Kapow kapow!

"Think you nailed him . . ."

Kapow kapow kapow kapow kapow! Kapow kapow!

"Two more . . . I see two more . . ."

Kapow kapow kapow kapow!

"Got any more ammo?"

Kapow kapow kapow! Kapow kapow!

As the first shots had come through the window, Sean's mind turned to the obvious comparison to the shootout in Muqdarubah. In today's firefight, the Americans were better armed—but so too was the foe. The sounds of both the incoming rounds and the return fire were incessant.

Kapow kapow kapow kapow kapow kapow kapow kapow kapow kapow!

Sean thought about St. Jude, the patron saint of lost causes.

Hey Jude . . . here we go again.

For the moment, though, the cause at Outpost Bravo did not *seem* lost. Difficult? Yes. Lost? Well, not yet.

In battle, however, things can unravel quickly.

Kapow kapow kapow! Kapow kapow! Kapow kapow!

There was no letup. There was a great deal of lead ripping harmlessly at the outside walls of the Outpost Bravo blockhouse—*but* there were also a lot of well-aimed shots pouring through the windows.

Kapow kapow kapow! Kapow kapow!

"Aaarrgh!"

Kapow kapow kapow kapow! Kapow kapow!

The gurgling grunt of pain from the courtyard said that another American had found himself in the sights of one of those well-aimed shots.

Kapow kapow kapow kapow kapow kapow kapow kapow!

As Sean scrambled out to help this man, he heard the sickening hum of a bullet very near his own face.

"Lord, protect us here," he whispered. "Please let your purpose for us all on this earth include something to do here *tomorrow.*"

Kapow kapow kapow! Kapow kapow!

Again, as in the room within the blockhouse, a badly injured man was being attended by one of his comrades. The bad guys knew the gruesome mathematical truth that inflicting wounds decreased the fighting effectiveness of the enemy exponentially. Every injury inflicted took out at least two men. This was why it was critical that one of the noncombatants—either the chaplain or the medic—get to the casualties as quickly as possible.

Kapow kapow kapow kapow! Kapow kapow!

It was a numbers game. The Americans were both surrounded *and* outnumbered, and these facts were made painfully more clear with each soldier wounded.

Kapow kapow kapow kapow kapow!

A half hour into the shooting, four soldiers were down, one of them dead. At least another four had been hit by ricochets, but were still able to fire their weapons. Among them was Tamlyn Schneider, the sole woman at Outpost Bravo.

Kapow kapow kapow! Kapow kapow!

Out on the street, the Americans were making the enemy pay a heavy price, but the al-Qaeda gunmen were still inching closer to Outpost Bravo.

Kapow kapow kapow kapow kapow kapow kapow! Kapow kapow!

"There! I see 'em running . . ."

Kapow kapow kapow kapow! Kapow kapow!

"Got 'em . . . got 'em!"

Kapow kapow kapow kapow kapow! Kapow kapow!

"You missed that one."

Kapow kapow kapow kapow kapow!

"Did not!"

Kapow kapow kapow! Kapow kapow!

"There he is again . . . get the SAW on him!"

Rrrrrrrrrrrrrip! Kapow kapow kapow kapow kapow! Kapow kapow!

The M249 squad automatic weapon was the heaviest and best weapon they had. Far more effective than the M16s, it could be used to keep the bad guys at bay wherever it was aimed, but it could be aimed at only one section of the perimeter at a time. The gunner moved from place to place, bringing its firepower briefly to bear before moving on.

Rrrrrrrrrrrrrip! Kapow kapow kapow kapow!

"Just missed him . . . can you see . . . ?

Rrrrrrrrrrrrrip! Kapow kapow kapow kapow! Kapow kapow!

"Think I got him . . ."

Kapow kapow kapow kapow! Kapow kapow! Kapow kapow!

"Keep shooting!"

Kapow kapow kapow kapow! Kapow kapow kapow! Kapow!

"Man . . . oh no!"

Kapow kapow kapow! Kapow kapow!

"What?"

Kapow kapow kapow kapow!

"I'm out of ammo for the SAW!"

Kapow kapow kapow! Kapow kapow kapow! Kapow kapow!

"Keep shooting!"

Kapow kapow kapow kapow!

"So many . . . where are they all comin' from?"

Kapow kapow kapow! Kapow kapow!

"Toss me some more mags," Lt. Jeremy Gamblin shouted across the room. He had burned through all of his M16 ammunition.

"Here's two," came the reply. "I'm almost out. Is there any more stashed around here anywhere?"

Kapow kapow kapow! Kapow kapow kapow kapow kapow kapow!

"I think so," said another man, but as he rose, an enemy round clipped him. Striking his helmet a glancing blow, it failed to penetrate, but it twisted his head violently and knocked him to the ground.

Kapow kapow kapow kapow kapow! Kapow kapow!

Sean was starting to turn to the aid of the downed soldier when panicked shouts were heard from the courtyard.

Kapow kapow kapow kapow kapow kapow! Kapow kapow!

"Oh no!"

Kapow kapow kapow kapow! Kapow kapow kapow kapow kapow!

"They're on top of us . . ."

Kapow kapow kapow kapow! Kapow kapow!

"Get the gun around . . ."

Kapow kapow kapow kapow kapow kapow! Kapow kapow!

"Noooo . . . !"

Kapow kapow kapow kapow! Kapow kapow kapow!

The sound of the commotion told everyone in the blockhouse that the enemy had breached Outpost Bravo's shorthanded outer defenses.

Kapow kapow kapow! Kapow kapow!

The SAW gunner, who had picked up the M16 of a fallen soldier, looked at Lt. Gamblin, and Gamblin looked at Sean.

Kapow! Kapow!

Two shots came from outside, and then the shooting stopped.

As the gunner raised his weapon and moved toward the doorway, there was a clattering sound and three men entered the blockhouse, and then another.

American M16s faced al-Qaeda AK-47s at close range.

Nobody fired.

The scene was frozen in time.

One of the al-Qaeda held a young American in a stranglehold as a human shield—with a dirty, long-bladed knife at a right angle to his throat.

"Don't shoot me," the man whispered.

The bearded man who held him just tightened his grip and shouted something in Arabic. The spittle that came with the remarks served only to underscore the anger.

Sean recognized the young American as David Menini, and recognized that the throat near which the knife danced was the one that produced a beautiful tenor at the FOB Lex chapel each Sunday.

One of the other al-Qaeda abruptly began scolding and berating the Americans, gesturing for them to drop their weapons. The suggestion seemed to be that the young American's throat would be cut if they did not.

"What'll we do?"

The Americans still wielded firepower that matched that of the al-Qaeda thugs, but it would be impossible to kill the one holding the tenor without doing irreparable harm.

Lt. Jeremy Gamblin faced one of those decisions that a twenty-something less than a year out of college should not have to face. It was a challenge that *no one* should have to face.

"We gotta buy David some time," Gamblin said. "We gotta buy all of us some time . . . drop 'em."

Sean saw the angry expressions as the weapons dropped to the floor. One M16 bounced slightly and came to rest near his own boot.

Kyle Lockhart let his own weapon fall gently, as though not wanting to damage it. Sean looked into his face, expecting fear and seeing only defiance from a man who had, as of only yesterday, spent his entire military career as a clerk.

Two other M16s fell, and Gamblin set down his M4, waiting to be the last.

The standoff was over. The al-Qaeda looked at one another and began laughing.

The one with the knife jerked David's head back and pressed the blade into his Adam's apple. There was one swift motion and a stream of blood poured down the gray-green uniform. His knees buckled, and David's body fell to the floor.

This was apparently very funny to the three bearded men, because they laughed even harder.

Before any of the Americans could react, more bearded men entered the room. Among them was a man with a great deal of gray in his beard and a jagged scar across his forehead. By the way he shouted at the others, Sean supposed that he was some kind of leader.

One by one, he sized up the Americans. He poked at Gamblin's lieutenant's bars. By his expression, they could tell that he understood Gamblin to be an officer. He regarded Tamlyn, the one woman among the Americans, with disgust.

At last, it was Sean's turn to be inspected.

In the Western movies, when the bad guys have "the drop" on you, the admonition is usually to *not* "try anything." However, as the man scrutinized the crosses on his lapels, Sean decided that it was time to "try something."

Looking the man in the eye, he said calmly, *"As-salaam alaikum."*

The greeting startled the man. It was so out of place.

Did this infidel speak Arabic?

Why would a man who was obviously about to die wish peace upon those who were about to kill him?

He looked again at the crosses on Sean's lapel and understood who he was and what he did.

"Hal tatakalum Al Arabiah?"

The man wanted to know if Sean spoke Arabic.

"Hal tatakalum Al Engleaziah?" Sean asked. Rather than answering the question, Sean turned it around. Did this guy understand English?

He shrugged in a way that suggested he knew a few words but was reticent to speak the language.

"Ayeena . . . where are you going to take us?" Sean asked. Better to ask that, and get them thinking of keeping the Americans alive, than asking when or whether they were to be killed.

A flicker of indecisiveness could be seen in the man's eye as he turned and shouted at the other al-Qaeda insurgents.

Kicking and prodding, they began binding the hands of the Americans with a roll of duct tape they found in the blockhouse.

In his mind, Sean said a prayer of thanksgiving. He would take being tied up with duct tape over a bullet in the back of the head—any day.

"The Lord is my shepherd . . . I shall not want," Sean said, out loud, beginning the Twenty-third Psalm and urging the others by his tone to join him.

"He maketh me to lie down in green pastures: He leadeth me beside the still waters . . . He restoreth my soul: He leadeth me in the paths of righteousness for his name's sake."

The al-Qaeda people looked at one another with bewildered expressions. Though the words the infidels spoke were merely gibberish to them, it was not hard to tell that they were prayers.

"Yea, though I walk through the valley of the shadow of death, I will fear no evil: For thou art with me; thy rod and thy staff they comfort me," he continued.

Most of the Americans joined him for the fourth verse. It was like the Lord's Prayer. Even for nonchurchgoers, these words were familiar.

"Thou preparest a table before me in the presence of mine enemies: Thou anointest my head with oil; my cup runneth over."

For the Americans, their cups were hardly running over at that moment, but they *did* still have their lives, and the al-Qaeda thugs *were* indeed surprised to hear the infidels actually praying.

How, Sean wondered, could religious people—even those who adhered to a violent perversion of their faith—kill people while they were in prayer?

The answer was that they certainly *could*, and perhaps they *would*. However, maybe, just *maybe*, they would think twice before doing it.

"Surely goodness and mercy shall follow me all the days of my life: And I will dwell in the house of the Lord for ever."

◆　◆　◆

Fiery and fierce the conflict,
Daring and swift the foe;
His hosts are found on the battle ground,
Where they wait to lay you low;

Sharp are his darts and deadly,
Keen is the strife and long,
Then arm for the fight in the armor of light,
Quit you like men, be strong!

Strive till the strife is over,
Fight till the fight is won,
Though sore oppressed, seek not for rest,
Until the day is done;

After the well fought battle
Join in the victor's song,
Your trophies bring to Christ your King,
Quit you like men, be strong!

FROM THE HYMN "RISE AT THE CRY OF BATTLE"
WORDS BY ADA R. GREENAWAY

30

Oh Lord,
What Shall I Do?

The second van never arrived.

Four American soldiers had been shoved into the first vehicle while three others began loading wounded comrades into the second. After some nervous bickering among the al-Qaeda who captured Outpost Bravo, the driver of the first took off alone. At one point, he had pulled into an alley and had watched his mirror anxiously for some minutes before resuming his dash through the squalid outer fringes of Safaliyah.

The plan had obviously unraveled.

Al-Qaeda had set out not just to overwhelm Outpost Bravo, but to abduct its defenders. The two vans were supposed to have carried the abductees away, but apparently only the first one had followed this plan.

Finally, after fifteen or twenty minutes of zigging and zagging, it seemed to the Americans inside that the van had reached its destination. The driver had shut off the engine. He and the man riding shotgun had gotten out. The four Americans listened for the second vehicle to arrive, but it had not.

Chaplain Sean Rasmunsen prayed for the others who were being loaded into it when last he saw them, and he prayed for his companions in the first van. He hadn't stopped praying since they careered wildly away from Outpost Bravo.

Why had the second van not come?

Was it going to another location?

If so, why did the driver of the first vehicle seem to pause and wait?

Were the other Americans victims of a friendly-fire incident?

Had an American attack helicopter seen the fast-moving white van and cut loose with a Hellfire missile?

Sean prayed not.

"What are they going to do with us?" Tamlyn Schneider whispered, looking fearfully at Lt. Jeremy Gamblin, and then at Sean.

She was a young private from rural Indiana, whom Sean knew from having seen her at chapel. Round faced and ruddy cheeked, she was the sort of person whom one might call jolly, although today her disposition was one of nervous apprehension.

Both the officers simply shook their heads as if to state the obvious—that they had no idea.

"Nothing, I hope," interjected Sgt. Kyle Lockhart.

"Amen," Gamblin added.

Wondering what was next was about all they could do.

Their abductors had parked the van in the shadow of a large building and had gotten out, leaving the four Americans to conjecture about an unknown future over which they had no control.

"Should we try to escape?" Kyle asked.

"Probably not a good idea . . . at least not for now," Gamblin said. "We don't know where we are . . . or whether they're standing just outside ready for any excuse to shoot us.

"I suppose it's a good sign that they *haven't* shot us," Sean said hopefully.

"Yet," Tamlyn said, choking back tears.

"We're gonna be okay," Sean said calmly.

Suddenly the back door jerked open, and the bearded men began dragging the Americans roughly from the van.

They were taken through a doorway, down a hallway, and pushed into a large dark room.

When the lights came on, they found themselves in a make-shift television studio. On one side of the room was a small cam-corder on a rickety tripod. On the opposite wall was a huge green banner with an Arabic inscription and a badly rendered marker illustration of what appeared to be crossed swords.

The Americans looked at one another. They each now knew what was coming next. They had all seen the grainy videos that originated in rooms such as this across Iraq.

A short, rotund man came into the room and began looking over his captive "on-air personalities."

As had the gray-bearded man back at Outpost Bravo, he re-garded Tamlyn with disgust. Was it her red hair, or the fact that she had tears on her round, freckled cheeks, or was it simply because she was a woman?

Again, the crosses on Sean's lapel attracted some attention.

Perhaps it was because of these that the chaplain was pulled away from the others and thrust into the folding chair that was positioned beneath the banner on the wall.

Pulling out a knife, he roughly slashed the duct tape with which the man of the Book had been bound. Sean rubbed his wrists and licked a couple of nicks on his thumb that had been made by the knife.

The man went to a backpack that was in a pile of junk near the camera, rummaged around, and took out a wad of papers. From this, he took one and handed it to Sean.

The top line read in English, *My name is.* This was followed by a blank space. It was obviously the script from which he was supposed to read. Beneath the space was a paragraph that began, *I am a crusader from the infidel army that preys upon the life of the people of Iraq . . .*

Sean weighed his options.

What if he read what was written on this paper?

What if he did not?

What would they do to him—and to the others?

Oh Lord, what shall I do?

As he debated his choices, three of the al-Qaeda thugs were fussing with the camera as the fat man scowled at them from the side of the room.

After a spate of angry expletives, they finally seemed to have figured it out.

A red light at the front of the camera came on.

It was showtime.

Oh Lord, what shall I do?

"*Asre'a!*" the fat man growled, scolding Sean to hurry up and read from the paper.

Oh Lord, what shall I do?

Sean glanced from the camera to the man, and as he looked into his angry face, a thought came to him.

His prayer was answered.

The man had spoken to him, so he would reply.

As Sean looked away from the camera and into this man's eyes, this seemed only natural, simply to reply.

"*Bismillah*," Sean said, smiling, using that phrase meaning "in the name of God" that had been spoken as a blessing before dinner on that night so long ago when he and Mareike and Tyler Kraus had dined in the peaceful home of young Bilal and his sister, Naja.

The fat man looked stunned, as though he could not believe that such a word had just come from these *ulooj* lips.

"*Allahumma ya mowlana antas-salaam, wa minkas-salaam*," Sean continued in a conversational tone, reciting the Muslim prayer that he had learned for his visit to Fahima and her family in Muqdarubah.

Sean watched the fat man's jaw drop.

What was this infidel saying?

Why was the infidel smiling calmly and telling *him* that Allah was eternal life and everlasting peace?

"*Wa ilaika yarjaus-salaam*," Sean continued. "*Haiyyina rabbana bis-salaam, wa adkhilna daras-salaam . . . tabarakta rabbana wa-ta'laita.*"

The camera rolled, recording images of an American—not of an American cowering and groveling, but of a smiling American speaking of Allah's infinite goodness.

"*Ya zal jalali wal ikram.*"

The fat man was impaled on a conundrum.

He had been defied by an infidel, but the infidel spoke words from the Qur'an, words that told of true peace.

What should he do to the infidel?

Should he kill him on camera while he spoke of Allah's infinite goodness?

Fortunately for Sean, circumstances intervened that gave the fat man more pressing concerns.

In an instant, the windowless room was plunged into darkness.

What happened?

Cursing came from behind the camera as eyes adjusted to the faint ambient light in the room.

Power failures were not uncommon in Safaliyah, as they were not uncommon throughout Iraq—but as far as Sean Rasmunsen was concerned, none had *ever* come at a more opportune moment.

The fat man leaped up from his chair and dashed out of the room, screaming to minions elsewhere in the building.

Perhaps he was one of those people who believed that screaming at his underlings would speed up a resolution of the sudden blackout. One of the three men behind the camera also left the room, but the other two stood up and lit cigarettes.

Tamlyn Schneider said something. Sean didn't hear exactly what, but it caught the attention of the two smokers.

Maybe she had asked for a cigarette.

Maybe she had told them that smoking indoors was impolite.

It mattered little.

It mattered only that their attention was drawn to her.

In the half light, Sean watched as the two men walked over to where she was seated against a wall about twelve feet from Kyle Lockhart and Lt. Gamblin.

"Get away from me!" Tamlyn shouted.

In the half light, Sean saw the glint of a knife blade. Everybody in al-Qaeda seemed to have a knife.

Oh Lord, protect us.

"Get away from me!" Tamlyn repeated.

Oh Lord, what shall I do?

What *could* Sean do?

Had the two men forgotten that there was an American in the room with his wrists no longer bound behind his back?

"Stop . . . No . . . Get *away!*"

Oh Lord, what shall I do?

In the half light, Sean could make out the AK-47 that had been left behind by the fat man.

Oh Lord, what shall I do?

Both Gamblin and Lockhart were bound and incapable of action.

Oh Lord, what shall I do?

The AK-47 lay just a few feet and a split second from his unshackled hands—but chaplains are noncombatants.

Oh Lord, what shall I do?

Sean thought of the words of Psalm 144 that say, "Blessed be the Lord my strength, which teacheth my hands to war, and my fingers to *fight*."

He gazed at the AK-47 that lay so near, yet so *far—far* because chaplains are noncombatants.

"Please . . . No . . . *Stop!*" Tamlyn moaned.

Oh Lord, what shall I do?

Tamlyn's screams, and the sounds of her kicking and struggling, echoed in the darkened room as Sean stood up and reached for the assault rifle.

He was no stranger to guns, having hunted ducks and deer as a boy. He was not even a stranger to assault rifles, having fired an M16 on a firing range at Fort Jackson during his basic training.

He was, however, a chaplain, and chaplains are noncombatants. As such, he was among that unique class of U.S. Army officers who are committed *never* to pick up a weapon.

Yet here he was, with an AK-47 in his hands and two bearded men now aware of this fact.

For a moment, all was quiet.

Oh Lord, what have I done?

The two men eyed the infidel who spoke of peace but now held a gun. Of course, neither of them were strangers to quoting the Qur'an one minute and drawing human blood the next.

Oh Lord, what have I done?

What I have *done*, Sean thought to himself, *is to have crossed the line. What I have done is to violate the inviolate to buy Tamlyn a few minutes of respite.* Any moment, the fat man and others would reenter the room, and the plight of the Americans would devolve into hopelessness.

Sean felt his hands tremble and saw the muzzle of the gun move.

For some reason, in the half light, the man with the knife misinterpreted this as a gesture that demanded he drop the knife.

He tossed it angrily, and it bounced to a resting place near Jeremy Gamblin. The lieutenant quickly wriggled his body atop the knife and slit the duct tape that held his hands immobile.

Having kicked the knife toward Kyle Lockhart, he walked toward Sean and relieved him of his terrible burden.

Both the chaplain and the infantry officer saw immense gratitude in the eyes of the other.

Lockhart cut the duct tape from Tamlyn's wrists and dragged her away from the two al-Qaeda.

"What now?" Kyle asked urgently, looking to Gamblin for answers.

"All we can do is . . ." the officer answered, grasping for a way to finish the sentence. With an unknown number of armed al-Qaeda just beyond the only doorway, the choices were invariably bleak.

". . . pray," Sean added, picking the choice of last resort, the only choice.

"In the words of that prayer from the Qur'an that I was reciting earlier, we can ask God to grant us a life in the home of true peace."

"Amen," Tamlyn said weakly.

From beyond the room came a sudden spike in the number of shouts and curses. This was combined with a rattling sound like tables and chairs being moved on a concrete floor. The noise from beyond the room began as a murmur and grew to a roar, like the sound of a sudden summer cloudburst.

As thunder within a rainstorm came the sound of explosions. As thunder within a rainstorm, the building shook.

The door flew open and the fat man was silhouetted in the doorway.

Seeing him, the two al-Qaeda in the room bolted for the doorway.

Three silhouettes became one.

There was the sound of gunfire, and this silhouette danced like a dervish, arms and legs flailing.

There was a sudden flash as the lights in the room came on.

Sean wondered why he did, but the first thing he noticed was that the red light on the camera was once again illuminated. Like an unthinking robot taking up its task as though no interval of inactivity had occurred, the camera slavishly resumed taping an empty chair positioned beneath the green banner on the wall.

As the four Americans looked at one another, another figure appeared in the doorway—and another and another.

The American flags on their shoulders were more than a welcome sight. They were like the answer to a prayer.

Even though they were a low-visibility suggestion of red, white, and blue, the flags represented so much beyond the fabric and the colors. They represented that something intangible that had once been explained to him by a young soldier on his first visit to Outpost Bravo, many, many months ago.

"My dad was in Nam," she had told him when he asked her why she had come here, into the unbearable heat and dust of a war zone. "He lost his arm, but he came home, got a job, did well at it, raised three kids, never complained about what happened. He was always proud of the country and had a lot of people looking up to him. I guess I sorta called myself to do something like this because of the example he set."

Sean had always thought of his calling as something bigger than himself, bigger than his personal wants, his personal desires. In their conversation earlier in the day, Mareike had brought it to

Sean's attention that his calling was far bigger than even he had imagined.

The official motto of the U.S. Army Chaplain Corps is the Latin phrase *Pro Deo et Patria*, "For God and Country," but few chaplains lose sight of the fact that their congregation is composed of the individual men and women in uniform with whom they are posted. For Sean, his motto might have read, "For the Soldiers of FOB Lex." Now his clientele was a much greater microcosm of soldiers, his mission much greater than once it had been. Men and women in uniform needed him; they needed their chaplain.

Far from being *egoistisch*, Mareike De Vries had selflessly shown him the way; she had told him what his blinded eyes could not see. Many months ago, he had felt it tugging him back to Iraq. Now, seeing the low-viz flags on the uniforms of the soldiers, he realized that she was right. He was being called to something far bigger than even he had imagined.

That afternoon, Mareike had brought Sean's calling into focus in a way that he could not see.

Now, he saw.

Now, *at last*, he saw.

She had suggested that he had been called back to Iraq only to be called back to Jackson.

He couldn't see it.

She had suggested that perhaps it was *her* calling to make him see this.

He couldn't see it—not then. But *now* he could.

Actually, these men, men who had ironically once looked for Sean's guidance at the FOB Lex chapel, were now the answer to *two* prayers. They had saved Sean's life and those of his companions, but they had also—just by the drama of their sudden appearance on the scene—answered that second prayer that went far beyond the immediate.

They had shown him—by their actions and Mareike's words—a milepost that would lead Sean Rasmunsen to the next step on the road toward fulfilling the purpose in his life.

◆　◆　◆

Mine eyes have seen the glory of the coming of the Lord;
He is trampling out the vintage where the grapes of wrath are stored;
He hath loosed the fateful lightning of His terrible swift sword;
His truth is marching on.

I have seen Him in the watch fires of a hundred circling camps
They have builded Him an altar in the evening dews and damps;
I can read His righteous sentence by the dim and flaring lamps;
His day is marching on.

Glory! Glory! Hallelujah! Glory! Glory! Hallelujah!
Glory! Glory! Hallelujah! While God is marching on.

FROM "THE BATTLE HYMN OF THE REPUBLIC"
WORDS BY JULIA WARD HOWE

31

Go with God

The line of armored Humvees moved slowly through Safaliyah, and the air was filled with the sounds of helicopters. Order, such as it was, had been restored to Saf City. After the carnage and destruction that he had seen at Outpost Bravo, Sean Rasmunsen was surprised—even shocked—to see that Safaliyah had emerged from the terrible day remarkably untouched by violence.

"Typical al-Qaeda operation," Capt. Ryan Clark said, glancing at Sean across the interior of the jostling vehicle. "Coordinated attacks. Coordinated and *vicious*, but isolated. Once they tip their hand, though, they've *played* their hand. They're through."

The captain had led the American response to the attack, securing all of the central part of the city within ninety minutes. Finding Sean and the others had been the last loose end.

"Wish we could have been to Outpost Bravo five minutes sooner," Clark said. "We just missed you."

"But all the others are okay?" Sean asked with concern.

"Except for the kid who got his throat cut, they'll all make it," Clark replied, obviously angry at David's pointless death. "Lucky for them the bad guys couldn't get that van started. If we hadn't found them, we wouldn't have known what happened to you guys."

"How did you find *us*?" Sean asked.

"Old-fashioned detective work . . . and old-fashioned bad luck for them. The folks at Bravo told us which direction you'd been taken. We picked up a trail of fresh oil. Figured that the van you were in must've had a loose gasket and was trailing oil . . . at least we *hoped* it was *that* van."

"So you just followed . . ."

"We just followed the 'Forty-Weight Road.'" Clark laughed, mimicking the chant from *The Wizard of Oz* about the Yellow Brick Road.

"I'm surprised by how little damage there is," Sean said. "From what we saw at Bravo, it seemed like the whole city was burning to the ground."

"Like I was saying, it was isolated. They hit Outpost November and Outpost Bravo . . . other than that, the biggest attack was at that school."

"School?" Sean said with alarm. "*What school?*"

"That school that the OEG people are at," Ryan said. "Wait a minute . . . you were involved with helping those folks down there, weren't you?"

"Yes, I was. What happened at the school? What did they . . . ?"

"We'll drive by there . . . you can see for yourself."

As Clark ordered the driver to divert the convoy route to pass the school, Sean's mind went blank, his thoughts replaced by a sheet of numbness.

They arrived a few minutes after the sun went down. The sky was deep blue, and the building was still illuminated by the light of dusk.

It was eerie. Across the street, lights burned in the shops and coffee bars, but the school was dark.

American soldiers and Iraqi cops stood guard near the open gate. Inside, Sean saw only darkness, but still he hastened to get in there.

One of the guards moved to block his entry but backed off and saluted when he saw the captain's bars and the chaplain's crosses. When he saw Capt. Clark, he saluted again and moved aside entirely.

They entered.

All was quiet except for the rumble of a gasoline generator that powered a few lights that Sean could see here and there. The main power had been knocked out, and the isolated lights merely made the place seem ghostly.

"What exactly happened here?" Sean asked a lieutenant who was standing with some other personnel in the courtyard. The last time Sean had stood in this spot—just a few hours ago—he had been surrounded by happy children.

"Al-Qaeda thought they could intimidate through bullying the kids."

"Anybody killed?" Sean asked hesitantly. He didn't want to hear the answer, but the question just came out.

The lieutenant just nodded and gestured toward a first-floor classroom that was lit by one of those ghostly white lights.

Inside was a neat row of about a dozen small bodies, each covered with a cloth, randomly gathered sheets and towels that afforded some small measure of privacy for the remains of young lives cut short by violence. In the far corner of the room, parents knelt sobbing with the body of their child.

Sean removed his helmet, handed it to Kyle Lockhart, and bowed his head in prayer.

He then moved across the room to offer condolences and a gentle hand on the shoulders of the grieving parents.

Tears welled in his own eyes when he recognized the young girl clutching the blue Dodgers cap.

"How many?" Sean asked the lieutenant when they stepped outside the classroom.

"We think that's most of them. Luckily, the majority got out . . . that way."

He nodded in the direction of the baseball diamond that had been the scene of so much joy.

The baseball diamond!

The fun!

The laughter!

Now *this!*

"They got out?"

"Most of 'em."

"I guess that *is* a blessing in all of this," Sean said, feeling the deep sadness in his own voice.

Thank God that Bilal and Naja hadn't come to school today!

"The kids were lucky, but you gotta thank the gals that helped get 'em out," the lieutenant said.

"Which gals?" Clark asked.

"There were two European teachers who ushered most of the kids out."

"Where are they now?" Sean asked. "The European teachers."

"Not sure," the lieutenant admitted. "We're still searching the place."

He shouted to a sergeant, repeating Sean's question.

The sergeant replied that they had gotten back into the building to try to get other kids up to the upper floors after the al-Qaeda took over the courtyard.

Flashlights on the stairway made the place seem haunted.

In a sense, it was.

Sean had never been here at night, and he found this familiar building eerie.

One by one, they checked empty classrooms.

In one, American soldiers were removing the bodies of dead al-Qaeda fighters. In most, it seemed as though the rooms were simply awaiting a class to come in and take their seats.

At last, they approached the room at the end of the hallway that Sean knew was Mareike's.

As he shone his flashlight into the room, it played first on the wall map of the United States that Sean had once used in his lecture on the Mississippi River and the great prairies that surrounded it. He remembered smiling, smirking faces that listened to his stories about the "Father of Waters," and how happy he had felt that day.

As he shifted the flashlight to the side, it was apparent that something terrible had happened in this room. Bullet holes pocked the chalkboard. Sections of it lay broken and pulverized on the floor.

Sean moved toward the front of the classroom, stepping over toppled desks.

He stooped to pick up a book that had fallen on the floor and saw a large, sticky, drying puddle of blood.

Blood looks peculiar in the unnatural glare of a flashlight. It looks strangely artificial, as though it is not quite real.

Walking around the puddle, he continued his grim search, lost in his own world, unaware of the others who accompanied him.

Near the desk in the corner of the room, his flashlight fell on a single grayish-purple shoe, a sneaker—it was unquestionably Mareike's aubergine sneaker.

He reached down to pick it up and found it damp and sticky.

In the strange, cold light of the flashlight, the color of the shoe hid the fact that it was soaked in blood.

Whose blood was on the sneaker?

Sean pretended to wonder abstractly over this question, as he avoided the obvious answer.

"Where are they?" Sean asked, his voice quavering. "There's blood . . . there must have been people in here."

"Must have been taken downstairs," the lieutenant suggested. "I thought all the bodies were in where those kids had been taken, but maybe there's another place. It's obviously real nuts around here. Let's go check."

With fragments of prayers running through his mind and tears in his eyes, Sean headed back down the stairs.

He was glad that it was dark.

Nobody wants to see the chaplain cry.

Where was she?

Could she be alive?

The lieutenant led them to a triage area near the office that Sean had not noticed when they had first entered the compound. Here, some of the wounded were being treated.

Sean's heart soared. Could Mareike be here somewhere?

"Chaplain Sean!"

He turned. It was one of the boys from Bilal's class.

Reaching up from a stretcher, he took Sean's hand.

"You're doin' good, buddy," Sean said, tears of joy streaming down his cheeks.

The boy smiled and returned Sean's thumbs-up.

Several others recognized Sean and called out to him. As he moved through the poorly lit tumult of people on stretchers, with medical personnel running here and there, he stopped at the side of each of the wounded to offer encouragement. All of the children knew his name and were happy to see "Chaplain Sean."

"Guess they know you here." Capt. Clark smiled, obviously impressed to see how well known and well liked the 2nd Battalion chaplain was at the school.

"They're all my buddies," Sean said. "They're all my . . . I guess you could say they're all my friends."

Off to his left, beyond the crowd, Sean heard a door slam and saw the flash of blue lights. An ambulance was just pulling out.

"Who's in that bus?" Sean asked, hurrying over to the place from which the ambulance had just departed.

"It's one of the people who worked here at the school," one of the American medics said.

"Who?"

"I dunno. Steve, do you know who that was that they're taking to the hospital?"

"Yeah," the other doctor said, looking at Sean's chaplain insignia. "It's a guy named Ilik. He ran the school."

"Is he gonna be okay?" Sean asked.

"He'll probably pull through," the doctor named Steve replied. "Got shot up pretty bad, though, protecting the kids."

"What about any other staff people here?" Sean asked. "Have any others been taken to the hospital?"

"Nope. He's the first. So far it's been only kids. This guy insisted that the kids be taken out ahead of him. Finally, I just had to overrule him; he was just too messed up. Most of the kids who are still here are noncritical. We're working through it."

"It's been a terrible thing," Sean said.

"I didn't realize how bad until I got down here," the medic named Steve replied. "Please say a prayer or two for these people."

"And some for you guys, too," Sean added.

Sean worked his way back into the triage area, looking desperately for the woman he loved, trying to balance the personal longings of Sean Rasmunsen with the requirements of his role as a pastor to his troops and as a man of the Book—and a friend—to all of these kids.

"Chaplain Sean!"

He looked up. It was Hala.

"Hala! It's so good to see you. Are you all right?"

"So good that you are here!"

As she hugged him with her left arm, he saw the bloodstained bandage on her right.

"Come," she said, taking his hand.

They entered the school's office and there, Sean saw Isabelle Laclerc. She lay on a desk. Sean had never seen the fiery Isabelle seem so peaceful. Her hands were crossed and her eyes were closed. Her long, dark, usually well-coiffed hair was a mess that she would never again be able to brush.

Even in death, her face was beautiful.

Before Sean could say anything, Hala took him by the hand and led him into Mustafa Ilik's darkened office, the same office where he had first met the headmaster so long ago.

Someone lay on the desk, someone covered by the orange and brown cloth that usually hung in the doorway. It was heavily stained with blood.

Blood looks peculiar in the unnatural glare of a flashlight. It looks strangely artificial, as though it is not quite real—but this blood was very, very real.

Walking toward the desk, Sean's flashlight fell on a pair of feet, protruding so silent and so motionless from beneath the cloth. One of the feet was bare, the toes appearing so white and so like marble.

On the other was a shoe, an aubergine sneaker.

For the first and probably last time in his military career, Sgt. Kyle Lockhart put his hand on the shoulder of a captain and gently nudged Ryan Clark out of Mustafa Ilik's office. He had no idea whether anything that Isabelle Laclerc had told him about Sean and Mareike was true. He probably never would—and he did not care. He knew, and Capt. Clark nodded that he understood.

The chaplain needed some privacy.

Alone in the dark office, Sean Rasmunsen reached for the hem of the cloth.

"I feel safe and protected with you around, Chaplain Sean," Mareike De Vries had said with a cheerful smile on that wonderful day so long ago when she had first reached out and wrapped her arms around Sean's neck, pulling him toward her.

So many, many weeks had passed since Sean had wrestled with his feelings, arguing with himself over whether to succumb to emotion.

"I have a thousand souls that I'm responsible for," he'd told her.

"And this means that you must shut out the feelings that you have for *me*?" Mareike had asked.

The way that she had said *me* had struck a chord. So simply had a simple word brought into focus that here stood a human being who had expressed her love, her willingness to give herself to him.

"Look at me," Mareike had said. "I'm just a human being . . . I'm just a woman . . . not a temptress sent to lure you into evil like Satan did to Jesus in the book of Matthew."

He had told her that he had other responsibilities, that her profession of love had caused him internal conflict. She was a woman whom he had not allowed himself to love, but who was willing to allow *herself* to share her love with him—and she had told him who *he* was.

"I fell in love with a man who was so good and caring," he could still hear her voice saying. "A man who the children love so much because he gives of himself . . . a man I love."

Sean had built himself into an emotional fortress to protect himself from the pain around him, the pain of disappointment, of loss, of hopelessness, of death, and of suicide. He had built himself into an emotional fortress, and Mareike had tried to break down the fortress walls.

She understood, as most women would not, the importance to him of his calling, of his ministry.

"You sharing your life with others is what I love . . . *part* of what I love about you," Mareike had said so happily on that day when they had first professed their love for one another.

Yet somehow he had not understood the importance to Mareike of *her* calling, her work. Mareike had said that she longed to be true to him, but she could not be true to herself at Fort Jackson.

She could have asked him to choose between her and his calling, but she had not.

"I cannot ask you to choose," she told him. "So *I have chosen* . . . you have so much to give . . . and Fort Jackson is where you must be."

Sean Rasmunsen realized that the most difficult choice of his life had been made for him. It was his final, unselfish, deeply caring gift from Mareike De Vries—sweet and loving and selfless Mareike.

Having given him the gift of not having to make this most difficult of choices, she had looked at him with tearful eyes that told him her love for him was not dead, and that their dream might one day come true.

"Go with God, my love."

Those were the last words that Mareike De Vries had spoken to Sean Rasmunsen.

"Go with God, my love."

They were the last words that Sean spoke on the night when he said good-bye to Mareike.

❖   ❖   ❖

Amazing grace! How sweet the sound
That saved a wretch like me!
I once was lost, but now am found;
Was blind, but now I see.

'Twas grace that taught my heart to fear,
And grace my fears relieved;
How precious did that grace appear
The hour I first believed!

Through many dangers, toils and snares,
I have already come;
'Tis grace hath brought me safe thus far,
And grace will lead me home.

FROM THE HYMN "AMAZING GRACE"
WORDS BY JOHN HENRY NEWTON

32

Full Circle

"Three days in a row below ninety . . . *man*, I'm gonna have to go find me some earmuffs," De Shawn Hughes said as he came into the chapel at Forward Operating Base Lexington.

"Definitely getting toward winter." Ashley Mariott laughed, moving some folding chairs aside so that the choir could begin practice.

"Sure was a fine going-away party last night," De Shawn said as he picked up a hymnal and began flipping through the pages to the hymn that was at the top of the list next to the podium.

"Sorry to see him go."

"Chaplain Sean, he was a righteous dude," De Shawn confirmed. "Still remember the day he told me to show up here for choir. Thought he was kiddin,' y'know. Then, when I figured out he wasn't kiddin', I thought he was *crazy*."

"Guess he was just recognizing talent, De Shawn."

"Guess so . . . but I'm sure gonna miss him."

"Wish I'd got to know him better," Bobby Budner interjected as he arrived for choir practice. "Didn't ever really talk to him until that morning that I came in to thank him for all what he did over in Mook . . . and he grabbed me and said, 'How'd ya like to come and sing?'"

"So, you like singing, Bobby?" Ashley asked.

"Yes, ma'am, sure do. Who woulda thought?"

"Thanks to Chaplain Sean, there's a whole lotta singers in this world that there wouldn't have been otherwise," De Shawn reflected.

"Was it just me, or did he look a little distracted at his party last night?" Bobby wondered.

"Probably sorry to be leavin' this fabulous choir," Ashley suggested. "Or sorry about what happened to David. I think he was actually cryin' a little bit when he said his little tribute to David. I know I had a few tears on my own cheeks."

"He was *there*, y'know . . . when David was killed," De Shawn reminded them. "He saw it happen. I was there, too, at Bravo, just before . . . got out just before they got surrounded. Had to shoot our way back. Sure wish I coulda been there to help save David."

"Sometimes there's not much anybody can do," Ashley said grimly.

"I think he was also thinking about that school down in Saf City where he used to go help out," Bobby added. "Those folks got themselves shot up real bad, too."

"Real bloodbath, from what I hear," De Shawn said, shaking his head. "Poor guy had to go in there and see all that . . ."

"I sure wouldn't want his job for nothing," Bobby said.

"Me neither," Ashley added. "Wouldn't want to see all that day after day and have to make sense of it all, and then have to be able to tell people *why* it all makes sense somehow."

"Have any idea when the new guy's comin' in?" De Shawn asked.

"Man's only out of Lex for a couple–three hours and you're wondering about his replacement?"

"Aren't *you*?"

"I suppose."

"Does anybody know *when* he's coming?" Bobby asked.

"Next couple of days, I heard."

"There's Kyle," Ashley said, pointing to Sgt. Lockhart, who had just come into the chapel. "Ask the chaplain's assistant."

"Hey, Sarge," De Shawn said. "Have any idea who the new guy's gonna be?"

"New chaplain?"

"Yeah."

"Haven't heard. I guess Colonel Folbright knows, but I haven't heard. I do know he might be coming in tomorrow . . . speaking of which, I need somebody to help me move some desks out of Chaplain Sean's tent."

Ashley and De Shawn looked at Bobby, and Bobby volunteered.

He followed Kyle Lockhart down the rows of tents and past the helipad from which Sean Rasmunsen had left FOB Lexington for the last time.

"Guess he must be in Baghdad by now," Budner surmised. "And tomorrow this time or the day after . . ."

"Nice green lawns and trees and birds."

"And fishing holes."

A cloud of dust swirling across the helipad underscored how true a contrast it would be back in South Carolina—where Sean would soon be speaking to young men fresh out of the seminary about the joy, the pain, *and the dust* that were part of a chaplain's life overseas.

The interior of what had been Chaplain Sean Rasmunsen's tent was eerily quiet, and sparse. His personal effects, his chaplain's kit and his gear, which were always stacked here or tucked there, were gone. His cot was here, along with two desks, two chairs, and the five file cabinets that Kyle Lockhart had long ago helped to scrounge. They saw that the chaplain's coffeemaker was still on his table, along with his pretty good desk lamp.

Lockhart and Budner had come today to remove one of the desks. Sean had borrowed it from the Charlie Company quartermaster with the promise that it would be returned. He had asked the sergeant to help him make good on that promise.

"What's that?" Bobby asked. "I didn't think Chaplain Sean was Catholic."

High on the wall was a crucifix.

"He wasn't. That belonged to Father Mike . . . Michael O'Malley. He was chaplain at Lex a *long* time ago. He left it behind and Chaplain Rasmunsen never took it down. Guess he's passing it along to the new guy."

"Looks like Chaplain Sean left some mail behind, too," Budner said, picking up a stack of letters that someone had laid on the desk they were about to move.

"Must have come in this morning after he left."

"What shall we do with it?"

"What is there?"

"Most are just addressed to 'Chaplain, FOB Lexington,' but there's one addressed to him personally from some religious supply place."

"Just leave 'em," Lockhart said. "Save 'em for the new guy."

"Oh, here's one that was stuck to that other one . . . hand addressed . . . hmmmm . . . pink envelope."

"Who's it from?"

"The postmark is Missouri . . . the return address is . . . hmmmm . . . It's from a Nicole somebody."

◆　◆　◆

There are loved ones in the glory,
Whose dear forms you often miss;
When you close your earthly story,
Will you join them in their bliss?

Will the circle be unbroken
By and by, by and by?
In a better home awaiting
In the sky, in the sky?

FROM THE HYMN "CAN THE CIRCLE BE UNBROKEN?"
WORDS BY ADA RUTH HABERSHON